TALE OF LOVE

With tantalizing slowness, he carried her to the brass bed. The soft rays of sunlight that filtered through the sheer material of the drapes reflected a glistening shimmer across her skin.

They came into each other's arms once more, and as his passion mounted, he embraced her boldly against his bare frame, a tender light shining through his eyes. His mouth moved down the length of her, sending hot shafts of desire racing unchecked through both of them.

Maybe nothing in the world could stop him from claiming her. Maybe these crazy feelings they were experiencing would turn out to be the real thing.

Maybe . . . she was finally in love.

POWER AND SEDUCTION

"I'm about to lose everything I own," Tina raged. "All because *you* refuse to advance me some of *my* money!"

"If you're going to lose everything you own, it's because you lavished what you did have on that slime you married. And I made up my mind the day you married him that he wasn't getting any of your money." A derisive smile twisted Dirk's lips. "And he didn't, did he?"

"No. He didn't last and I blame you for the breakup of my marriage."

"Good." Dirk smiled at her serenely.

Tina glared at him. "What do you mean, good?"

Dirk laughed. "I mean if my tight hold on the purse strings had anything to do with the demise of your misalliance, well, then I'm glad. Couldn't be happier."

"You really are a cad!" she whispered angrily.

"I do try," he answered, amusement dancing in his eyes.

VALENTINE SAMPLER

Lori Copeland
TALE OF LOVE

Amii Lorin
POWER AND SEDUCTION

LEISURE BOOKS NEW YORK CITY

A LEISURE BOOK®

February 1992

Published by

Dorchester Publishing Co., Inc.
276 Fifth Avenue
New York, NY 10001

Lori Copeland

TALE OF LOVE

To Emily Reichert:
for her support, guidance, and enthusiasm

Chapter One

THE SNOW WAS COMING DOWN IN heavy sheets at O'Hare International Airport. Perched in the glassed-in birdcage that was known as the tower, weary flight controllers were going into the last hour of their shift.

It had been one hell of a night.

During the past few hours the controllers had efficiently handled close to four hundred incoming and outgoing flights. Now, the controllers were enjoying a welcome lull in the frenzied air traffic. Planes were sitting at the gates, others systematically coming down on landing strips; but the rush was nothing compared to what it had been earlier.

From his vantage point high atop the airport terminal, Garth Redmond looked out on the red beacon lights moving about the runway and wished his shift were over. The cold he'd come down with two days ago was making him feel headachy and irritable. He still had another hour left before he'd be free to go home, kick back, and relax.

Garth glanced at the ground-surveillance radar and suddenly sat up straighter. A quick reading on the bright display indicated that a Pan American Boeing 747, still ten miles out, was coming in faster than usual. Garth quickly flipped a switch on the panel before him. "Approach, this is Ground. Clipper 242 looks to be coming in pretty fast. Does he have a problem?"

"Ground, this is Approach. Yeah, he's picking up heavy ice. He's been cleared to approach."

Garth glanced at the airport-surface radar and frowned. If Tim Matthews, the Approach controller, had accurate information, they were in trouble. Garth's ground-surveillance screen indicated an unidentified radar target taxiing toward the approach end of the active runway.

Garth hurriedly reached for the binoculars and scanned the snow-covered taxiway. He swore under his breath as he saw the lighted section of a Global Airways DC-9 disappearing toward Runway 36 in the heavy snow.

"Global, this is Ground..." The sharp crackling at the other end took Garth by surprise. "Global, this is Ground. Do you read me?" The question was met with an ominous silence. Flipping a second button, Garth said curtly, "Local, we've got a problem. I've got a Global Airways DC-9 taxiing on parallel taxiway, and I'm not talking to him."

"What's he doing out there?" Jack Lindley shot back.

"That's what I'm trying to find out. Better advise the Clipper."

"Roger." The Local controller flipped a button on his panel. "Clipper 242, be advised we have a no-radio Global DC-9 taxiing southbound on Runway 36 parallel taxiway. Be prepared for a go-around."

Even while the Local controller was advising the Pan American pilot, Garth realized that the huge Boeing 747 coming in from Anchorage was on the final mile to mile-and-a-half approach. He seriously doubted he could go around.

"Local, what's the Global doing there?" the pilot of the Clipper demanded.

"That's what we're trying to find out."

Garth listened to the tense exchange as he kept a close eye on the runway visual-radar indicator. Visibility was down to two thousand, four hundred feet. For the past four and a half hours, the pilots had been relying solely on instruments.

Garth concentrated on the monitors. The nerves between his shoulder blades squeezed together painfully as he hit a button again.

"Global DC-9, this is Ground. Exit runway *immediately!* A Boeing 747 shot final!"

While the media focused on midair collisions and near misses midair, the more frequent problem that faced a flight controller was the kind of situation Garth now found himself monitoring. Wiping a shaky hand across the back of his neck, he eased forward in his chair as the tower supervisor threw down the papers he had been reading and came over to stand behind Garth's chair.

"What's going on?"

"I've got an unauthorized DC-9 taxiing into reserved runway, and I'm not talking to him."

Joel Anderson's seasoned eyes quickly sized up the developing situation. He frowned.

"The fool apparently thinks he's been cleared to taxi," Garth muttered. He tried to reach the DC-9 again. "Global DC-9, exit to taxiway *immediately!* Repeat. Exit to taxiway *immediately!*"

Joel leaned over Garth's shoulder and watched the screen as the two planes continued on their landing courses, both simultaneously approaching Runway 36.

"Tell Local to advise Clipper to go around," Joel warned as Garth automatically started pressing the necessary buttons.

"Local, this is Ground. Advise Clipper 242. Unauthorized DC-9 still on runway. Go around *immediately!* Repeat. Go around *immediately!*"

"Roger!" Local quickly activated another button. "Clipper 242, this is Local. Aircraft on runway. Go around. Repeat. Go around."

Garth could hear Local talking to the Clipper. Then he heard the pilot's grim refusal. "I'd love to oblige, Local, but this ain't no crop duster I'm flying!"

"Oh, hell!" Garth's voice echoed bleakly in the darkened room as he sagged back in his chair. The DC-9 was about to cross the path reserved for the incoming Clipper; and with radio contact to the DC-9 gone, it was out of the flight controller's hands and up to a Higher Power.

All Garth could hope for was that the timing

of the two aircraft would be split second and a collision would be avoided.

Joel hurriedly reached for the crash phone to alert the fire station and emergency crew to the pending crisis. Garth tried to raise the Global DC-9 again.

"Global, exit to taxiway immediately! Repeat. Exit to taxiway immediately!"

Eyes riveted to the screen, Garth and Joel watched in tense silence as the two blips on the radar screen rushed closer and closer together. The room had grown unnaturally quiet as the other flight controllers performed their duties in hushed tones.

"Well, start praying," Joel advised.

The wide-bodied Boeing 747 touched down on the landing strip and came streaking along the runway as the DC-9 began to ease its way across. The pilot of the DC-9 was still unaware of what was happening.

"Move, damn it!" Garth spoke tautly to the DC-9, then held his breath as the plane continued to roll laboriously across the path of the incoming 747.

"Get out of the way, buddy!" The strained voice of the Clipper pilot cracked over the wire as he, too, tried to will the DC-9 out of his pathway.

The dots closed in on each other as the Clipper roared down the landing strip at a speed of more than two hundred miles an hour. The blips came closer and closer.

Suddenly, they split apart, and the DC-9 eased

off the runway as the 747 shot by him in a screech of flying mud and snow.

Garth threw down his pencil angrily as Joel let out a loud war whoop.

"Holy shi...What was that?" the expletive slipped out as the pilot of the DC-9 finally came in over the wire. He was obviously shaken.

"Global, you're on unauthorized taxiway!" Garth snapped, then curtly explained what had just happened.

The pilot made his apologies, then requested to return to the terminal. "We've had a radio malfunction."

Garth granted the necessary clearance and abruptly severed contact with the pilot.

For a moment Garth fought to overcome an unreasonable sense of frustration. He fumbled for his handkerchief as Joel laid his hands on his shoulders and gave them a supportive squeeze. "Good work!"

Emotionally and physically drained, Garth could not will himself to respond to Joel's encouragement. He mopped the moisture from his forehead. There was no longer any doubt about it: The pressure of the job was getting to him.

True, Garth had experienced closer calls, but his heartbeat had never raced as fast as it was now.

"Another close one!" Garth's voice echoed hollowly in the dimly lit room.

Joel thought Garth sounded unusually tired and emotionally drained—not at all like the self-confident, cocksure young kid Joel had hired nine years ago. There had been a time when Garth would have brushed off this sort of incident without another thought, considering it just a part of the business. Tonight, though, was different. Garth seemed brooding, uncertain, troubled . . .

Joel's eyes met Garth's sympathetically. Garth was one of the most competent young men he had ever had the pleasure of working with. He was alert, intelligent, a seasoned professional. But as his supervisor, Joel couldn't sit back and ignore the situation any longer.

All the symptoms of burnout were there. Anxiety, stress, and the pressures of the demanding position were obviously taking their toll on Garth.

Joel clapped a friendly hand on the younger man's shoulder. "Step into my office when you get a minute."

Garth's pulse jumped erratically. "Sure, Joel." His eyes remained fixed on the screen as he spoke, but he knew what was coming. Joel had noticed his odd behavior, and he wanted an explanation. But Garth didn't have one.

By the time he entered Joel Anderson's cluttered cubicle a half hour later, he'd decided that he was blowing the situation out of proportion. He was fine. Joel wasn't going to yell at him. He probably just wanted to shoot the breeze for a while.

Joel was on the phone when Garth arrived. He glanced up and motioned him to help himself to the coffee.

Garth shook his head. The last thing he needed was more caffeine in his system. He settled his large frame in the chair opposite the desk.

In a few moments Joel finished his conversation and replaced the receiver. "Sorry about the delay. Those idiots in the office drive me up a wall."

Garth smiled. "No problem."

Joel got up and walked to the hot plate. "I shouldn't drink another cup of this stuff. Wanda would have a fit if she knew how many I've had today...but what the hell." He poured the strong black coffee into his cup and added a couple of packets of sugar. "I'm going to die of something, so I figure I might as well go happy."

Garth acknowledged Joel's attempt at levity with a wan smile and waited patiently until he sat down again.

Joel was always worrying about what his wife would say about his bad habits but never enough to change them, Garth thought with halfhearted amusement. He just wished Joel would get on with whatever he had on his mind.

It seemed to Garth that Joel was doing a lot of fidgeting before he got to the point. "You're doing one hell of a job, Garth," he finally said, lighting a cigarette absentmindedly.

Garth glanced up, surprised by the unexpected praise. He was still half expecting to be chewed out for his performance during the past few weeks. Joel hadn't missed his edginess—Garth would bet on that. But compliments?

"Thanks. I appreciate it."

"But you're going on excused leave." The statement was firm and straight to the point.

Garth shook his head. "No...I can't. Not right now."

"Sure you can. You're on leave beginning tomorrow morning."

"Come on, Joel . . ." He was about to argue the point, when he saw the look of determination in his superior's eyes.

Garth realized he could sit there and argue all day, but in the end Joel would have the last word.

"No buts, Garth." His tone might have softened, but his resolution hadn't. "I've sat by and watched what's been going on for weeks now, and I think it's time we did something about it."

Garth didn't have the heart to disagree or to press Joel for details. They both knew Garth hadn't been himself lately. But, damn, his ego sure hated to accept the fact that he was stressed out.

"I'm sorry. I know I haven't been giving you my best lately," he admitted.

Joel leaned back in his chair and studied his coffee cup thoughtfully. "I've never felt that you didn't give me your best. You're one of the most valued men I have. I'm only trying to see that you stay that way. You're tired and stressed out. I want you to get a little R and R. Relax, have some fun. Forget about the job and its pressures."

"Are you worried because of what happened a few minutes ago?" Garth asked. "Because if you are, I can explain. I have this miserable cold—"

Joel interrupted gently. "No, this is a decision I've been avoiding for weeks."

"You think I'm no longer competent?" The mute appeal in Garth's eyes was hard for Joel to ignore.

"Of course not. I just think you need a little

rest." He could see that Garth was wrestling with his pride. "It's nothing to be ashamed of. We all have our limits. A few weeks of lying in the sun, and you'll be back complaining you've used up all your vacation time," Joel promised.

"Well, I can't say I agree, but you're the boss." Garth conceded, though he hated to.

"Then you agree to the leave?"

"I don't think it's a good time. It'll leave you in a bind," Garth reminded him. "I think if I could just get over this cold—"

"You will. A couple of weeks will work wonders for you." He leaned forward in his chair and stubbed out his cigarette. "Damn things are going to kill me," he complained under his breath. "Wanda would have a fit if she knew how many I've smoked today."

Garth stood up, openly disturbed by the unexpected turn of events. He felt resentful and deprived; yet at the same time he felt a strange sense of relief. Two weeks without coping... without worrying... without sitting on the edge of his chair...Maybe that *was* all he needed.

"Well, I don't suppose it would do any good to argue with you."

"Nope. None at all. Soon as Randy gets here, consider yourself out of work for the next two weeks. Or longer, if you need it. You let me worry about your replacement. That's what I get paid for."

"Joel...I appreciate this...." He reached over to shake his superior's hand, gratified for the other man's concern.

"Don't worry about it," Joel said absently.

"Oh, Lord, look at the time! I've got to call Wanda and tell her I'm going to be a few minutes late." He flashed Garth an apologetic grin. "The woman's terrified I've dropped dead if I don't get home by six on the dot."

Garth knew exactly where he would go to find the privacy he wanted: his grandparents' beachfront cottage in West Creek, North Carolina.

Silas and Grace Redmond would be in Florida for the winter, but Garth knew how to reach them.

It didn't matter that he wouldn't be able to lie around in the sun—in West Creek, it was, after all, the end of December. All he needed was a good book, a couple of packages of Oreo cookies, and complete solitude for the next two weeks.

Keep the sun and sand—give me the seclusion of that cozy three-room cottage, he thought as he drove home to pack a couple of bags.

The time off would enable him to get his priorities back in line and his head on straight again. The weather wouldn't be all that bad in West Creek, and at least he'd be able get away from all this miserable snow for a few days.

Garth wasted no time in securing a plane reservation, packing, and calling a taxi. He figured it would be better if he left Chicago before the storm turned into a full-scale blizzard. Because of the holiday rush, Garth considered himself extremely fortunate to get a seat on the next plane. Fortunately, he had connections with a cute blonde at the ticket counter.

The nine-thirty flight would take him to Raleigh,

where he'd have a brief layover before he could get a commuter hop to West Creek.

He decided to wait to call his grandmother from the terminal to ask her permission to use the cottage. If he called at the last minute, Garth knew she wouldn't have time to make half a dozen entertainment plans on his behalf.

Grace and Silas were well-meaning, but they always felt that Garth had to be entertained. Just because they were vacationing in Florida didn't mean Grace would be deterred from getting on the phone and lining up some of their friends to entertain her grandson in their absence.

At the last minute Garth made a hurried call to Lisa Matthews, the woman he'd been dating for the past few months. Lisa was another pressure that had been nagging at him lately. She wanted to get serious; Garth, on the other hand, was perfectly content to let the relationship drift along, with no strings attached. The unexpected change in plans would give him some desperately needed breathing space.

Garth hurriedly made the call, explaining to Lisa that he was going away for a few days.

She was upset but made Garth promise to call her the minute he arrived at his grandparents' cottage.

"Why don't I fly down for the weekend?" she suggested.

"No, I think I need the time alone, Lisa." They'd been spending so much of their time arguing lately that Garth felt he needed a reprieve.

"Well . . . if that's how you feel." Garth could

hear the petulance creeping into Lisa's voice, but he chose to ignore it.

"I'll call you later in the week." It was Garth's one concession.

"Make sure that you do."

Fierce winds blowing off icy Lake Michigan raced a bone-rattling chill down Garth's slightly feverish body as he left his apartment thirty minutes later, lugging the suitcases. He paused, sneezed, then blew his nose before going on.

A heavy blanket of snow made a dull, crunching noise beneath his boots as he trudged through the white powder to the waiting taxi. With six inches already on the frozen ground, the National Weather Service wasn't calling for an end to the storm until late tomorrow night.

Garth cautiously shuffled along what he assumed was the unshoveled sidewalk. Getting through the wet snow proved to be no easy task—but, then, nothing had been easy lately.

The sound of the cabbie impatiently leaning on the horn made Garth quicken his steps. Struggling to retain his balance as well as the luggage, he felt his temper flare when he thought of how he had waited for that cab driver for more than an hour, and now the man had the audacity to honk for *him* to hurry!

Garth reached the cab and tried to jiggle open the door, which had frozen shut fifteen minutes earlier. Hoping to free a hand and pry the stubborn latch loose, he set one suitcase down beside him, where it promptly sank out of sight in a growing snowdrift.

Expecting the door to require a hefty-sized tug, Garth obliged with a hearty jerk that sent the door flying open. He suddenly found himself lying flat on his back.

"Oh, Lord, give me a break!" Garth pleaded as he lay staring up at the cab's muddy underside. Glancing around to see if anyone other than the cabbie had seen the humiliating incident, he slowly rolled back onto his feet.

Convinced that the driver wasn't overly interested in his welfare, Garth grabbed the suitcases and pitched them into the backseat. He had to slam the door twice before it finally latched.

The plump cabbie wrestled a nasty stub of cigar butt between his lips and asked with a distinct Jersey accent, "What's ya pleasure, Mac?"

"O'Hare," Garth requested curtly. *And, believe me, nothing's my pleasure at the moment!* he thought irritably.

The cabbie shot a sympathetic glance in the rearview mirror. "Rough day, huh?" He rolled down the window and reached out to wipe the thick frost from the windshield with a large rag.

Garth viewed the action with growing dismay. No defrosters in this kind of weather? "You can see where you're going, can't you?"

"Huh? Oh, sure. The darn defroster went on the fritz about an hour ago. No sweat, though. I can get ya to O'Hare with my eyes closed." He gunned the engine, and the cab fishtailed onto the busy street.

The transmission sputtered as the driver raked through the gears. Every time the gears caught, the back of the taxi spun out, forcing Garth to grab the back of the seat for support.

"Hold on! This baby runs like a dream once you get her hummin'," the cabby called back between speed shifts.

Garth rested his head wearily against the seat and shot another squirt of decongestant up to his clogged sinuses.

As the cab neared the airport the traffic became congested and slowed to a snail's pace. Garth was sneezing with appalling regularity now.

"Sounds like you got a lulu of a cold there."

"Yeah, I think it's getting worse." Garth blew his nose, then glanced at his watch. He was going to be cutting it close. He was tempted to tell the driver to step on it, but he wasn't suicidal yet.

A good mile and a half from O'Hare the traffic came to a complete halt. Garth kept glancing uneasily at his watch. Twenty minutes later not a single car had budged.

"Hey, listen! I have an eight-o'clock plane to catch," he reminded the driver.

"Just keep your shirt on! I'll get you there, bub."

Another ten minutes passed, and Garth realized that time was running out. The plane would leave in twenty minutes, and he was still a half-mile from the airport.

Heaving a resigned sigh, Garth reached into his pocket, withdrew a wad of bills, and hurriedly paid the driver.

"Hey! Where you goin'?"

"I'll have to make a run for it." Garth sneezed again and grabbed the two pieces of luggage.

The long, cold run to the airport was a nightmare. The drifts were piling up, and the temperature was in the low teens. The tip of Garth's nose was beet-red, and his cheeks looked like two blazing cherries by the time he reached the terminal. He ran inside, wheezing like an overworked locomotive.

It was still a long sprint to his boarding gate. Garth was convinced that it was only through an act of divine intervention that the jetway was still attached to the plane when he arrived.

Stepping inside the plane, Garth was greeted by a friendly flight attendant. "Good evening. Welcome aboard American Airlines."

Garth fumbled in his pocket for his soggy handkerchief and tried to return her smile without his frozen face cracking into a million pieces. "Good evening . . . Terrible weather . . ." he returned lamely.

"I hope you enjoy your flight, sir."

I hope so too, Garth thought grimly as he dragged his baggage down the aisle—there had been no time to check it. He wedged the suitcases tightly into the crowded compartment at the rear of the plane.

Moments later, he sank wearily into his assigned seat. The two-year-old sitting next to him promptly started screaming as his mother tried to fasten him into a seat belt.

Short of a plane crash, Garth knew the flight had to be more enjoyable than the past four hours had been.

Chapter Two

HILARY BROOKFIELD WIPED HER teary eyes and tossed another soaked tissue into her purse. It joined nine crumpled others.

She hated herself for being so weak—so out of control—so asinine! She wiped angrily at the icy particles forming on the window and stared out of the cab into the blinding snow. Hilary had always considered herself an "in-charge person," but today's events had proved her to be anything *but* in control.

The yellow cab slowly inched its way through the snow-covered streets of Denver. The worsening weather had rendered the rush-hour traffic more snarled and congested than usual.

"How much longer before we get to the air . . . airport?" she asked, trying to subdue her sobs. Her warm breath turned frosty in the arctic air.

"I'll have you there in another twenty minutes. Sorry about the heater. It was working fine an hour ago. Can't imagine what could've happened to it," the driver apologized.

Hilary sighed. She could explain the malfunction—she'd been in the backseat for the last forty-five minutes of that hour. Why *shouldn't* the heater fall apart? Everything else in her life had, she thought, succumbing to another onslaught of self-pity. She bawled into her wadded tissue for a few minutes, then blew her nose again.

The taxi driver peered expectantly into the rearview mirror. If there was one thing that made Max Stinson nervous, it was a squalling female. Not that Max was hard-hearted. He was considered a real softie, but the poor soul in the backseat hadn't turned off the tap since he'd picked her up.

"Um . . . miss? Are you all right back th—"

KAABOOMMM!

Hilary squealed, then ducked at the sound of the sudden explosion.

"Oh, boy! I think we've got ourselves a flat tire, miss." The driver fought the steering wheel and finally managed to ease the cab over to the side of the road.

After bringing the crippled taxi to a halt, the man turned to reassure his passenger. "Now, don't you worry. I'll get you to Stapleton on time."

Hilary sat up and blew into her tissue again, skeptical of his optimism. Why should she hope she'd make her plane on time? Nothing else had gone right today.

She'd lost a button off her new coat and the stud to her gold earring; there had been a fifteen-hundred-dollar discrepancy in the books at work; and she'd been dumped.

A mere flat tire shouldn't upset her. Hilary leaned over and bawled harder into the tear-sodden tissue.

Every snowplow in Denver had been working nonstop for the past twenty-four hours. Six-feet-high drifts made curbside parking impossible, but the cab driver had managed to pull as far off the road as possible. There was an endless string of irritated motorists inching past the disabled vehicle. They leaned on their horns as if that would somehow even the score for their frayed tempers.

"I'll have the tire changed in a jiffy," the driver promised as he got out and slammed the door behind him.

Hilary worked to stem the flow of her streaming eyes. With yet another Kleenex having bitten the dust, she dumped it into her coat pocket and fished out a clean one.

While the driver changed the tire, she sat in the frosty silence of the cab, watching the snow drift past the car window. The hypnotic effect of the swirling flakes dredged up thoughts of the unpleasant emotional scene she'd experienced only a few hours earlier.

Lenny Ricetrum. Lenny Ricetrum the Rat, she corrected herself. The big dirty rat, she corrected herself again, as if calling Lenny names would help.

Hilary had dated Lenny steadily for the past few months. And she had grown to care very deeply for him—or at least she thought she had until this morning.

Wasn't that just like love? Hilary agonized against the cold pane of the window, indulging in her own private pity party. You think everything is wonderful, and the next thing you know ...it all blows up in your face!

Oh, she'd seen it coming, though she hadn't wanted to believe it. Lenny had always had a roving eye. Maybe that's why she'd found him so attractive, so exciting, so much fun to be with, despite his being brash and rough around the edges.

Hilary readily admitted that Lenny was a novelty. She'd never dated anyone like him, and she'd found the experience exhilarating.

But Meredith Lowry had apparently found him equally attractive.

Meredith was always hanging around the construction site where Hilary and Lenny worked. Ralph, an electrician at O'Connor's, had noticed that the bold redhead was making an obvious play for Lenny's attention. He had called it to Hilary's attention once or twice.

"Hey, Hilary! Ya better keep an eye on that little redhead. Looks like she's mapping out your man!" Ralph had tried to sound as though he were teasing, but even then Hilary had detected the underlying tone of seriousness in his words.

Hilary had kept telling herself that Lenny's case of roaming eyes was just a passing thing. Nothing to get herself in an uproar over. Besides, she'd always prided herself on not being a jealous or possessive person.

But deep down, Hilary knew the reason she hadn't confronted Lenny and demanded he put a stop to his womanizing; she thought she loved him. Consequently, the problem hadn't gone away.

This morning she'd barely seated herself at her desk when Lenny had come into her office and dropped the bombshell.

He hadn't minced words or tried to lighten the impact of his cruel announcement. Without batting an eye, he'd announced that their relationship was over. He'd left a stunned Hilary slumped over her IBM, wondering what had gone wrong.

"Hilary . . . I'm sorry." Michael O'Connor, the owner of the construction company, had tried to comfort her. "I was afraid this would happen."

Hilary cried on his broad shoulder, praying he wouldn't say "I told you so."

"Mr. O'Connor, Lenny didn't even say why . . ." Hilary dissolved into tears as Michael put a strong arm around her shoulders.

"Sh, sh, little girl." Michael gently tried to soothe her tattered pride. "Men like Lenny don't usually explain anything they do. I say good riddance to bad rubbish, as far as that bum is concerned."

Hilary tried to still her sobbing. She was a grown woman acting like a child. But at that moment, she'd felt like a street urchin. One who had just been stepped on.

At Mr. O'Connor's suggestion, Hilary had taken the rest of the day off. Sitting alone in her apartment she had knocked a big dent in her supply of tissues. She spent two hours crying, pacing the floor, crying, drinking coffee, and crying.

Realizing the situation wasn't improving, Hilary decided that what she needed was time away from the whole ugly situation. If she went back to the office, she would be forced to see Lenny at least a couple of times a day. She just didn't feel up to that right now.

With grim determination, she phoned Michael O'Connor and asked for a week's vacation to try and collect her thoughts.

"You go right ahead. A little time away is just what you need to put this thing in perspective," Michael agreed. "And don't feel guilty. Construction work is never booming this time of year. Enjoy your week."

Hilary decided she shouldn't waste precious time trying to decide where to spend her unscheduled vacation.

A good friend, Marsha Terrill, had moved to West Creek, North Carolina, a year ago. Hilary and Marsha hadn't been able to visit each other since Marsha's move, although they'd kept in close touch. Hilary decided that now would be the perfect time to visit Marsha.

The airline booked her on a nine-thirty flight. Hilary spent the next thirty minutes trying to reach Marsha. Each time she'd gotten a busy signal.

Hilary tried again before she left for the airport, but the line was still busy. Assuring herself that the layover in Raleigh would give her a chance to phone Marsha from the terminal, Hilary wasn't concerned. Marsha loved surprises, and besides, Hilary wasn't sure if she could control her emotions long enough to explain the unexpected visit.

Hilary's thoughts were interrupted as the cab driver got back into the cab. His clothing was covered with a thick dusting of snow.

"All fixed," he announced.

"Do you think we can still make it to the airport on time?"

"You bet! Even if I have to make this taxi sprout wings to get you there. I've never caused any passenger to miss a flight yet."

Yes, but you've never had me in your cab before, Hilary thought fatalistically.

Max was true to his word. He delivered Hilary to the airport ten minutes before her plane departed. What he neglected to mention was that *she'd* have to sprout wings to make it through the gates in time to catch her flight.

She raced feverishly through the crowded terminal, dodging through the throng of holiday travelers. As she breathlessly neared the boarding gate, a slow-moving elderly gentleman ahead of her dropped his boarding pass. He came to an abrupt halt.

Hilary had no choice but to do the same. She drew in her breath painfully as she felt her right ankle twist as she struggled to regain her balance. The ankle had been broken in a skiing accident three years earlier, and the renewed pain was breathtaking. Fighting the hot sting of the wrenched muscles, Hilary started trying to pick up the luggage she had dropped.

"You okay, little lady?" The elderly man

turned around, unaware that he had been the cause of her newest crisis.

"Yes...thanks...I'll be fine." Hilary gritted her teeth in agony.

"Shouldn't be in such a big hurry. That's what's wrong with the world today. Everyone's in such an all-fired hurry," the man complained as he proceeded down the corridor.

"And happy holidays to you too," Hilary muttered.

She carefully tested part of her weight on the injured ankle. The searing throb was horrible. She realized that the only way she could make the flight was to swallow her misery and hobble on.

By grace alone, Hilary managed to make it to the jetway seconds before it was detached from the plane.

Sinking gratefully into her assigned seat, Hilary buckled her belt to prepare for takeoff. She fought back the hot swell of tears that threatened to overcome her again.

Hilary, you have to stop this, she warned herself. Other women had been dumped and had lived through it. She would too.

Hilary gently rubbed her swollen ankle and wondered if she would be able to get her shoe back on if she slipped it off during the flight. Deciding to take the chance, she kicked off the two-inch black heel and wearily leaned her head back on the headrest.

If she'd had even the slightest inkling of how this day was going to turn out, she would never have gotten out of bed that morning.

Chapter Three

AT PRECISELY TEN THIRTY-SEVEN, the Boeing 727 carrying Hilary Brookfield landed in Raleigh, North Carolina.

A light snow was falling, and because it was beginning to cover the ground, Hilary couldn't help but wonder if the two-hour scheduled lay-over would drag out endlessly. She quickly dismissed the disturbing thought. Surely fate had been cruel enough to her today, she reasoned.

By now her ankle had swollen to nearly twice its normal size. She sighed as she thought about how she'd detained the man sitting beside her while she'd had to slowly force her shoe back on, groaning in agony.

Her ankle hung over the shoe like sagging elephant hide. If she'd thought the pain was bad before—well, it was worse now. Recalling the catastrophic course her life had recently taken, Hilary tried to summon up a hint of optimism as she hobbled painfully down the jetway.

At least I can still hobble, she told herself. *And I can still see where I'm going,* she added encouragingly. As a rule, her contacts would be bothering her by now, but they felt pretty good. Hilary limped on with grim determination.

Her improved spirits lasted until she entered the terminal. Her eyes widened when she saw the energetic preschooler who was throwing a temper tantrum. He bolted rebelliously from his mother and dashed headlong in her direction. Trying to sidestep the oncoming human missile, Hilary felt a body hurl against her. The sudden impact knocked her breathless for a moment.

Purse and makeup kit went flying at the same time that Hilary's right eye went blurry. Her hand flew up to try and catch the contact that had been dislodged, but the automatic reflex came too late.

"Frederick Lee! You stop that this moment!" The child's mother marched over to take the little boy by the scruff of the neck. "Just you wait until your father hears about this! Say you're sorry to this nice lady for bumping into her!" The woman turned apologetically to Hilary, who by now had dropped frantically down on her knees and was crawling around the floor of the terminal, searching for the missing contact.

"It's all right...I'm sure Frederick didn't mean any harm..." Hilary was as blind as a bat without her contacts. She welcomed the assistance of several thoughtful travelers who offered to help with the search. In the end, however, the contact was lost forever.

"I'm really sorry about your contact," the harried mother assured Hilary again. She had a firm clasp on the child now. Fascinated, little Frederick was watching Hilary crawl around on the floor.

"Don't worry," Hilary assured the young mother. "I have an extra pair at home." The misfortune meant that she would be half-blind during her stay with Marsha. But only *half*, she consoled herself, still fighting to hold on to her earlier spurt of optimism.

"I saweee wadeee." Frederick had turned sullen in the face of adversity.

"It's quite all right." Hilary's smile was tolerant as one of the gentlemen helping to search for the missing contact took her arm and assisted her to her feet. A renewed surge of pain shot through her ankle, and she bit her lower lip to keep from moaning. Smiling, she thanked the gentleman.

The lady and child merged into the crowd as Hilary gathered her belongings and limped steadfastly toward Gate 78.

As Garth stepped off the plane, he noticed that the runway was crowded with emergency vehicles and personnel. There were two ambulances, two fire trucks, and various pieces of emergency equipment poised on the landing strip Garth's plane had just come in on.

Garth frowned as he noticed Hank Resin coming down the jetway with a hurried stride. Hank had been employed at O'Hare years ago. He'd since married and moved to Raleigh. Garth recalled that Hank had been one of O'Hare's top mechanics.

"Hey, Garth, ol' man! Were *you* on this plane?" Hank's friendly grin was spread all over his face as he reached out to clasp Garth's hand.

"Yes. How are you, Hank?" Garth's frown deepened. "What's going on?"

"Are you serious? You don't know?"

"Know what?"

"There was a little mechanical trouble with the landing gears. The pilot managed to get them working in time...but only seconds before he had to touch down. The ol' wheels popped out of the belly like a roasted turkey!"

Garth grinned lamely, but Hank noticed that his face had turned two shades paler. "No kidding? We were coming in under emergency conditions?"

"Yeah. Flying's a real hair-raiser sometimes, ain't it?"

Garth felt his stomach grow queasy. He'd noticed that the pilot had circled the airport several times, but the idea that the plane was in trouble had never entered his mind. He felt himself go weak with relief at the close call. With his nerves already ragged, he'd have been peeling the paint from the plane's interior had he suspected he was in the middle of a "hair-raiser."

It didn't matter that it was snowing again. All that mattered was that his feet were back on solid ground. At least for now, Garth thought. In another couple of hours he would be airborne again. The flight to West Creek would surely be without incident, he hoped fervently.

As he emerged into the brightly lit terminal, Garth was mumbling under his breath a reassuring litany of statistics proving that the skies were safer now than ever before.

He had to deftly sidestep a woman who was down on her hands and knees in the middle of the floor. Garth swore under his breath and wondered where some of the weirdos he saw in airline terminals ever got the money for a plane ticket.

A few steps later he felt his shoe crunch down on what felt like a piece of glass. He paused momentarily and lifted the sole of his shoe up for inspection. He frowned as he discovered the remnants of a piece of hard candy. On closer inspection, he decided it was a contact lens.

Flicking the lens off his sole, he hurried in the direction of Gate 78.

Hilary stopped at the first pay phone she found. She rummaged in her purse for change to make the call to Marsha. All she could come up with was six pennies, a nasty-looking nickel that had part of a breath mint stuck on it, and a Canadian coin she had picked up somewhere.

By the time she had limped to the nearest coffee shop for change, and limped back, all the phones were in use again. Hilary waited patiently while a frazzled housewife gave final instructions to her husband and children. Hilary was sure the woman's family must have been as happy to have seen her leave as Hilary herself was when the lady finally ran out of time and had to dash to catch her plane.

Hilary dropped the newly acquired coins in the

slot and tapped the numbers. She breathed a sigh of relief when she heard the phone begin to ring.

"Hello! This is Marsha!" Marsha's familiar voice came over the line on the second ring.

"Hi, Marsh! This is—"

Marsha's voice continued. "I'm sorry I can't come to the phone right now. Get this—I'm lying on the warm beaches of sunny Jamaica! At the sound of the tone, please leave your name and number, and I'll return your call when I get home in two glorious weeks!" Following the recorded message, there was a beep.

Hilary clamped her eyes shut in disgust and clenched the receiver tightly in her hands. Jamaica! How could Marsha do this to her!

Hilary hooked the receiver back in place and broke out into a new round of desperate sobs. With her right hand she fumbled blindly through the muddle of wadded tissues overflowing her purse. A clean one was not to be found.

Garth was just about to call his grandparents' number, when he heard the young woman using the phone beside him suddenly burst into tears. He eyed Hilary apprehensively and continued punching out the numbers.

Hilary laid her head on her coat sleeve and cried harder, oblivious to the crowd she was drawing.

Garth watched her from the corner of his eye, noting her unproductive search for a tissue. He reached for his handkerchief and offered it to her.

"Thank you," Hilary accepted the handkerchief gratefully. She promptly wiped her eyes, and Garth resigned himself to the fact that the white linen would be soiled with black mascara. Then he turned his attention away as he heard his grandmother's voice come over the wire.

"Gram? Hi, it's Garth."

"Garthy! How nice to hear from you!" Grace Redmond's matronly voice drifted reassuringly over the wire.

"It's good to hear your voice too, Gram. Listen, I've got some time off and I was wondering if you'd care if I used the beach house."

Garth came right to the point, certain that his grandparents wouldn't object to the loan of the cottage.

"Well, of course you may use the cottage, dear. This is just wonderful! Your cousins are down there right now. If you can get there in the next couple of days, it'll give you a chance to visit with Dorothy, Frank, and the children."

Garth felt the tiny hairs on his neck bristle. Lord! Talk about topping off a rotten day. *Not Dorothy and Frank!* he pleaded silently. "They're using the cottage?" he asked.

"Yes, dear. Isn't it marvelous? They'll be there until ... oh, dear, let me see ... I believe until the day after tomorrow. When did you say your vacation started?"

Garth knew he couldn't tolerate two days locked inside a three-room cabin with his cousin Dorothy, her boastful husband Frank, and five of the rowdiest kids God had ever put on earth. He wasn't about to hurt Gram's feelings, but there was no way he was going anywhere near that cottage until Frank and Dorothy were gone.

"Gee, Gram, that sounds nice, but I'm afraid

I can't make it before Sunday night. I guess by then Dorothy and the family will already have left."

Garth hated to lie, but he would if he had to.

"Oh, dear, I'm afraid they will have. Frank has to be at work on Monday. What a shame! Well, maybe you can visit with them next time," Grace said soothingly.

"Oh, sure thing. Tell them I'm sorry I'll miss them."

"Well, the key's under the mat, Garthy. Now, listen, you will come and see your grandma and grandpa before the winter's over, won't you? We'll be glad to send you a plane ticket."

Garth assured his grandmother that he'd try to make the visit. He thanked her for the use of the cottage and hung up wondering what he would do for the next two days.

The thought of having to spend time in a hotel room wasn't pleasant, but it was his only choice. It beat having to tolerate good ol' hot-winded Frank and his five curtain climbers.

Hilary made a final swipe at her teary eyes as Garth finished his phone conversation. She promptly offered the return of his soiled hand-kerchief.

"Thanks...but just keep it." Garth told her.

"I'm sorry about the mascara. I think it'll come out in cold water," Hilary said, realizing why he was reluctant to accept it back.

"No, really, I don't need it," Garth replied. "Are you all right?"

"I'm fine, thank you."

Garth thought the woman looked as if someone

had just shot her dog. Glancing around for the nearest lounge to wait out the layover, he eventually melted into the crowd as Hilary hobbled over to the waiting area and sat down.

Withdrawing a magazine from her purse, she began to read to pass the time until her plane left for West Creek. She had no idea what she would do when she got there, but she supposed she'd rent a cheap hotel room and try to rest a few days while she gathered her thoughts. Then she'd be forced to make the return trip home.

What was supposed to be a two-hour layover gradually dragged into eight. The lengthy delay didn't surprise her. In view of the past few hours, nothing surprised her.

Having purchased a fresh supply of Kleenex and a cup of hot chocolate around two o'clock, Hilary went back to her seat in the boarding area. By now, she was numb with fatigue, but her ankle didn't throb as much.

Garth spent the time in the lounge, eating bag after bag of corn chips. He had no idea why he was eating them. With his cold, he couldn't taste a thing. He supposed he was bored. The chaotic turn of events he'd encountered the last few hours had numbed him. He sneezed and reached into his pocket for another couple of antihistamines.

Around seven P.M., Flight 263 to West Creek was asked to begin boarding.

Garth boarded the plane last. He walked down the aisle, pausing before seat 3a in the nonsmoking section. He glanced down, and his heart sank. He saw the woman who'd been crying at the pay phone. She was sitting in the seat next to him.

"Hello again." Garth joined her and fastened the belt tightly around his waist. Damn! He hoped she wasn't going to bawl all the way to West Creek. He'd like to catch a few winks of sleep during the short flight.

"Oh...hello." Hilary sniffed and sat up straighter, wiping at her crimson-colored nose. She fought to stem the flow of tears.

Though the endless waterworks were beginning to wear on Garth's nerves, he was determined to be nice.

She was winsomely attractive—even if her eyes did look like two burnt holes in a blanket from all that crying. Shoulder-length dark brown hair framed her face in a soft cloud. Her eyes were a large watery blue, lined with spiky black lashes. She looked like a little pup that had just been kicked.

Under different circumstances Garth would have asked her name, but right now he was bone-weary. Socializing was the last thing on his mind.

"Are you all right?" He finally grumbled under his breath as he reached for the pamphlet the stewardess was holding up.

"Oh, yes. I'm...fine, thank you."

If this was fine, I'd hate to see her when something's really bothering her, Garth thought fleetingly.

Hilary realized she was making him nervous. He was just too polite to say anything. The poor man had been subjected to her blubbering long enough. He had to be getting a little tired of it.

And he had been so nice, lending her his handkerchief and all. Hilary shut her eyes and drew a deep breath. She promised herself she would not think of Lenny Ricetrum. She would allow herself only pleasant thoughts.

"Magazine?" Garth offered, trying to take her mind off her troubles.

"No, thank you. I lost one of my contacts at the airport, and I can't see very well."

"Oh." Garth went back to riffling through the pages of the pamphlet. Hilary noticed that he suddenly paused and stared off into space. He glanced back at her, then quickly back down at the pamphlet.

"Did you lose your contact at this airport?" Garth asked in what he hoped sounded like a casual voice.

"Yes. Why?"

Garth grinned lamely. "Oh, no reason."

Settling back comfortably in her seat, Hilary tried to concentrate on something pleasant.

Moments later she found herself focusing on the man sitting next to her. He was good-looking. Crisp, clean-cut—even though he could stand a shave. His hair was a pretty chestnut color, with red highlights, and his eyes were a nice doe-brown. The build beneath the leather jacket he was wearing was impressive.

He works out, Hilary decided. She turned her gaze back to the window as she caught him looking at her over the top of his magazine.

He wouldn't dump a girl without an explanation the way Lenny had, Hilary thought intuitively. Tears began rolling out of the corners of her eyes.

She fumbled in her purse for a clean tissue but discovered that, as usual, she didn't have one. A few minutes later Hilary heard a resigned sigh, and another snowy-white handkerchief magically appeared in her hand. *No*, she thought as she blew her nose for the hundredth time, *he wouldn't treat a girl that way*.

When the plane touched down in West Creek, Hilary took her makeup kit straight to the ladies' room, where she applied fresh makeup and combed her hair. She was doing better. She hadn't shed a tear for almost thirty minutes, and she was optimistic that the crisis had finally passed.

Nearing the baggage pickup, Hilary witnessed a tender good-bye kiss shared by a young couple who were obviously in love. Her newly acquired "chin-up" attitude wavered, but she quickly diverted her attention and began looking for her luggage.

The revolving rack carouseled one fuzzy-looking suitcase after another past her blurred vision. Finally, Hilary thought she caught sight of two familiar pieces of Samsonite. She reached for the bags and was stunned when a large male hand hastily snaked in from behind her.

"Excuse me, but I believe this is my luggage," Garth apologized.

He groaned when he recognized her again.

Hilary turned to correct the mistaken intruder coolly. "I'm sorry, but I think you must be mistak—Oh, hello! It's you again!" Her face broke into a pleasant smile. "As I was saying, I think you must be mistaken. This is my luggage."

Garth returned her smile tolerantly. "No, I think you're mistaken. This is my luggage."

"Wait just a minute!" Suddenly Hilary had had it with being pushed around. She wasn't about to let this stranger take advantage of her, no matter how nice he'd been earlier. "This is my luggage, and I want you to let go of it!" she demanded.

"This can be settled easily enough." Garth stood his ground. "All we have to do is read the nametags. I'm sure you'll see you're mistaken. It's my luggage."

Hilary glanced around uneasily. The dispute was being closely watched by several other weary travelers eager to retrieve their own baggage. "Oh...yes, of course. That's the sensible thing to do."

Garth lifted the bags off the rack and carried them to the doorway. "Let's see what we have here." He silently read the first tag, and though he was disappointed to find it wasn't his, he found himself grinning devilishly. Glancing up at Hilary, he said solemnly, "I guess I was wrong. The bag isn't mine."

"I know." Hilary forced the smugness out of her voice. "That's what I've been trying to tell you."

Garth picked up the piece of luggage and extended it to her courteously. "Here you go, Harry."

Hilary accepted the bag graciously, then frowned. "Harry?"

Garth lifted one brow questioningly. "You *are* Harry Hasseltine?"

"I certainly am not."

Garth grinned, displaying two of the most delightful dimples Hilary had ever seen. "You're not. That's too bad," he said dryly, "because this bag belongs to Harry Hasseltine."

"What? Let me see that!" Hilary felt her cheeks flush beet-red. On closer examination, Hilary discovered Garth was correct. The bags belonged to Harry Hasseltine. "What about the other one?" she challenged. Hilary thought she should know her own luggage.

Garth read the other tag. This time he was less pleased with the information it provided.

"Well?"

"Yours," he conceded humbly.

"I knew it!"

"Don't gloat."

Hilary forced herself not to. "Well, I suppose my other bag is still on the rack somewhere," she conceded.

They went back to the revolving rack and waited until every single piece of luggage had been claimed. Their three bags failed to appear.

"Damn. There must have been a mix-up somewhere," Garth complained as he picked up her bag and they made their way to the baggage-claims department.

Garth noticed that Hilary was limping as they walked. "What's the matter with your foot?"

Color flooded Hilary's cheeks again. She'd hoped he wouldn't notice her swollen ankle. It strongly resembled an oversized softball now.

"I twisted my ankle earlier," she explained.

"That's too bad."

It took half an hour to inch their way to the claims window. They filled out the proper forms concerning lost luggage. Garth finished first and left a few minutes ahead of her. Hilary experienced a pang of disappointment as she watched him walk away. He'd been nice enough to ask if she needed help getting a cab. She'd gracefully declined his offer, and he'd left her leaning on the counter. He'd smiled at her and said, "Take it easy, Harry!"

When Hilary had completed her form she hobbled outside to summon a taxi. West Creek's weather was considerably better than Raleigh's. The skies were overcast, but there was no sign of snow.

"Hi, again." Hilary set her bag down on the curb. She smiled at Garth, who was still trying to hail a cab.

"Hi. Get the forms filled out?"

"Yes. I hope it doesn't take long to locate the missing luggage."

"Me too. They have practically everything I own," Garth admitted.

Several cabs whizzed by before either Garth or Hilary could bring one to a halt. Garth finally made the first catch.

He opened the door and started to hop in, when he caught sight of Hilary standing on the curb, trying to balance on one leg. With a resigned grin, Garth slid back out of the cab and held the door open for her. "You take this one," he offered. He felt he owed her that much.

"Oh, no...please, I couldn't. You take it. I'll be fine."

"I insist."

"No, *I* insist."

Realizing they'd gone this route before with neither giving an inch, Garth gave in first to save time. "Look, if we don't decide soon, the cab will leave without either one of us."

"I suppose we could share the ride," Hilary conceded. She could feel the exhaustion of the past few hours creeping up on her.

"Fine," Garth agreed. "I'll get your bags for you."

"Thanks." Hilary gratefully handed him her suitcase and makeup kit and limped over to the curb.

As the cab pulled away, Garth instructed the driver to take him to the West Creek Sheraton.

Hilary was grateful the driver assumed they both had the same destination. The hotel sounded terribly expensive to Hilary, who was quietly reassessing her limited funds, but perhaps if she were frugal, she could manage for a few days.

When the driver brought the taxi to a halt outside the Sheraton's elaborate front doors, Hilary knew she wasn't going to be able to afford the hotel.

Garth paid his fare and ducked out the door with a quick "Nice meeting you." The puzzled driver shot Hilary a questioning glance in the rearview mirror.

Hilary grinned back lamely. "Can you recommend a modestly priced hotel? One that's clean," she added quickly.

"Well, let's see . . . The Merrymont isn't bad.

It's a nice family-type place about a mile on down the road."

"Thanks. The Merrymont will do nicely."

About the time Hilary's taxi had pulled up in front of the Merrymont, the management at the Sheraton was informing Garth that they had no available rooms. Had he booked even a day earlier, they could have accommodated him, they said with regret. But no rooms were vacant for tonight.

The manager offered to inquire about vacancies at other establishments, and Garth wearily thanked him. All he cared about was a bed that, hopefully, the roaches wouldn't carry off during the night.

After making several calls, the manager cheerfully informed Garth that he'd secured a room for him at the Merrymont.

"That's fine. How far is it?"

"Just down the road, sir. I'll get you a taxi."

When Hilary entered the Merrymont there were plenty of rooms. There was only one minor problem: The employees of the hotel had gone out on strike two hours earlier. The management assured her that, despite the inconvenience, they would extend every effort to make her stay as comfortable as possible.

"Would you phone the airport for me?" Hilary asked a clerk as she signed the register. "The airline has misplaced one of my bags. As soon as they're able to locate it, I'd like to have it sent directly to my room."

"Yes, ma'am. Your room is 402, and we hope you enjoy your stay." The inexperienced young desk clerk made a wholehearted attempt at professionalism as he handed her the key.

At this point, Hilary didn't care if they put her on the sofa in the lobby. She had to rest her ankle.

"Where are the elevators, please?"

"Oh . . . uh . . . sorry, ma'am. That's another little difficulty we're experiencing. The elevators are out of order right now, but we've called a repairman. He's due anytime. I'm sure he'll have them running in a jiffy. If you'd like to wait in the lobby, you're certainly welcome to do so."

Hilary looked at him in disbelief. "No, thanks. I'll take the stairs."

She silently thanked the airlines for losing her other bag as she limped up four flights of stairs, lugging the makeup kit and dragging the heavy suitcase along behind her.

When she reached the fourth floor she sagged against the wall, gasping for breath. Her heartbeat had to be at least two hundred and sixty-five. She never realized how miserably out of shape she was.

Working her way down the dimly lit hallway, she found her room—the one farthest from the stairway. Hilary unlocked the door, flicked on the lamp, and fell across the bed in exhaustion. It was several moments before she could will herself to get up off the bed and close the door.

Sinking back on the bed, she surveyed the room and found it to be clean and adequately furnished.

A half hour later Hilary finally rolled off the

side of the bed and went in search of the bathroom. The thought of soaking her ankle in a nice hot tub had become her newest priority.

With the tub brimming, its tantalizing warmth inviting, Hilary was mere inches away from submerging her throbbing ankle in the healing waters when a sharp rap at the door sounded.

She groaned and grabbed for the side of the tub. "Who is it?"

The rap sounded again, and she reluctantly reached for her robe. Seconds later she hobbled to the door.

"Yes?" Hilary called from behind the dead bolt.

Silence reigned supreme now.

She waited a few moments, then slid the bolt out of place and eased the door open cautiously.

Sitting before her were three pieces of blue Samsonite.

Realizing that only one could be hers, Hilary stepped into the hall to stop the bellhop. Whoever was responsible for their delivery, however, was long gone by now.

She knelt down to squint at the tags and found that one of the bags was indeed hers. The other two belonged to a Mr. Garth · Redmond . . . whoever he might be.

Hilary sighed and began to drag the luggage into the room. She closed the door and went back in the bathroom. When she was through with her bath, she'd call the desk and inform the clerk of the error. As far as Hilary was concerned, Garth Redmond was going to be without luggage for another hour.

Chapter Four

HILARY LAY IN THE TUB AND soaked the injured ankle for more than an hour. She finally summoned enough energy to dry off and apply cream and powder. She was relieved to have her personal articles back in her possession. She decided that the bath had been just the thing to cheer her up.

Her gaze caught the two pieces of Samsonite still sitting beside the bed. Garth what's-his-name would probably appreciate having his possessions, Hilary conceded with a pang of guilt. She should have reported the mistake earlier.

The teenybopper who was manning the front desk answered her call in a California Valley-voice that Hilary found difficult to decipher.

"Yoah! What is it?" The exuberant greeting caught Hilary off guard. The teen's voice was undergoing rapid adolescent changes. Hilary wasn't sure what he'd said, much less what he'd meant.

"Yes . . . this is Hilary Brookfield in Room 402. Two pieces of luggage have been delivered to my room by mistake."

"No joke?"

"Yes, no joke. Would you please send someone to get them?"

"Sure thing, lady. Do they have a name on 'em?"

"Yes. They belong to Garth Redmond."

"Redmond, Redmond . . ." The young man repeated the name. Hilary could hear him frantically rummaging through his registration forms.

"Yeah, here ya go . . . Garth Redmond. He's in Room 404. Uh, sorry 'bout the mix-up there, lady. Tell ya what I'm gonna do. Soon as I can put a fix on that bellhop guy, I'll send him up to get 'em."

Hilary thought of the hour she'd already wasted. Mr. Redmond would want to have his personal toiletries as soon as possible. Since he was next door, Hilary decided to deliver the bags herself. She'd bet dollars to doughnuts that Mr. Redmond was a kindly old gent who would deeply appreciate her act of kindness.

Besides, there was the staff strike to consider. The few employees the hotel had managed to recruit were inexperienced and, understandably, overworked. With the elevator still on the blink, the least Hilary could do was offer to help.

"If it isn't against hotel policy, I could set Mr. Redmond's luggage outside his door," she said.

"Lady I don't know nothin' about no hotel policy—know what I mean? But if you're sure it wouldn't be too much of a hassle, hop to it." The clerk accepted her offer eagerly.

"All right," Hilary said. "I'll take care of it immediately."

"Gee, thanks a wad, lady."

Hilary hurriedly dressed, then gathered the luggage. Gingerly placing her weight on the injured ankle, she smiled when she discovered that the pain was tolerable. Adding just a fraction more of her weight, she suddenly winced and cried out in pain. The injury was better but far from healed. Hilary didn't need to remind herself a second time to keep most of her weight off that ankle.

Talk about weight! Hilary complained to herself as she grunted and tugged the two bulging suitcases to the door. *Poor old Mr. Redmond must have packed his respirator in one of these things!*

Hilary toyed with the idea of knocking on the door of Room 404 and abandoning the baggage. That's how hers had been delivered. Then she decided against it.

If Mr. Redmond is in ill health, she told herself, *he won't be able to manage the bags by himself.* By now Hilary had convinced herself that Garth Redmond was a senior citizen. He could even be napping and not hear the knock on the door. The bags could be stolen before Mr. Redmond realized they'd even been returned. Hilary decided to knock on the door and assist with the heavy luggage. She tapped lightly, allowing ample time for the aging man to respond.

Mr. Redmond would appreciate her thought-fulness, Hilary told herself again. And it would be nice to hear a man say thank you, for a change. Her morale could use the boost. *Perhaps he's hard of hearing*, Hilary thought as she rapped a second time.

Garth rolled over on the bed and tried to clear his mind. Lack of sleep and the multitude of cold pills he'd been taking were making him so groggy he could hardly wake up. Was someone trying to beat the door down, or was he dreaming?

Annoyed and still half asleep, Garth rolled out of bed as the knock sounded again. He stumbled toward the door, grumbling under his breath about never being able to get any rest, when his big toe found the straight pin that had been care-lessly dropped on the carpeted floor by the last occupant of the room.

"Oh, damn!" Garth sucked in his breath and dropped to one knee as he tried to identify the object that had just harpooned him. A moment later he gingerly plucked the pin from his throb-bing toe. The trickle of blood that oozed from the tiny prick made him feel light-headed. Garth had never been able to stand the sight of blood—especially not his own.

A third knock on the door brought him to his feet again, and he hurried across the room.

"Okay! Okay! Don't knock the thing off its hinges!" Garth shouted irritably. He undid the lock and opened the door a fraction.

Hilary saw one blazing eye peering back at her. "Mr. Redmond? I'm sorry to bother you, but— oh, hi there!" Hilary was shocked yet delighted to see the man from the airport standing in the doorway.

Garth finally managed to focus his bleary gaze on the person standing in the doorway.

It was her again.

"My goodness, what a surprise!" Hilary exclaimed.

"Yeah...How you doing?" Garth tried to remain civil as every bone in his body cried for mercy.

"Well, how do you like that! I thought you were an old man!" she said brightly.

"A what?" Garth sagged against the doorframe, wondering where she got her energy. He knew she had been up all night crying, but she looked as fresh as a daisy. He envied her stamina.

"Are *you* Garth Redmond?"

"I was a few hours ago. I'm not too sure right now."

"Well, I'm Hilary Brookfield. I thought you were staying at the Sheraton., What happened?"

"They didn't have any vacancies." Garth yawned.

"Well, guess what?" Hilary exclaimed.

"I haven't the faintest."

"I have a surprise."

Garth caught himself swáying forward as he felt his energy draining. "You were banging on my door to tell me you have a surprise?" He couldn't believe the woman. "Couldn't it have waited until later?"

"Yes, but I thought you'd want to know right away. Of course, I didn't know *you* were Garth

Redmond, or I wouldn't have bothered you until you had rested a while ..."

Noting his cool indifference, Hilary felt her lower lip begin to quiver, a warning sign Garth had come to recognize and fear. He was acting as if she were bothering him instead of doing him a favor, Hilary thought resentfully.

The ungrateful clod! She'd only wanted to help. All she'd gotten for her efforts was a sarcastic "You were banging on my door to tell me that?" It wasn't fair.

Hilary's injured pride ballooned as she recalled every injustice fate had dealt her in the past twenty-four hours—most of which she considered undeserved.

No one appreciated her. No one. Not Lenny Ricetrum—he'd dumped her for a redhead. Not Marsha—she'd deserted her for Jamaica. A strong wave of self-pity flooded over Hilary, and lack of sleep was not adding to her usual good disposition.

Hilary told herself that she was one giant doormat for the whole world to wipe their dirty feet on. Not even Mr. O'Connor appreciated her, she concluded. If the truth were known, he'd probably agreed to the unscheduled vacation just to get her out of the office.

And now, this ... this *ingrate* didn't even appreciate the effort it took for her to deliver his missing luggage—in person. What did he care that she had a swollen ankle, was blind in one eye, not to mention that she was still in shock from having had her heart ripped right out of her chest!

The list could go on forever and the disinterested look on Garth Redmond's face was the last straw! She began to cry again.

Garth suddenly came to life. He flung open the door and pointed his finger sternly in her direction. "Don't start that again," he warned. He knew that once she was wound up the tears wouldn't stop for hours.

"I bothered you to return your luggage, Mr. Redmond! I was 'banging' on your door because I thought you might appreciate having clean clothes." Hilary stiffened her lower lip defensively. "I can see I was mistaken."

Garth glanced down, and he saw the two bags sitting at her feet. "Oh...well...thanks." He felt like a heel for shouting at her.

"Thanks?"

Garth bristled at the sharp accusation in her voice. "Yes, thanks! I appreciate it!" Lord, what did the woman want? Blood?

"Well, all I can say is, if I had known they were your bags, I wouldn't have put myself out to deliver them," Hilary declared.

"I said I appreciate it. Do you want me to get down on my knees and say it again?"

"That won't be necessary...but do you realize the elevator's out," Hilary reminded him.

"You carried the bags up four flights of stairs?" Garth didn't know why she had his bags or why she would want to carry them up four flights of stairs on a twisted ankle, just to bring them to him.

Hilary refused to answer. He could come to whatever conclusion he wanted. She hadn't carried the bags up four flights of stairs, but she was feeling just neglected and irritated enough to let him think she had.

"All right," Garth conceded. "I appreciate your delivering the bags, okay? I was half asleep, and I didn't mean to snap at you." He'd feel awful if anyone had seen her dragging his luggage up the stairs—at least anyone who could connect the bags to him. She couldn't weigh more than a hundred pounds soaking wet...And with that twisted ankle...Garth flinched.

"I accept your apology, and you can rest assured I'll not be bothering you again," Hilary promised. She was still visibly miffed at what she considered his bad manners. She turned and began to hobble back to her room.

"You staying here?"

The slamming of a door gave Garth his answer; she was right next door.

Garth glanced around, feeling that he was being watched. He noted the piercing surveillance of a middle-aged woman across the hall. Her dark eyes impaled him from behind her half-opened door, and it was evident that she'd monitored the whole conversation.

"Look, I'm sorry," Garth apologized. He turned his palms up helplessly. "I didn't ask her to bring my luggage. Okay?"

The woman, whose hair was wrapped tightly in pink curlers, gave him a nasty look before she slammed her door shut as well.

When Hilary returned to her room she flung herself across the bed. The unnerving encounter

59

with Garth Redmond had only served to remind her of how alone she was. She buried her face in the depths of the pillow and wished she had never made this miserable trip. It was just another harrowing episode on her growing list of mistakes.

Feeling a stab of homesickness, Hilary considered returning to Denver on the next available flight. Obviously she wasn't going to be able to forget Lenny. A week's vacation would have been nice, but with Marsha gone, it seemed pointless.

Hilary felt that she might as well go home and face the problem head on. It wouldn't be pleasant, but she was sure she would survive. She decided to rest just a few minutes before she called the airport . . .

Giving the woman across the hall a mental raspberry, Garth picked up the two bags and carried them into his room.

He realized he'd been sharp with . . . what was the girl's name? Hilda . . . Holly . . . Heidi? He couldn't remember, but he regretted having made her cry again.

The woman had problems, but so did he. Garth absentmindedly touched the heavy stubble on his face. What he needed was a shower, a shave, and twenty-four hours of undisturbed sleep.

The shower worked like a shot of adrenaline. Garth shaved, then dressed, but his conscience still nagged him.

Maybe he should step next door and thank the girl again for bringing his luggage. Garth shook his head admiringly. *Four* flights of stairs! With a twisted ankle, dragging two bags that weighed as much as she did!

The woman had guts.

Garth knew he would sleep better if he checked on her first. He sighed, slapped on a musky-smelling aftershave, combed his hair, and quickly left the room.

He tapped softly on the door of Room 402, praying that the woman in the pink curlers across the hall wouldn't hear him. He waited several minutes before he tapped again. Still no response.

Well, so much for chivalry, Garth thought as he turned to go back to his room. Heidi was probably down in the bar having a drink; she must have forgotten all about the incident.

As Garth entered his room again he hung the Do Not Disturb sign on the doorknob outside. Seconds later he climbed wearily back into bed. For the next forty-eight hours he was going to do what he'd been sent here to do: Relax.

Chapter Five

STARTLED BY SHOUTS AND POUNDing on doors, Garth sat bolt upright in bed. Fighting off the cobwebs of a deep sleep, he shook his head several times. He tried to focus his vision. *Now* what was going on, he wondered irritably.

If he'd felt annoyed at the earlier interruption, Garth was inclined to be furious this time. He had been so tired that it had taken him an hour to relax and finally doze off.

Garth was sure he couldn't have slept more than a moment, even if the clock on the nightstand told him otherwise. He had slept for at least ten hours. It was morning now, almost six-thirty A.M.

Grabbing the rumpled sheet, Garth gave it a good jerk and tossed it aside. His feet hit the floor at the same time a loud knock sounded at the door. He grabbed his pants off the back of a chair.

If Heidi was back again, he'd personally strangle her, he vowed as he fumbled for his shoes. Mumbling a few choice threats under his breath, he searched frantically under the bed for the missing mate. He wasn't going to take the chance of being harpooned again.

There was another sharp rap at the door, followed by a man's voice. "Open up!" he shouted.

Garth retrieved the missing shoe as another sudden loud thump at the door sent his head banging into the frame of the bed.

"Damn!" Garth ran his tongue over his bleeding lip as he clutched the shoe and crawled to freedom.

Rubbing the goose egg-sized lump that was beginning to rise on top of his head, he hopped to the door while trying to put his shoe on at the same time. He jerked the door open, vowing to take revenge on the knucklehead responsible for the invasion of his privacy. Garth was totally unprepared to see a fireman standing in his doorway.

"Yes?"

"Sorry to disturb you, sir, but we're going to have to ask you to vacate the building."

He noted the man's fire-fighting gear. The man stood, ax in hand, in the hallway reeking now with thick foul-smelling smoke. Coughing, Garth had a sinking feeling that this wasn't a fire drill.

As if his nerves weren't already dangling by threads! The thought of being fried alive didn't help the situation any!

"Oh, hell!" Garth turned four shades paler. "What's going on?"

Recognizing the panic etched on Garth's face,

the fireman tried to calm him down. "We have a small fire here on the fourth floor, sir. We're asking all the guests to vacate the premises immediately."

"Ah . . . yeah . . . sure. I just need to get my things first." Garth whirled around when the man's sharp rebuttal stopped him.

"Leave them!"

"But—"

"Look, mister, right now we've got this thing under control. But it's possible that could change."

"Oh . . . yeah. I'm going."

"Take the stairs at the end of the hall, buddy. *Don't* use the elevator!" The fireman warned. Then he continued down the hall to alert the other guests.

Moving in a daze, Garth headed for the end of the hallway. As he passed Room 402 the door flew open, and Hilary came rushing out. She was clutching something to her chest.

Garth noticed she was wearing her nightie. "Are you still here?" He realized that the fireman should have knocked on the door of 402 before banging on his.

"I had to go back for my makeup," Hilary said breathlessly.

"Your *what?*"

"My makeup." She looked at Garth guiltily. "I look terrible without it . . ." Her lame reply was drowned out by the harsh demands of the fireman shouting.

"Hey, you two! Out of the building. *Now!*"

Garth took Hilary firmly by the arm and propelled her toward the stairway. "Come on, we have to take the stairs!" As he opened the door to the stairway he drew her back protectively into his arms when he saw the cloud of thick smoke blocking the fire exit. "We can't take the stairs," he said needlessly.

"Oh, my gosh! What'll we do?" Garth could feel Hilary trembling as he drew her closer to him.

"Come on." Garth grabbed her hand and pulled Hilary along behind him. Remembering her injured ankle, Garth finally stopped and scooped her up in his arms, then raced down the hall to the outside fire escape.

As he stepped onto the metal steps, a gust of frigid air rippled up the back of the thin shirt he was wearing.

"I wish you'd brought a coat while you were at it," Garth bantered, trying to ease the look of horror on Hilary's face. He felt her arms tighten around his neck more securely.

"What's wrong?"

Wide-eyed, Hilary shook her head. "No...I can't..." She was looking down, shaking her head, her arms wrapped around his neck so tightly he could barely breathe.

"Oh, yes, *we* can," Garth assured her, trying to loosen the stranglehold she had on his throat.

Too petrified to speak, Hilary fervently shook her head, no!

"Just hold on. I'll carry you down—"

"Down? On, no! You can't..." she pleaded. "I'm terrified of heights!"

Heights! Garth thought. *It's not as though we're*

on top of the Eiffel Tower, for crying out loud!
Seeing fresh tears surfacing in her eyes, Garth
sighed.

"And I'm not overly fond of being burned
alive," he said, "so let's compromise. You shut
your eyes and don't look down, and I'll get us out
of here before the whole building goes up in
flames."

With a horrified gasp, Hilary buried her face
in his neck. "I'm scared, Garth."

"I'm scared, too," he admitted. "Just hold on."

She nodded. "Please walk slowly."

"It depends on how hot it gets." Garth hefted
her up more comfortably in his arms, then began
to ease his way down the metal stairway.

The wind was gusty, and it was getting colder.
The streets below were teeming with activity as
sirens wailed and flashing red lights lit up the
darkened sky.

"It's all right. We're only four floors up. It's
really not that high." He encouraged her as he
took each step slowly. He was careful to keep his
voice calm as he cautiously wound his way
around the narrow staircase. Heights were not
exactly Garth's favorite thing either, and the
small patches of ice he encountered occasionally
on the steps were not exactly comforting.

"Are you all right?"

"Are we almost down?"

"Not quite. Three floors to go."

"Three!"

"You're doing fine. Don't look down."

"I'm not looking in any direction."

It wasn't until his feet had touched solid

ground that Hilary stopped shaking and she dared to open her eyes.

The impact of what was happening finally hit her like a ton of bricks.

"Oh, my gosh! What about my clothes? I'm not even dressed!"

Shivering with cold, Garth set her on her feet. "I don't know. We'll have to see how bad the fire turns out to be. The fireman talked as if they had it under control."

Volunteers from the Red Cross hurried over to drape warm blankets around their shoulders. Cups of hot coffee were placed in their hands, and they gratefully sipped as they were pushed aside by the milling crowd.

They wandered across the street and sat down on the curb, drinking the coffee and staring up at the fourth floor where all their personal belongings were.

"There's an awful lot of smoke coming out of those windows," Hilary observed.

"Not that much. You know how safety-conscious hotels are. They'll have us back in our rooms in a few hours at the most," Garth predicted.

As he spoke, angry flames began to belch out of several windows on the fourth floor.

"Oh, dear," Hilary winced. "I think we've had it."

Had it they had.

The fire developed into a major one. While Garth and Hilary sat and sipped coffee, the entire fourth and fifth floors of the hotel went up in flames.

Every stitch of clothing they had brought with them, except for the few pieces they had on their backs, burned before their eyes.

Garth took the disaster with resignation. "You know, Heidi—"

"It's Hilary," she corrected him. "Hilary Brookfield."

"Oh, I'm sorry. I've been trying to remember," Garth apologized. "Anyway, as I was saying, I've had one hell of a twenty-four hours. What about you?"

Hilary nodded. "Miserable! And I came here to get away from it all!"

Garth looked at her and began to chuckle. A deep, nice sound. One that brought an immediate smile to Hilary's face. "You too?"

They both broke out into laughter, relieving the tension that had been building for hours.

"Well . . ." Garth leaned his elbows back on the curb when their amusement finally subsided. He stared up at the burning fourth and fifth floors of the hotel. "Things could be worse. Material possessions can be replaced. At least no lives were lost."

Hilary had to agree. He was right . . . It could have been much worse.

"Wonder how it started?"

"I heard someone say a man was smoking in bed."

"That's sad."

"Well . . ." Garth yawned and stretched lazily. "I don't know about you, but I could use something to eat. Are you hungry?" He smiled, determined to make the best out of a bad situation.

Hilary realized that she hadn't eaten a thing in the last twenty-four hours. "Yes, I'm starved."

Having spotted a small diner across the street earlier, they wandered away from the scene of the fire.

"I shouldn't go in looking like this," Hilary fretted. She clutched the blanket more tightly around her chin.

"No one will care," Garth promised. He ushered her into the warmth of the small building. It was almost deserted; everyone was watching the fire.

The menu didn't offer a large selection, but after pondering the choices they settled for grilled cheese sandwiches and Cokes.

Sharing a broken-down booth, they ate the meal slowly, savoring the warmth of the diner as they watched the frenzied activity outside.

Eventually the conversation drifted to the reason they were both in West Creek, and once more Hilary felt the hot sting of tears.

Garth glanced up from his plate expectantly, surprised to see that she was crying again. "Hey, what are the tears for? I thought we agreed we were pretty lucky."

"Oh, it isn't the fire..." Hilary fumbled for a tissue, waving one hand dismissively as she blew her nose. "Just ignore me. It'll pass in a minute."

"Look..." Garth reached in his pocket and retrieved the handkerchief she had used earlier. He handed it to her. "I've watched you crying for twenty-four hours. I don't know what's wrong, but it surely can't be all that bad."

"But it is," she sobbed, burying her face in the

handkerchief for another good cry. "I've been dumped!"

"Dumped?" Garth looked at her blankly. *Dumped. What was that supposed to mean?*

When the tears finally subsided, Hilary found herself telling Garth about her recent breakup with Lenny, the harrowing ride to the airport, how she'd twisted her ankle, lost a contact, and Marsha's unexpected exit to Jamaica.

Instead of dismissing her troubles as minor and unworthy of such a concentration of despair, Garth was surprisingly understanding.

"I know how you feel," he admitted. "The reason I'm here is because my boss thinks I'm stressed out."

"Well, I thought I had stress before," Hilary confessed, trying to find a dry spot on the handkerchief to blow her nose. "But since I left Denver, it's been Trauma City."

Garth nodded. "I know." It hadn't exactly been Christmas morning for him either. "Well, look,"—Garth reached over to take her hand supportively—"It's been rough, but the worst is over. As soon as we can, we'll look for new accommodations, and then we'll both get that rest we came for."

"Yes, I suppose so."

Funny, Hilary would have thought that a man holding her hand would upset her so soon after Lenny. Instead, she found the unexpected gesture comforting. Garth had nice hands, large and protective. For the first time in hours, Hilary felt the world beginning to turn right side up again.

"Do you have any idea what you're planning

to do, now that your friend is in Jamaica?" Garth asked.

"I was planning on taking the next flight home—before the fire." Hilary surveyed her bathrobe dismally. "Now, I don't know. I'll have to have clothes before I get on a plane."

"Well, I suppose we can—" Garth's words were severed in midsentence as he felt a steel hand clamp down on his shirt collar. He glanced up, and his eyes widened as he was jerked out of the booth by the scruff of his neck.

"What the—" Garth yelled as a man twice his size—twice anyone's size—dangled him in the air by his collar. The intruder glared at Garth as if he were about to disassemble him—piece by piece.

The burly character looked Garth squarely in the eye without blinking and stated in a voice that sounded like creek gravel, "The question is, what do *you* think you're doing, chump!"

By now Garth was red-faced and gasping for breath. He was clearly in no condition to answer the man's question.

"Hey! You want to put me down!" Garth finally managed to wheeze out. He had no idea who this maniac was or what he'd done to antagonize him. The only thing he *was* sure of was that he had no intention of provoking him further.

Like a bolt of lightning, Hilary sprang to her one good foot. "You put him *down* this instant!" she demanded. "Who do you think you are?"

Oh, please, Hilary don't get him any madder!

Lori Copeland

Garth willed silently as he watched her go nose-to-nose with the giant.

"I'm warning you! *Put him down!*" Hilary threatened. She snapped her fingers, then pointed at the giant authoritatively.

Maybe she knows karate, Garth prayed. His face was beginning to turn a splotchy blue. No, even if she knew karate, kung fu and had a Sears, Roebuck chain saw in the pocket of her bathrobe, Garth realized, she still was no match for this bonzo burger.

To Garth's astonishment, Hilary got her point across. The giant dropped Garth like a sack of grain, and he fell limply into the booth as the man confronted Hilary, still eye-to-eye.

Garth began sucking in deep gulps of air as Hilary spoke to the bully curtly. "Just what do you think you're doing?"

"I came looking for you, babe." The man's deep voice had suddenly taken on a tone of boyish pleading as he stepped forward and tried to take Hilary in his arms.

"Wait a minute!" Garth moved to protect Hilary, but she gently pushed him back down in the booth.

"It's all right," she said. "I'll take care of this."

"Are you sure?" Garth was confident there wasn't a lot he could do anyway—given the hundred-pound difference in size between himself and the giant—but he was willing to try.

"How did you know where to find me?" Hilary asked calmly, ignoring Garth's struggle to get to his feet again.

Garth had a tight feeling in the pit of his stom-

72

ach, coinciding with the one he still had around his neck. All he'd ever heard about "a lover scorned" came rushing back to him. This undoubtedly must be "the rat," Lenny Ricetrum.

"I called the boss, and he said you'd gone to West Creek to spend some time with a girlfriend. Some girlfriend!" Lenny sneered. He glanced at Garth disdainfully, then back to Hilary and demanded, "Where's your clothes?"

"On the fourth floor of that burning hotel!"

Lenny shot a hurried glance out of the window. Assured that she was telling him the truth, his scowl began to slowly recede.

"Mr. O'Connor told *you* where I was?" Hilary demanded.

"Well, not me exactly. I had a friend call. Jake told Michael that he was your cousin from out of town," Lenny admitted.

It infuriated Hilary to think that Lenny had stooped to such low-down tactics. Especially after having treated her so badly.

"I realized I made a mistake, babe." Lenny smiled at her persuasively. "I came all this way just so we could patch things up."

"Oh, what a shame! Did you bring the little redhead too?" Hilary asked pleasantly.

Garth found it hard to believe that this was the man Hilary had wept through three boxes of Kleenex for. Lenny didn't appear to be her type.

"I don't want the redhead, Hilary. I want you," Lenny admitted contritely. He tapped a tightly clenched fist against his leg and shot Garth another nasty look. His voice dropped repentantly. "I made a mistake, okay?"

"Well, Lenny, we all make mistakes, but I'm afraid this one can't be corrected that easily," Hilary told him.

Reconciling with Lenny? After he had treated her so shabbily? Hilary realized that was something she was going to have to think about.

"Come on, honey," Lenny coaxed. "Let's go somewhere and talk this thing over." He shot Garth another warning look.

Hilary looked at Garth, then back at Lenny.

"Go ahead. Don't worry about me," Garth offered, hoping they would leave him out of it.

Hilary realized she was about to do a devious thing, but she needed time to think. She just hoped Garth would play along.

"No, I don't think so. I'm here for vacation, and I'm staying." She slid in the booth next to Garth and slipped her arm through his. "With Garth."

Garth's eyes widened.

Lenny's upper lip curled ominously as his snapping black eyes openly accused Garth of trifling with his woman.

"I thought you were going to take the next plane," Garth reminded Hilary as he casually removed her arm from his.

Garth liked Hilary, and he would have helped her out if he could have. But he wasn't prepared to lose his life for her.

"I'm staying!" Hilary said. She firmly linked her arm back with his.

"Now, look"—Garth was beginning to lose his patience—"I don't want to get involved in this..."

Lenny's face resembled an approaching cloudburst. "Well, well, well! Ain't this cozy! You work fast, buddy boy!"

"No, this isn't what you think." Garth tried to explain, but Hilary was doing nothing to help. In fact, she seemed to be deliberately egging him on. "Tell him, Hilary . . ."

"Tell him what?" Hilary asked unconcernedly. She picked up the menu to study it.

"Tell him why we happen to be together." Garth decided to be firm with her. "Right now! I've grown fond of my neck!"

Lenny looked as if he were ready to blow a fuse.

"Leave Garth alone, Lenny. You're making him nervous," Hilary said obediently.

"Are you coming with me, or are you staying here with this jerk?" Lenny demanded. He was getting tired of begging. Lenny Ricetrum had never begged a woman in his life, and he sure wasn't about to start now.

Hilary carefully placed the menu back on the rack. "I'm staying with the jerk," she announced.

"Now just a minute . . ." Garth said resentfully.

Hilary patted Garth's arm reassuringly. "Go away, Lenny. Garth and I want to be alone."

Garth was dismayed. Every word Hilary said was clearly designed to give the erroneous impression that he and she were together. Really *together!* Garth had the growing suspicion that Lenny Ricetrum planned to squeeze him to death . . . slowly and painfully.

Hilary's reaction left Garth bewildered and just a little irritated. He had enough trouble without having an irate boyfriend on his tail. Not only was Hilary deliberately aggravating a man who weighed twice what Garth did, she seemed to be enjoying it!

The sound of a meaty fist crashing down on the table convinced Garth that Lenny was aware of the goading.

"Look, Ricetrum. I haven't moved in on your territory, but if the lady doesn't want to go with you, she doesn't want to go," Garth said. He stood up to face his adversary, trying to remember if he had ever made out a will.

Garth winced as the meaty fist hit the table a second time, rattling the dishes loudly again.

"Hey, you, back there! What are you trying to do, tear down the joint?" The proprietor of the diner shouted. "Either put a lid on it, or take it down the street!"

Thank God! Reinforcements! Garth's knees sagged with relief. He'd wondered just how long the owner would continue to keep his eyes glued to the football game on the portable black-and-white television set.

Lenny eyed Garth coldly. Hilary glared at Lenny with a look that could freeze hell over, and Garth wished to high heaven he'd never left Chicago.

"Well, you and ol' lover boy better watch your step," Lenny warned, deciding to let the matter lie for the moment. "But let me warn you, sweetheart, you'd better reconsider."

Garth put his arm around Hilary protectively. "Why don't you bug off, Ricetrum. Can't you see the lady's not interested?"

Garth's eyes suddenly bulged as Lenny pulled him up again and jerked the collar of his shirt into a tight knot, choking off his breath once more.

"Hilary, dammit! Tell him you'll at least think about it!" Garth gasped.

"Never," Hilary stated calmly.

"You better hope she gives it another thought, sucker. You'd just better hope she does!"

Lenny dropped Garth back down onto his feet, pivoted on the ball of his foot, and marched out of the restaurant angrily.

Garth grabbed his swollen neck and fell back in the booth limply.

He shot Hilary a murderous look as she sat calmly sucking up what was left of her Coke through a straw.

Stress? Joel Anderson had thought Garth was suffering from stress before? He should see him now.

Chapter Six

"OKAY, YOU WANT TO TELL ME what *that* was all about."

Garth was still shaken by the events of the past five minutes. From the moment he'd first laid eyes on Hilary, he'd wondered if she wasn't an apple short of being a bushel.

Now he strongly suspected she was—and it was beginning to look as if she were harboring a silent death wish for him.

Rubbing his aching throat, Garth waited while Hilary nervously twisted her straw into the shape of a distressed pretzel.

"That was Lenny—the man I told you about."

"I just about had that figured out."

Guiltily, Hilary dropped her eyes away from Garth's. "I should have warned you. Lenny has a nasty temper."

"I noticed that right away, too. What I didn't notice was that we were together—I mean, as in *personally* together!" Garth challenged.

Hilary hung her head sheepishly. "Oh, that ... Well, I had to think fast. I'm sorry I involved you, but I knew Lenny would insist I return to Denver with him ... and I don't want to."

"You don't want to!" Garth shook his head in disbelief. "I thought that's what all the water-works were about."

"Yes ... but I need time to think." Hilary deposited the mangled straw in the ashtray. "Lenny needs to be taught a lesson. He can't just up and dump me, then waltz back into my life as if nothing happened." She had a little pride left.

"Fine! But from now on, pick another guinea pig," Garth warned. He reached for the check. "I came here looking for a little peace and quiet, and I don't plan to get involved in a lovers' spat."

"Lenny isn't my lover," Hilary stated flatly.

"Well, he sure isn't mine!"

Hilary's face suddenly softened. "I'm sorry, Garth ... really."

"It's okay ... And I don't want you to take this personally, but I think it's time we went our separate ways." Garth didn't mean to sound harsh, yet he felt it imperative to let her know where he stood. Fate had thrown them together constantly, but the time had come to part.

"Oh, I don't take it personally," Hilary assured him. "I think you're right ... and I'm sorry about involving you the way I did. It won't happen again."

Garth straightened his collar petulantly, wincing when the material rubbed his bruised neck. "It's all right ... but don't do it again."

"I wouldn't think of it." Hilary slid out of the booth and reached for the check. "Please, I insist on paying."

"That isn't necessary," Garth said dismissively. "I'll get it." He reached over and absent-mindedly tucked the blanket up closer around her neck. "You're...uh...you're showing too much..." Garth was finding it increasingly hard to keep his eyes off the tantalizing sight of the soft swell of creamy flesh the blanket was doing an inadequate job of concealing.

"Oh," Hilary glanced down, wondering exactly how much of her "uh's" had been exposed. "Thank you."

"You're welcome." *She sure has some figure,* Garth thought. He ran his eyes lazily over her petite form, which was draped enchantingly in the dark blanket. No wonder Ricetrum had blown his cool.

"About the check...I really wish you'd let me pay," Hilary persisted as she reached for her purse.

"It's not necessary," Garth repeated. He didn't want to stand there all night and argue over four dollars and twenty-eight cents.

"But I want to," Hilary insisted, and Garth found himself returning her smile.

He reached over and ruffled her hair good-naturedly. She had pretty hair, thick and lustrous. "I'll get the check," he stated firmly.

"You've been awfully nice about all of this." With a sparkle in her eyes that Garth found disturbingly appealing, Hilary reached for her makeup kit, and the blanket slipped a notch lower. She glanced up and smiled guiltily as Garth quickly averted his eyes. She tugged the blanket primly back in place.

"Oh, dear!"

"What now?" Garth noticed she was looking askance at the makeup kit.

"My purse . . . it's still in the hotel room."

"You mean you saved the makeup kit and left your purse?" He found that sort of feminine behavior hard to comprehend.

Hilary nodded miserably. "It had my plane ticket and all my money in it."

"Oh, bother!" Garth swore under his breath, realizing what her loss could mean.

She lifted her eyes hopefully. "What do you think I should do?"

"I don't know." Garth wasn't sure what *he* was going to do, but he knew one thing: He wasn't in any shape to be responsible for her too. "I'll take care of the check; then we'll try to figure out something."

"Thanks . . . I'll pay you back."

While he was paying the cashier, Hilary tried to decide what to do next. She couldn't expect Garth to take care of her. They barely knew each other, and he had made it clear that he was in West Creek for complete relaxation. He had been wonderful to her, but she couldn't continue to impose upon him.

She would have to call her parents and ask them to wire money, but she realized even that could take time. What was she to do in the meantime?

Garth returned from the cashier. They stood

for a moment. He smiled lamely, and she smiled back.

Garth barely knew her, yet he couldn't just leave her sitting in a diner wrapped in a blanket. But if he took her with him, he'd never get any rest. Her luck seemed to be as incredibly rotten as his.

"Do you know anyone else in West Creek you can call?"

"No." Hilary shook her head sadly. "I'll have to call my parents and have them wire me some money."

"That sounds good."

"It might take a few hours to get it."

Garth was relieved to hear she at least had a plan. "That shouldn't be a problem." Two hours . . . two measly hours and then he could be on his way again.

"What will you do?" Hilary asked politely.

"I'll check with the hotel, but I think our clothes are gone for good. I was thinking maybe I should walk down to one of the department stores and pick out a few pieces of clothing to tide me over."

"Oh . . . that sounds nice. Would you mind if I tagged along until my money gets here?"

"No, I suppose not," Garth agreed cautiously. He eyed her blanket worriedly. "Just be sure you keep that thing pulled up."

"Maybe I shouldn't go." Hilary quickly reassessed her state of undress. "I might embarrass you . . ."

"I don't see that you have much choice. Besides, if anyone asks why you're wearing the blanket, we'll explain what's happened. Just keep the thing pulled up tight."

Obediently, Hilary hitched the blanket higher. "I will." She smiled up at him through lowered lashes, and Garth felt his pulse quicken.

Don't be getting any ideas about her, he warned himself. *She's nothing but bad news, Redmond. All you have to do is see that she's taken care of for another two hours; then it's so long, sweetheart.*

The reassuring thought made Garth feel better.

While Garth browsed through the men's department, Hilary phoned her parents in Denver. They quickly assured her they would send the money.

"Hotel fire! Are you sure you're all right? We thought you were going to be staying with Marsha!" Maxie Brookfield exclaimed.

"I'm fine, Mom. Honest. It was so late when I arrived that I thought I'd just stay at a hotel tonight," Hilary fabricated. She hated to mislead her mother, but she didn't want her to know her true predicament. Although Hilary had lived away from home for four years, her parents were still protective enough to worry about her if they thought she was alone in West Creek. Fortunately, Maxie didn't press the issue.

"Honey, don't you worry!" Simon Brookfield's voice came over the line to comfort his daughter. "We'll take care of the problem immediately. You're sure you're all right?"

"I'm fine, Dad. Just wire the money, and I'll pay you back when I get home."

As Hilary replaced the receiver a few minutes

later, she thought how nice it was to have parents. Especially understanding ones who asked very few questions.

Garth was examining a black-and-red flannel shirt when Hilary found him in the men's department.

He thoughtfully eyed his reflection in the full-length mirror, then turned and lifted his brows expectantly. "What do you think?"

"It's nice. You look good in red." *Actually, he would look good in anything,* Hilary found herself thinking. *Or in absolutely nothing . . .* She was shocked to have such thoughts about a complete stranger.

"Did you get through to your parents?"

"Yes. Daddy's making all the arrangements. He'll be calling me back as soon as the transaction is completed. I gave him the number of the store, and the manager said he would be happy to page me when the call comes through."

"Good." Garth said absently. He decided to take the shirt. "We'll just kill time until he calls back."

Glancing at Hilary, Garth felt a tug of compassion. She looked pitiful standing there in that blanket.

"Hey, why don't you pick yourself out a few things? I'll lend you the money, and you can pay me back when your money gets here," Garth offered casually.

"Oh, I couldn't. You've been too kind already."

"No, go ahead. You can't run around that way." He was beginning to resent some of the suggestive looks a few of the male shoppers had already given her. "Buy whatever you need."

"It would be so nice...if you're sure you wouldn't mind." Hilary jumped at the opportunity to rid herself of the embarrassing blanket.

"I'm sure." Garth disappeared into the dressing room to try on a pair of black trousers while Hilary went off to make her own selections.

She was trying to decide on an inexpensive coat when the saleswoman approached her. "Miss Brookfield?"

"Yes."

"You have a call at the counter."

"Thanks." She grabbed the midcalf-length burgundy coat and added it to the jeans, undies, gloves, and blouse she had already selected. Then she eagerly trailed behind the elderly woman to the service counter.

"Hi, Dad. Is everything taken care of?"

"Honey, now don't worry...They're having some sort of a computer malfunction at the Western Union office here, but the money's on its way."

"Good. How long will it take?"

"Well, that's the catch. You won't be able to pick it up until tomorrow morning," Simon explained apologetically.

"Tomorrow morning!" Hilary exclaimed, trying unsuccessfully to hide her disappointment. "Oh, Dad! Can't they get it here sooner than that?"

"I'm afraid not. Just have Marsha drive you to the Western Union office anytime after eight tomorrow morning. The money will be there waiting."

"But Marsha . . ." Hilary caught herself just in time. She realized she couldn't tell him Marsha was in Jamaica, while *she* was stranded in West Creek, penniless, with nowhere to spend the night.

"Hilary? Are you still there?"

"Yes. Tomorrow morning will be fine, Daddy. Thanks. I'll call you and let you know when I get the money," she promised. She quickly hung up before her courage failed.

The saleswoman had overheard the conversation, and Hilary suddenly found herself telling her about her miserable plight. She burst out into a fresh round of tears.

The clerk was just handing her a fresh tissue when Garth approached the counter with his arms loaded with garments.

"What's wrong now?" He dropped the bundle and automatically reached into his back pocket for a handkerchief. He knew Hilary well enough by now to know that she would go through her tissue in a matter of minutes.

Between sobs, Hilary recounted the details of her conversation with her father. At the conclusion of her tearful report, the saleswoman shot Garth an expectant look and leaned across the counter. "The poor little thing is in an awful predicament," she said sympathetically.

"I'm aware of that."

"Good! Then you won't just walk off and leave her?"

Garth eyed the salesclerk coolly. "I hadn't planned on it."

"There, there, dear! I'm sure everything will

work out all right." The motherly clerk tried to soothe Hilary. "This gentleman said he would stay with you."

"Oh, thank you, but I've been enough trouble to him as it is." Hilary accepted the handkerchief and blew her nose.

"Let's not panic," Garth said—for the sake of both women. He reached into his billfold for a credit card. "Put her purchases on here too."

The clerk nodded pleasantly. "If you'd like to slip into the dressing room and put these on, I'll make out the tickets," she told Hilary as she handed her a complete change of clothing.

While Hilary dressed, Garth paid for their purchases, then walked over to the elevator. Leaning down for a drink of water from the fountain, he started and jumped back as the flow spurted up to hit him full in the face. Reaching for his handkerchief, he remembered it was gone.

Sighing, Garth mopped the water off his face with the sleeve of his shirt. He found it hard to believe that just the day before he had been in Chicago—only mildly stressed out.

Hilary came out of the dressing room carrying the neatly folded blanket, her nightie, and her makeup kit. She located Garth and smiled, and he felt his stomach flutter. The jeans and blouse she was wearing fit her like a glove, and he was forced to admit to himself how attractive she was.

"You look better," he complimented her. He handed her the shopping bag with her other purchases inside.

"Thanks. What's that all over the front of your

shirt?'' Hilary opened the bag and retrieved the coat and gloves. She slipped them on as he punched the button for the elevator.

"Water."

"Oh." Hilary didn't dare ask him how it got there.

They got on the elevator and rode to the ground floor. As they emerged from the revolving doors a blast of frigid air hit them in the face.

"It's getting colder," Hilary observed.

Pulling up the collar of his new jacket, Garth scanned the sky thoughtfully. "Yeah, it looks like rain."

They paused beside a streetlight, each sneaking an uneasy glance at the other. It would be the opportune time to part company.

"Well . . ."

"Well . . ." The thought of having to spend the night at a bus station or all-night café flashed horrifyingly before Hilary's eyes.

"I suppose we should check with the hotel and see what they suggest," Garth offered.

"Yes, that's a good idea."

They walked back to the Merrymont at a brisk pace, seeking shelter deep in the linings of their coats from the rising wind.

When they arrived it didn't surprise them to learn that the hotel had ceased operations for the time being. There was still a thick plume of black smoke drifting out of the windows of the fourth and fifth floors.

"Well, back to square one," Garth said as they walked back out to the street.

Feeling like an anchor around his neck, Hilary

knew the time had come to set him free. He had been nicer than the average person would have been, but she couldn't impose on him any longer. Already she was feeling a dependency on him that she shouldn't feel.

"Garth..." He paused and she turned to face him. She had to raise her voice above the rising wind. "You go on. I'll just hang around the lobby of the hotel until tomorrow morning."

"No, I couldn't do that—"

"Yes, you can. I insist. Just leave me your name and where I can return the money you loaned me, and I'll mail you a check when I get back home."

The thought was tempting, and she was making it easy for him. Still, Garth didn't feel he could just walk off and leave her. But Hilary insisted. She made him write down his name and address; then he stepped off the sidewalk to hail a passing cab.

"I promise I'll send the money as soon as I get home," she assured Garth as he hesitantly got into the waiting cab.

"You sure you'll be all right?" Garth felt torn. He didn't want to be responsible for her, yet he found himself reluctant to leave her.

"I'll be fine. Really!"

Garth reached into his back pocket and hastily withdrew his billfold. "Here's seventy-five dollars. See that you get a nice room at one of the other hotels and a good breakfast in the morning." He shoved the money into her hand before she could protest.

"Garth, I couldn't..."

Garth slammed the door and rolled down the window. "You can pay me back. Just be careful. There are a lot of weirdos around."

Hilary smiled and clutched the money to her heart. She was suddenly very sad to see her Good Samaritan go. "I will. You be careful too."

"I will."

She leaned over impetuously and kissed him. Her mouth felt warm and sweet on his. Garth closed his eyes, and he felt himself respond to the unexpected reward. The kiss sent a surge of desire through him. He was surprised at his reaction. A simple kiss shouldn't affect him that way.

The embrace was over before Garth knew it, and the cab was pulling away from the curb. He twisted around in the seat, watching as Hilary's now familiar figure grew smaller in the distance.

A feeling of loss came over him as the cab turned the corner and she disappeared from his view.

All the "what ifs?" imaginable flooded his mind as he sank wearily back in the seat. He had a headache; his nose was raw from his miserable cold; and now he felt like a complete ass for deserting her.

Suppose she couldn't find a hotel room? Suppose she ran into that airhead Ricetrum again. Suppose someone tried to pick her up . . . Garth's mind was spinning with all the ugly possibilities. He couldn't be her keeper! He was having a hard enough time coping with his own problems.

But the image of Hilary standing alone on a dark street corner rose up to haunt him. *Damn it, Redmond! You wouldn't leave a dog standing on a corner in this kind of weather, alone, unprotected...*

Unable to shake the guilt feelings, Garth suddenly leaned forward and tapped the driver on the shoulder. "Go back to the Merrymont."

"Did you forget something?"

"I guess you could say that." Garth sighed. He had no idea what he was going to do with her. He just knew he couldn't leave her standing on some corner.

As the taxi neared the hotel, Garth shook his head wearily when he saw she was sitting alone on a bus bench, her makeup kit and the shopping bag from the department store propped beside her. The wind was tossing her hair about, and just as he'd suspected, she was crying again.

Garth rolled down his window as the cab eased up to the curb. "Hi, good-looking. You fool around?"

Hilary glanced up, and her eyes brightened. "Only when I'm asked," she sniffed. She tried to make light of her misery, but she had *never* been so glad to see anyone.

"Well, I suppose you could get in, and we could discuss the possibilities," Garth suggested dryly.

He knew he was flirting with her, and for the life of him, he didn't know why.

Hilary grinned and hurriedly reached for the makeup kit and shopping bag before he changed his mind. "I suppose it's worth discussing," she conceded.

After all, she reasoned as she slid into the backseat of the cab next to his comforting warmth, she really didn't have much choice. And she had missed him like the devil the two and a half minutes he had been gone!

Chapter Seven

AS THE TAXI PULLED BACK INTO the line of traffic, Hilary jerked her gloves off with her teeth and unbuttoned her coat. "Where're we going?"

"Beats me. You got any suggestions?"

"Sorry, I ran dry several calamities ago," Hilary confessed. "Listen, I really appreciate your coming back for me."

"I thought you were going to get a hotel room," Garth reminded.

"I was...but I didn't know where to begin looking." Hilary's face suddenly broke out in a relieved grin. "Honestly, who would ever think two people could run into so many obstacles just trying to spend a quiet vacation?"

Garth was busy looking out of the window for a hotel or motel with a vacancy sign. He was barely listening to her prattle. "Yeah, who would ever think," he answered absentmindedly.

Hilary edged forward on the seat and peered

at him intently. "You're doing okay, aren't you?
I mean, all this hasn't been too much for you,
has it?" If the poor man had been under stress
before, Hilary knew the last few hours couldn't
have helped.

"No, I'm fine. How about you?"

She sighed. "I'm adjusting."

"Where to, buddy?" The cabbie peered in his
rearview mirror, waiting for directions.

"To tell you the truth, I don't know," Garth
confessed. "Would you have any idea where we
can get a room for the night?"

"Around here?"

No, in Honolulu! Garth thought irritably.
"Yeah, around here."

"For the entire night?" The driver sneaked another peek in the mirror and noted that neither
one of them had luggage. They were both carrying shopping bags from Garfield's. It must be
whoopee time again.

"There's a meat-packers' convention over at
the Bellview and a pharmaceutical convention
over at the Bell Tower." The cabbie took off his
hat and scratched his head. "What with the Merrymont fire, I think just about everything in
town's full up this evening." The cab turned the
corner and shot down Gamin Boulevard.
"'Course, I know a little place over on Fairfax
that rents out rooms for a couple of hours or
so..."

Garth felt his face turning a bright red at the
cabbie's mistaken interpretation of his request.
"Uh, no, we need something for the night," he
mumbled.

The cabbie's mouth turned up at the corners in a tiny smirk. "Well, like I said, that's gonna be tough."

"Ask him if he knows someone who would just rent us a room for a little while," Hilary whispered.

Garth's gaze slid up guiltily to meet the cabbie's in the rearview mirror. "Are you serious?" he snapped out of the corner of his mouth. "He already thinks the worst."

"But if there's no hotel or motel vacancies, maybe there's a boarding house around that would be willing to rent us a room." Hilary realized it was a long shot, but at this point she was ready to concede they were desperate.

Seeing the immediate color flood Garth's face again, she added, "I wouldn't mind sleeping on the floor . . . if you'll just spend the night with me."

"Uh . . . Hilary . . ." Garth knew the driver was listening to their conversation.

The cabbie grinned as he reached into his shirt pocket for a cigarette.

"No, really! I'll do anything you say if you'll just stay with me tonight, Garth."

While sitting on the lonely bus bench, Hilary discovered she'd lost whatever self-confidence she thought she'd possessed. She wasn't beyond begging Garth to stay with her. It hadn't taken but a few minutes to realize just how disconcerting it was to be completely alone in a strange town. Hilary would gladly sacrifice her pride if he would promise not to leave her alone again.

"I'll even pay you"—Hilary upped the ante hopefully—"as soon as I get my money."

Lucky devil! the cabbie thought enviously.

Garth's face turned several shades of red as he diverted his attention to staring out of the window again. "Why don't we stop at a restaurant and have a cup of coffee? We need to discuss this in private." Garth was determined to avoid the cabbie's widening smirk in the rearview mirror.

"Oh . . . Well, sure," Hilary agreed, wondering why both men suddenly had such strange looks on their faces. "You won't try to get away from me again, will you?"

"No . . . and I didn't try to get away from you earlier," Garth said quietly. He wished she would change the subject.

Hilary leaned back in the seat and let out a sigh of relief. "Good. I'd hate to have to call Daddy again."

Garth leaned forward and spoke curtly to the cabbie. "She means she had to call her father for money and . . ." He broke off lamely, realizing he could never explain the confusing situation. "Just pull over at the first restaurant."

"Whatever you say, Romeo!"

The taxi screeched to a halt a few minutes later in front of Red's Sirloin Parlor. Garth paid the amused driver as Hilary got out of the cab. He noticed she was limping again.

"How's the ankle?" he asked as he held the door open for her to enter the restaurant.

"I think it's getting worse."

"It looks as if it's swelling more."

That didn't surprise her. It was throbbing to beat the band.

"You get us a table, and I'll grab a newspaper."

Garth spotted the vending machines at the corner. As crazy as it sounded, Hilary's earlier suggestion of a boarding house might be their only chance to avoid sleeping on a park bench tonight.

While Garth went for the paper, Hilary asked for a table for two, and was promptly seated. As she sank into the comfortable red leather seat, exhaustion overcame her again. She realized she couldn't take much more of this merry-go-round. She was tired and grimy, and she longed for a hot tub where she could soak her ankle and a soft bed on which to rest. Was it only hours ago that she had experienced all those wonderful luxuries she had always taken for granted?

Hilary absently picked up one of the bread sticks the restaurant had provided and bit into it. Her eyes widened as she crunched down on something grainy.

Removing the foreign object from her mouth, she was dismayed to find it was a small piece of enamel from a tooth. She deposited what she had chewed in a napkin, and with her tongue she probed the jagged edge of a molar. She groaned out loud.

This had been the worst day of her life!

When Garth returned with the papers Hilary told him about the latest catastrophe, and he shook his head compassionately.

"I ordered coffee," she told him as he unfolded the paper and began scanning the classified ads.

"Good." He handed her a section of the ads. "Here, see what you can find."

"Okay."

"By the way, what time is it?"

97

Hilary glanced at her watch. "Eight-thirty."

"Brother!"

"What's wrong?"

"Nothing. I was just thinking that it's getting late to go looking for a room at a boarding house."

"Yes, I know."

The waitress brought their coffee and set it down before them. "Anything else I can get you?"

Hilary smiled. "No, thanks . . . unless you can recommend a good eye doctor, an ankle doctor, a dentist, and a place to stay the night."

The waitress walked away, smiling as if she thought Hilary was kidding. Hilary wished she had been.

"She didn't believe me."

"Who in their right mind would?"

They sipped their coffee and browsed through the ads, reading one out loud every few minutes.

"Here . . ." Hilary leaned forward and pointed to an ad in the third column. "This sounds like a nice one."

"I should hope to shout it does!" Garth protested. "Look at the price."

"Oh, yes. Sorry." She was leaning so close that he could detect a faint whiff of her perfume. For some crazy reason Garth suddenly felt himself becoming aroused.

Now that was *all* he needed to make his day, he thought irritably. he folded the paper shut.

"You keep looking. I'll call and check on a couple of these." He slid out of the booth and walked to the pay phone.

Hilary picked up her coffee cup and studied

him from under lowered lashes. She was enjoying his company. He was wearing a nice, clean-smelling aftershave...intriguing and sensuous. She took another sip of coffee. It seemed to her he got better-looking by the minute. Not pretty-boy handsome, but his face had enough interesting planes and angles to make a woman look twice.

Hilary wondered how many women there were in Garth Redmond's life, and she was surprised to feel an unreasonable twinge of jealousy at the thought. She barely knew him; yet she found herself feeling almost possessive.

Garth returned to the table in a few minutes, waving a piece of paper at her triumphantly. "These two are still available."

"Wonderful! Can we look at them right away?"

"I told them we'd be there within the hour."

The taxi pulled up in front of the first house, and Hilary looked at Garth and smiled. "It looks lovely."

"Right now, I'd settle for a pup tent," Garth confessed.

The landlady greeted them at the door with a warm and friendly hello. "My name is Mrs. Biggerton, but you can call me Mary," she said.

Hilary and Garth nodded and smiled politely.

"Mr. Biggerton always said our guests should call us John and Mary—God rest his soul." Mary dabbed at the corners of her eyes. "John was such a good man."

Lamely, Hilary and Garth nodded again.

"The room...?" Garth prompted.

"Oh, yes, the room. Just follow me, dearies."

My, my, Mary thought. *What a lovely couple they make.* She was reminded of herself and her late husband. She and John had been just about this young couple's age when they had bought this old house. *How grand first love is!* she thought as she led them up the carpeted stairway.

"It's a lovely, lovely room. Nice big windows facing the south. Very quiet. Old Mr. Whitlock has the adjoining room, but he doesn't give anyone a minute's trouble," Mary promised as she unlocked the door and motioned them into the room.

Garth saw all he needed to make a quick decision. The room had a bed, and it appeared to be clean. He turned to Hilary who quickly gave her approval with a hasty nod.

"It looks good to me," she agreed.

"Good. We'll take it."

"Oh, my!" The landlady smiled at them benevolently. "I was hoping you would say that. Now if you and the missus will follow me, we'll take care of the registration."

Garth was about to clarify the *missus,* when he saw Hilary's warning look.

They walked back down the stairway, listening to Mary chat about her pet canary, Wiladeen, who was feeling under the weather. "I'm afraid she's caught a draft, poor thing. And with the weather predicted to turn so bad...well...I only hope Dr. Saddler can drop by before too much longer."

Garth glanced at Hilary. He wondered if a draft could be fatal to a canary.

Hilary lifted her shoulder bitterly. If it were *her* canary, it would be.

As they entered the front hallway, Mary glanced out of the picture window and noticed that the taxi was still waiting at the curb. "Oh, dear! If you'd like to get your luggage, I'll wait here for you," she offered. The cab's meter was running, and the poor little things were probably having to watch every penny, Mary reasoned. She felt sorry for young people today. Everything was so expensive.

Hilary appreciated Mary's concern but quickly pointed out, "We don't have any luggage ..."

She realized immediately that she'd said the wrong thing.

A giant iceberg suddenly floated into Mary's eyes. "You don't have any luggage?" she asked.

"No ... You see, we actually need the room for just one night ... because all the hotels are full ..." Hilary's voice trailed off lamely as the iceberg suddenly grew in size.

"One night?"

"Yes, you see—"

"Why, the two of you should be ashamed of yourselves!" Mary marched over to the door and yanked it open self-righteously. "Go! Out of here with you! I run a decent, God-fearing establishment, and I don't hold with any of this kinky one-night stuff."

"Excuse me, Mary, but we're not—" Garth started to protest, but Mary cut him off abruptly.

"*Mrs*. Biggerton to you! Why, John would roll over in his grave if he thought I was party to such goings-on. The very nerve!" Mary stuck her nose in the air. "Out!"

"But, Mary..." Hilary tried to explain again, embarrassed by the woman's mistaken impression. "You see...no, we aren't married, but we were staying at the Merrymont and—"

"Oh, *please*, young lady! Spare me the details!" Mary pressed a hand over her thundering heart. "Mind you now, I'm not one to moralize, but you two should be ashamed of yourselves. Your parents certainly would be!"

"You don't understand..."

But Hilary's attempted explanation was ignored as Mary pivoted on one foot and stalked away. "I'll have no part of this! No, sir, not in this house! And I'll thank you to show yourselves out!" Mary was still ranting about "today's decadent society" as she disappeared through the kitchen doorway.

Hilary turned to confront a red-faced Garth. "You devil, you! Are you trying to corrupt me?" she deadpanned.

Garth sighed as he ran one hand through his hair. "I have the distinct feeling the room isn't available anymore."

"Strange, I have that same feeling."

They quietly let themselves out the front door.

"I don't know what you're laughing about," Garth admonished as they got back into the cab. "It's close to ten o'clock, and we still don't have a place to spend the night."

"I know." Hilary settled herself in the backseat and picked up the classified ads again. "But we will," she predicted optimistically.

At the next stop they were admitted inside the house by a big burly man who constantly winked at Hilary whenever Garth's head was turned. Recalling the bad impression they'd made on Mary Biggerton, Hilary cringed to think how this insinuating clod would misconstrue the situation.

Hilary heard Garth's quick intake of breath as the man unlocked the door to the apartment and let it swing open.

The small room was appalling. Beer cans were strewn across the coffee table, and there were several bags of trash standing in the middle of the kitchen floor. Just how long they'd been there, only heaven knew. If the sight hadn't nauseated Hilary, the smell certainly did.

She tried not to breathe as she trailed closely behind Garth. She hoped he was as horrified as she was, yet she was resolved to yield to his decision. Whatever he decided, she would have to accept.

Glancing at the soiled spread that was draped haphazardly across the sagging bed, Hilary reminded herself that she really wasn't *that* tired. She could sit up in a chair all night and let *him* have the bed.

Garth continued to pretend polite interest in the room. True, they were desperate, but nobody could be *this* desperate, he thought glumly. He was surprised that the man had the nerve to show the apartment without first having bulldozed the place out.

"It's a little messy," the landlord granted. "The ol' lady don't get off work till eleven, but if you want the room, I'll send her up as soon as she gets home. She can spruce it up a little." He ripped the tab off a beer can and took a long swallow as his eyes ran over Hilary suggestively. "Won't take long, once she gets her butt in gear."

Hilary clamped her hand over Garth's arm and began to squeeze tightly.

Garth glanced at her questioningly.

"My foot..." Hilary shuddered as a large brown roach scurried across her shoe and disappeared under the bed.

"Damn bugs! The exterminator was here last week, and the little varmints have been runnin' wild ever since." The landlord set his beer can down, jerked the metal bed away from the corner, and proceeded to stomp the offending creature into a greasy pulp.

So much for available room number two.

"Well, now what?"

In the taxi once more, Hilary sucked in the welcome fresh air and tried to forget the unspeakable carnage they had just witnessed.

Garth struggled to make a decision he'd avoided all evening. It looked as if he'd be forced to make it now.

"My grandparents have a beach house," he finally admitted.

Hilary glanced at him in disbelief. "Here...in West Creek?"

"Yes...but I didn't want to go there until tomorrow night."

"Why not?"

"My cousin Dorothy, her husband Frank, and the most obnoxious kids I've ever encountered—

that's why not," Garth confessed. "But even *they* are beginning to sound good."

"Are they staying at the cottage?"

"Yes, but they're supposed to leave tomorrow night. As much as I hate to admit it, I don't think we have any choice but to join them."

"I can stand it if you can," Hilary assured him.

Garth wasn't sure he could, but he figured his options had just run out.

The taxi eased to a stop in front of the cottage on Oceanside Drive. The weathered bungalow was surrounded by neatly manicured hedges. Garth paid the driver, grabbed the two Garfield shopping bags, and escorted Hilary up the sidewalk.

"What are we going to tell your cousin?" Hilary fretted. She could imagine how Dorothy would view her staying with Garth.

"I don't know about you, but I'm telling them good night. Then I'm going straight to bed."

"Not me. I'm heading straight for a hot bath."

"I don't see Frank's station wagon around anywhere. They must be out sightseeing." Garth reached under the mat to retrieve the extra key.

"I feel terrible just barging in like this."

"Wait until you meet Frank and Dorothy. You'll get over it."

"Garth!" Hilary frowned, and he grinned.

They stepped through the doorway, and Garth flipped on the lights. Setting the shopping bags on the small love seat, he walked into the living room, switching on lamps as he went. Hilary followed closely behind as her eyes appreciatively scanned the homey cottage.

"This is really nice," she said gratefully.

"Yeah, I always thought so. It has all of Gram's personal touches." Garth's smile was affectionate as he pointed toward the multicolored afghan that was draped across the back of the sofa.

"Did she do these?" Hilary was closely examining the finely detailed cross-stitched pictures that adorned the south wall.

"Yeah, those too. Wait until you see the kitchen—if the kids have left it standing. Grandpa is a carpenter by trade, or at least he was until he retired. He did all the cabinetwork."

Hilary followed him into the kitchen, and Garth switched on the lights.

If the living room echoed Garth's grandmother's creativity, the kitchen proved that his grandfather was equally talented. "My goodness, this is lovely!"

"You really like it?"

Hilary walked over to the cabinets and ran her hand over the polished oak admiringly. "This is exactly the sort of cabinet I'd like in my own home someday."

Garth smiled and thought of how Lisa would hate the cabinets. They wouldn't be modern enough for her. "Grandpa always says when I get married he'll build me a house."

Hilary's gaze met his shyly. "And are you planning on getting married soon?"

"No...not soon. How about you?" Garth regretted mentioning the subject as he saw the sadness come into her eyes. "Sorry, I didn't mean to remind you of Lenny."

"That's all right. Lenny and I never discussed marriage," she admitted.

"I date a woman who'd like to discuss it, but I'm not ready yet," Garth said.

"Oh."

Glancing at the kitchen table, Garth noticed a note propped against the ceramic salt shaker. He picked it up and read it, then released an audible sigh of relief. "Looks like we may have gotten our first piece of good luck."

Hilary glanced at her watch. "Let's note the hour, for posterity's sake," she joked.

"Looks like Frank decided to leave a day early so he could rest up before going back to the office."

"Oh. Well, at least that will make it easier for you." Hilary pulled a chair away from the kitchen table and sank onto it gratefully. She began absentmindedly rubbing her swollen ankle.

"That ankle still bothering you?"

"A little."

Garth knelt down and took her foot in his hand. The ankle was red and swollen to twice its normal size.

"Sit right there, and I'll have you fixed up in no time," he promised.

He rummaged beneath the kitchen sink and produced a small porcelain pan. He put the tea kettle on the burner to heat water, then poured a small amount into the pan a few minutes later. After adding cold water, he tested the temperature, then carefully slipped her shoe and ankle hose off and lowered her foot into the basin.

"How's that?"

"Fine." Actually, Hilary thought it was pretty close to heaven.

While she soaked her ankle, Garth rummaged through the pantry and retrieved a small first-aid kit. "Gram's always prepared," he explained as he opened the lid and reached for the Ace bandage. "When you're through, I'll wrap it for you."

While Hilary indulged herself, Garth made them each a cup of tea, and they lapsed into an easy, relaxed conversation.

"So you're a flight controller," Hilary mused aloud. "That must be very interesting."

"Yes, I've always liked my job, but it can get hectic at times."

"Tell me something—how in the world do you keep all those planes from running into one another?" Hilary asked.

Garth laughed. "Well, I don't. At least, I'm not responsible for *all* of them. Let's see, how can I explain it simply? The east-bound flights fly at odd altitudes—twenty-seven hundred, twenty-nine hundred, or thirty-one hundred feet, etcetera. West-bound flights fly at even altitudes."

"But doesn't that bring them dangerously close to one another?"

"No, not at all. They're separated by distances of a thousand feet vertically, and ten miles laterally."

"Then you agree that flying is the safest way to go?"

"The safest way *to go?*" Garth grinned. "We try to avoid that phrase, but yes, I believe the skies are safer than they've ever been, despite what you hear to the contrary. Between 1981 and 1985, the airlines flew one billion passengers through twenty-six million takeoffs and landings, with an average fatality rate of ninety per year. Compare that to the hundred and twenty-three people killed daily in car accidents—that's an average of forty-five thousand deaths a year. And flying is even safer than walking, which takes seven thousand lives a year."

"I don't mind the flying. It's the circling—when my plane hasn't been cleared to land—that makes me nervous," Hilary confessed.

"It shouldn't worry you. It's just a normal holding pattern when traffic's stacked up. The planes are still separated by a thousand feet, and they're being closely monitored on radar. When a plane at the bottom of the stack is cleared to approach and land, then the others are individually and systematically instructed to descend a thousand feet."

"Simple," Hilary jested.

"At times," he agreed.

It was nice to talk to each other. Hilary and Garth's moods were less pessimistic by the time Hilary had removed her foot from the basin a half hour later. She surveyed the foot and grinned. "It's beginning to shrivel." She gingerly lifted the waterlogged foot, and Garth reached for the towel. "I'll get that for you," he said.

"You don't have to. I can . . ." Hilary began to protest. She suddenly felt extremely shy. She reached for the towel, knocking it from his hand.

Bending to retrieve the linen, they found their

faces inches apart. The unexpected closeness caught them both by surprise.

"I can do that," she said softly.

"I'd like to do it for you."

Hilary had a fluttery feeling in the pit of her stomach. Garth's look was warm and suggestively intense.

As if a magnet were drawing them together, their mouths slowly moved toward each other. They touched.

His lips were sweet and inviting as they lingered on hers, caressing and light. Hilary closed her eyes and felt the room begin to tilt crazily. She held her breath, hoping he would take her in his arms and deepen the kiss. But as suddenly as it had begun, the embrace ended.

Garth cleared his throat and handed the towel to her. "Maybe you're right. You dry the foot, and I'll wrap it."

Hilary touched her tongue to her lips. She could still taste his presence. "All right."

When the ankle was properly wrapped, Garth suggested they go straight to bed. "There's only one bedroom, so I'll take the sofa," he offered.

"Please, take the bed. I don't mind sleeping on the sofa."

"The sofa will be fine. I'm so tense I'll have to take a sleeping pill to relax. Believe me . . . I'll be out in five minutes," Garth assured her.

Rummaging through the shopping bags, Garth found the package of T-shirts he'd purchased earlier. "You can sleep in one of these."

"Thanks. Would you care if I took a bath first?"

Visions of Hilary naked, soaking in a hot tub, rose up to tantalize Garth.

"No. Make yourself at home. There's a bathroom second door to the right. I'll use the one off the utility room."

"Thanks. Well, I guess I'll see you first thing in the morning."

"Yeah..." Garth's eyes moved over her lazily. "If you're up first, Gram keeps the coffee in the refrigerator."

"How do you like your eggs?"

Garth's eyes unwillingly dropped to the gentle swell of her breasts, and he was mortified to hear *his* voice saying, "Fried ... with double yolks."

Chapter Eight

HILARY AND GARTH SAID GOOD night, and Hilary walked down the hall to Garth's grandparents' bedroom. She was still smiling.

The way Garth had looked at her a few minutes ago and the crazy way her pulse had jumped when his gaze slid admiringly over her breasts ... Well, maybe Lenny wasn't going to be as hard to forget as she'd first thought.

Hilary opened the door and switched on the lamp beside the bed. The small bedroom emerged in a warm light. The furnishings were homey and comfortable, and the full-sized brass bed beckoned invitingly.

In minutes Hilary had slipped out of her blouse and jeans and had drawn a tub of hot water in the adjoining bath. Instead of a leisurely soak, however, she found she wanted to wash as quickly as possible and get into bed.

At Garth's suggestion, she availed herself of

Grace Redmond's liberal assortment of creams and lotions sitting on the vanity. Then she slipped into the T-shirt he'd handed her earlier.

The garment totally engulfed her petite frame, and Hilary found herself running her fingers sensually over the soft material, thinking about its owner.

Hilary knew Garth had never worn the shirt, yet she found herself visualizing how the material would lie against the broad expanse of his chest . . . the way it would mold and cling to all those muscles . . . With that tantalizing thought, she felt the beginnings of desire. It was strange. She would ordinarily be thinking about Lenny; yet now it was Garth—a man she had known for such a short time—who suddenly dominated her fantasies.

She pulled back the fluffy comforter on the bed and climbed between the crisp sheets. The mattress welcomed her tired body with a cushioning embrace. Outside, a shutter banged against the side of the cottage, and Hilary could hear the breakers rolling in from the Atlantic.

It seemed as if the wind had been picking up steadily all evening. Hilary hoped it wouldn't interfere with plane departures the following morning. She planned to go to Western Union and collect her money, then call the airport and book a flight to Denver. Soon this whole crazy escapade would be a memory . . . with the exception of Garth. Hilary had a feeling he was going to linger in her mind a good deal longer.

She lay in the dark, going over the past few hectic hours with a surprising fondness. How unexpectedly they'd come into each other's life.

Had his pulse raced as erratically as hers did when they touched? Snuggling more deeply within the folds of the comforter, Hilary warned herself that she was becoming much too attached to Garth Redmond.

For all she knew, he could be in love with the "Lisa" he had mentioned earlier...And there was Lenny to contend with...And Hilary didn't know a thing about Garth, other than the fact he was attractive...kind...understanding...incredibly gentle.

The memory of his unexpected kiss set off a series of flutters in the bottom of her stomach as she eventually drifted off to sleep.

Garth had to manhandle the stubborn sofa cushions. He unfolded the thin foam mattress from the metal cage of the sofa, then rummaged for ten minutes before he found an extra blanket and pillow in the hall closet.

As he passed Hilary's room, he wondered if she was asleep. He had heard her moving about earlier, but all was quiet now.

Running his tongue over his lips, he could still taste the faint traces of her lipstick. Why was it that one kiss had aroused him so swiftly, so unexpectedly, so fully that he had had to fight the urge to make a pass at her? Crazy, that's what it was. The woman was not only dangerous to his libido but together they made a dangerous couple. It was as if a curse were on both of them, yet Garth found Hilary increasingly appealing.

Slipping off his shoes, he climbed into bed,

then tried to remove his pants beneath the sheet. Snagging his sore toe in the metal frame of the sleeper, he bit his lower lip to stifle an agonizing moan.

Damn! Might as well try sleeping on a bed of nails!

The thin slice of foam rubber, which someone had mistakenly labeled a mattress, had a tendency to curl up slightly at either end; and the metal support bar across the middle seemed determined to become embedded in the base of his spine.

Rolling back out onto the floor, Garth reached for his trousers and withdrew the small packet a doctor had given him a few months ago when he'd complained of a succession of sleepless nights. The strong medication was to be taken only when necessary, but Garth knew, at the rate he was going, he had to have it now.

He walked into the kitchen, drew a glass of water, and popped one of the pills into his mouth. A few moments later he was back in bed, trying to find a safe harbor away from the tormenting support bar.

As the sleeping pill began to take effect, Garth's eyelids drooped heavily. Hilary's image floated temptingly before him. Hilary ... sleeping in the next room, in his shirt ... unrestricted ... unencompassed ... eggs ...

Garth groaned and rolled onto his stomach. He slammed the pillow over his head to block out the sound of the wind and his confused thoughts.

* * *

Sometime around three in the morning, Garth flipped over on his back. He could hear the wind howling outside the beach house.

Ordinarily he was a light sleeper; but under the influence of the medication, he found it nearly impossible to open his eyes. Trying to fight off the effects of the sleeping pill, Garth finally managed to sit upright in bed.

He shook his head in an effort to clear his vision. His eyes narrowed as he focused on the large protuberance at the bottom of his bed. Groping at the bulge in the blankets, he jumped when he heard a feminine voice respond in a sleepy tone.

Sometime during the night, Hilary had crawled into bed with him. She recoiled when a hand touched her bare bottom.

"What in the . . . Hilary, is that you?" Garth leaned over and heatedly addressed the bulge.

"Yes" came the muffled reply.

"What are you doing?"

"Trying to sleep."

"In *my* bed?"

"Yes."

Garth sighed and ran his hand through his tousled hair. "You want to come out of there?"

It was hard enough for Garth to ignore his growing attraction to her. Now she was in his bed . . .

There was a slight pause; then Hilary slowly emerged from beneath the blanket. She was embarrassed he'd caught her, but she quickly decided that the sense of security she'd felt while snuggled safely under the covers was worth the sacrifice. It had been either join Garth in his bed, or continue to lie petrified in her own while her mind amplified the sound of the wind as it slapped angrily at the beach house.

Hilary crept out of the sheets, up the long, muscular length of his body, and settled easily on his chest. It was much wider than she had first estimated. He was bare-chested and undeniably gorgeous. Hilary wasn't usually so audacious; yet she felt completely at ease lying on top of him.

Garth's eyes met hers distraughtly. "*Now* what are you doing?" The feel of her lying pressed tightly against his bare chest sent his hormones on a rampage.

"The wind is blowing," Hilary explained lamely, realizing that he was probably going to demand that she go back to her own room.

"So?" His voice was still thick with sleep.

"So . . . I was frightened . . ." Her fingers slipped through the thick mat of hair on his chest and lingered there.

"Frightened? Why were you . . . Stop that!" Garth removed her hands, but she quickly wrapped her arms around him and buried her face in his neck.

"Please, I've always been terrified of the wind," Hilary pleaded. "Just let me stay here with you for a while."

Garth tried to shift her, aware that she was going to be shocked if she moved in the wrong direction.

"Look"—he eased her to his side, settling her in his arms as he would a small child—"there's nothing to be afraid of. It's just a little wind."

"I was in a tornado once," she confessed, trying

to offer him some sort of explanation for her radical change in behavior. "I was terrified."

Garth felt a shudder ripple through her, and he pulled her closer. "Okay, if it makes you feel any better, you can stay with me for a while." He was too tired to think straight, and she was doing crazy things to his libido. But it was a mistake to let her stay, and he knew it.

Hilary sighed, and her arms tightened around his neck appreciatively. "Thank you."

Garth lay back on the pillow and closed his eyes for a moment. He felt fuzzy and lightheaded from the medication. He drifted off for a moment, thinking about Hilary in his arms. He desired her. Wouldn't any man in his right mind? But he wasn't thinking clearly. They'd known each other only a few hours, and Garth wasn't about to jump into what could easily become a sticky situation.

But she felt incredibly good in his arms. Soft and tiny like a kitten ... and she smelled so feminine. The tantalizing scent drifted over Garth ... Her bare legs were next to his, and they felt as smooth as silk next to his hair-roughened ones.

Garth stirred restlessly. "Hilary ... about you and Lenny Ricetrum—"

"Please, I don't want to talk about Lenny."

"Are you sure? You've been pretty upset about him." Garth absentmindedly began to caress the outline of her bare thigh. Maybe if he reminded her of Lenny she'd realize that they were putting themselves in a dangerous position, lying this close ...

"Lenny seems like a million years ago," Hilary confessed as she snuggled more deeply into his arms. It wasn't Lenny who was upsetting her. It was Garth. Hilary was afraid he would realize what his hand was doing—and stop.

But his hand continued to meander slowly up the silken length of her. Supple fingers paused once or twice to massage the small of her back.

Hilary, secure in the realization that he *did* realize what he was doing, began to relax.

"You shouldn't do that," she protested half-heartedly when he touched pleasure points, causing a quickening of her pulse. She hated herself because she couldn't manage to sound more convincing.

"Just relax," he murmured smoothly, and his hand continued its alluring path up her spine, sensuously kneading and exploring her satiny skin. Even in his sluggish state, Garth knew he should stop. But he couldn't—even if he'd wanted to. Wasn't she openly inviting him to take advantage of the situation? Together in the same bed, she was clinging to him as if they were already lovers.

His mouth lowered slowly to search for hers, and a thrill shot through him when he found hers eagerly waiting.

They kissed, their soft murmurs of pleasure blending as his hand moved under the T-shirt to her bare breasts.

The kiss deepened, and Hilary felt herself go limp in his arms as the gusts shook the house with growing ferocity.

She realized that what she was doing was rash and totally out of character, yet she was returning his kiss with a reckless abandon, pressing ever closer ... encouraging his advances ... almost begging for them.

Had the past few hours indeed pushed her over the brink to insanity?

Garth shifted his weight, and his kisses became more ardent as he pressed her back against the pillows.

"Garth ..." Hilary murmured as their mouths parted a few moments later. He nibbled warm kisses down the column of her neck. "Is there another woman ... ?"

"Another woman?"

"Is there someone special in your life?" Hilary hesitated to ask, but the answer could make a difference.

"No." Garth started to kiss her again, and then he paused. Lisa seemed so distant since he'd left Chicago. Almost as if she no longer existed in his life. "No, that's not quite true." He amended what he'd said. "I've been seeing a woman for the past few months, but we're not engaged."

"Do you plan to marry her?"

"No." The finality of his answer surprised him. A heavy weight felt as if it had suddenly been lifted off his shoulders. "No, I don't," Garth repeated again more firmly. "I just realized that."

"What we're doing is reckless," Hilary warned, teasing his mouth with the tip of her tongue. "We barely know each other."

"I know."

"I don't make a habit of this."

"That's nice to know." He rolled over with her in his arms and began to slide the T-shirt up over her head.

"Garth." Hilary's eyes met his, and he saw confusion clouding the pools of glistening blue sapphires. "I don't want you to think I'm easy." She had gone mad. There was no longer any doubt in Hilary's mind.

"I don't think that." He kissed the tip of her nose, then took her mouth again as his fingers began to arouse her with an expertise that left her breathless. Garth was careful to keep his own desire in check as their passions began to soar. Hilary heard his suppressed moan, and her own spiraling needs urged him on.

Garth murmured her name urgently as the storm continued to build.

Hilary was suddenly seized with panic. What was she doing in his arms, about to let him make love to her? She didn't know a thing about him. It seemed imperative that they know *something* about each other!

"How many children are there in your family?"

"What?"

"Children . . . do you have any brothers and sisters?"

"Two younger brothers."

"I have an older sister. What's your favorite dessert?"

"Cheesecake."

"I favor lemon pie."

"That's nice." Garth's mouth took hers fiercely.

"School?"

"What?"

"Where did you go to school?"

"In Chicago . . . Why?"

"Are you a college graduate?"

"Yes . . . Are you?"

"Yes." They rolled over, and Garth lay on top of her now.

"What about your grades?"

"They were okay . . . I made the Dean's honor roll."

Hilary felt her heart sink. She'd been lucky to eke out passing grades.

"What kind of a car do you drive?"

"Damn it, Hilary! Do we have to discuss this right now?"

"No, I just thought we should know something about each other."

"I know I'm going crazy," Garth whispered. "Let's talk later."

Hilary decided she'd found out all she needed to know.

In his arms she found a joy, an awareness she had never known before. He was gentle yet firm, demanding yet giving, eager to have her experience the ultimate fulfillment along with him. She knew she was falling in love and was powerless to stop it.

Garth suddenly groaned as he lost control. He joined her in completion, and they soared and spiraled in the climax of their loving. Tears rolled unabashedly down Hilary's cheeks at the beauty of the moment.

"What's the matter?" Garth whispered once the tides of passion had crested explosively, then slowly began to ebb.

"It was so . . . perfect."

He smiled and wiped the wetness off her cheeks

with his thumbs. "It isn't anything to cry about."

"I cry when I'm happy."

"And when you're sad . . . and when you're hungry . . . and when you're—"

Hilary tenderly covered his mouth with her hand. "True. I'm a mess."

"No, you're beautiful," Garth corrected her. Hilary was sure she saw something very close to love in his eyes. "And you've made me very happy." Their mouths met again affectionately.

"The wind is getting worse," Hilary murmured a few moments later as Garth settled her in the crook of his arm.

"If it'll make you feel better, I'll take a look outside," Garth offered sleepily. "Those old shutters have always been loose, and when they rattle it makes the wind sound worse than it really is."

"I would feel better . . . but be careful."

"I planned on it." Garth slid out of bed and immediately stubbed his sore toe on the metal leg of the bed. He hopped painfully on one foot as Hilary wadded the corner of the sheet in her mouth to keep from laughing.

He looked at her incredulously. "You think this is funny?"

Hilary quickly sobered up. She shook her head, no.

Garth stepped into his pants and yanked the zipper closed. "I'm going to lose that toe if I hit it one more time!" he grumbled.

Hilary agreed and stuffed the sheet into her mouth again, her eyes crinkling with suppressed laughter.

Garth reached over to tickle her ribs, and she

collapsed on the pillow. They wrestled on the unsteady frame for a few minutes before it threatened to collapse. He finally kissed her again and got up. His head spun like a top, and he groped for support.

"Damn! I should never have taken that sleeping pill."

"How strong was it?"

"Enough to knock a bull moose out cold for twenty-four hours."

Hilary grinned. "Go check the shutters; then we'll both try and get some sleep."

"Believe me, Ms. Brookfield, there are very few women I would go out at this hour to check a shutter for," Garth complained.

He slipped his jacket on and opened the front door. The sudden impact of the violent wind threatened to knock him off his feet. "Holy..." he exclaimed. It was pitch-black, but from where Garth stood he could see that the trees lining the cobblestone walk were practically bent over double in their surrender to the strong gales. In the distance he could hear the roar of the breakers rolling in from the ocean.

"What's the matter?" Hilary was waiting just inside the door.

"The wind...It's going crazy."

"I told you so."

"Those breakers have to be at least four feet high," he exclaimed.

"Is it a hurricane?"

"I don't know. Stay where you are." Garth shut the door, and Hilary crept back into the warmth of the bed.

She plumped the pillow, keeping one ear tuned to the wind as she thought about the way Garth had made love to her. Was it possible that only a few hours ago she was crying over a lost love, and now she could barely remember what Lenny looked like?

Was it possible to fall in love with a man so totally, so completely, in such a short span of time? Or was it merely the strange set of circumstances she and Garth found themselves in that caused the strong attraction? Hilary wasn't sure.

Intimacy was an act she'd never taken lightly. She viewed sex as a serious commitment moment, but she didn't know how Garth felt about the subject. Hilary rolled over and stared at the front door. Where was he? He'd been gone only for a few minutes, she reminded herself. He couldn't possibly have had time to fix the shutters . . . But then it was so dark and windy out there. What if something had happened to him? Panic seized her as she hurriedly slipped out of bed. Wrapping herself in the blanket, she hobbled to the door and pulled it open.

Oh, my gosh! She held her breath in awe. She had never seen such violent winds. "What is it?" Hilary had to shout to make herself heard.

Garth was busy trying to secure one of the flapping shutters. "What?" He cupped a hand to his ear questioningly.

"I said is it a hurricane?" Hilary shouted.

"Hurricane?"

She nodded.

"I don't think so. I think the season's over." Garth leapt back up on the porch as an icy rain started to plummet down from the overcast sky.

Hilary went in search of a towel as he shrugged out of his wet jacket. Moments later she returned and handed him the towel.

"If it isn't a hurricane, what is it?"

"I have no idea. I suppose it could be a hurricane, but they're usually over by mid-November." Garth vigorously rubbed his hair dry with the towel. "But by the looks of things, I'd say we're in for something more than a typical winter storm."

"With the way our luck's been running, I'd have to agree."

Garth glanced up and grinned. "Let's see . . . What could be worse than a hurricane?" he prompted.

"Typhoon?"

"I doubt it. We're on the Atlantic side."

"Not for long," Hilary predicted. "Not the way that wind is blowing."

Garth pitched the towel on a chair and walked into the kitchen to switch on the radio. He scanned the range of the dial but couldn't find a weather report. He set the dial on an easy-listening station, realizing that most stations have periodic weather announcements.

Hilary kept glancing out of the window and pacing back and forth across the floor nervously. Garth was still trying to fight off the effect of the sleeping pill, so he wandered back into the living room and draped himself across the sofa.

"Are you going to sleep—in this storm?" Hilary asked.

"No." Garth yawned. "I'm just resting my

eyes." His voice trailed off sleepily as he began to get warm.

Hilary shook her head in disbelief, then went into the kitchen to get closer to the radio.

Garth nodded off briefly, only to be awakened a few minutes later by Hilary tapping on his shoulder.

"Huh?" He tried to force his heavy lids to open.

"What's a 'ziggy'?"

"A what?"

"A *ziggy*."

"Some sort of a model...I think." Both eyes drooped shut again.

Hilary shook his shoulder. "No, that was Twiggy! What's a *ziggy*?"

"Damned if I know." Garth tried to cover his ears with a pillow, but Hilary blocked the effort.

"Listen, Garth. There's something really strange going on. Wake up!" She reached over and turned up the volume of the small radio she had brought in from the kitchen.

"...We interrupt this broadcast again for an updated report on the winter-storm watch. The National Weather Service has issued a severe winter-storm warning for the entire coastal region. Winds gusting up to fifty miles per hour, unusually high tides, and surging waves are expected. The National Weather Service has urged residents to complete all safety precautions and evacuate to higher ground inland as soon as possible."

Hilary listened wide-eyed as the weather forecaster continued his gloomy report.

"The severe coastal storm is being attributed

to the nearly straight-line configuration of the earth, sun, and moon. It is estimated that this alignment takes place once in every eighteen and a half years. *Syzygy* is the technical term for this celestial lineup, which occurs when the moon is aligned directly opposite the earth and sun, or between the two bodies. Both sun and moon are far south of the equator; and the moon is at perigee—its closest approach to the earth in a month. Either alignment causes a bulging of the tides in some areas of the earth. Keep tuned for updated reports—"

Having heard all he needed to for the time being, Garth reached over and switched off the radio.

"What are you doing?"

"Eighteen and a half years! And the syzygy picks this time to show up again!" Garth smacked his pillow angrily.

Hilary watched as he slowly rolled to his feet, trying to focus his vision.

"Where are you going?"

"Apparently this thing is going to get a whole lot worse before it gets any better. We've got work to do."

"Don't you think we should leave?" Hilary trailed helplessly along behind him as he went in search of a rain slicker.

"And how do you suggest we do that—call a taxi?" he asked dryly.

"We could try."

"Check the phones. I'm betting most of the lines are down in this area."

When Hilary picked up the receiver, she was

met with an ominous silence. Her face grew pale. "What will we do?"

Garth paused and pulled her up to his chest. He tipped her face up to give her a brief, reassuring kiss. "I'm sorry. I know you're scared, and I have to admit I'm a little concerned myself. But we'll be fine."

"I'm frightened."

"After what we've been through? Living through a little 'ziggy' should be a breeze!" He made light of their predicament.

"Are you going out again?"

"Yes. We can't just sit here. My grandparents keep a good supply of plywood out in the garage. They've lived through a few coastal storms in their time." Garth smiled encouragingly. "Quit worrying."

"Oh, Garth! This is all my fault."

"Why?"

"I saw that 'ziggy' word mentioned in the newspaper, but I didn't bother to read what it meant."

"It's *syzygy*." Garth pronounced the word *SIZ-uh-jee*. "And don't feel guilty. I'm the one who's at fault. I knew about the storm watch for this area, but as of yesterday the forecasters hadn't been able to predict how serious it would be. Besides, I was so preoccupied with my own problems that I didn't pay much attention."

Hilary appreciated Garth's attempts to minimize her fear. "Do you really think we'll be safe here?"

Garth nodded. "I'd better get at it, though. I've got a lot of nails to drive."

"I'll help."

"What about your ankle?"

"It's fine." Hilary forced herself not to limp as she turned toward the bedroom to get dressed.

Garth caught her arm to detain her. "Hey, lady"—he pulled her back into his embrace and kissed her again with incredible tenderness— "you're okay, you know that?" he asked when their lips finally parted.

"Thank you. I've been hoping you'd notice." They kissed once more; then he swatted her bottom playfully and sent her on to get dressed.

Nailing the bulky sheets of plywood over the windows was a slow, tedious process. Especially when one of the carpenters was trying to fight off the sluggish aftermath of a sleeping pill, and the other one was trying to keep her weight off the sprained ankle she kept forgetting about.

Despite deep yawns and countless ouches, the work was eventually completed.

Around midnight the tired twosome stood back to assess their work. Garth watched Hilary's eyes as they reflected pride in their accomplishment.

She'd sure proved to be made of stronger stuff than he would have expected from the weeping, helpless girl he'd encountered twenty-four hours ago. If she hadn't held the awkward sheets of plywood, Garth would still be struggling to nail them to the window frames. She'd taken time out to brew a pot of strong coffee, and they had drunk several cups as they continued to work.

"I wish we'd had enough plywood to cover the garage windows," Hilary brooded.

"They'll be easy enough to replace."

With the work completed, Garth changed his mind about staying through the brunt of the storm. "Maybe we should try to get to higher ground, now that the house is secured."

"All right. But first"—Hilary pointed to a faint light in the distance—"we need to see if those people need our help."

Garth glanced at the cottage occupied year-round by the Johnsons. They were near his grandparents' age; and the last time Garth had seen Ben, arthritis had taken its toll on the aging man's hands.

The self-designated rescue team hurriedly headed into the wind and crossed the yard.

Ben and Esther Johnson welcomed the offer of assistance. Hilary and Garth pitched in and worked throughout the night, praying that their efforts would save the cottage from complete destruction.

"Don't you think we should try to get to higher ground, Ben?" Garth asked as the last of the windows was sealed off.

"Nope. Me and Esther's been through some pretty rough times. We'll be staying."

Garth glanced at Hilary, who smiled. The strain of the past few hours was evident on her pretty features. "We'll be staying with you—if you don't mind," Garth said.

"Nope. Welcome the company."

The brunt of the storm was predicted to hit around three that morning. Ben, Esther, Hilary, and Garth sat huddled in the Johnsons' living room to wait out the raging winter storm.

Around two o'clock, Esther and Ben nodded off to sleep.

"Are you doing okay?" Garth whispered as he cradled Hilary in his arms. They were sitting on the sofa, listening to the rain pounding on the weathered roof.

"I'm fine. Just a little tired." Hilary yawned as she rested her head on Garth's shoulder. She was exhausted, but she had never been happier. "How's your cold?"

"I hadn't thought much about it. I guess it's better."

"Good. You tired?"

"Yeah, bushed." Garth sighed as he stretched long legs out in front of him and rested his head against hers.

"Garth . . . about what happened earlier."

Garth didn't answer for a moment. Somehow he sensed he wanted to talk about the intimacy they'd shared, but he wasn't sure he did. He needed time to sort through his mixed feelings. Though he couldn't explain it, he knew Hilary had touched a portion of his heart that no other woman had ever touched before. Finally, he responded to her prompting. "What about it?" he asked softly.

Hilary moved her head until it rested comfortably on his chest. Her finger toyed lightly with the button on his shirt. "I'll never forget tonight . . . or you."

Garth stroked her hair affectionately. "I won't forget either." She felt so small and helpless in his arms . . . so *right!*

"Will you call me occasionally?"

Garth chuckled. "What do you want me to call you?"

Hilary sighed. "Darling . . . sweetheart . . . honey . . ."

He sighed and buried his face in her hair. He wasn't sure if she was teasing or not.

Hilary laughed, and she could tell he was considerably relieved. "Just call to say hello once in a while. Let me know how you are . . . where you are . . ."

Hilary couldn't imagine not ever seeing him again, but she knew it was entirely possible, once they went their separate ways.

"Sure. Why not? And you can give me a ring every now and then."

She decided to pay him back for his earlier jibe. "What sort of ring do you want?"

"Is this where I'm supposed to say 'a wedding ring'?" Garth asked calmly.

Hilary raised her face to meet his, her heart suddenly in her eyes. "Of course not . . . Unless you want to."

Garth chuckled at her candor and kissed her deeply, drawing a response from deep within.

When their lips parted many long moments later, he promised softly, "I'll think of you often."

"Make sure that you do!" Hilary wanted more—much more. But it was a start.

"I'm hungry."

"Me too." Their mouths touched, lingered, reluctant to part.

"We'll eat a steak ten inches thick when this is all over," he promised, trailing a finger through a damp strand of her hair.

"You'll have to buy it for me," she reminded him.

"I'll buy you the moon if you want it." His mouth closed hungrily over hers again, sealing the promise with another long kiss.

Exhausted from the hard work and the all-night exposure to cold winds, they settled down in each other's arms and dozed, secure in the knowledge that, at least for the moment, they still had each other.

Chapter Nine

THE WINTER STORM RAGED FOR hours. Fierce winds pounded at the thin sheets of plywood nailed to the windows, and cold rain poured from repeated cloudbursts, promising the aftermath of severe flooding.

It seemed Mother Nature was intent upon showing the true force of the power she held over the elements. Even the salty sea responded to her show of uncompromising strength as it hurled its brutal waves against the deserted shoreline.

Hilary lay listening to the wind. Her stomach rolled turbulently as she thought of being devoured by the angry ocean. The only thing that kept her from succumbing to her terror was the comfort of Garth's arms. With him by her side, she felt she could endure anything.

The storm continued for what seemed like endless hours before it finally began to abate. With dawn came the calming of the ruthless winds, although the rising sun was still obscured behind a thick mass of clouds.

"It looks like it's about over." Ben stood at the front door of the cottage and viewed the aftermath of destruction, thankful that the cottage had survived another onslaught.

Garth stirred on the sofa and gently nudged Hilary. "Come on sleepyhead. We need to check on Gram's cottage."

"Is it finally over?" Hilary sat up self-consciously, trying to arrange her tousled hair into some semblance of order.

"It's still raining, but the winds are beginning to let up." Garth was anxious to view the storm's damage.

Hilary and Garth stepped out onto the porch a few minutes later. The ravaged remains that greeted them were distressing.

Trees were down, their sharp, splintery ends a mere mockery of the splendid strength they had once possessed. The front lawn of the cottage had been turned into a small lake.

Garth and Hilary descended the steps to wade ankle-deep in icy water. It was no longer pouring, just an icy drizzle fell from the clouds.

"Your cold, Garth . . . It will get worse," Hilary fretted as they sloshed their way across the yard.

Garth sneezed and pulled the slicker up closer to his face. "Watch where you're going. There's a lot of debris."

Shattered pieces of wood drifted past, fragments of small abandoned boats that had fallen prey to the pulverizing winds. In the distance they could see a deserted beach house bobbing, roofless, in the turgid waters. The structure had been too weak to withstand the main onslaught of the storm.

Garth threaded his way along the beach while Hilary followed, clinging to his jacket for stability.

"And what, fair lady, should we do on this third day of our lovely vacation?" Garth joked as he stopped long enough to sneeze a couple of times into his handkerchief. "I'm sick of all this relaxation! Let's do something exciting!"

Going along with his sudden spurt of joviality, Hilary pretended to give the matter serious thought. "Oh, dear, I don't know. There's so much we haven't done, yet. Earthquakes, locust plagues, aviational disasters—"

"Oh, sorry. I almost covered that one on my flight to Raleigh, but everything turned out all right at the last minute."

"Honestly?"

"Honestly. The landing gear malfunctioned on my plane," Garth admitted.

"Well, I suppose that makes up for the blowout my cab had on the way to Stapleton . . . and for my sprained ankle."

"Yeah, I suppose that makes us even-up on good times."

They looked at each other and grinned. "At least *you* aren't half blind," Hilary said accusingly. "I lost my contact at the airport."

"I know. I stepped on it."

Her mouth dropped open. "You *what!*"

"I can see . . ."—Garth ignored her astonishment and went on listing his miseries—"I just can't breathe because of the pneumonia I got when my cab was stuck in traffic, and I was forced to run the rest of the way to O'Hare."

By now, each of them was striving hard to keep a straight face.

"You had plenty of time to buy cold pills during the layover in Raleigh," she said reproachfully.

"No, I spent those particular eight hours handing out clean handkerchiefs to some strange— and I do mean strange—woman who was crying every time I looked up."

"How sad!" Hilary's grin widened. "You didn't have cold pills in your luggage?"

"I didn't *have* luggage by that time."

"But you could have purchased some when you arrived at your hotel."

"Oh, by then I had my luggage back," he conceded.

"You did?"

"Yes, only the hotel burned down, and I lost it again."

They lost their composure at the same time and began laughing over their ridiculous string of bad luck. Hilary sagged weakly against him, and he almost went down in the water.

"You should have seen your face when Lenny grabbed you around the throat!"

Garth steadied himself and looked at her incredulously, shocked that she would have the gall to mention the humiliating incident. Hilary dissolved in a new round of merriment.

"You thought that was funny? You're sick! That baboon could have broken my neck!"

Hilary nodded sympathetically. "I know!"

She dissolved in laughter again, but Garth shook his head in disgust. He hadn't found Lenny Ricetrum all that amusing.

When Hilary's giddiness had finally passed, Garth reached over and pulled her to him for an overdue good-morning kiss.

"Hell of a vacation, Ms. Brookfield, but you've definitely made it worthwhile," he said a few moments later.

"Thank you, Mr. Redmond. We must do it again sometime."

As they neared the Redmond cottage, they were relieved to see that it was still standing. Garth didn't even mind that its shingles were all curled or that the windows of the garage had been blown out during the night. As they drew nearer, the waters were beginning to recede.

"My feet are like blocks of ice," Hilary complained. She huddled more deeply into the lining of her jacket.

"Mine too." Garth sneezed again.

Until last night his cold had seemed to be getting better. This morning there was a tightness in his chest, and the cold water he was standing in set him shivering with a renewed chill.

Garth reached over and took Hilary's hand as they walked around the corner of the garage. "I want a hot cup of coffee and some dry clothing."

The sight of Lenny Ricetrum sitting on the front porch was the last thing Garth had expected. Hilary stopped abruptly when she saw him. She tugged warningly on Garth's jacket as he trudged on toward the porch, ignoring the unwelcomed visitor.

"Uh-oh . . . Look who's here."

"I noticed, but *he* can move on this time."

"But, Garth . . ."

Garth ignored her protests, and they continued walking toward the cottage. Personally he planned to ignore the two hundred and twenty pounds of foreboding flesh sitting on the doorstep.

Lenny stood up and crossed his arms. His look openly dared them to try and walk past him.

Garth had just about had it. What was supposed to have been a relaxing vacation had turned into a nightmare of unbelievable proportions. From the very start of this bizarre journey two days ago—*just two days ago*, Garth thought despairingly—he'd run into one disaster after another. Now, to add to his problems, he'd become intimate with Hilary Brookfield, who just happened to have an ex-boyfriend who was big enough to hunt bear with a switch.

What had he done to deserve this?

The sight of the baboon who had earlier tried to twist his neck off, who was now trying to block the entrance to *his* home, kindled a spark of anger in Garth.

"How did you find us, Lenny?" Hilary demanded as they approached the porch.

"Let's just say I'm not as dumb as you think I am."

"I didn't say I thought you were dumb. I just thought I had made it clear that I was going to need a little time to think about our situation—"

"Can it, Hilary!" Lenny interrupted curtly. "This is between me and ol' lover boy right now."

"My name is not *lover boy*, Ricetrum, and I don't appreciate your talking to Hilary in that tone of voice," Garth warned. His brown eyes sparkled with a stubbornness Hilary had never seen there before.

"Lenny, I want you to leave." Hilary hurriedly stepped between the two men. She was afraid Lenny would actually hurt Garth this time.

Garth calmly set her aside.

"But, Garth!"

"I can take care of this, Hilary."

"Hilary, I told you to can it!" Lenny snapped.

"And I told you, I don't want you talking to Hilary like that." Garth stepped forward, meeting Lenny's cold stare with one equally glacial.

"Oh, yeah? How would you like me to talk to you—with these!" Lenny doubled up his two beefy fists and shook them threateningly at Garth.

Garth stiffened with resentment. "Be my guest!"

Hilary clamped her hand over her mouth as Lenny suddenly sprang from the porch like a panther.

The force of a man twice his weight slamming into him so abruptly promptly knocked Garth back flat on his back. Lenny gripped Garth's head, landing a brutal punch to the right eye. It split the skin wide open on impact. Blinded by mud and blood, Garth struggled to deliver his own blows.

Hilary stood paralyzed with fear, watching the

unfairly matched pair as they rolled around in the mud. The tumbling finally halted with Lenny sitting straddled across Garth's chest.

"Come on, Ricetrum! Can't we discuss this like two adults—" Garth's plea was cut off as another meaty fist slammed into his mouth. He swore and rolled his head to one side to spit blood.

The two began frantically wallowing around again at Hilary's feet. She realized she'd have to do something—and fast.

The sight of blood oozing from the cuts on Garth's face gave her the strength she needed. She crouched aggressively as her temper surfaced in full force.

"Lenny, you get off him this instant!" Like a mean bantam rooster, Hilary flew between the two struggling men.

In her eagerness to assist Garth, she slipped and fell facedown in the mud. She paused only long enough to rake away the gook from her eyes. Crawling the rest of the way on her hands and knees, she pounced on Lenny's back.

"What are you doing?" Lenny tried to shake the unexpected wildcat off his back. But Hilary's fingers grabbed a hunk of his black hair and jerked painfully. Lenny let out a yell, and the momentary distraction afforded Garth a well-targeted right to Lenny's face.

As Lenny's hands shot up to protect his nose, Garth was busy trying to free himself. Lenny's fruitless efforts to sling Hilary off his back left her head spinning long after his attempts had slowed down.

"I said let him go, Lenny!" Hilary enunciated

in an ominous voice just before she yanked hard on his hair again.

"*Ouch!* All right, all right! Damn it, Hilary! Let go of my hair!"

Finally giving up on his hoped-for reconciliation, Lenny lifted himself from Garth, whose face was completely covered with mud.

Lenny made a feeble attempt to straighten his dishevelled clothing. He could take a hint. It was obvious that Hilary was no longer interested in him.

Reaching up to rub his smarting head, Lenny gave it one more try. "I'm warning you, Hilary. I'm flying back to Denver in an hour, and if you don't come with me right now I'm washing my hands of you—permanently."

Hilary rose to her feet unsteadily, her clothing covered with thick mud. "Well, happy trails to you!"

Lenny shot her a dirty look and stalked off angrily to his rented car. Moments later he wheeled out of sight.

Garth sat up and stared at the muddy woman who had come to his rescue. Even with her hair dripping filth, Hilary was nothing short of beautiful as she hovered over him and offered her hand in assistance.

Garth lifted one brow wryly. "Happy trails to you?"

Hilary shrugged. "I couldn't think of anything better."

Though he realized he would have a shiner later on, Garth couldn't remember when his spirits had been higher. Hilary had flatly refused to go back with the jerk.

Hilary put a protective arm around Garth and helped him carefully to his feet. "We'd better get you into some dry clothes."

"*We?*" Garth grinned.

"You're sure a frisky little devil—right after the tar's been beaten out of you!" Hilary chided. She decided to ignore his suggestive tone. "Lean on me."

"I didn't get the tar beaten out of me," Garth protested. "Ricetrum's going to have a black eye too." He draped his arm around her neck and nuzzled her ear playfully. "Um . . . you taste like mud!"

Hilary avoided his amorous advances and pointed him in the direction of the cottage. "Let's get you into the shower and rinse off some of this mud before it sets like cement."

"Will you get in with me?"

She blushed. "You're getting awfully bold."

"It's our vacation! We should have a little fun," Garth complained. He felt good. She'd actually refused to go back with Ricetrum!

While Hilary adjusted the water temperature in the shower, Garth examined his injuries in the mirror. He decided he hadn't come out all that badly. He could've been dead!

He licked the salty blood off his split lower lip and frowned. "Why couldn't you have been dating a hundred-pound weakling?"

Hilary grinned. "You did okay."

"I did, didn't I? Did you see that right punch I threw at him?"

"I saw. It was impressive. Come over here."

Garth obeyed and she helped him—clothes and all—into the shower. When he was safely in the stall she started to close the door, but he reached out and grabbed her hand.

"Now, stop—"

"Get in with me."

"No!"

"Yes! You know something?" His eyes met hers, and Hilary felt she could see right into his soul. And it looked as if he had feelings that he couldn't comprehend himself.

"No, what?" She knew she shouldn't take the bait, but she did anyway.

"For a minute I was afraid you would go back with Ricetrum," he confessed.

"Would that have bothered you?"

He smiled back at her. "Yes ... I think it would have."

Hilary felt the return of butterflies in her stomach. "I'm glad. Lenny Ricetrum is history, as far as I'm concerned. I'm not sure what I ever saw in him."

"I'm not either. I didn't think he was your type," Garth admitted as he pulled her into the shower with him. He wrapped his arms around her waist possessively. "Kiss me."

Hilary didn't wait to be invited twice. She moved into his waiting arms, and they exchanged a long, satisfying kiss.

"Are you hungry?" he murmured sexily against her lips.

"Ravenous!"

"Me too!"

They both knew they weren't talking about food.

With a control that had his insides trembling, Garth's hand captured her chin and his thumb gently caressed her lips. "Thank you."

"For what?"

"For standing up for me against Lenny."

Hilary could feel the sweet pulse of desire coursing through her as he began to peel away her muddy clothing. "I can't explain how I felt when I saw you were in danger..."

"Try!" Garth urged as he quickly stripped out of his clothing, then pulled her close so that her bare body was pressed against his.

"I was frightened...I was so afraid Lenny would hurt you...and I didn't know what I would do if he did." Hilary's words dissolved as she felt the touch of his lips on her breast.

"You're beautiful," he whispered as the tip of his tongue moved with unbearable lightness across her skin. Waves of pleasure surged through her as he continued the sensuous assault. "And desirable...exciting..."

Hilary curled her fingers into the thick mass of his hair, pressing her body against his solid, comforting length. Nibbling lightly at the lobe of his ear, she added one other description, which only served to send a hot shaft of desire ricocheting through him.

"And very wicked!" Garth scolded.

"That wasn't wicked."

"Who told you it wasn't?" His mouth caught hers demandingly.

After a long, arousing kiss Garth whispered his

own observation, and she laughed softly.

"You're terrible!"

Garth chuckled and gave her a big bear hug. "You know what?"

"No, what?"

"This has been a terrible vacation, but I can't remember ever feeling as good as I do right now."

Hilary laughed, sharing his jubilant mood. She was happy, but she had to remind herself to keep the whirlwind relationship in perspective. The feelings were still too new for her to hope they could ever last.

As the hot-water heater's supply began to run out, Garth lifted her into his arms and stepped out of the shower.

"Garth . . . we shouldn't," Hilary warned. Barely controlled passion was clearly evident in his eyes now.

"Why not?"

"Well, last night . . . was last night. When you go back to Chicago, and I return to Denver . . ." Her voice trailed off lamely. Her body throbbed with longing; she wanted him as badly as he wanted her.

He looked into her face, full of defenseless love, and assured her gently, "I can't imagine ever forgetting you."

He moved to the brass bed and laid her down tenderly. Then his hands were in her hair, drawing her closer and stilling her murmured protests with the perfect union of their mouths. Soft rays of sunlight filtered through the sheer material of the drapes as he sought to weaken her resistance as surely as she was weakening his.

He brought her body flush against him, proving his need for her. A tender light shone in his eyes as he whispered in a voice made more urgent with desire. "If it's the short period of time we've known each other that bothers you, then I won't make love to you again," he promised. "But I'm afraid you'll have to be the one to make that decision."

"Until I met you, I would have never dreamed I could be so reckless," Hilary confessed.

"Reckless? I don't think what we have is reckless."

"It is for me, Garth. I want permanence in life ... and I think it's too soon for us to commit ourselves to such a relationship. We barely know each other."

"No, not yet. But in time ..." Garth lowered his mouth to take hers. The rational words lingered, but the desires of the flesh were more persuasive.

Lavishing her throat with feather kisses, he warned again. "Say the word and I'll stop."

Hilary thought he wasn't being fair. Her hazy mind didn't have the slightest idea of what "the word" would be.

"I don't want you to stop," she confessed and drew a shuddering breath. He was kissing her with a seductive torment that was more eloquent than words.

"Maybe there isn't any word that could stop me," he conceded. His mouth moved down the perfumed length of her, touching her here ... and there ... and there ...

Maybe nothing could stop him from claiming her again, Garth realized.

Maybe this crazy roller coaster he had been on would turn out to be the real thing.

Maybe . . . He would think about it later.

Chapter Ten

HILARY WAS THE FIRST TO awaken. Her hand moved to caress the warm form lying next to her. When it came in contact with a masculine, hair-roughened thigh, she smiled. She hadn't been dreaming. Garth had made love to her again—no, it had been more than making love. Something wonderful and exciting had taken place last night, and she was sure he'd felt it too.

She sighed and rolled toward him as his arms drew her tightly against his bare length. He was still asleep, and he looked so peaceful that she was sure there was still a special warmth that lingered from their spent passion.

The little clock sitting on the nightstand drew her attention. She gasped softly when she realized they'd slept for a straight fourteen hours!

Turning back to Garth, she teasingly traced the dark circle under his left eye—Lenny's legacy.

Black eye or not, he was the most handsome

man in the world, she thought wistfully. More important, he was a good man...perfect husband material. Hilary sensed he would be wonderful with children, and she'd bet her last her dollar he would even love his mother-in-law. He just seemed to be the type.

Propping herself up on her elbows, she tenderly brushed her lips across his bare shoulder. "Mrs. Garth Redmond. Hilary Redmond. Garth and Hilary Redmond," she whispered, liking the sound of all three.

Garth moved and his eyes opened slowly. Hilary smiled and kissed the tip of his nose affectionately.

"What are you doing?"

Sorry that she'd disturbed him, mostly because she'd been caught, Hilary said guiltily, "Tasting."

"Tasting?"

"Yeah." She poked the tip of her tongue in the crease of one of his dimples and licked him playfully.

"What do I taste like?" he mumbled.

"Um...like...gentleness, passion, kindness—things like that." Her mouth found his, and they kissed a long, leisurely good morning kiss.

When their lips parted, Garth gazed into her eyes lovingly. "I didn't know you could taste things like gentleness and kindness."

"Not all men taste like that." She absent-mindedly traced his lower lip with the tip of her finger. "But you do, Garth."

"You give me too much credit."

"No, I don't. You're wonderful."

Garth was embarrassed by her praise, but he loved it. "You think so? Come here." He pulled her on top of his chest and kissed her again. "Let's see what you taste like."

Hilary closed her eyes and savored the butterfly kisses that he sprinkled across her forehead, her nose, finally coming to rest against the fullness of her lips, his tongue gently probing the warm moistness of her mouth.

"So . . . what do I taste like?"

Garth gazed into her passion-laden eyes and said softly, "Let's see." He paused, gliding his tongue back across her lips, tasting, sampling her sweetness. "I think you taste like . . . gentleness, kindness, and passion."

"But I don't have all those qualities. I anger too easily; I have no patience at times; and while I'm not a mean person, I'm not necessarily overly kind." She hated to admit it, but it was all true.

"What about passion?"

"Well now, passion is possible," she confessed humbly.

"Possible!" Garth lifted a dark brow dubiously, and she grinned.

"Well, maybe probable," she amended, vividly recalling the night before.

"I should think so!"

"Want me to prove it?"

"I thought you'd never ask!"

Entwined in the warm embrace of each other's arms, they gently rolled over, and Garth hungrily captured her mouth again. As their insatiable need for each other flared up again, Garth buried his face in the full softness of her hair and confessed she actually tasted sweet—very sweet. For the next thirty minutes they made love with such ardor that it left them both spent.

With passion temporarily appeased again, Hilary lay quietly in his arms. Garth wondered why she'd suddenly grown so still. He glanced down and nudged her gently. "Hey, sleepyhead, don't drift off on me. It's getting late."

"Um . . . just a few minutes . . . two winks at the most," she pleaded.

Garth glanced at the clock and was astounded to see the time. "Not a chance! I'm starving. Let's forget breakfast and find ourselves a nice thick steak."

The thought of food enticed Hilary to move ever so slightly beneath the sheet. Prying one eye open, she bargained, "And a hot, fat, baked potato—drenched in butter and sour cream?"

Garth nodded sleepily.

"Salad, rolls, and lemon pie?"

"Cheesecake."

"Both!"

"Good Lord!" He smacked her on her bare fanny and rolled out of bed. "How do you keep your figure, eating like that?"

"I just don't worry about it. I usually eat anything I want and suffer terrible guilt later."

Garth chuckled, recalling how Lisa forever counted calories and became outraged when he refused to do the same. "I'll buy you anything you want. Let's just get a move on."

"All right, but I get the shower first." She playfully tossed her pillow at him as she sprang to her feet and headed toward the bathroom.

Intercepting the flying pillow with one hand, Garth sat up in the bed and watched as she disappeared through the doorway. "Want some help?"

"No. Not if you want to get to the restaurant anytime in the near future," she called back.

Garth rolled out of bed and went over to the door. He rapped loudly. He could hear the sound of water running, so he knew she would be standing beneath the warm spray now.

He remembered all too well how beautiful she looked with her silky skin glistening, the gleaming beads of water sliding down the length of her supple frame . . .

"Just a shower—I promise I won't start anything," he pleaded as he pressed his face against the closed door.

Hilary laughed and shouted above the stream of hot water, "Not a chance. You could be lying."

"No, I promise."

"I thought you were hungry!"

There was a meaningful pause. Then, "I am."

At the suggestive innuendo in his voice, Hilary felt herself weakening. The hot-water heater did tend to empty its supply rapidly—and he did have that miserable cold . . . She tried desperately to rationalize what she was about to do.

"Please!"

With a resigned sigh, she stepped out of the shower and unlocked the door.

"I knew you'd break down." Garth grinned and reached for her slippery body as she tumbled willingly into his arms.

"I told you I was weak."

"I remembered." Garth ran his hands exquisitely over her bottom while he kissed her, then let them drop back to his sides repentantly. "Okay, I promised. But may I at least soap your back?"

"Only if you'll shampoo my hair too," she bartered as she stepped back into the shower and turned to face the spray of warm water.

"I don't know how to shampoo your hair," he protested.

"You shampoo yours, don't you?"

"I don't think it will be the same."

By the time Garth had lathered her hair, Hilary looked like a creature from outer space.

"Garth! You've used too much shampoo," she complained, spitting the soap bubbles out of her mouth.

He was unconcerned. He was too busy sculpting various animal shapes out of the white froth.

"And here is an attack zebra!" he announced, scooping up a handful of the soap suds and backing her into the corner of the shower.

"Garth, no!" She dodged as he—and the attack zebra—masterminded an offensive on her body that eventually ended with another round of lovemaking.

Later, while she dried her hair, Garth dressed and headed for the Johnsons' cottage to call a taxi.

The level of the small lake in the front yard had descended more rapidly than he'd expected. He was glad its icy waters no longer sloshed over the tops of Silas's old rubber boots.

It was more than two hours before the cab arrived.

As they settled themselves in the backseat, it occurred to Hilary that she hadn't phoned her parents as she'd promised. She'd even forgotten to pick up the money they'd wired her.

"Garth, before we find a place to eat, could we stop by the Western Union office and pick up my money? I was supposed to have picked it up hours ago. My parents are probably sick with worry."

"Of course. I had forgotten all about the money. I suppose we'd better stop by the Merrymont and file an insurance claim while we're at it."

"I suppose so." Hilary snuggled closer to him.

"After we've had dinner." Garth leaned over and nibbled on her ear.

"By all means. Let's eat first."

By the looks of things, the small town of West Creek was still in a state of emergency. Utility workmen were busy repairing fallen power lines, and merchants were removing the bulky sheets of plywood that had saved their plate-glass windows. In the lower-lying areas, families could be seen sweeping the icy waters out of their flooded homes.

Hilary's money was waiting when they arrived at the Western Union office. She signed the required forms, collected her funds, then phoned her parents in Denver.

"Daddy?" Hilary began hesitantly. She wasn't sure if her parents knew of the storm.

"Hilary! What on earth happened to you? We

heard on the news about a storm back there, and we were worried sick when we didn't hear from you!" The sharp tone of her father's normally mild voice assured her they knew the full extent of the damage caused by the syzygy.

"Daddy, I'm fine," Hilary said soothingly. She glanced at Garth and made a patient face. "The storm wasn't as bad as the news media made it sound."

Garth grinned, realizing she was trying to downplay the extent of the nightmare they had just weathered.

"When you didn't call us back, naturally we assumed the worst. Your mother's been having fits!"

"I'm sorry, Daddy. Lines are down, and I wasn't near a phone that worked. Tell Mama I'm fine. Really!"

"I will, baby. Is Marsha all right?"

Hilary looked at Garth and smiled. "She's fine, Daddy. Couldn't be better."

"Are you going to cut your vacation short because of the storm?"

"I think so. I'll let you know what I decide."

When Hilary said good-bye and hung up the phone, Garth looked at her tenderly. "That was nice of you."

Lisa would have played the crisis to the hilt; yet Hilary had gone out of her way to spare her parent's feelings. Garth admired her more every hour.

"What was nice?"

"The way you deliberately spared them extra worry."

"Why should I worry them? The storm's over, and I'm still in one piece."

"It was still nice of you." Garth leaned over and kissed her.

"Well..." Hilary wrinkled her nose at him lovingly. "I've had a good example to live by lately."

The taxi left the Western Union office and drove to the restaurant. Fortunately for their growling stomachs, the Steak House had escaped severe damage.

Garth eyed the broken neon sign outside the restaurant. "How do you want your *teak*?" he teased, making playful reference to the S that had been sucked away by the strong winds.

Hilary smiled, thinking how nice it was to be able to enjoy life again.

Garth escorted her from the taxi and offered her his arm. Hilary graciously accepted it, and with a look of pride etched on his face, he guided her into the restaurant.

"How's the ankle feeling?" He had almost forgotten about her injury.

"What ankle?" she grinned. "How's the cold?"

"What cold?" Garth bantered. The words were barely past his lips when another sneeze hit him.

In no time the hostess had them seated and served. Hilary couldn't remember when a baked potato had ever tasted so good. Garth remarked that his steak was prepared exactly the way he liked it, and he savored every bite with exaggerated pleasure.

Over coffee and cheesecake, the lightness of

their mood slowly shifted, becoming more serious.

Garth reached over and picked up her hand, then kissed the back of it gently. "I'm glad we've had this time together."

Hilary sensed that the hour she'd been dreading had finally arrived. For a second she considered confessing that she had fallen in love with him. But at the last moment she changed her mind. She wasn't sure he was ready to hear that yet. He had never talked of the future.

"I'm glad we have too, Garth."

"The past few days have made me think about a lot of things . . ." His words faded as he groped for a way to express his feelings. He wasn't exactly sure what they were himself. She'd just come out of a bad relationship, and it was too soon for her to start a new one. As for him, he certainly didn't want to jump into anything he couldn't get out of later if he wanted to.

Hilary absentmindedly toyed with her coffee cup, keeping her gaze from his. She wanted desperately to tell him how she felt, but she was afraid. If she expressed her love, and he didn't share the feeling . . .

"Hilary, I guess what I'm trying to say is . . ." Garth paused, poking his fork at the half-eaten cheesecake.

"Garth, you don't have to say anything," Hilary told him. She didn't want to hear the dreaded "It's been nice, but see you later, kid" routine. She'd rather part with the fragile hope that what they'd had was real. Maybe with a little time, Garth would realize it too.

"Hilary...I need a little time—"

"Garth"—she reached over and covered his hand with hers—"you don't have to explain. I know." He was struggling with his doubts, and she wasn't going to push.

"I'll call you...And you stay in touch with me." Garth's troubled eyes searched hers for an answer she didn't have. "Okay?"

Hilary sighed. At least he wasn't shutting the door entirely. It was more than she'd expected but achingly less than she wanted.

"Okay."

Garth felt a sinking sensation in the pit of his stomach. Had he hoped she might argue with him? "Okay, we agree to keep in touch?"

"Yes, of course." Hilary squeezed his hand reassuringly.

His gaze grew incredibly tender, and he held on to her hand tightly. "You're one hell of a woman."

"Thank you." Her own eyes glistened brightly with unshed tears. "You're quite a man."

Forcing a front of bravery, Hilary quietly excused herself and left for the sanctuary of the ladies' room before the telltale tears could slip down her cheeks. Once she was safely behind closed doors, she gave into the heartfelt sobs. She would never see him again, she agonized. He would go back to Chicago and forget that Hilary Brookfield had ever existed.

Torn between an aching heart, which told her to stay and try to change his mind, and a rational mind, which cautioned her to leave before she got in any more deeply, Hilary reluctantly admitted to herself what she had to do.

She'd go back to Denver first thing in the morning. Maybe getting back to a normal routine would help her get her life in order.

When Hilary returned to the table, she was dry-eyed and wearing a bright smile. Over second cups of coffee, she told Garth of her plans to leave for Denver on the early-morning flight, reasoning that she really should be getting back to the office. "I left on such short notice, and with Marsha gone..." Hilary shrugged. "I think I've had all the 'vacation' I can stand."

They both laughed nervously.

"I guess maybe I'll do the same thing," Garth admitted.

They looked at each other, and Hilary wasn't sure if she had the strength to leave.

"I'll get the check," she said softly. "I have the money this time."

Later they rode to the Merrymont and quietly filled out the small mountain of insurance forms, then called the airport and made their reservations for the next morning's flight.

As they left the counter Garth put his arm around her and drew her close to his side. "Stay with me tonight."

"I was thinking about getting a room in town," she confessed. She knew that if she spent the night with him, she'd be helpless to leave when morning came.

"Please...one more night," Garth urged.

Hilary shook her head ruefully. "What am I going to do with you?"

Garth's adoring eyes sent her the silent answer.

"Oh, I almost forgot." She rummaged through her purse after they were seated in the taxi. "Your money."

"Keep it. Consider it a get-acquainted present." Garth smiled.

"Thank you, but I couldn't." Hilary tucked the wad of bills into his jacket pocket.

Garth removed the money and pressed it firmly into her hand. "If you insist on paying me back, wait until you get home. Please."

"Okay, but I will pay you back," she insisted, realizing she didn't want to spend their last few precious hours together arguing. "I'll put a check in the mail tomorrow."

She suddenly sneezed.

"You getting sick?"

"I think I'm getting your cold."

"Hm!" He grinned and winked. "I wonder why!"

They shared their last few hours together in the beach house beneath a darkened sky now ablaze with glittering stars.

"It feels like I'm saying good-bye to my best friend," Garth confessed as he cupped her face and tried to memorize every feature in the soft rays cast by the lamp at the bedside.

"I'd like to be your best friend," Hilary whispered.

Garth sipped at her lips as if they were warm wine. "Granted, my fair lady . . ."

It was a long time before their passion could be appeased. It was late when they finally dropped into an uneasy sleep, still entwined in each other's arms.

During the night they slept fitfully, waking every hour to look at the hands on the clock.

When daybreak arrived, few words were exchanged as they rose and dressed for their early-morning flight. They carefully avoided looking at each other as they packed in strained silence.

At the municipal airport on the outskirts of West Creek, they sat quietly as they awaited the plane.

The short flight was uneventful, and all too quickly they had landed at Raleigh-Durham.

This time a lengthy delay, such as the one they had experienced three days earlier, would have been welcome, but both departures were running right on time.

Hilary's plane was the first scheduled to leave.

"Well, I guess this is it." She forced her voice to remain cheerful, although her insides were tied in knots.

"Yes, I guess it is." Garth ran a hand uneasily through his hair. "You will keep in touch?"

"Sure." Hilary smiled and patted the side of her purse. "I've got your number written in three different places." She knew she didn't need the reminders. She'd memorized the number before the ink had dried.

"Well, they're playing my song," she said as the second call for Flight 527 come over the intercom.

Garth suddenly reached out and caught her to him. "Take care of yourself..."

"You too..." She was suddenly crushed against his broad chest.

Even through the thick fabric of his jacket she

could detect the beat of his heart. It was all she could do to refrain from crying out her pent-up love as he lifted her off her feet and kissed her more passionately than ever before. She was breathless and teary-eyed when the final boarding call sounded.

He gently lowered her back to her feet, and his eyes met hers solemnly. "I'm holding you to your word, Hilary. Don't forget me."

"I won't," she promised, and they kissed one last time before she broke away and ran blindly down the jetway.

Chapter Eleven

THE FOLLOWING DAYS PASSED with painful slowness. Hilary spent long hours at O'Connor Construction Company, where she was preoccupied with agonizing memories of Garth.

They both had remained true to their promise to keep in touch. They corresponded via telephone or cards almost daily.

Even Lenny Ricetrum had kept his promise to wash his hands of Hilary. He'd quit his job at O'Connor's, and someone had mentioned that Lenny was seeing a recently divorced brunette.

The news didn't bother Hilary. She discovered she didn't care if Lenny's newest flame had purple hair—as long as he stayed away from her.

The sound of the five-o'clock whistle signaled Hilary that Day Number Ten had passed. Feeling disheartened, she put on her coat and headed to her empty apartment. Gary Franks had called earlier and asked her out for dinner, but Hilary confessed she would be terrible company.

It was becoming harder and harder to face the four walls that had become her self-imposed prison. She fantasized that Garth would magically be there waiting for her one night, but she knew that wasn't likely to happen.

Hilary arrived home and held her breath with anticipation as she checked the mailbox. When her trembling fingers retrieved the large manila envelope with Garth's return address scrawled across the corner, she felt her heart soar. A big fat letter was stuffed inside. Hilary unfolded its neatly written pages, and a pink check slipped to the floor. She frowned, scooping up the check she'd sent to him for the clothing he'd bought her.

Trying to read the letter and unlock the door at the same time proved to be impossible, so she paused in savoring every word just long enough to jiggle the door to her apartment open. Once inside, she didn't bother to remove her coat as she sank down on the sofa to finish the letter.

"Oh, Garth, I miss you," she whispered, wiping the back of her hand over eyes that were now filling with tears as she read his casual chitchat.

The telephone rang, forcing her to restrain her tears. She grabbed for a tissue and prayed the caller would be Garth.

"Hi, honey!" Simon Brookfield's voice came cheerfully over the wire.

Feeling her heart take a nosedive, Hilary sighed. "Oh, hi, Daddy."

"What's this 'oh, hi, Daddy' stuff? Are you all right?" Simon had noticed that something had been bothering his daughter ever since she'd returned from vacation.

"I'm sorry. It's been a long day." Hilary apologized for her obvious distraction. "How's Mama?"

"Fine. She wants to know if you'd like to come for dinner tonight. We haven't seen much of you since you got home."

"Dinner? Tonight?" What if Garth should call while she was away? No, she couldn't take the chance. It was foolish to sit and wait for his call, but then Hilary would be the first to admit Garth had that effect on her.

"Thanks, Daddy, but I'm really tired tonight. I thought I'd take a nice hot bath and go to bed early."

"Are you sure, honey? You've been spending a great deal of time tucked away in that apartment of yours lately. We miss you."

"I'll make it up to you, I promise. Maybe one night next week."

"Okay, hon. Anytime will be fine with your mother and me. Just give us a call."

"I will."

"How's the cold?"

"I think I'm finally getting over it."

"You're sure nothing's wrong?"

"Dad, I'm not a child," Hilary reminded him patiently.

"I know, I know. But just because you're grown doesn't mean we don't still worry about you. You just wait—"

"Until you have children of your own!" Hilary finished for him, then laughed softly. "Okay, I'll make sure they keep me up nights worrying, just the way I do the two of you."

"You won't have to go out of your way to do that," Simon chuckled. "It comes with the job."

"Good night, Dad."

"Good night, dear. Don't forget about dinner next week."

"I won't."

Hilary hadn't much more than placed the receiver back onto its cradle when the phone rang again.

"Hello." She was careful not to allow her expectations to soar again.

"Hi, babe!" The familiar baritone voice immediately turned her knees to pulp.

"Well, hi there!" Hilary deliberately kept her voice casual, although she had to sink onto the nearest chair. "I just got your letter...and my check. What's the big idea?"

"Don't panic. I can explain."

"Then start explaining. And it'd better be good. If not, this check goes back in the mail—first thing tomorrow morning," she warned.

"You'd actually be so crass as to send a present back?"

"Present? What's the occasion for such a generous present?"

"Your birthday?" he offered.

"Uh-uh. My birthday isn't until July. How quickly one forgets," Hilary teased.

"I didn't forget...You never told me," Garth said softly.

"You never asked."

"Okay, I'm asking you now. When's your birthday?"

"July twenty-eighth."

"So I'm a little early. Take the check and buy yourself something nice."

"Oh, Garth! I love you!" The words were out before Hilary realized what she'd said.

There was a significant pause. Then, "You what?"

Hilary realized that her impulsive declaration of love had completely stunned him, so she tried to patch up the confession by appearing to make it more of a blanket observation. "Of course I love you. How could I not love a man who helped me through three of the most miserable days of my life?"

"Oh . . . that kind of love."

Had she heard a distinct let-down in his voice, or had she only imagined it?

"Exactly when do you think it happened? Was it when you soiled my handkerchiefs, or when we hand-wrestled for the Samsonite?" Garth tried to mask his disappointment with teasing.

"I think it was shortly after you called me Harry," Hilary decided.

For a moment there was another silence; then Garth said, "Well, I guess I'd better get myself in gear and get ready for work. I just thought I'd call and see what you were up to."

"Garth . . ." Hilary stalled, wanting to tell him she did love him—and not just because he had shared those three days with her. She loved him because he was special. She loved him because he was Garth.

"Yes?"

"I'm glad you called."

Hilary was positive she detected a slight un-evenness in his voice this time. "I think about you a lot, Hilary."

"I think about you, too."

"Lenny giving you any trouble?"

"No, I haven't seen Lenny lately."

"Well, I need to go. We've been in school re-cently. They've started a new landing program that's designed to clear up the lengthy delays in flight schedules." Hilary heard his weary sigh. "It's been a nightmare."

"Is the weather bad?" She wanted to prolong the conversation, yet she knew she shouldn't de-lay him.

"It snowed a little today."

"Well, thanks for my birthday present."

"Yeah, keep in touch."

"Yes . . . you too."

"Good night."

"Good night."

The following week more presents arrived. First, Hilary received three dozen white roses. Garth called that evening to explain that their arrival was an early Valentine's Day gift.

Hilary accepted that. Valentine's Day was only three weeks away, she rationalized, wondering if he really thought the flowers would last until then.

When a large flacon of Joy was delivered two days later, it was Hilary who called Garth. Her jubilant thank you was casually dismissed with the assurance that the perfume was an early Christmas present.

"Garth, it's only the last day of January!" Hilary protested.

"Yeah, I know. But I like to get my shopping done early. I beat the rush of last-minute shoppers that way."

As the days turned into a full month, Hilary knew their phone bills would be astronomical. She dreaded the day when AT&T tallied up their conversations.

The weather in Denver took a turn for the worse, dumping a record-breaking snowfall the first week in February. More diligently than she watched *Dallas* or *Falcon Crest*, Hilary found herself watching the weather report every night to see what the weather was doing in Chicago.

Until she'd met Garth, she'd never cared about the forecast. But with the increased pressures bad weather brought to the air-traffic controllers, Hilary's nightly prayers now ended with a Please, let there be clear skies in Chicago tomorrow!

Garth came to dread the long nights. After having spent two nights in Hilary's arms, he had yet to experience the restful sleep he'd shared with her in West Creek.

Scanning the forecast printout sheets for the Denver area, he wondered if his "snow bunny" would ever again melt in his arms the way she had at the beach house.

Sometimes Garth would call Denver on his break when he could feel the pressures mounting. Hilary could always tell when he was calling from the control tower. His voice would be tense. But after five minutes of chatting he seemed to relax and become his old self again.

"You're good for me," Garth confessed one night, and Hilary assured him that the feeling was mutual. She always felt warm and needed after they hung up, even in the loneliness of her apartment.

March arrived, and with it came Hilary's first phone bill. She let it sit on the coffee table for two days before she had enough courage to open it.

"Good grief!"

She knew she couldn't afford to keep up with the tremendous cost of calling Illinois every other night. It would be cheaper to fly there and talk to Garth in person.

She paused as she seriously toyed with the idea. Well, why not? For much less than one month's telephone bill, she could fly to Chicago and spend an entire weekend with him. She threw the bill in the air exuberantly. Why not?

It wasn't the huge phone bill that convinced Garth it was time to put a stop to the cat-and-mouse game.

He'd always come home tired, even before Hilary came into his life. But now he'd always wake up feeling exhausted, having spent night after night tossing and turning.

Garth didn't mind obsessing about Hilary during his every waking moment . . . he just preferred that she be in his arms while he was doing it.

He tried dating Lisa a few times but finally admitted that she was out of the picture. Lisa had taken the breakup as he'd expected—very badly. She was furious and nasty.

But Garth didn't care. All he could think of was Hilary.

Hilary, in the meantime, frequently drove out to Stapleton International Airport, where she would gaze longingly at the control tower. She tried to visualize Garth's world.

She was still debating whether or not to fly to Chicago. Suppose Garth would resent her for just dropping by. It was possible. He'd never once suggested they try to see each other again. In the end, Hilary decided that was a chance she'd simply have to take. She couldn't endure another week without seeing him. As she gazed at the distant tower, she thought of the man she loved who was hundreds and hundreds of miles away. The constant roar of jets taking off and landing reminded her of the awesome responsibility of Garth's job, and she felt the sting of tears filling her eyes.

Garth needed her. He needed someone to come home to...someone who could share his life, someone who would love him...care for him... nurture him...

Garth Redmond needed her.

On her lunch hour the following Friday, Hilary purchased a ticket on a late-night flight to Chicago.

It was the day before Valentine's Day. She would plead that she couldn't find a stamp and wanted to deliver his card personally. Garth could hardly object, since he had used much flimsier excuses himself when her presents had been delivered.

The afternoon seemed to drag by without end. Hilary spent most of the time correcting one typo after another on the countless stacks of invoices she'd attempted to type.

Ten minutes before the five-o'clock whistle blew, Hilary was out warming the engine of her car. She figured there was no sense in wasting precious time. This way, the motor would be purring like a kitten when she punched the time clock.

At exactly one minute after five she was out the office door. She was home by five-thirty, a new record for a drive that usually took close to an hour.

She packed a sufficient amount of clothing and personal items to get her through the weekend, then took a taxi to the airport.

The night before Valentine's Day! Hilary's heart raced wildly with the knowledge that, with any luck, she would be spending it in Garth's arms. She prayed he wouldn't have other plans for the weekend. The thought was too disturbing to dwell upon.

Hilary exited the cab and raced toward the busy terminal, paying no heed to the small patches of ice still lingering on the walkways. All of a sudden she found herself slip-sliding across the frozen glaze, groping wildly to retain her balance.

Dropping the suitcase, Hilary grabbed for a handrail just moments before she would have spilled to the ground. But not quickly enough to prevent her left ankle from twisting painfully.

She grabbed the injured ankle and groaned out loud. There was something about Stapleton and her ankles that just didn't mix! She thought of the last "fly the friendly skies" effort she'd attempted and prayed this wouldn't be another disaster.

She took small comfort in the fact that the right ankle had since healed. It was her left one that was killing her now. Retrieving her suitcase, she hobbled on, praying that she wasn't on another roll of bad luck.

In a rush to board her flight, she limped right past the handsome man who was just dashing out another door.

Garth stopped abruptly and whirled around as he saw Hilary limping in the opposite direction.

He saw that she was carrying a suitcase, and his heart nearly stopped. She was on her way out of town just as he was coming in. The realization shot a surge of panic through Garth, and he called out to her hastily retreating form the first thing that came into his mind.

"Hey, what's wrong with your ankle?" he shouted, puzzled that, after all this time, she was still hobbling.

The sound of Garth's voice brought Hilary to a skidding halt. He *had* come for her! She knew it even before she turned around.

"Garth!" Hilary's eyes lit up like two Christmas trees as she dropped the suitcase and came flying toward him, forgetting all about her throbbing ankle.

Garth caught her up in his arms, and they

kissed long and hungrily, ignoring the way they were blocking the flow of traffic.

"Garth, darling! What in the world are you doing here?" Hilary exclaimed as their mouths finally parted long enough to exchange a few brief words between snatches of eager kisses.

"I could ask you the same thing." Garth grinned. She looked even better than he had remembered.

"I...I was on my...I asked you first!"

"I'm here to see my girl," Garth said simply, then took her mouth in another possessive kiss.

It was forever before they could will their mouths apart long enough to step aside finally and let the other passengers pass.

"No kidding—why are you here?" Hilary insisted as he carried their bags over to the side and set them down.

"I was just passing through Denver, and I thought I'd stop in and ask you to..."

"I would love to have dinner with you." Hilary accepted before he could finish the invitation.

Garth grinned and kissed her once more. "Who said anything about dinner?"

"Oh, uh...I thought you were going to ask me ...to have dinner with you." Hilary could feel an embarrassed flush spreading across her face.

"No. Dinner isn't exactly what I had in mind."

"I'm sorry...What were you going to suggest?"

"Well, since I couldn't find a stamp to mail your Valentine card I thought I would personally deliver it, and then—"

"Oh, Garth! That was my line!"

"Your line?"

"Yes! I was on my way to see *you*, and I was going to say I couldn't find a stamp for your card, so—"

Garth laughed and they were suddenly kissing again. When their lips parted much, much later, he gently cupped her chin and lifted her face to meet his. "I was on my way to ask you if you weren't busy this weekend, would you consider marrying me?" he finished.

"Marry you?"

"That's right."

"Well . . . yes. Of course."

"I was hoping you'd say that." Slowly his mouth covered hers.

All of a sudden his words sank in, and Hilary's eyes widened in disbelief. She broke off the kiss and let out a shriek of delight as she threw her arms around his neck and hugged him so tightly he found it hard to breathe. "Marry you! I can't believe it! When? Now? Of course I will!"

Garth chuckled and tried to loosen her grasp but finally gave up and hugged her back. "Why do you find that so hard to believe?"

"You've never said you loved me," she said accusingly, still finding his proposal hard to believe. Garth had just asked her to marry him!

"Maybe I've never said it in so many words, but I thought you might get the hint," Garth chided. He thought of the horrendous stack of florist, phone, and department-store bills lying on his desk at home.

"Oh, I love you!" Hilary kissed him over and over, not caring in the least that they were making a scene. "To heck with all these flimsy excuses! Let's go to my apartment," she suggested in a breathy whisper against his ear. "I want to give you your Valentine's gift . . . in person."

Garth growled suggestively. "I hope it's what I've been wanting for weeks."

Hilary winked. "I would have sent it earlier if I could have found a big enough stamp."

Garth quickly picked up both pieces of luggage, and they started out of the airport, with Hilary clinging possessively to his arm.

"Is your ankle still bothering you?" he asked.

"Would you believe I slipped on the ice and sprained it again?" she complained.

"Same one?"

"No, the other one this time."

Garth threw his head back and laughed, feeling like a million dollars as they walked out of the terminal into the frigid night air.

Snow was beginning to fall in thick, puffy flakes that stuck to the frozen ground the moment they landed.

"The weatherman's calling for eight inches by morning," Hilary warned.

"Well, naturally!" Garth looked at her wryly. "What else would Brookfield and Redmond expect when they're together?"

Hilary grinned and wrinkled her nose at him. "Say what you want, but I think we'll make a perfect team."

Garth leaned over and tenderly kissed away the remains of the large snowflake that had just landed on her cheek. "You bet we will, Brookfield. The *very* best."

Amii Lorin

POWER AND SEDUCTION

For my beautiful girls:
Lori, Amy, and Erica Leigh.
Have fun, my loves!

CHAPTER ONE

Her long, elegant legs carrying her slender body swiftly along the sidewalk, Tina Holden Merritt was oblivious to the appreciative male glances she received as she strode by. Come to that, Tina was entirely oblivious to her surroundings, the cold bite of the late November air, and even the lowering gray clouds that threatened rain, sleet, snow . . . or possibly all three.

Though her classically structured, beautiful face appeared serenely composed, Tina's mind seethed with a hot fury that was becoming as familiar to her as her own body.

Damn him!

Her brown-and-white tweed cape swirling around the tops of her brown suede knee-high boots, Tina swung through the entrance doors to her apartment building. Smiling vaguely at the security guard, she crossed the plushly carpeted lobby to stand before the elevator, impatiently tapping one narrow foot as she waited for the doors to open. In an effort to calm herself, Tina forced slow, deep breaths through her slightly parted, perfectly shaped lips.

Damn him to hell!

Fully aware that the breathing exercise wasn't working, she stepped into the elevator when the doors swished open and stabbed agitatedly at the floor button marked six. As the car ascended, Tina closed her anger-brightened brown eyes and deliberately conjured an image of the object of her fury as she'd last seen him.

Even viewed through anger-clouded eyes, there was no denying that Dirk Tanger was one attractive specimen of masculine virility. Tina didn't even attempt to deny it; she simply hated the man too much to be affected by it.

Who cared that he'd attained a height of at least six foot, three inches of near physical perfection? Or that every one of those inches was covered by taut, healthy-looking skin the exact shade of a gleaming bronze coin? Or, for that matter, that his tan face contrasted so gorgeously with his straight white teeth and complemented his burnished gold hair and beautiful, sapphire blue eyes.

Very likely hordes of misguided, not too awfully bright females cared, Tina thought nastily, grimacing as she strode out of the elevator and along the carpeted hall to her apartment door.

But then, the poor dears didn't know Dirk as she did. Tina forgave the unknown females pityingly. Tossing her supple leather handbag onto the nearest chair, she withdrew a crumpled paper from a deep pocket in the cape before flinging the garment after the bag. Smoothing the wrinkled paper out, she read the politely worded message for perhaps the fifteenth time, teeth grinding as her eyes scanned the neatly typed lines.

At that particular moment, Tina was positive she could easily strangle one overbearing, arrogant Dirk Tanger . . . even if she had to stand on a ladder to reach his throat. Which was a bit of an exaggeration as she was only about seven inches shorter than he.

How dare that man refuse her access to her own

money . . . again! Tina raged inwardly. And it wasn't as if Dirk could possibly have misunderstood the situation, either. The letter she had written to him had been clear and distinct, informing him of the fact that if he did not advance her the sum of money she requested she would very likely lose everything; the emphasis being on the word "everything."

And as if his refusal hadn't been hard enough to swallow, the beast had had his secretary send out a damned form letter!

Crumpling the letter—again—Tina tossed it onto her desk, then stormed to the wide window that framed the tall spires of Manhattan. Staring sightlessly through the pane, Tina curled long, slender fingers into her palm; oval nails digging into her flesh, she bit down hard on her lower lip. None of her ploys to stem the flow of stinging tears worked. Overspilling her lids, the tears trickled then ran down her artfully made-up face, leaving black trails of watered mascara all the way to her usually determinedly set chin.

She had to get away before she started screaming, she realized. Drawing a ragged breath, Tina wiped at her wet face. She'd begun snapping at everybody in the shop after reading the letter this morning, and had actually come to within a hair's breadth of firing Paul Rambeau, her most talented stylist. If she kept on like this there would be nobody left to keep the shop running—not that it mattered much, since she was probably going to lose it anyway if she couldn't come up with some fast cash.

But where could she get the money? Resting her flushed face against the cold pane, Tina closed her eyes. She had borrowed to the hilt from the banks, and she'd be darned if she'd go to any of her friends for a loan; her friends weren't aware she was having money problems. Tina would just as soon keep them in the dark. So, that left one source: Dirk Tanger, Tina's financial guardian.

Raising her head, Tina looked down at her trembling hands. A bitter smile twisting her lips, she decided she could not—*would* not—go begging to Dirk looking like a washed-out, worn-out nervous wreck.

Walking slowly into her bedroom, Tina stood frowning at the pale reflection of her own image in the mirror above her dresser. The smudged mascara gave her the appearance of a woebegone raccoon, but even after she cleaned her face, Tina knew that she would still look pale and drawn, with dark circles under her eyes.

That couldn't possibly be from sleeping a mere two to two and a half hours at any given stretch, now, could it? she silently asked the pathetic woman in the mirror. Lifting her hand, she raked her fingers through the wind-tossed mane of dark red hair that waved gently to her shoulders.

You need a rest, my girl, Tina advised her reflection wryly. A long rest in a quiet place; a place without pressures or hassles or bills stamped overdue. But where . . . other than an institution? The vacation house in the mountains had been a victim of the divorce she'd been a party to nine months before, so scratch the eagerly purchased, painfully given-up hideaway in the hills.

Stepping out of her boots, then her tan wool wraparound skirt, Tina mulled escape locations while preparing for a warm shower. The ice-green nubby-knit pullover sweater was pulled off, then the lacy mint-green bra sailed through the air in the general direction of the clothes hamper. Slipping off sheer panty hose and lacy mint-green bikini briefs, Tina left them where they lay and walked into the bathroom adjoining her bedroom.

Tina loved the white-and-gold tiled bathroom. In fact, Tina loved the entire apartment. Glancing around as she briskly applied a toothbrush to her even white teeth, she sighed regretfully. The apartment would have to go; she simply couldn't afford the rent on the place much longer. Blinking against a fresh onslaught of tears, she stepped under the shower, head bent to allow the warm spray to beat against the tense muscles in her neck.

First her car, she thought dejectedly, and soon her apartment. And if she didn't come up with some money—a lot of money—she was going to lose the whole ball of wax, Tina raged silently.

And all because *that* man liked playing God with *her* inheritance. Actually gnashing her teeth, Tina turned the water off and grabbed a gold-trimmed, white bath sheet, drying herself carefully before stepping onto the deep-pile bath mat that covered a portion of the white-and-gold marbleized tiles.

"I could just murder that man!"

Saying the words aloud eased the tightness in Tina's chest somewhat and, strolling into the bedroom, she smiled as various methods of bringing about Dirk Tanger's demise rose to tantalize her imagination. Contemplating the gorier of those methods, Tina absently tidied the room, a grim smile playing on her lips.

The room once again cleared of discarded clothing, she shimmied into a flowing, blue-and-green patterned caftan and drifted, shoulders drooping wearily, from the bedroom to the bright orange-and-white kitchen.

Where could she go to get some rest while strengthening herself to clash with the ogre in charge of her funds?

Thinking of, then discarding, several sites, Tina prepared a cold tuna salad supper . . . knowing full well she would probably not eat it. Tina had eaten less and less each day as the financial bonds had slowly tightened around her. At five feet eight, she had sported a svelte figure mere weeks ago. Now she was beginning to look hollow and fragile, and she knew it.

Where can I go? she wondered distractedly, dipping an herbal tea bag up and down in a cup of hot water.

Go home.

Hand paused in midair above the steaming cup, Tina frowned at the answer her subconscious had provided.

Home?

Not even tasting the forkful of salad she'd put into her mouth, Tina chewed methodically as she rolled the word around in her mind.

Home.

Of course! Raising the cup to lips smiling with natural ease for the first time in months, Tina nodded her head briefly, decisively. What more perfect place to crawl into a hole to lick raw emotional wounds than a small seaside town in November?

None whatever, Tina told herself firmly, spirits rising. Polishing off the salad with renewed appetite, she sat back in the cane chair and sipped meditatively at her tea, a faraway expression in her eyes as she mused on the perfection of her hometown as a retreat.

Tina had been born in Cape May, New Jersey, and had always been proud of the fact that it was the nation's oldest seashore resort town and a historic national landmark. Smiling reminiscently, she remembered singing her hometown's praises while away at school, informing anyone and everyone of its famed Victorian architecture and its legendary visitors, from six presidents to John Philip Sousa and even Ford and Chevrolet, who, it was claimed, raced on the beaches.

188

Sighing with sudden, unaccountable homesickness, Tina jumped up and strode to the burnt-orange wall phone. Without hesitation she lifted the receiver and punched out the home number of Paul Rambeau, her second-in-command at the shop she'd worked so hard to establish.

Paul answered on the third ring, his naturally deep voice pitched even lower than during working hours.

"It's only me, Paul," Tina said in a voice laced with amusement. "No need to strain your vocal cords." Grinning at his inelegant snort of disappointment, she purred, "Which one of your latest conquests were you expecting to call this evening?" Paul always kept at least three eager women on his emotional string, each woman fully aware of the other two. In that way Paul adroitly avoided any deep involvement with any one female.

"Serena," Paul replied in a tone of utter boredom that Tina knew was part of his who-the-hell-cares act. "What's on your mind, boss lady? Or did you just this minute think of something you forgot to chew me out about this afternoon?" Paul drawled wryly. But then, of course, Paul could afford to sound unconcerned. To Tina's knowledge there were at least four of her competitors dangling lucrative bait under his nose in a bid to steal the very talented stylist away from her.

Tina winced. Had she behaved like a raving ogress that day? No, she asserted in answer to her own question, she behaved like a raving ogress *every* day! In all honesty, she couldn't blame Paul if he bit the proffered bait and left her salon.

"I'm sorry about this afternoon, Paul." Tina gave a poor excuse for a laugh. "I'm sorry about every afternoon," she said expanding her apology.

"No sweat, honey." As usual, in private, Paul dropped the phony French accent he affected so well and slipped into the vernacular. "I know the heat's been on you lately to come up with a lot of folding green. Just hang lose, babe. Something'll turn up."

Tina was at once torn between laughter and tears. The idea of the ridiculously handsome, aristocratically austere-looking Paul Rambeau spouting slang brought a bubbling giggle to her throat; her comprehension of the support within that slang brought moisture to her eyes.

"Paul, I . . . I have to get away for a while," Tina said, swallowing the lump that had risen at his understanding.

"Tell me about it," Paul murmured in an exaggerated drawl.

"Can I dump the whole shooting match into your lap for a few weeks?" she asked, already sure of his answer.

"Can birds fly?" Paul queried dryly. "Can fish swim? Can Rex Reed—?"

Tina groaned theatrically. "Is that a yes?" she prodded.

"That is most definitely a yes, beautiful," Paul assured with genuine seriousness. "Get the hell out of town for a few weeks, or even a few months, and figuratively at any rate, tell your creditors to back it up for a while." Paul chuckled softly. "I'll keep the clientele happy . . . one way or another."

Tina was still shaking her head in amusement as she hung up the receiver a few minutes later. As the majority of the shop's clientele were female, Paul had not had to draw Tina a verbal diagram of exactly how he'd go about keeping them happy if all professional services failed.

Tina's final request of Paul had been for the loan of his car, a sporty little Nissan he valued more than any woman he'd yet found. Paul's unhesitatingly swift granting of the favor said reams about the trust and friendship that had grown between them over the three years he'd worked for her. Interwoven with the friendship they shared was a deep mutual respect. Proof of this was in the fact that not at any time had Paul exerted his undeniably sexy charm on Tina.

With a lighter spring to her step, Tina swept back to her bedroom. As the arrangements were for Paul to drop his car off at her apartment in the morning before he went to open the shop, Tina decided to pack and make it an early night. Who knows, she thought wryly, dragging her suitcase from the closet, I might even sleep the night through for once!

The speedometer needle hovering at fifty-five, Tina held the steering wheel loosely as she cruised along the Garden State Parkway. A smile softened the somber slant of her lipline as she passed the exit sign for Ocean City's business district.

And none too soon, she mused, surprised at the hunger pangs grumbling in her stomach. In less than an hour she should not only be at home but out again, shopping for food to stock the fridge. Excitement reinforced the hunger pains building inside Tina. By the time she finally drove the little car down the quiet tree-lined street, she felt half sick with anticipation.

Slowing to make the turn onto the curved street, Tina crept along, her misty gaze caressing the familiarity of it all. And then, near the very end of the street, stood her home, smaller, not as impressive as some of the other, more famous Victorian homes in the quaint community, but home just the same.

Parking along the curb, Tina sat still a moment, staring at the house she hadn't seen in over five years. Would it seem considerably smaller to her now? she wondered. Then, more practically: Would it be in terrible disrepair? Only one way to find out, she chided herself, go have a look!

Set into action by her own advice, Tina slid out of the car, strode across the pavement and up the front steps to the veranda—and stopped dead in her tracks, blinking at what had to be a hallucination. She *had* to be seeing things, Tina assured herself, for that could not have been a face peering out the narrow living-room window at her!

When Tina opened her eyes, the face was gone, the lace curtain in place again. Laughing shakily to herself, Tina delved into the capacious handbag slung over her shoulder, finally extracting a large, old-fashioned door key. You need a rest even more than you thought, she chided herself, stepping to the door. Before the key touched the lock, the door swung open.

"Oh!" Tina gasped, staring in disbelief at the face she'd seen peering out the window. The face was part of a neatly shaped gray-haired head that rested on a thin neck connected to a tiny, trim body.

"May I help you?" the small woman asked pleasantly, a smile of welcome on her plain face.

"Yes . . . ah, that is, I—"

"You're looking for a room to rent?" the woman cut in.

Room to rent? Tina frowned. In my own house? Tina opened her mouth to speak; then not knowing exactly what to say, closed it again. What was going on here? Deciding to try to find the answer, Tina returned the woman's smile.

"Do you have a room for rent?" she inquired curiously.

"In November?" The woman's laugh was every bit as pleasant as her smile. "I have a house full of empty rooms." Stepping back, the woman motioned Tina inside. "And I'm aching for some company," she continued as a dazed Tina entered the beautifully preserved foyer. "The place is a little dull right now, but it will liven up closer to the holidays when the tourists arrive for the Christmas festivities."

"Ah, yes, I suppose so," Tina murmured vaguely, all too aware of the seasonal attractions the town had to offer at Christmastime. But for now Tina was too distracted with glancing around, noting the changes, to dwell on the holiday that was still over six weeks away. Suddenly realizing she'd been staring much too long, she returned her attention to the woman.

"Have you been here long?" Tina asked carefully.

"Going on five years now," the woman replied, waving Tina into the living room. "I'm Elizabeth Harkness, but every one calls me Beth." She smiled, then went on, nudgingly, "And what's your name?"

"Oh, ah, Tina . . . Tina Merritt."

Beth extended one tiny hand. "What a pretty name. How do you do? It'll be a joy to have you in the house." Beth made a face. "It does tend to get a little lonely here along about the middle of November. How long were you planning to stay?" Lively dark eyes studied Tina hopefully.

Captivated by the small, friendly woman, Tina laughed. "I have no definite date in mind, as a matter of fact. A few weeks or so I guess." She shrugged at her own ambiguity.

The woman's dark eyes glowed. "That's wonderful! Have a seat, dear. No! Don't!" Beth smiled at her own change of instructions. "Let's get you settled first." Whipping around, she headed for the front door. Tina had little choice but to follow in Beth's wake. "Do you have much luggage?" Beth asked as she opened the door.

"No." Tina was beside the smaller woman with a few long strides. "Just a suitcase and a carryall."

Trailing Beth across the veranda and down the steps to the pavement, Tina glanced up and down the nearly deserted street. "I suppose the car will be all right here," she mused, thinking she'd be in big trouble if anything happened to Paul's car.

"It'll be fine, dear," Beth assured her dryly. "As you can see, there's not an awful lot of traffic!"

Laughing together, they carried the cases into the house, Tina following Beth up the curved staircase that joined the building's three floors. The bedroom that Beth ushered Tina into was different, yet familiar. Tina had spent her childhood in that very room, as it had been her own bedroom from the day her mother had decided Tina was ready to graduate from the small nursery next to the master bedroom.

"It's . . . it's lovely." Swallowing against the thickness clogging her throat, and widening her eyes to contain the sudden welling up of tears, Tina strolled to the room's one narrow window which overlooked the back garden, now lonely-looking in its bare starkness. "Yes," she murmured. "Quite lovely."

"Well, then," Beth said briskly. "I'll leave you to get settled." Her hand on the doorknob, Beth paused. "Did you stop for lunch along the way?"

"No." Shaking her head absently, Tina turned to smile at Beth. "I was hoping to find some place to have lunch after I'd arrived."

"Well, you have." Beth smiled. "Lunch will be ready in fifteen minutes." She started out the door, then paused again, as if in afterthought. "Will that give you enough time?"

"Plenty." Tina nodded in agreement. "I just want to freshen up a little. I can unpack later."

"Oh, that reminds me!" Beth's eyebrows flew into an arch. "There are no private bathrooms. There's a central bath on each floor. The one on this floor is two doors down the hall." Again, Beth moved to go out, and again she paused, a chuckle running through her voice. "Of course, you'll have the bath all to yourself—at least for a week or so." This time she did leave, closing the door quietly behind her.

Standing at the window, Tina glanced slowly around the room, the thickness in her throat expanding as the tears escaped her lids to trace rivulets down her face. When she had occupied the room before, the walls had been painted a bright sunshine-yellow and the furniture had been white French provincial.

Now it was completely changed. The walls were covered with paper patterned with tiny blue periwinkle flowers, and the furniture was oak and wicker. Potted and hanging plants added a dash of freshness to the charming decor.

Closing her gritty eyes, Tina had the feeling that if she listened hard enough she'd hear her mother or father calling her for lunch or dinner. Shaking her head, Tina brushed at her wet face and walked out of the room and along the hall to the bathroom, noting the changes there as well.

No, she told herself sadly, her parents would never call to her again.

By the time Tina had splashed cool water on her face and washed her hands, she had her emotions firmly under control, and was determined to find out how her house had become a bed-and-breakfast. With a grace that was natural to her, she ran down the curved staircase and moved unerringly toward the kitchen . . . which, like the entire house, was changed but still familiar.

"Something smells delicious!" Tina exclaimed as she entered the big, old-fashioned kitchen in which

the most modern of conveniences were cleverly camouflaged to appear turn-of-the-century.

"Clam chowder." Beth smiled. "Manhattan style.
And spinach salad"—her smile grew into a grin—"my
style. Have a seat." Beth waved at the sturdy oak table.
"Would you like a cup of coffee? It's fresh."

"I'd love some, thank you." Tina slid a ladder-back
chair from under the table and sat down. "I drove
straight through from New York and I'm beginning to
feel parched." She didn't add that her tears had left
her throat feeling raw and dry as well. "Is there anything I can help you with?" The question came as
naturally as breathing; Tina had always helped her
mother in the kitchen.

"Not a thing, dear." Beth shook her head as she set
a steaming cup of coffee in front of Tina. "You're the
paying guest, just sit and enjoy."

Bending over the cup, Tina inhaled the aromatic
steam. Sipping the best coffee she'd tasted in years,
Tina studied Beth as she bustled about getting lunch.
A very nice person, Tina decided, but how did she get
here? In my house? Tina determined once again to get
some answers.

After three spoonfuls of the rich, savory soup, Tina
changed her opinion of Beth; Beth was not just a nice
person, she was an absolute treasure!

Never reticent in lavishing praise where she thought
it was due, Tina complimented Beth on both the soup
and the salad—a dream with chunks of tomato, bits of
crisp, real bacon, croutons, and English walnuts
tossed among the dark green spinach leaves and
ranch-style dressing.

Tina held her counsel until after the meal was finished when she and Beth were sipping from fresh cups
of coffee; then she began probing gently.

"Does running a bed-and-breakfast rooming house

pay when there are obviously off periods, like now?" Tina asked with what she thought was commendable casualness.

"It does for me." Beth laughed. "I receive my salary every week whether the house is full or empty."

"Oh, I see," Tina murmured, positive now that she really did. "You run the place for an absentee owner?" Even though she'd posed it as a question, there was no longer one in Tina's mind. And her mind was beginning to churn with the anger that had been banked by the novelty of meeting Beth Harkness.

Beth nodded. "I receive a check in the mail every week to cover my salary and whatever expenses I may have incurred—you know, for repairs and such." She smiled softly. "Dirk never questions the amount."

Tina swallowed the groan that rose to her throat. Keeping her tone coolly modulated, she repeated quietly, "Dirk?"

"Yes." Beth's smile was positively motherly. "Dirk Tanger. A wonderful man."

Tina gagged on the mouthful of coffee she'd unfortunately sipped while Beth was speaking. *Wonderful!* Sure . . . old Dirk could afford to be wonderful—and generous: the rat was spending *her* money. With the thought came the realization that she would be expected to pay for her room—*her* room!

Controlling her temper was not the easiest thing Tina had ever done but, by gritting her teeth, she accomplished it.

"How much do I owe you for one week's rent?" she asked, in a muffled tone owing to the fact that she was speaking through gritted teeth.

Smiling benignly, Beth quoted a sum that was in truth very reasonable, Tina knew—unless one was up against a financial wall, which Tina was. Doing a swift mental computation of rent, gas for the car, and the possibility of meals taken outside the rooming house, Tina figured she could stay at the house until the first or second week of January. Sighing ruefully to herself, Tina withdrew her wallet from her purse.

Beth wrote a receipt for the money Tina handed to her, then said, "The price includes all meals whenever you're here." The smile that spread over her face was pure imp. "Usually only breakfast is included, but"—Beth shrugged—"I'm so delighted to have the company, I'm throwing lunch and dinner in as a bonus."

Tina helped Beth tidy the kitchen, then she went to her room to unpack. The anger she'd felt the day before was on her again, riding her mind unmercifully. Carefully *not* slamming drawers, muttering imprecations against arrogant jerks who played lord of the manor with other people's money, Tina stashed her foldables into dresser drawers and hung the few dresses and skirts she'd packed into the one shallow closet the room contained.

When Tina was finished unpacking, she slid the suitcase and carryall under the bed, then stood, uncertain, in the center of the room. Now what? she wondered, rubbing her palms down over the expensive denim sheathing her hips. You came to rest, didn't you? Tina mutely replied to her own query: So, rest.

Shoulders drooping, she walked to the window. Dully examining the changes time and a different point of view had wrought, she let her gaze rest on a delicate-looking white-painted iron bench placed under the wide, bare branches of a tree Tina knew was over one hundred years old.

Near the bench was a brick path that ran the length of the back garden. The path had been there for as long as Tina could remember; only the placing of the dormant rosebushes and rows of hedge were changed.

The same, yet not the same. Like me, Tina thought

moodily, swinging away from the window. I'm the same Tina who slept in this room and the same Tina who dreamed away rainy days sitting by that window. And yet I'm a different Tina, grown up, mature, the galling fact of a divorce in my past.

The last consideration sent Tina striding across the room. Scooping her suede jacket from the foot of the bed, she left the room and ran down the stairs. She paused only long enough to give a sweeping glance to the living room; not spotting Beth, she walked out of the house, hoping a vigorous walk would burn off some of her renewed anger.

Moving with quick, rhythmic precision, Tina's legs made short work of the streets as she roamed around, reacquainting herself with the town. Her boots kicking leaves as dry and dusty as her memories, Tina presented a calm exterior to the occasional person she passed. Inside, she was boiling again.

It was all Dirk's fault. Everything that had happened to her since her father died was Dirk's fault, she fumed, jamming her chilled hands into her pockets. At least, Tina qualified, everything *bad* that had happened to her. Even the failure of her marriage could be placed at Dirk's door!

Entering the quaint bygone-era ambience of the Washington Street Mall, Tina slowed her breakneck pace. Breathing heavily, she strolled through the mall, glancing into shop windows, seeing nothing. She passed a coffee shop, then turned back and went inside.

Over a cup of coffee she didn't really want, Tina was immune to the charm of Victorian decor as she railed against the one man on the earth who held her entire future in his hands. Thoughtfully sipping the dark brew, Tina set her mind to work on various ways of getting what was rightfully hers from Dirk Tanger—her own money and her own life.

Rejecting each and every idea that swam into her tired mind, Tina paid for her coffee and left the shop. The sun was beginning to throw long shadows along the ground, but there was one more place she wanted to go before returning to the house.

Walking slowly now, Tina covered the short distance from the mall to the beach. Standing on the sand, she gazed out over the constantly moving ocean, her mind swept clear by the stiff wind whipping off the water.

"Makes you feel insignificant, doesn't it . . . the sea?"

At the sound of that voice, still too familiar, Tina whirled around, her breath catching in her chest.

Dirk Tanger was leaning against the beachfront promenade, his burnished hair ruffled by the wind, his blue eyes intent and alive with amusement, his lips curved into a wry smile. He looked arousingly attractive, muscularly fit, and more than ready for anything.

"Hello, big-city girl," Dirk said softly. "Slumming?"

CHAPTER TWO

Surprised, shocked, mentally rattled by the sight Dirk made as he leaned indolently against the rocky base of the promenade, Tina stared at him in disbelief. Where the devil had he sprung from . . . hell?

"Not at all." When Tina finally responded to Dirk's taunt she was rather proud of the casual note she'd managed to inject into her voice—in actual fact, she was trembling like a leaf inside. "I might ask what you're doing here."

"You might at that." Smiling lazily, Dirk pushed his deceptively slim body away from the large rock. Hands coming to rest lightly on his hips, he arched a brow that was more brown than gold. "I might even tell you." His white teeth flashed against his tanned face as his smile widened. "Over a beer," he added challengingly.

About to fling a frosty no at him, Tina caught herself just in time. In a bid to gain time to consider her options, she tilted her head, her expression blatantly bored as she slowly made a visual inventory of him. And Dirk inventoried to a staggering amount of pluses!

Even attired casually in brown corduroys, a fisherman's knit pullover in a shade that reflected the sapphire blue of his eyes, a wide-wale corduroy jacket in an antique gold color, and tan desert boots, Dirk Tanger contrived to appear elegant . . . damn him.

For some inexplicable reason the tremor inside Tina deepened. I'm not ready to deal with him yet! she cried in silent protest. And yet, what better way to form a battle plan than to get behind the enemy's lines? Undecided, Tina stared down at the suede boot toe she was ruining, grinding it into the moist sand.

"Hello?" Dirk's bored tone snagged at her attention. "Is anyone home?"

Head snapping up, Tina glared at him, her eyes shooting sparks of annoyance. "You always were dreadfully amusing," she drawled with deliberate nastiness.

"I'm glad you remember," Dirk taunted softly.

"Or were you merely dreadful?" she continued sweetly, a thrill of an emotion quite like fear curling in her midriff as Dirk's eyes narrowed with anger.

"I was never dreadful to you," he retorted sharply, as if deeply stung by the barb.

"Oh, really?" Tina was suddenly consumed by the rage of memory, rage that inundated the fear. "Would you like me to quote you chapter and verse?" she asked, gaining strength from the flush of red that crept up his throat.

"Dammit, Tina," Dirk exclaimed harshly. Then as if catching himself, he lowered his voice. "Are you going to have a beer with me or not?" he asked with a sigh.

"Why not?" Tina lifted her shoulders in a careless shrug. "If . . ." Her voice trailed off. There were many if's Tina could have demanded of Dirk, if's like: If you guarantee we'll have the drink in a public place; if you promise not to badger me; or, most important of all, if you give me your word you'll keep your hands to yourself.

"If?" Dirk prompted warily.

Deciding to be prudent, Tina shrugged again. "If you'll allow me wine instead of beer," she lied with forced unconcern.

The blue gaze that raked over her was dark with inner speculation. Dirk didn't believe for one second that she'd hedged over his choice of a drink, and Tina knew it. The sardonic smile that curved his lips promised trouble ahead for her, and Tina knew that too.

"My dear Tina," Dirk said smoothly, "you can have champagne if you like." There was a brief, telling pause, then he let fly a barb of his own. "Since I'll be paying the check with your money anyway."

Tina choked off the gasp that sprang from her throat, and swallowed the bitter taste of gall. You arrogant bastard! she seethed. You overbearing son of a—

"I did mean today." Fortunately, Dirk's prodding drawl interrupted Tina's less than ladylike ravings. Extending one large hand, he cupped her elbow. "Shall we?" His hand dropped as Tina jerked her arm away.

"I can manage very well by myself, thank you," she said coldly, moving around him toward the street.

Tina was striding haughtily when Dirk drew alongside her, matching his gait to hers. Rigidly facing forward, Tina gave him a sidelong glance, a rush of satisfaction washing through her at the sight of his taut features.

"You really are mad because of that letter I sent you," Dirk said. "Aren't you?"

"Not at all," Tina corrected coldly. "I'm mad because of *every* letter you've *ever* sent me!"

They were approaching a restaurant-lounge that fronted on Washington Mall and, as Tina would have walked by, Dirk caught her upper arm, turning her in her tracks.

"We can have our drinks in here," he instructed

tersely, when she threw him an angry look. Swinging the side entrance door open, he motioned her in.

Even now, nearing dinner time, in the off-season the back dining room contained few patrons, and those few had clustered together in one corner. Choosing a table at the other end of the room, Dirk slid a chair out for Tina. When she was seated, he circled around to sit facing her. A waiter appeared at their table as they were still adjusting their chairs.

"Maybe every letter I've ever sent you made you angry because I simply refused to let you squander all your money," Dirk suggested dryly, after the waiter had taken their order and departed.

"Squander?" Tina stared at him incredulously, "You—you—" Sputtering, and fully aware that she was, Tina paused to draw a deep breath and lower her voice. "Damn you, Dirk! You have no right to say that. I do not squander money," she insisted with soft force. Tina's quietly outraged tone gained her an arched expression of mockery from Dirk.

"Well, at least not as often as you'd like to," he sparred verbally. "But that's only because I won't let you."

Tina opened her mouth to dispute his claim, then immediately closed it again when the waiter delivered the drinks to their table. She played with her cocktail napkin until he'd retreated to the bar again, then she launched into an attack.

"I am on the verge of losing every damn thing I own," Tina spat at him. "All because *you* refuse to advance me some of *my* money!"

"Not so." Shaking his head in denial, Dirk leaned back comfortably and drank deeply from his frosted mug of beer. "If you're about to lose *any* damn thing you own, it's because you lavished what you did have on that slime you married." Dirk's smooth tone was contradicted by the fierce light in his eyes. "And I made up my mind the day you married him that *he* wasn't getting any of *your* money." A derisive smile twisted his lips. "Not until you were twenty-five, at any rate." Dirk's smile turned downright nasty. "And he didn't, did he?"

Tina glared across the table at him. Twenty-five was the magic number for her, because when she turned twenty-five she took control of her inheritance. Of course, her marriage hadn't endured that long. Right or wrong, Tina held Dirk responsible for the failure of her marriage. Now, staring not daggers but swords at him, she let her hate show.

"No, Chuck didn't last." Tina emphasized her former husband's name deliberately. "But I blame you for the breakup of my marriage." If she had hoped to shame him by her charge—and she most definitely had —Tina was rudely shaken by his response.

"Good." Smiling serenely over her gasp, Dirk swallowed the last of his beer. Catching the waiter's attention, he indicated his desire for a refill, then lifted his brow at Tina's barely touched wine. "Not thirsty?" Dirk's gaze mocked her rising flush of anger.

Ignoring his question, Tina narrowed her eyes and glared at him. "What do you mean, good?"

Dirk laughed. "I mean . . . good." Exchanging the empty mug for the full one the waiter brought to the table, Dirk silently toasted her. "If my tight hold on the purse strings had anything whatever to do with the demise of your misalliance, well, then . . . good. I'm glad. Couldn't be happier." He smiled companionably. "Have I defined my expression fully now?"

"You really are a bastard!" Tina snarled in a whisper.

"I do try." Dirk's shrug spoke volumes about his indifference.

Frustrated by her failure to get at him, Tina raised her glass and gulped some wine, barely noticing the crisp taste of the drink Dirk had ordered for her.

Dirk observed her quietly, his eyes dancing with amusement, until she placed the glass carefully on the tiny napkin.

"Would you like another?"

Inside he was laughing at her, and Tina knew it. The knowledge infuriated her all the more. "Since I'm paying for it, why not?" Tina let all the bitterness and anger she was feeling show in her rough-edged tone.

Dirk was unimpressed, as he proved by grinning at her wickedly. "Would you like something to eat with it? Since it is dinner time . . . and you *are* paying for it?"

Dinner time. Beth Harkness. *Her* house. The thoughts tumbled into Tina's mind, reminding her of another very sore spot. Accepting a fresh drink from the waiter, she sipped daintily.

"Dinner." Tina's rough-edged tone had smoothed to a purr, somewhat like the noise one hears from a wildcat an instant before it springs. "That reminds me. Do you know, I'm paying rent to sleep in my own house?" She raised one brow delicately. "Isn't that amusing?"

Anyone who really knew Tina would have been justified in becoming uncomfortable at her soft, chiding tone. Dirk was not merely anyone, nor was he in the least uncomfortable—if his lounging form and smiling face could be believed.

"A regular riot," he concurred teasingly.

"Of course, Beth is throwing meals in with the rent." Tina's voice grew even more pleasant, and even more dangerous.

"Kind of her," Dirk observed agreeably. "But then, Beth's one of a kind."

Tina's fingers tightened their grip on the fragile stem of the glass.

"If you throw that wine at me," Dirk warned softly, "I'll shampoo your hair with this beer."

Stalemate. Tina gritted her teeth and hated him with her eyes. Dirk smiled benignly into her hate. The tension humming between them was a palpable thing, tightening Tina's already taut nerves, exciting her senses, and interfering with her breathing.

"I want to kiss you so badly I can taste you on my mouth."

Tina stopped breathing entirely. Shivering inside the warmth of the jacket she had not bothered to remove, she stared at him in mute shock. Dirk was no longer laughing, or lounging. Sitting erectly, his gaze intent, he was watching closely for her reaction.

"Tha—that's not funny." Tina deplored the weakness of her tone, but the strength she strove for just wasn't there.

"No, it isn't." Dirk's low tone certainly didn't lack strength. "As a matter of fact, it aches like hell."

Tina recoiled against her chair as though he'd struck her. It was so unfair of him! The memory was there; had been there from the moment she'd spun around on the beach to face him. But it simply was not fair of him to bring it into the open. Protesting inwardly, Tina stared at him in anguish. Why, she wondered in sudden weariness, had she ever expected Dirk to be fair?

"You ache too, don't you?" Leaning across the table, Dirk grasped her hands with his. "Don't try to deny it, Tina. Your eyes betray you."

Oh, damn . . . what Dirk said was true, though she'd endure mental and physical torture before she'd ever admit it, especially to him. Merely feeling his heated gaze roam over her body set her on fire.

"You really are a son of a—"

"Oh, honey, you don't know the half of it." Dirk's soft laughter sliced across her hoarse voice. "I can be real mean when I'm hungry," he whispered, the caressing movement of his fingers on her at variance with his threat. "And I'm getting hungrier by the minute." Surprisingly, confusingly, he released her hands and sat back. "So, shall we order dinner?"

If Dirk had hoped to throw her completely off balance he'd succeeded admirably, Tina conceded wryly, clamping her teeth together to keep them from rattling. Her breath coming in shallow little gasps, she raked her mind for a suitably scathing put-down and came up blank.

"I'm going home now." Pushing her chair back, Tina moved to stand up.

"Sit down, Tina." There was no menace at all in Dirk's tone; no warning, no threat. Still, there was something, an elusive something that touched her deep inside. Tina sat down.

"Do you have any idea how much I despise you?" Tina made herself meet his stare directly.

"Yes." Dirk's brilliant eyes clouded for an instant, as if with deep pain, then they cleared, glittering with a sexuality that was as terrifying as it was exciting. "And while you're away from me, you can hate me with the fervor of a purist." His lips curved in a knowing smile. "Isn't it a bitch that when we're near each other, the hate gets muddled by physical attraction?"

Tina wanted to scream a denial to his face. She wanted to but could not, simply because she knew he'd know she was lying. In an effort to combat the strange sensation that she was crumbling inside, Tina raised her glass and drank thirstily.

"My room is directly across the hall from yours."

Tina choked on her wine. Coughing, she gaped at him helplessly.

"Oh, Tina." Shaking his head, Dirk got to his feet to walk to the bar area. When he returned he was carrying a glass of water and two menus.

"Here, drink this and calm down," he advised almost tenderly. "I have no intention of kicking your door down in the middle of the night to have my evil way with you." One eyebrow arched in devilment. "Even though the idea is rather intriguing." Dirk watched in amusement as she sipped gratefully at the cool water. When the choking spell was drowned, he returned to his chair.

"No, Tina. You'll never find yourself in the position of having literally to fight your way out of my arms." Dirk's eyes caressed every feature of her face, setting off a tingling shiver she was beyond masking. The evidence of her response to his visual lovemaking lit a flame in the depths of his eyes and curved his lips in a smile.

"Ah, no, Tina." Dirk's tone of rough velvet ignited a blaze in her body. "You won't have to fight me."

Dirk had no need to elaborate and he knew it. Tina was well aware the battle was with her own unbridled response to him. Dirk was as aware of the fact as she.

Biting her lip, Tina drank more carefully, riling at the fate that had sent him to Cape May at this particular time. If she'd had more time to pull herself together, to rest and get a grip on the despair and anger driving her to near exhaustion, she felt sure she could have controlled this physical thing between them. Sighing, she watched him warily, knowing that if he touched her she'd go up in flames, and then she'd hate herself as well as him.

"Settle down, honey, and choose your dinner." Dirk

handed her a menu. "You didn't think I was considering a wrestling match here, did you?"

"You're disgusting!" Snatching up the menu, Tina hid her hot face behind it, hating him even more because she knew that, were he to attempt seduction in a very public dining room, he'd very likely succeed!

"We could begin with oysters." Dirk's dry tone drew her suspicious glance. "Never know when you'll need fortification."

"I'll start with onion soup." Tina smiled sweetly.

Dirk's laughter, when natural and free, was a sound of beauty. "Thanks, honey. I haven't laughed that easily in a very long time."

His eyes were so honest, so open, Tina hated having to sink a needle, but she couldn't pass up the opportunity.

"Trouble with the little woman, Dirk"—she hesitated briefly—"honey?"

Dirk's reaction was immediate, and chilling. A coldness settled over his face that froze his features and hardened his eyes. And he used those hard-looking eyes to advantage, slicing through to Tina's core.

"Not anymore." His tone was as hard as his eyes. "And I'm not planning to have any with you, either."

"No?" Tina dared to smile. "Then I'd advise you to rethink your plans . . . *honey*. I'm going to give you more trouble than your wife ever dreamed of." Leaning an elbow on the table, Tina propped her chin on her hand and smiled beguilingly. "I think I'll have grilled ham"—she fluttered her lashes flirtatiously—"as my main course."

From behind her teasing pose, Tina watched as the tension eased out of Dirk's strong body, her chest heaving along with his in a long sigh of release.

"Excellent choice." He applauded her tactics.

"Oddly, I'd forgotten how much fun it is to fight with you."

Pretending interest in the patrons on the other side of the room, Tina glanced away from him. "I can assure you, this time the fight will not be fun," she said tightly, damning him once more for raking up the past.

"Maybe not for you," he observed blandly. "But that's understandable, you're going to lose."

Turning her head very slowly, Tina stared into his incredibly blue eyes. "Rather than divorce you," she said scathingly, "I'm amazed your wife didn't kill you."

"She didn't divorce me." Dirk's lips curved with scorn . . . for his wife or her? Tina wondered. He cleared the issue bluntly and succinctly. "I divorced her."

Tina had never met his wife, had never wanted to meet her, yet at that moment she felt compassion for the woman who'd made the mistake of loving such a ruthless man. Glancing down at the menu still clutched in her hands, she sighed and closed it.

"Suddenly not hungry?" Dirk taunted.

Tina shook her head briefly. "I just remembered that Beth will be expecting me for dinner," she lied, longing for nothing more than to get away from him.

The movement of Dirk's head reflected hers. "No, she won't. I told her we'd be having dinner out."

"You told her?" Tina blinked. "When? I only left the house a few hours ago!"

"And I arrived less than fifteen minutes after you left." Dirk blinked back at her mockingly.

Again cursing providence for sending him here at this time, Tina deplored the necessity but asked the obvious. "But how did you know I was staying there? Did Beth tell you?"

"Of course." His gaze roamed her face, lighting

with amusement at the evidence of anger tingeing her cheeks. "But I already knew. Where else would you have gone?"

Adding one and one, Tina came up with the obvious: Dirk had known she was coming home. And there was only one person who could have provided him with the information. Gritting her teeth, Tina promised herself she'd fire Paul Rambeau the moment she returned to New York.

"I asked Paul not to tell anyone where I would be." Tina sighed. "How did you get the information out of him?"

"Is that his name? The one with the bogus French accent?"

Tina nodded curtly.

Dirk's eyes glittered with some emotion Tina couldn't quite identify. "Your new boyfriend?" His tone was as smooth as glass—or ice. Refusing to give him the benefit of any reaction at all, she simply stared at him. "What does he do?" Dirk's brow arched. "At the shop, I mean?"

"He's my top stylist." Tina replied grudgingly, fully aware of what his reaction would be. Dirk's bark of laughter proved her correct.

"A stylist!" Dirk's condescending tone grated on Tina's nerves. Still, she maintained a stoic silence. "How sweet." His laughter subsiding to a deep chuckle, Dirk raised his glass in a mock salute. "Here's to Paul . . . just one of the girls."

"You fatuous jerk!" Bristling, Tina jumped to Paul's defense, conveniently forgetting her vow to fire him moments ago. "Paul is not only one of the most sought-after hairstylists in New York, he's one of the most sought after bachelors! He has more women than a rich Arab sheikh!" Her lip curled jeeringly. "Save your ridicule—or apply it to yourself."

212

Dirk's eyes glittered warningly. "Are you one of those women?" he asked very softly.

Her expression haughty, Tina mirrored his action by raising her glass mockingly in a salute to him. "Mind your own business," she said pleasantly.

With a deceptively frightening calm, Dirk placed his glass on the table, then leaned forward in his chair. Only the flash in his sapphire eyes revealed the fury raging inside him. Lifting his hand, he grasped her chin with his thumb and forefinger, drawing her face close to his.

"Are you sleeping with him?"

Incensed, Tina glared into the shocking blue depths of Dirk's eyes, hating him—and suddenly wanting him more than she wanted air to breathe. Determined not to humiliate herself by struggling against his hold, she sat perfectly still, refusing to answer, defying him with her eyes.

"Answer me, damn you!" Dirk's voice had gone very low and scratchy. "Are you sleeping with him?" His grasp tightening, he shook her head slightly.

"No!" Tina spat the word through gritted teeth. "Paul's an employee and a friend, nothing more. Now take your hand off me."

Though Dirk obeyed her command, he did so with a lingering caress, trailing his fingertips over the satiny texture of her cheek. The shivering response Tina could not hide brought a satisfied smile to his lips. The tips of his fingers still burning her skin, he leaned closer to her.

"Come, Tina," he whispered coaxingly. "Come one inch nearer and kiss me."

God, she was tempted! Her senses exploding from the musky, arousing male scent of him, her lips tingling with the need to taste his, Tina stared at him, inwardly fighting the urge to lose herself inside the blue depths of his eyes. She was losing the battle when Dirk inadvertently turned the tide.

"Come, my love, let me have your mouth."

A spasm of agony slashed through Tina at his hoarsely voiced endearment. The sudden urge she had to fight was violent. Dirk had called her "my love" that afternoon five years ago. Like the young fool she'd been, Tina had taken the endearment at face value, living to regret it with ever fiber of her being. The impulse to strike out at him searing through her body, Tina drew a deep breath and slowly sat back, putting a measure of distance between them.

"Go to hell." A confusing mixture of pleasure and pain washed over Tina at the way Dirk's head jerked back, as if she'd struck him a physical rather than a verbal blow.

"I've been there." Dirk's smile held bitter humor. "I prefer taking you to heaven." Tina's involuntary gasp made his smile real and breathtaking. "I distinctly remember being there with you." His gaze caressed her paling face. "Have you been there since, Tina?"

The implication contained in Dirk's question was unnerving and insulting at the same time: unnerving for Tina and insulting to her former husband. Recoiling, yet determined not to reveal how deeply his shot had penetrated, Tina forced herself to be still.

"You really are a conceited beast," she grated coldly.

"Very likely," Dirk surprisingly agreed. "But along with my enormous conceit, I am also very honest." He smiled with wry self-derision. "And in that honesty I must confess that my king-sized marriage bed never afforded me the exquisite pleasure I found in your narrow, virginal twin-sized one."

Abruptly Tina was on her feet and moving to the door. She had to get away from him or face the consequences he'd most assuredly mete out when she hit him . . . which she was sorely tempted to do!

Tina was halfway down the next block before Dirk caught up to her. Grasping her upper arm, he brought her to a jarring halt.

"You're always running," he said in an exasperated tone. "Haven't you learned yet that you can't run away from the truth?"

"Truth?" Amazing herself, Tina dragged a ripple of laughter from the depths of her churning emotions. "One man's truth is another woman's fiction." Feeling the encroachment of hysteria, she jerked her arm sharply in a bid for freedom; Dirk's hold remained firm. "Damn you, let me go!"

"No." Dirk's tone was adamant. "Not now. Not ever again."

Before Tina could find the breath to question his rather ominous statement, he began walking, forcing her into motion beside him. "You didn't have your dinner." Glancing at her, he added, "And I think you're beginning to get a little light-headed." Without pausing, he started back to the restaurant.

"Dirk! Stop this!" Tina's voice held an edge of shrillness that carried clearly on the cold night air. Digging her heels in, she attempted to slow his determined stride. "I want to go home. I'll get something to eat there."

Surprisingly, Dirk stopped. Turning to face her, he caught her other arm and held her still. "Okay, Tina, we'll go home." His tone went low with emphasis. "*We'll* go home." Ignoring her gasp of outrage, he released her arms only to capture her hand inside his own. Striding along once again, this time toward home, he pulled her along with him.

Even with the long stride Tina possessed, there was no way she could match Dirk's loping gait. Impelled into a trot to keep up with him, she was robbed of the breath necessary to vent her anger and frustration at him. By the time they had traversed the few blocks to her house, Tina was panting from exertion and seething with fury. Presenting a composed exterior to Beth Harkness was one of the most difficult things Tina had ever done in her life.

"You two back already?" Beth smiled in surprise when Tina was practically flung into the living room by a less than gentle shove at the back of her waist.

"We decided to come home for dinner," Dirk informed the older woman tersely.

Beth's smile vanished. "Oh, dear! I've already cleared everything away—not that there was all that much to clear away." Her shoulders moved in a helpless shrug. "I wasn't very hungry." Laying aside the large lap rug she was knitting, Beth moved to get to her feet.

"Don't get up." Dirk's gently voiced order arrested Beth's movement. "We can help ourselves. Can't we, Ms. Merritt?" He slanted a warning glance at Tina.

"Yes, of course," Tina responded, somehow managing a smile for the other woman. "Is there any of that soup left from lunch?"

"Yes, it's in the plastic container on the top shelf of the fridge." Beth frowned. "Oh, Miss Merritt," she murmured reproachfully, "why didn't you tell me who you were?" Before Tina could reply, she moaned, "And I charged you rent!"

Tina shot a glance of sheer rage at Dirk before crossing the room to Beth. "I guess I was too surprised," she admitted candidly. "I expected to find the house empty." As Beth continued to frown, Tina added softly, "I might add that receiving such a warm welcome was a very pleasant surprise . . . and I'm still Tina," she chided gently.

"Of course she's still Tina," Dirk drawled from right behind her, his nearness causing a tremor along her spine. "And now Tina and I are going to raid the fridge." Curling his arm around her waist, he drew her close to his hard, warm length. "Come on, kid, let's dump some food into you." Tina smothered a gasp as he slid his hand over her hip. "We've got to fatten this gal up, Beth," he tossed over his shoulder as he led Tina toward the kitchen. "She feels like a bag of Tinkertoys."

"We'll do our best, Dirk." Beth's delighted laughter followed them out of the room.

Tina wasn't laughing; she was hanging on to her temper by sheer willpower. The instant they were out of Beth's sight and hearing, Tina pulled away from Dirk's encircling hold.

"Tinkertoys?" Tina hissed, swinging away. "You—"

"Can it, honey." Dirk cut her off with a chuckle. "You're skinny, kid. It's as simple as that."

On the point of opening the refrigerator door, Tina spun to glare at him. "I am not skinny," she snapped, planting her hands on her hips aggressively. "I'm fashionably slender."

Dirk's chuckle grew into full-throated laughter. "Call it what you will, honey." Walking to her, he brushed her hands from her hips and grasped them with his own. "You still feel skinny to me." Although Tina stiffened with resistance, he drew her rigid body into contact with the angular contours of his. "Very exciting," he whispered, his smile fading. "I actually like the sensation of being prodded by your pelvic bones."

Against her will, against her simmering anger, against all common sense, Tina's heartbeat kicked into high gear. Her sense of self-preservation urged her to protest this intimacy, to step away from him and ridi-

217

cule the fire of passion flaring in his eyes. Staring into the heat of that passion, Tina's breathing became shallow as she slipped beyond protest. Feeling her skin grow warm from the blaze in his eyes, she watched, mesmerized, as Dirk lowered his head to hers.

CHAPTER THREE

Dirk's kiss was everything Tina remembered—and much, much more.

Drowning in the sweetness of his persuasive mouth, Tina sighed and parted her lips to the searing probe of his tongue. As she softened against him, Dirk slid his hands from her hips to imprison her within the tight circle of his arms, crushing her to his chest with a growl in his throat.

"Tina."

Tina felt more than heard the aching sound of her name groaned into her mouth and, at the same time, felt a liquid flame race wildly through her veins. Oh, Lord, she wanted him. And the wanting was as much of heaven as she ever hoped to know, and more of hell than she ever wished to experience.

Tina knew, somewhere deep inside, that she had to stop him, and she would, soon . . . but first, she had to taste him, just this once.

Curling her arms around Dirk's strong neck, she drank as greedily from his mouth as he did from hers, thrilling to the shudder of responsive need that shook his long body. Clinging to him a moment longer, Tina parried the urgent thrust of his tongue, then dipped daintily with her own. When the restless movement of his hands brushed the outer curve of her breasts, Tina broke free of his arms and ran for the safety of the stairs and her room.

Locking the door behind her, Tina slumped back against it, dragging deep, sobbing breaths into her chest. Slowly, testingly, she glided the tip of her tongue over her kiss-bruised lips, yearning for more of him.

"Tina." Dirk's soft call from the other side of the door sent a chill to mingle with the heat in her veins. "Open the door, love. We've got to talk."

No. No. Moving her head back and forth on the solid barrier between them, Tina closed her eyes and mind to the entreaty in his voice. Dirk's use of that particular endearment again quenched the blaze his kiss had ignited.

"Tina!" Though still soft, Dirk's tone had taken on the edge of impatience. "Open this door."

"No." This time Tina said the word aloud, if in a strained whisper.

Even so, Dirk heard her. Cursing softly, he rattled the doorknob. "Honey, come on! You haven't eaten. Come have some supper with me."

Supper? Sure. He wanted *her* for supper! Biting her lip, Tina shook her head more fiercely. "I'm not hungry," she declared truthfully. "Go away, Dirk. I'm not going to unlock the door." Pushing herself away from the door, she straightened her shoulders. "I'll talk to you tomorrow . . . maybe."

"What do you mean, maybe?" Dirk snapped angrily. "You can't hide in your room forever, Tina." There was a pause. Then, his voice menacing, he warned, "And don't even think of running back to New York during the night, because this time I'll come after you." He paused again. "I mean it, Tina. If you run I'll find you, wherever you go to hide. You're not a kid anymore." Dirk lowered his voice, pitching it so she could hear him while Beth, downstairs, could not. "I want you, and I'm going to have you. Even if it means following you straight to hell."

Beginning to shiver, Tina clasped her upper arms, hugging herself as she stared at the door. After a moment, cursing again, Dirk strode purposefully down the hall.

This time I'll come after you. Hearing his promise reverberate inside her head, Tina walked to the window and sank onto the brightly patterned cushion on the white wicker chair placed to one side of it.

You're not a kid anymore. A kid. Tina swallowed in an attempt to dislodge the lump of emotion in her throat. It seemed like forever since she'd been a kid. Closing her eyes, she conjured a picture of the kid she'd been —the kid Dirk had indulged more than he ever had his own younger sister.

Tina could hardly remember a time when Dirk had not been around. Yet she knew that he'd first come onto her scene the summer she was five years old and he was fourteen. Tina had fallen into a very bad case of hero worship that summer. Her hero had been Dirk. She had never really fallen out of it.

Smiling sadly, Tina sent her mind skipping down memory lane in much the same manner she had skipped along that summer she was five. In point of fact, she'd been skipping around the kitchen table as her mother prepared lunch when her father entered the room, a tall, gangly, towheaded boy trailing at his heels.

"Here's Dirk . . . finally, Pam." George Holden drew the youth forward to meet his wife.

Eyes wide with awe, Tina stared up at the young man who, at least to her eyes, looked like the prince charming in her picture book.

221

"How do you do, Mrs. Holden?" Dirk said very formally, sticking out a bony right hand to grasp hers.

A gentle smile played on Pam's lips. "I'm very well, thank you," she replied softly. "And delighted to, as George correctly put it, finally meet you." Her smile grew wide. "I've heard many good things about you, Dirk."

"And you're as beautiful as Mr. Holden claimed!" Dirk blurted, a red stain flushing his cheeks. "Ah, I mean . . ."

"Don't be embarrassed." Pam laughed softly. "It's very nice to hear that George still thinks I'm attractive after all these years."

"I think you'll always be beautiful," Dirk responded with quiet dignity.

"Didn't I tell you this boy was something else?" George laughed heartily. "And this little imp here"—he reached out to draw Tina to his side—"is our Tina." Parental pride was evident in his tone.

"Hello, Tina," Dirk said soberly, shaking her little hand as formally as he had Pam's.

It was at that moment that Tina had fallen in love.

Dirk was invited to lunch and accepted readily. Pulling out the chair next to Tina's, he kidded, "I'll sit beside scrawny here."

At Tina's stricken face, Pam consoled, "Don't fret, love, you're merely growing faster than your weight can keep up with. I'm sure Dirk was only teasing." Lifting her hand, Pam smoothed her palm over Tina's one long braid. "You're going to be a real beauty some day."

"And then I'll marry you." Grinning boyishly, Dirk yanked on her braid.

The terribly heartbreaking thing was, Tina had believed him.

From that day on Dirk seemed to become a permanent fixture around Tina's home, at least during the summer months. From the Saturday before Memorial Day until the day after Labor Day, he spent more time at the Holden house than he did at his own parents' summer home a block and a half away. For Tina, Dirk became friend, brother, protector, and knight in shining armor all wrapped up in one tall, lanky frame.

That first summer, his already broad hand holding the padded seat securely, Dirk taught Tina how to balance and ride a two wheeler without training wheels. Subsequent summers brought lessons in swimming, bodysurfing, sailing, kite-flying, and fishing from a pier and from a deep-sea boat.

The rest of the year, except for Christmas, which always arrived with a gift under the tree for her from him, Tina heard nothing from Dirk—not a card, not a note, not a telephone call. When, during the course of that first winter, Tina became moody because of Dirk's lack of communication, her father had drawn her onto his lap, stroking her hair as he explained the circumstances of Dirk's life.

"You probably won't understand all this," George began, correctly. "You see, honey, Dirk's winter months are very busy and full, much more so than the average boy of his age."

Being a normal five and a half, Tina had gazed up at him owlishly. "Why?" she demanded sulkily.

"Well, for one, he attends a private school instead of a public school like most of the children you know." George tickled her under her chin in an attempt to tease her out of the blue devils. "He is very bright, you know."

Well, of course, Tina had known that. Her hero was the smartest person in her world . . . at least *she* thought he was. Tina nodded solemnly.

"His daddy owns a bank in Wilmington and, even at

the age of fourteen, Dirk is being trained to take over for his father someday." At that point George smiled in a way that meant nothing to Tina, but would have conveyed empathy to a more mature person. "Summertime is the only time Dirk has to be young," he continued with a sigh. "And I know he wanted very badly to play football," he'd gone on softly, before smiling down at her. "Oh, well, I'm sure Dirk's father knows what he's doing."

"Indeed!"

It was the unusual acerbic note in Pam's tone that drew Tina's glance to her mother, not the meaning behind the single word she'd spoken. There would be many years after that January evening before Tina would come to understand the brief conversation that had followed between her parents.

"Now, Pam," George cautioned mildly. "Howard Tanger is a fine man, and he's been a very good friend to me, as you well know." His smile was tender, as it always was for Pam. "Where do you think I'd be today if it hadn't been for Howard?"

"Really, George," Pam scolded gently, "I know and understand the esteem you have for Howard. And your loyalty is commendable, but—"

"But—without Howard, I'd still be working for someone else," George interrupted gently.

Pam sighed. "All right, yes, the man was the only banker with enough faith in your idea to approve a loan for you to start your own business, but I will not accept the premise that you would be a failure today if it weren't for him!" She held up a dainty hand when he would have interrupted again. "No, dear, let me finish. It might have taken you longer without Howard, but you would eventually have found a way to start the business. As to Dirk"—Pam sighed more deeply—"he's everything you wanted in a son." Her voice trailed to a faint whisper. "The son I couldn't give you."

"Darling, don't." George would have jumped to his feet to go to her had he not been holding Tina. "You know I wouldn't have traded you for half a dozen sons."

"Yes, I do know." Pam smiled brightly. "And now you have Dirk, at least from June until the beginning of September. It simply saddens me that the boy has only three short months every year to *be* a boy. Childhood is such a short period of time as it is, and he's missing it!"

As nothing her parents were talking about made any sense at all to Tina, she had chosen that moment to fall asleep on her father's lap, still missing her new friend Dirk.

Winter wore on, but as summer always does, it came again to the seaside town, and with it came Dirk, a little taller but as gangly as before. And so the years of their childhood spun out, more quickly for Dirk than for Tina. And with each successive summer, the changes were noted as to wintertime-acquired height and filling out, again more quickly for Dirk than Tina.

For Tina, the memories of summer were precious gems to be hoarded more greedily than any miser ever hoarded his gold—for Tina the memories *were* pure gold.

Gold! The noise Tina made deep in her throat was part sob, part derisive snort. On closer inspection, the gold proved to be cheap spray paint that had chipped away badly over the last four years, Tina thought tiredly.

Shivering with a chill that had more to do with her mental sojourn than the wind rising outside the window, Tina stood up stiffly, then froze. The footsteps coming along the polished hardwood hallway were not really heavy, yet not light enough to be those of Beth Harkness. In the seconds the steps paused outside her door, Tina ceased to breathe. The ragged breath that eased past her lips when the steps resumed again hurt her chest, and her heart. At the soft click of a door closing across the hall, Tina sighed and switched on her bedside lamp. It was safe for her to get ready for bed now: Dirk had retired for the night. Scooping her nightgown from the foot of the bed and her robe from the narrow closet, she inched open her door, then crept along the hall to the bathroom. Five minutes later she scurried back into her room, locked the door, and dove under the covers, switching the light off even as she burrowed into the warmth of the down-filled comforter that covered the bed.

By the time Tina finally fell into a fitful slumber hours later, the comforter and bedsheets were a tangled mass around her slender body, and her eyelashes fanned over smudges of exhaustion under her eyes.

Sometime during the morning a ringing phone drew Tina partially from the depths of the deep sleep she'd drifted into after bouts of lighter, dream-disturbed rest. For some time after the ringing stopped, she hovered in that dark tunnel between wakefulness and sleep. She was sinking into the arms of peace again when she dreamed she felt gentle fingers smoothing errant strands of tousled hair from her temple and brow and heard a soft, familiar voice close to her ear.

"Don't run away. Please, wait for me, love," the dream voice pleaded. "This time, wait for me."

When Tina woke fully, it was on the heavy side of midmorning. Her eyes still closed sleepily, she frowned. There was a strangeness here, but what was it? The muted, mournful cry of a sea gull turned the frown to a wistful smile; she was home, not in the

226

apartment above the crowded streets of New York City.

Dirk.

The smile faded and Tina closed her eyes again. She would have to leave, go back to the city and the shop; she simply could not deal with Dirk in the state she was in.

But would Dirk let her go? The question nagged at the edge of Tina's mind as she pushed herself from the tangled bedcovers and made her way to the bathroom.

As she bathed, Tina recalled Dirk's warning the night before. A prickling sensation ran down her spine as her mind replayed the low, intense sound of his voice.

I want you, and I'm going to have you. Even if it means following you straight to hell.

Dirk had meant what he'd said, and Tina knew he'd meant it. She also knew precisely what he'd meant by it.

Beginning to shiver, she stepped out of the old-fashioned tub, firmly assuring herself the tremor coursing through her was caused by revulsion and *not* anticipation.

Catching sight of her reflection in the medicine-cabinet mirror, Tina frowned at the shimmer of excitement flaring in her sherry-brown eyes.

"Grow up, you fool!"

The reflection blinked at the scathing sound of the advice she muttered aloud.

"If you want to commit emotional suicide, there has got to be a better way to do it than through Dirk Tanger!"

Tearing her gaze from the mirror, Tina quickly dried herself, shrugged into her robe, and after carefully scanning the hallway, dashed back to the relative safety of her room.

Tina was midway to the bed where she'd laid out her clothes when she stopped short, a puzzled expression stealing over her face. The day had progressed to within striking distance of noon . . . why was the house so very quiet? Was she alone in the house?

Her curiosity aroused, Tina dressed in lacy underwear, a deep pink, cowl-necked sweater that should have clashed with her dark red hair but didn't, and jeans. After putting on her boots, she punished her unruly mane with a brush; then, her face free of makeup, she descended the curving staircase slowly, warily searching for Dirk.

At the bottom of the stairs she glanced around; the house did indeed appear deserted. The aroma of freshly brewed coffee told her it wasn't.

Feeling ridiculously like a child again, Tina tiptoed through the dining room to the kitchen, steeling herself for the sight of her nemesis.

"Whatever are you doing?" Standing at the refrigerator, Beth tilted her head and leveled a quizzical look at Tina. "Why are you pussyfooting through the house? You don't need to worry about waking anyone. You're the last one up."

Her cheeks growing pink with embarrassment, Tina sighed with relief at finding Beth alone in the room. "I . . . ah . . . didn't know," she said lamely. "It was so quiet, I thought perhaps Dirk was still asleep."

Beth chuckled. "Heaven's, Tina, he's been gone for hours."

Tina sauntered into the room with her more usual loose stride. "Gone?" she repeated, almost afraid to hope. "Gone where?"

"Back to Wilmington." Taking a carton of orange juice from the fridge, Beth closed the door, then glanced at Tina, shaking her head. "Poor dear, and he only arrived late yesterday. I don't believe that man has had a vacation in three years."

"Really?" Trying to sound and look casually interested, Tina dropped into a chair. The odd sinking inside couldn't be caused by disappointment . . . could it? Lifting a slender hand, Tina flipped her hair back over her shoulder in a defiant gesture; of course she wasn't disappointed. Dismissing the strange hollow feeling, she forced her concentration on what Beth was saying.

". . . And he works so hard too." Beth was now at the slate-topped counter next to the sink, pouring orange juice into a delicate-looking stemmed glass. "Did you hear the phone ringing this morning?" Her eyebrows arched as she set the glass in front of Tina.

"Umm." Tina sipped at the juice before murmuring, "Vaguely."

Beth smiled understandingly. "Sleep is rarely restful the first night away from home." Moving with what Tina was beginning to recognize as her normal briskness, she crossed to the stove. "Now, what would you like for breakfast?"

Information. Tina bit back the response. If she was patient, maybe, just maybe, Beth would get around to telling her why Dirk had left so precipitously.

"I'm not really much of a breakfast person." Tilting the glass, she finished the juice. "Toast will be fine." Rising with a fluid grace that was both unconscious and natural, she carried the glass to the sink.

Beth ran an assessing glance over Tina's too slender form. "It seems to me you're not much of an *any* meal person," she chided gently. "Tina, I really think you should eat something substantial. You have an absolutely fragile look." Beth smiled coaxingly. "I have waffle batter all ready to pour into the iron and, if I do

229

say so myself, I make heavenly waffles." Her eyes twinkled. "There's blueberry sauce to top it off with."

"Hot blueberry sauce?" Tina's mouth actually watered; she hadn't had waffles with hot blueberry sauce in ages.

"Hot blueberry sauce," Beth concurred with a grin, sensing a victory.

"Sold." Tina grinned back.

Awash in a pool of buttery-colored sunlight, Tina savored every bite of the berry-drenched light-as-air made-from-scratch waffles. Her fork spearing through the last small piece, she mopped up the remaining sauce before popping it into her mouth.

"Oh, Lord," she moaned, sipping at the coffee Beth had set in front of her. "That was so good." Gazing at Beth, Tina smiled. "I don't suppose you'd consider coming back to New York with me, would you?" she asked hopefully.

Although she shook her head, Beth flushed with pleasure. "I couldn't do that. Dirk would have a fit!" Refilling Tina's cup, she chided, "Especially after he practically ordered me to find a way to get some food into you."

Tina's pulses leaped. With anger, she assured herself, staring at Beth with eyes widened with incredulity.

"Dirk did . . . what?"

"Asked me to at least try to get you to eat," Beth replied complacently.

Tina shook her head in confusion. "When?"

"This morning, before he left." Beth flashed a smile as she poured a cup of coffee for herself. "While *he* was mopping up the sauce with his last piece of waffle."

Ridiculous as she knew it was, Tina felt a glow of pleasure at the idea that she and Dirk had enjoyed the same breakfasts. The glow was short-lived as she ruthlessly asked herself, So what? Curiosity finally getting the better of her, Tina asked, too offhandedly, "Why did Dirk have to cut short his first vacation in years?" Try as she might, she didn't succeed in keeping her tone free of sarcasm. Beth's startled expression caused a twinge of remorse in Tina's conscience. Watch your mouth, her better self warned. It's not Beth's fault you detest the man; *she* obviously adores the beast.

"That phone call this morning was from his secretary," Beth explained in a tone that conveyed consternation. "It seems that some sort of a deal that was simmering on a back burner came to a boil sooner than expected." Her shoulders lifted in a helpless shrug. "He had to go back, since he's the president of the bank, you know."

Oh, yes, Tina grimaced inwardly. *She* knew better than most. President and controlling stockholder. Tina swallowed an unladylike, disdainful snort.

"Yes, I know," she managed to reply with commendable calm. "Too bad his deal cooked over at the start of his vacation." How very like Beth to equate business with what she knew best, Tina thought with amusement.

"Yes, well." Beth sighed. "That's the way it goes. Dirk did say he'd be back, though."

As Beth had offered that tidbit while she was rising from the table, she missed the spasm of shock that shuddered through Tina's slight frame. Her haunted gaze following the older woman's progress to the sink, she moistened her suddenly dry lips.

"He did?" she asked carefully.

"Mm, hmm." Beth turned to smile at her. "Left a message for you too."

"What . . . sort of message?" No amount of applied willpower could keep the wary note from Tina's voice.

"Dirk said you were to rest and eat to build up your strength for when he returns." The smile Beth gave Tina was beautiful, and innocent. "He must be planning something exciting for the two of you."

Exciting? Oh, God! Tina shivered in the warmth of the fall sunshine. Dirk's message was equivalent to a declaration of war.

Run!

The command screamed through Tina's mind as she stared at Beth with deceptive composure. Where could she run to that Dirk would not eventually find her? Not for an instant did Tina even try to convince herself that Dirk's warning of the night before had been issued capriciously; he had been serious. Whatever his reason, Dirk was determined on a course of action. And *she* was the target at the end of that course.

Suddenly feeling crowded and stifled in the large room, Tina jumped to her feet. "I think I'll take a walk," she said with forced brightness. Starting for the door, she paused as her glance skimmed the dishes in the sink. "Oh, would you like help with the dishes?" she asked contritely.

"Tina!" Beth laughed. "Let's not get things confused here. I work for you, remember? I get paid for doing the dishes." She made a small, shooing motion with her hand. "Go drink in some fresh sea air, it just might give you an appetite for dinner." She favored Tina with her pixieish grin. "I'm preparing chicken and dumplings. That should put a little meat on your bones."

Hands jammed into her jacket pockets, Tina strolled the quiet streets of her childhood, the familiarity of it all tugging on her memory and emotions.

Much like any tourist in a city, but without the usual

guidebook in hand, she wandered about, up one street then down another, falling in love with her hometown all over again.

Standing across the street from the stately Chalfonte Hotel, Tina chuckled aloud as whispers from the past tickled her memory. The chuckle faded to a loving smile as her gaze caressed the ornate Italian style of the town's oldest hotel, which had always made Tina think of New Orleans for some reason.

Steeped deeply in the past, her own and the town's, Tina continued her stroll through memory's byways.

There was the Queen Victoria, as regal-looking as ever. And over there The Mainstay Inn, Cape May's Victorian mansion. Oh, how she loved each and every one of the town's beautifully restored homes in the historic district. But as deeply as the old structures touched her, there was an even older love that lured Tina. Having paid due homage to the town, she turned her steps to the sea.

For some time Tina ambled along the long promenade, filling her lungs with the tangy sea air, and her senses with the lost and lonely cry of the gulls. At that moment Tina felt in complete empathy with the swooping sea birds. Only civilization's veneer kept her from issuing a lost and lonely cry of her own.

Turning her back on the imposing old hotels and newer motels that were strung out like jewels along Beach Avenue, Tina loped down the steps to the beach and the swishy siren call of the ocean.

The tide was out, revealing a width of sand that Tina quickly crossed. Walking along the edge of the foaming surf, she tried to visualize the bygone activities that had taken place on the broad strand. How often, she mused, had she heard the tale of how Henry Ford and Louis Chevrolet, among many others, had raced their cars on the then wide beaches? Or of the sailing sloops and later the steamers that had journeyed from Phila-delphia, New York, Baltimore, and Washington full of summer visitors? On reflection, Tina humorously wished she had a dollar for every time she'd heard those and a host of other turn-of-the-century stories.

And all the stories, all the sights and sounds, and the ever-restless, ever-mesmerizing sea added up to one irrefutable fact: Tina was home.

And home, to Tina, meant Dirk. A less palatable, but irrefutable, fact.

A bittersweet smile played along Tina's suddenly vulnerable-looking lips. Feeling her lower lip begin-ning to tremble, she caught it between her teeth.

If nothing else, Dirk had been correct about one thing, Tina thought tiredly. She most assuredly did need to rest, and very likely needed several good solid meals to fortify her. In truth, she couldn't remember ever feeling quite so tired before.

But were a few days of rest and food enough fortifi-cation for the clash of wills she knew was coming? Somehow Tina doubted it.

The chill that permeated Tina's entire body had little to do with the November air or the cold ocean spray that set her dark red hair shimmering with tiny beads of moisture. Even so, Tina chose to believe it did. Walking at an angle, she scuffed through the sand toward the promenade, but instead of remounting the steps, she leaned against a huge supporting boulder in much the same way Dirk had the previous afternoon.

Had coming back here been a mistake? Sighing, Tina raised her face to the westering sun. This place, and its special ambience, held far too many memories for her, both good and bad.

Yes, perhaps coming home had been a mistake. What she needed was time to regroup her strengths, shore up her weaknesses, and gird herself for the battle that was approaching as surely as sunset.

Here, in this town where she had laughed and cried and come early to the emotion of innocent adoration, Tina felt her chances of winning were cut by half. And the biggest undermining factor was the object of that youthful adoration, Dirk himself.

Her own inner speculation startled Tina into awareness. What in the world was she thinking of? she berated herself. The time of naive hero worship was long since past. The braided Tina was no longer alive. She had emerged from the chrysalis a sleek, independent businesswoman. Yesterday could not hurt her, it was tomorrow that held danger.

Pushing her lethargic body erect, Tina walked up the steps to the promenade, then down the ramp to the street. As the road was practically devoid of traffic, she crossed against the light, grinning at a patrolman who called to her to be careful.

Run. The earlier panic came back to tease her mind. Lifting her head, Tina thrust out her delicately formed chin. Run? Ha! No way! She had a business to save from financial ruin. And what promised to be a battle royal with the only man who could help her save that business was yet to be faced.

Tina unconsciously straightened her spine as she walked. She had worked damned hard for her shop. And nothing, nobody, was going to take it from her—not even the overbearing, arrogant Dirk Tanger.

As she turned the corner onto her street, Tina decided that whatever she had to do, she'd do, but save the shop she would.

CHAPTER FOUR

In a conference room rich with the gleaming patina of dark wood and expensive plush carpeting, Dirk sat unmoving in a leather curved-arm chair.

His hands resting lightly on the smooth table, his features set into austere lines, Dirk's sapphire-bright gaze was fixed on the middle-aged businessman who was presenting his request for a large loan to save his company from a takeover.

To the rest of the men at the long conference table Dirk's concentration appeared as usual: unnervingly direct. The rest of the gentlemen at the table would have been shocked out of their staid minds if they knew Dirk's thoughts.

She's going to run. In fact, she's probably on her way to New York right now—if she hasn't arrived there already. Dammit! Why did this takeover panic have to come to a head today?

Revealing nothing of his inner turmoil, Dirk tuned the older man's voice out, fully aware that he was going to grant the loan. His eyes as clear as a bottomless blue pool, Dirk stared at the man sightlessly.

So, the very elegant, very independent Ms. Tina Holden Merritt needed money, did she? Blasting angry and ready for war, is she? Absolutely detests Dirk Tanger, does she? How very interesting.

Catching a smile of satisfaction before it reached his

uncompromisingly straight lips, Dirk savored the warmth of the smile as it curled and wended its way through his taut body.

He would go after her, of course. Hadn't he warned her that he would? The thought of the chase turned the curl of satisfaction to a wave of heat. For a moment, Dirk found it difficult to remain motionless in his chair.

This time, you fool, don't let her get away from you! Dirk chastised himself mercilessly. If you had kept your head together five years ago, she never would have rushed into the avaricious arms of that—that *user*. She was yours, and you let her slip away. Don't make the same mistake again.

His gaze riveted to the man speaking across the table from him, Dirk made himself a solemn promise. If he had to follow Tina halfway around the world, if he had to force her to do things his way, he would do it. Nothing was going to stand in his way this time. Not his conscience. Not her antipathy for him. Nothing.

Groaning with repletion, Tina sat back in the kitchen chair and lifted her coffee cup in a salute to Beth.

"Oh, Beth, that meal was fabulous! I believe you whipped those dumplings out of clouds and air." Relaxed, Tina sipped her coffee. "And that sour-cream salad dressing is delicious. I feel as if I've gained five pounds!"

"I seriously doubt it." Beth's sparkling eyes belied her dry tone. "But I'm glad you enjoyed it. Cooking for one gets pretty boring." Beth beamed at Tina. "Now, how about dessert?"

"Dessert!" Tina exclaimed, shaking her head. "I'd absolutely explode!" Her voice softened, coaxingly.

"Are you sure you wouldn't like to come back to New York with me?"

"Yes, Tina, I'm sure." Beth chuckled, and pinked like a young girl. "But thank you anyway. It's always nice to hear compliments."

The two women were quiet for several minutes, savoring the rich-bodied flavor of the coffee. As she refilled their cups, Beth gave Tina a quizzical look. "What do you do in New York, Tina?" Before Tina could reply, she added, "If you're not, you should be a model."

Tina's soft laughter danced around the quiet room. "I'm not a model, Beth. I own and operate a salon."

"A beauty salon?"

"Well, sort of," Tina explained, "but not exactly. It's more like a spa, but not exactly that, either."

Beth's expression drew laughter from Tina. "Well, goodness! What exactly is it then?"

"I suppose you could call it a combination of the two," Tina replied with a slight shrug. "We offer all the services of both, from a simple haircut to a personal detailed fitness program. The name of the shop is The Total Person, and that's what we cater to—for women, men, and children." Tina smiled. "We even have individual sessions on fashion."

"Very expensive?" Beth teased.

Again Tina's laugh lit up the room. "Of course! I employ some of the best in all the various fields: cosmetology, physical fitness, and fashion." Her laughter faded to a soft smile. "I have one stylist who can do the most fantastic things with the most problematic head of hair." Tina's voice was tinged with awe. "I swear, Paul is a stylistic genius!"

"A man?" Beth looked skeptical.

"Oh, yes." Tina chuckled. "Very definitely a man."

"How intriguing," Beth said interestedly. "In fact, I

find the whole idea of your salon intriguing. Tell me more."

Beth's request was like dangling a carrot in front of a race horse. Tina happily lunged at the bait. All through the kitchen clean-up routine, Tina expounded on the whys and wherefores of how she'd conceived and then executed her idea for the salon. The only thing Tina didn't tell Beth was that, unless she could pry her money out of Dirk, the reality was doomed to fade into never-never land.

Tina and Beth spent the remainder of the evening quietly in the comfortable Victorian-decorated living room. While Beth's knitting needles clicked away at an amazing rate of speed, Tina sat engrossed in a recently published book on nutrition.

Having slept restlessly the night before, Tina was smothering yawns midway through the eleven o'clock news on the small television set that was neatly concealed inside a delicate cabinet with beveled-glass doors when not in use.

"I'm for bed," Tina declared, giving up the effort of keeping her eyes open.

"You'll miss the weather forecast," Beth observed teasingly.

"Hmm." Getting to her feet, Tina stretched her long, limber body. "I'll stick my head out the window tomorrow morning." She yawned again. "That method is more accurate anyway."

Beth's commiserating laugh followed Tina as she slowly mounted the curved staircase, her hand trailing loosely along the polished wood banister. Within minutes of entering her room, she was crawling under the cocooning comforter, no longer making even a token attempt to cover her yawn. Settling onto the welcoming mattress, Tina closed her eyes wearily . . . and suddenly found herself wide awake.

After shifting restlessly for a few minutes, she threw the covers back and slid out of bed, deciding the room was airless and stuffy. Crossing to the window, she ran the shade up, flipped back the latch, and opened the window a few inches, drawing deep gulps of sea air into her chest.

The room quickly lost its stuffiness; Tina quickly lost her desire to sleep altogether. Sighing, she drifted back to the bed, burrowing her cold feet under the covers.

Now what?

Lacing her hands behind her head, Tina stared at the ceiling. She was tired, extremely tired, yet her mind raced at a speed that obstructed sleep. Her problem was that she didn't want to examine the subject her mind raced with. Frowning into the darkness, Tina tested the name of her nemesis on her tongue. "Dirk."

What did he want with her? Tina's lips twisted wryly. Well, of course she knew *what* he wanted! The question was, Why? And why now? For, other than two abrasive meetings, she'd had no contact with him for five long years. They had both married during that time. The twist to her lips grew bitter. She had no idea what had gone wrong with Dirk's married life, but she knew what had interfered with hers.

The grating noise of Tina's teeth grinding together sounded loud in the quiet bedroom. If it hadn't been for Dirk's obstinacy, she would still be married to Chuck.

Indeed? Tina winced at the nagging, ridiculing nudge from her conscience. Well, she temporized, perhaps the failure of her marriage wasn't *all* Dirk's fault. But his firm refusals to release her funds had certainly contributed greatly to it.

And Chuck's other women? her conscience persisted. Tina's soft sigh betrayed a sense of an inadequacy she would never reveal to anyone else. Squirming in discomfort caused more by her thoughts than the awkward position she was lying in, Tina clamped her lips against a cry of despair. Why? Why? What had she lacked, how had she failed Chuck so very badly that he sought comfort with other women?

Was she too strong? Too weak? Too outgoing? Too retiring? Had she laughed too often? Too little? Had she disappointed him both emotionally and physically? Had she failed to fill his needs?

But what about her needs?

Tina closed her lids over the hot moisture welling in her eyes. Didn't her needs count? If Chuck had felt unfulfilled he had certainly not been alone!

While Tina had looked forward to recreating the same type of homey atmosphere she had grown up in, Chuck had insisted on an exorbitantly priced showplace, a frame for his spectacular good looks. While she had hoped for intimate evenings at home, with quiet dinners and communicative conversation, he had demanded bright lights and hordes of flashy people. But in the final analysis, Tina's biggest shock came when she finally pinned Chuck down to a discussion about children. She admitted to longing for at least two, ideally a boy and a girl. Chuck laughed in her face. Tina was sure she'd remember his taunt for the rest of her life.

"Children! Are you serious?" Chuck had actually sneered. "Procreation is for the middle-class mentality. The last thing I want is even one of the little brats cluttering up my life."

What an absolute fool she'd been to allow Chuck to sweep her off her feet and into a whirlwind marriage. As is usually the case when one acts on impulse, Tina found the product fell far short of its gorgeous outer wrapping. Besides which, Chuck had been an unimaginative if not downright lousy lover.

Of course, Tina had had only one previous encounter on which to base a comparison. Dirk.

Tina's head moved reflexively in denial of the memory that rose to torment her. No, she would not think of it! She could not bear to think of it. She was simply too vulnerable now, too tired, too burnt out. Curling into a ball of misery, Tina erected a mental roadblock against the memory of Dirk and that beautiful afternoon they had shared.

Love's young dream! An impressionable teenager's romanticizing of a very basic physical act, Tina chastised herself ruthlessly.

Bitter laughter shattered the midnight peace of the bedroom. Rejection at any age is emotionally demeaning; at nineteen it had been traumatic. In sheer self-defense, Tina had pushed the incident out of her conscious mind for a long time.

Now here it was, back to torment her, undermine her anger and hatred, and make her burn for him all over again.

Unaware of the tears that ran down her flushed cheeks, Tina clenched her hands, viciously digging her nails into her palms in an attempt to neutralize one pain by the infliction of another.

"Oh, damn you, Dirk Tanger." The muffled cry sliced through the night and Tina's heart. For, damn him as she often had—and would again—the truth was as undeniable as the pulse that beat through her bloodstream: she loved him.

"I won't love him!" Angrily.

"I don't want to love him!" Rebelliously.

"He doesn't love me." Despairingly.

Exposed, the wound throbbed and bled in the form

of hot tears. Her face turned to the pillow, she sobbed herself to sleep like an abandoned child.

Tina woke to the pervading chill of an early morning mist creeping on gray padded feet through the open window, and the ever-present soulful calls of the gulls. Her own emotions echoing the cries, she dragged her tired body from the bed, moaning a protest as she caught her reflection in the cheval mirror that stood near the wall opposite the bed.

Walking slowly to the glass, she peered at her reflection, frowning at the telltale signs of too many restless nights.

"Exercise, and plenty of it," she murmured to the pale face staring back at her. "That's what you need, my friend."

Still clad in the short pullover nightie, Tina moved fluidly into her warm-up routine, stretching and bending to wake up her muscles. After half an hour of the workout, she dressed in jogging pants and jacket, socks and running shoes, and put a terry sweatband around her forehead. After leaving her room, she made a quick stop in the bathroom to scrub her teeth and splash cold water on her face. Then, draping a towel around her neck, she ran lightly down the stairs and out the front door, heading for the beach with the determination of a lemming.

Arms loose at her sides, elbows bent, Tina shook her hands lightly as she jogged at an easy pace to the promenade. Standing on the walkway, she drew deep drafts of the misty air into her lungs before skipping down onto the beach.

Once again Tina went through a warm-up of stretching and bending. Once the nighttime kinks loosened, she took off on the packed yet resilient sand near the water.

There were a few hardy souls like herself on the

beach, jogging at various speeds from a fast walk to a flat-out dash. Tina, in for the long haul, maintained a steady, rhythmic pace.

She really didn't like to jog; in fact, she loathed it. It hurt. And the longer she ran, the more it hurt. Working like a bellows, her lungs burned and screamed for air, her heart pounded until she thought it would burst from her chest, and she became light-headed. No, Tina did not enjoy running; Tina enjoyed feeling fit. Tina ran, each and every day—as a rule—to stay in shape.

This morning, Tina was paying dearly for laying off the previous two days. What she really wanted was a steaming cup of Beth's coffee. What she was getting was the result of two days laxity. Still, the soles of her shoes beat a regulated slap on the sand. When her mind whispered that with just a tiny bit more effort on her part she could very likely fly, Tina packed it in and went home.

"That you, Tina?" Beth called from the kitchen at the sound of the front door closing.

"Yes," Tina called back from the foot of the stairs.

"Are you ready for breakfast?" Beth came to stand in the doorway to the dining room. At the sight of Tina her eyebrows arched. "Oh. Have you been jogging?"

"I'll say!" Tina rolled her eyes. "Give me ten minutes to shower and dress and I'll be ready to consume anything you put in front of me. I'm starving!"

"Take your time." Beth laughed. "I'm not going anywhere."

Neither am I. The realization flashed into Tina's mind as she dashed up the stairs. She had been working, sometimes nonstop, for so very long, the idea of not having *anything* to do was unsettling.

How in the world was she going to fill up all the hours in the day? Tina wondered, turning her face into the shower spray. Perhaps she could help Beth with some of the housework. In actuality, the responsibility for the property *was* hers. After all, she owned the place.

On reflection, a warm glow of ownership seeped into Tina. Too bad the house was so far away from New York. If it were just a little closer, she could live here and commute. Then it wouldn't matter so very much that she had to give up her apartment.

At the consideration, Tina went still, oblivious to the water cooling as it cascaded over her body. What was she thinking of? she chided herself harshly. She loved her apartment. Hadn't she come here with the firm intention to rest and gear herself for a showdown over money with Dirk? Had she lost sight of her goal after only two days?

Twisting the water faucet off, Tina shook her head sharply. Get your act together, she advised herself grimly, stepping onto the bath mat. Hold fast to your original plan to have the final round with Dirk.

And it's not merely a question of the apartment, remember, Tina continued her silent lecture as she patted her glistening limbs dry. It's your business, the car you loved that you had to give up, all the years of begging for what is yours, and all the years that arrogant man laughed in your face as he turned you down!

Turned you down. The phrase revolved in Tina's mind as she dressed in soft wool slacks and a long-sleeved tailored shirt.

Damn him! Tina stamped her narrow foot into a supple leather boot.

Double damn him! Tina repeated the process with the other foot.

How dare he turn her down? Although Tina refused to examine the exact cause of the fury searing her mind, the issue had grown cloudy. Five years. Five long years, and still it hurt so very badly that Tina masked the pain with fury. But deep inside, where she absolutely would not look, a tiny voice wept with anguish.

Why did he reject me?

If I were a man, I'd beat him up! Uncaring of the childishness of the thought, Tina savored the idea of it as she dried her hair, then brushed it out. Fiery strands crackled with electricity as she stroked the bristles through the shoulder-length mass. Tossing the brush onto the dresser, she met her own stormy eyes in the mirror. The very idea of her administering a thrashing to Dirk brought a rueful smile to Tina's soft, delicate lips, and her sherry eyes lighted with grudging humor.

Okay, scratch the much-needed thrashing, but she'd find a way to make him pay for all the indignities he'd heaped on her over the past five years. Her mouth set in a grim smile, Tina made a silent vow. She'd get Dirk . . . somehow. He'd been leading her on a merry dance long enough. The time had come to pay the fiddler. And in this instance, Tina Holden Merritt *was* the fiddler . . . and it was her time to call the tune!

Feeling extraordinarily light, as though a weight had lifted from her shoulders, Tina began humming softly to herself as she went down the stairs. She was still humming as she time-stepped into the kitchen.

"Well, how do you do?" Beth smiled. "If jogging has that kind of effect on everyone, maybe I'll take it up myself."

The laughter that rippled from Tina's smooth throat widened the smile on Beth's lips. "Actually, I'm feeling great!" she admitted, the delightful sound of her laughter ringing out again. "Ready to face just about anything . . . or anybody!"

"I'm so pleased." Beth's chest heaved with a sigh of relief. "To tell you the truth, Tina, you looked just about beat to your knees when you arrived here two days ago." Tilting her head, she scrutinized Tina's glowing face. "I know Dirk will be pleased when he gets back. He was very concerned about you, my dear."

Talk about crash landings. Tina came down to earth with a decided bang. Dirk, Dirk, Dirk. All things considered, she was thoroughly sick of hearing his name. With a dismissive shrug, she plopped onto a kitchen chair.

"Dirk is not my keeper, Beth." Though mild, Tina's tone had an edge of impatience to it. "I can't say I care whether or not Dirk is pleased."

In the process of pouring grapefruit juice into a glass, Beth's hand paused in midair as she glanced down at Tina in shock. "But . . . Tina, Dirk is obviously very worried about you," she exclaimed. "And isn't he your guardian or something?"

"No!" Immediately contrite for the sharpness of her tone, Tina bit her lip in vexation. "Beth, I'm sorry." Tina sighed, thinking, good-bye good humor. "Dirk has control of my inheritance until I'm twenty-five, but that's all he has control of."

"But he's so fond of you," Beth protested, chidingly. "Why, anyone could see that! It's as plain as the nose on your face."

"My nose is plain?" Tina made a weak attempt at changing the topic of conversation. "And here I always thought it was rather patrician."

"Your nose is elegant . . . as are all your features, and you know it." Beth frowned fiercely at Tina. "And don't try getting away from the subject, either. Dirk Tanger is a very nice man." A grin flirted with her thin lips. "Not bad to look at, either."

Wrong. The last thing Dirk is, is not bad to look at,

247

Tina thought exasperatedly. Dirk Tanger is downright devastating. Damn his hide!

Against her will, a picture of her tormentor rose in Tina's mind, burnished-gold hair glinting in the sunlight, sapphire-blue eyes laughing at her, white teeth flashing in a teasing grin. The vivid image sent a sensuous chill tiptoeing the length of her spine.

"Be that as it may," Tina said repressively, whether to herself or Beth was beside the point, "Dirk's attractiveness has nothing to do with it. And I'm not convinced about his concern for me. Dirk looks out for number one—always."

The carton of juice landed on the table with force. "Tina, really! I think you are being terribly unfair. Why, I've known Dirk for over four years now, and he's never been less than a gentleman."

Yes, but then you have no money under his control. Prudently, Tina kept the indictment to herself. Mentally shrugging, she decided to leave the bubble-bursting to Dirk; raining on parades was simply not Tina's style. Holding up her hands in a gesture of surrender, she smiled conciliatorily at Beth.

"If I agree that Dirk is definitely a gentleman," she teased, "may I then have some breakfast?"

"Oh, good grief!" Beth went into her bustling routine. "I am sorry. What would you like? Eggs? Pancakes? Swiss breakfast?"

The last suggestion stopped Tina. "Swiss breakfast?" she repeated blankly. "What in the world is that?"

"I can see you've never had breakfast in Atlantic City," Beth retorted.

"I haven't been in Atlantic City since I was twelve," Tina admitted somewhat ruefully. "First because I was too busy getting an education, then starting my business, and later, because I simply couldn't afford taking a chance of gambling away my money." Tina frowned. "But what has that got to do with this Swiss breakfast?"

"I first ate it there," Beth replied. "And I've since concocted my own version." Lifting the carton, she filled the glass in front of Tina. "What I make is pretty close to the original, if I do say so myself."

"I believe you." Tina hid a smile. "But what is it?"

"Oh." Beth grinned sheepishly. "Cold oatmeal."

"Cold oatmeal?" Tina shuddered delicately. "I think I'll pass."

Beth's smile turned smug. "Would you trust me enough to take one taste?" Without waiting for Tina to reply, Beth went to the refrigerator and removed a small dish. On the way back to the table, she scooped a spoon from the cutlery drawer. Dipping the spoon into the cereal, she passed it to Tina, who sampled it very cautiously.

Prepared to hate the stuff, Tina chewed slowly, then an expression of amazement spread over her face. "This is delicious!" she exclaimed in astonishment. "What the devil have you got in there?" Accepting the bowl from Beth, Tina dug in hungrily.

"All good things." Beth smiled serenely. "Bits of pear, peaches, apricots, raisins, and pecans, all mixed together with cream."

"Hmmm," Tina murmured. "Heavenly."

"I thought you'd like it." Beth poured cups of coffee for Tina and herself. "It's one of Dirk's favorites."

Dirk—again! Fortunately, Tina was sliding the last spoonful into her mouth; her appetite went flat. "Then it's too bad he isn't here to enjoy it," she observed diplomatically.

"Yes." Beth sighed. "I was hoping he could return today."

Tina wasn't, but refrained from offering her opinion.

"The man works too hard." Beth's tone held conviction. "Has ever since I've known him."

That did it. Rising, Tina went to the counter where the coffeepot was placed and refilled her cup. The absolute last thing she wanted was a running account of Dirk's virtues. As far as she could ascertain, Dirk had none. Suddenly deciding she needed to talk to her shop manager, she headed for the doorway.

"If you'll excuse me, Beth"—Tina flashed her a smile—"I have to check in with the shop. I'll clear out of your road." Her glance rested on the old-fashioned–style wall phone. "If there's another phone?"

"Oh, yes, of course." Beth waved her hand to indicate the second floor. "It's in Dirk's room, across the hall from you." Just as Tina was gritting her molars, Beth continued, "You can take it into your own room, if you like. There's a jack on the baseboard behind the desk."

Though Tina dreaded having to enter Dirk's bedroom, she did so boldly; after all, it was her house, she assured herself bracingly. The pep talk was not necessary, however, as the room held not a trace of his person or things. Breathing easier, she disconnected the jack, crossed to her room, and sighing as though she'd escaped some danger, plugged it into the jack she found exactly where Beth had said she would.

Paul Rambeau answered the phone in the shop on the third ring, which immediately set Tina to wondering where their receptionist was.

"The great Rambeau answering the phone?" Tina asked. "What will people say?"

"People better keep their sayings to themselves," Paul retorted. "Except you, of course. But then, you're not people, you be the boss."

"And I think you be a trifle strange." Tina laughed.

"I can't call to mind a single living soul who'd refute that statement." Paul joined in on Tina's laughter. "What can I do for you, Ms. Employer?"

"Keep your mouth shut for starters." Though mild, Tina's voice conveyed her displeasure.

"Hit me with that again, my pet, you missed the bull's-eye entirely." Paul's bafflement was genuine. "What am I supposed to have done wrong?"

"I distinctly remember asking you not to tell anyone —like in not a soul—where I was going," Tina said carefully.

There was a pause, then, "And I distinctly remember following your instructions to the letter," Paul shot back. "Which, come to think of it, hasn't been extremely difficult, as there's only been one call to that effect."

"So, how did he know where to find me?"

"The banker? How the hell should I know?" Paul's tone drew a clear picture of his frown for Tina. "Are you telling me he did find you?"

Tina relaxed at the note of sincerity in his voice; she'd hated the idea of Paul's betraying her. "He arrived here mere hours after I did."

"No sh—kidding!" Paul laughed. "That son of a—gun!"

Her sentiments exactly. Tina smiled wryly. Aloud, she probed, "You didn't give him a hint?"

"Honey, I wouldn't give him the time of day," Paul scolded. "You know that."

"I'm sorry, Paul," Tina apologized contritely. "Knowing him, I thought he'd strong-armed you into confessing."

"Over the phone?" Paul laughed. "I'd pay hard-earned money to see that trick!"

Don't be so glib, Tina advised silently, Dirk could

probably do it. "Everything going all right there?" She changed the subject. "No problems or anything? Like Janise quitting, maybe?"

"I chased Janise out for an Orange Julius for me." Paul smacked his lips loudly. "I'm a sucker for that stuff. And yes, everything's perking along as usual here." His voice lowered with concern. "Will you loosen up, beautiful? You needed this break. Enjoy it. I'll hold down the fort."

For several moments after she'd replaced the receiver, Tina sat staring at the phone. How would she have ever gotten through the last year without Paul's concern and affection? she wondered, rising slowly. Come to that, she thought, Paul had been the only undemanding constant in her life ever since she'd hired him.

Paul deserves a raise, Tina decided, leaving the room. And I'm going to give him one—five minutes after I shake Dirk's dust from my boots!

Tina filled the hours of the day by running errands for Beth, a pleasant chore, since she did the running seated inside Paul's car. After consuming another of Beth's delicious dinners, she and Beth retired to the living room.

"I wonder what happened to my collection of books?" Tina mused aloud, frowning as she glanced around the room.

"Everything of yours is here, dear." Beth looked up from her knitting. "Stored up on the third floor."

Tina snapped at the idea of something to do. "I think I'll go investigate," she said, uncurling her legs and rising.

"You'll need the key, the storeroom is always kept locked." Beth smiled at her. "Dirk's orders. The key's in the cellar way, hanging on a nail."

After retrieving the key, Tina ran up the stairs to the

third floor, which consisted of one large room. Unlocking the door, she pushed it open, then groped for the wall switch. The room sprang to life and a soft, shocked "Oh" whispered through Tina's lips.

Beth had not been exaggerating. Everything of Tina's was in the room, not boxed and shoved out of the way, but neatly arranged, exactly as it all had been in her room on the floor below when she'd left the house for the last time.

Transfixed, Tina's startled gaze roamed over the room as she blinked furiously against a rush of tears. All her furniture was there, placed as closely as possible to the way it had always been, as were her books and the little china pieces she'd collected as a teenager.

But the object that riveted Tina's attention was the single-sized canopy bed, looking exactly as it had years ago, the ruffled canopy crisply laundered, the matching spread smoothed over the mattress.

Biting her lip, Tina stared at the bed, unable to move as memory washed over her, flooding her senses. Five years ago, she had lost—no given—her virginity on that very bed. The recipient of her gift had used it and then thrown it back at her, tarnished forever. The recipient of her gift had been her hero from the first time she had seen him at age five, the recipient of her gift had been Dirk.

Spinning on her heel, Tina rushed down the stairs as though the room were possessed by demons, when, in truth, it was her own mind that was possessed. Crying freely, she entered her room and threw herself into the wicker chair by the window, her brain whirling with images she could no longer keep at bay.

CHAPTER FIVE

Tina had been curled up in a chair that afternoon five years before too. She had also been crying. The tears were of loss for her only remaining parent, her father. Although Tina had known that her father had never recovered from the death of his wife two years before, she hadn't dreamed that he'd simply work himself to death in his grief. Yet that was precisely what George Holden had done. At the age of nineteen, Tina had buried her father.

Friends had been kind, and Tina truly appreciated their kindness, but there was an emptiness, an ache deep inside, that seemed to be tearing her apart. And Dirk, her champion, her dearest friend, her secret love, was thousands of miles away in Germany. Dirk had teasingly kissed her good-bye less than a month earlier when she'd returned to the college she was attending in North Jersey; Tina's childhood love knew nothing of the secret she held close to her heart.

The late September afternoon back then was dark with angry storm clouds. The window was awash with the heavy flow of rain, as if the pane of glass were weeping with the pale face in its reflection. So deep into her misery was Tina that she didn't even hear the first light tap at her door. The only reason she noticed the second tap was that it was accompanied by the sound of a voice—the most beloved voice in the world to Tina now that both her parents were gone. Afraid to believe her sense of hearing, her head spun toward the door even as it opened.

"Tina."

Sounding as though the one word hurt him inside, Dirk closed the door quietly and strode across the room to lift her gently out of the chair and into his arms.

After being strong for three days, Tina fell apart at Dirk's touch.

"Dirk." She sobbed against his chest. "He's dead. Daddy's dead. And I wasn't even here. He wouldn't let them send for me until it was too late. Oh, Dirk. Daddy's dead!"

"I know, honey, I know." Dirk's voice had an unfamiliar gravelly sound. "I came as soon as I heard." For a moment, his body tensed. "Dammit, they should have notified me. I should have been here with you!"

Dirk's concern, his gentle embrace, set the tears flowing again, and Tina cried like a lost child, her arms clasped around his waist, her tears wetting his shirt.

Turning carefully, Dirk sank into the chair, drawing Tina onto his lap. "Cry, honey," he murmured into her hair as his hands stroked her arms and back. "Cry it all out. I'll cry with you." And he did. Tina knew because she could feel the warm tears as they dropped off his face onto her cheek.

The afternoon waned as Dirk sat holding Tina securely against his strength, stroking her, rocking her, murmuring to her. Even after Tina had stopped crying, and then sniffing, he held her, brushing his lips over her temple, crooning a wordless song of sympathy. The change came to both of them at the same time, innocently, naturally.

Seeking more of Dirk's warmth and strength, Tina curled into him, raising her face as he lowered his to murmur his empathy. Their lips brushed, parted, brushed again . . . then clung.

"No." The whispered protest came from deep inside Dirk's throat, a protest against himself, not Tina. Slowly, reluctantly, he drew his mouth from hers. "Tina . . . honey, I—"

Her lips burning with a strange but pleasant sting, Tina silenced Dirk's plea for reason with her mouth, her soft gasp of delight mingling with his sigh.

Reacting instinctively, Tina parted her lips, thrilling to the new and wonderful sensations radiating through her body from the sudden hard pressure of Dirk's mouth. A soft, melting moan slipped from her at the first, tentative touch of the tip of his tongue as it slid along her lower lip, igniting an overwhelming need deep within her body.

Her hands groping unsurely, Tina found the strong, taut column of his neck, and then her fingers speared into his burnished hair, the tips kneading his scalp, urging him closer still.

"Honey, I shouldn't," Dirk groaned, sliding his mouth from hers. "You're so very young, so very . . . oh, God, I want you so!" This last as Tina sent her tongue gliding along his lip in an action reflecting his.

Their mouths touched again, then fused, short circuiting the wires connecting mind to reason. In an instant the kiss went from sweet to wild. Set free of restraint, Dirk's tongue scoured the honey-coated recesses of Tina's mouth, his teeth nipped hungrily at her lips, and his hands moved with restless abandon over her shoulders and down her back.

Within seconds the storm raging inside Tina was far more spectacular than the one flinging rain against the window. Consumed by a molten heat unlike anything she'd ever experienced before, her hands moved frantically over Dirk's chest and arms, propelled by a driving need to explore him everywhere.

His mouth locked to the sweetness of hers, Dirk deepened the kiss, teaching her the sensuously erotic love play of dueling tongues. Stroking, thrusting, his tongue ripped the fabric of Tina's senses as devastatingly as the lightning outside rent the black clouds.

"Tina!" Dirk's voice was thick, a strangled cry of pain. "Sweet, love, help me. Stop me—I can't stop myself!" Even as he pleaded for her intervention, his mouth took hers again, and one strong, gentle hand curved over her breast, cupping it possessively.

The effect of Dirk's stroking fingers on her breast was like a torch to tinder, setting off a blaze that ran like wildfire throughout Tina's entire body. Reality drowned in the rising tide of first passion, and Tina blindly followed the lead of emotions out of control.

Her fingers trembling with the need to touch him, Tina fumbled at the buttons on his white shirt until, with a sigh of pleasure, she found the warm skin beneath the silky material. The touch of Tina's fingers to his bared chest shattered the last of Dirk's reserve.

A growl-like sound grating in his throat, Dirk gathered Tina into his arms and stood up to carry her to the narrow canopy bed. Beside the bed he let her go, to slide down the length of his taut, aroused body as if in warning.

"You can still stop me, love, if you want to." His warm breath feathered her ear, sending a shiver creeping enticingly down her spine. Feeling her response, Dirk groaned in defeat. "I'll try not to hurt you, love. I'd rather be tortured than hurt you."

Gently, tenderly, exquisitely, Dirk removed the barrier of clothing that separated their yearning bodies. When, at last, they stood before each other, naked,

Dirk's adoring gaze worshiped the budding perfection of Tina's body.

"You're so very beautiful," he breathed raggedly. "As beautiful as I always knew you would be." Not making the slightest move toward her, he held out his arms. "Come to me, love . . . if you still want to."

Tina didn't hesitate. Her sherry eyes soft and glowing with love, she stepped into his arms, wrapping her arms around his slim waist possessively, sensuously gliding her body against his until her curves fitted perfectly his angular shape.

The move from standing beside the bed to lying on the bed was made smoothly, effortlessly, and for Tina, excitingly. The feel of Dirk's warm, naked skin sliding along hers set off tiny explosions at her nerve endings, demolishing the last of her inhibitions.

Whimpering a siren song that needed no lyrics, Tina flowed like satin under the tightened muscles of Dirk's body, her senses absorbing, flaring to the hoarse, gritty sound of his voice.

"Slowly, love, slowly." His lips roamed over her face to her neck, then down, down. His tongue bathed the wildly fluttering pulse in her throat before leaving a moist trail to the tip of her breast. When his lips closed over that quivering tip, Tina cried out in delight at her first encounter with the promise of ecstasy.

"You're so satiny soft here"— his finger stroked the curve of her breast—"and so excitingly hard here." His teeth raked the tight nipple with gentle savagery. "I want to kiss you, and bite you, and slide my tongue over every inch of you." And as he whispered his desire, he carried out his designs, tantalizing her, driving her deeper into love madness with the biting kisses and teasing tongue he sent on a languid exploration from her breasts to the soles of her feet.

And all the while Dirk paid homage to the perfection

of Tina's long, satiny body with his hands and mouth, he adored her verbally in a voice that spoke of a desire long repressed.

"I've dreamed—been afraid to dream—of doing this since the summer you were sixteen." The ragged sound of his voice fanned the flames roaring through Tina. "When I went home the fall before, you were still a twittering, gawky girl. Then when I came back the next year, I found an emerging young woman."

"Oh, Dirk. Yes!" Tina's gasped response was not in answer to his huskily murmured statement, but to the melting sensation of his teeth sinking gently into the soft inner flesh of her thigh. Writhing beneath his love bites, she was beyond coherent articulation.

"How many nights!" Dirk's groan misted her fine skin with his sweet breath. "God, love, the nights were hell since that summer . . . every night since then!"

Completely lost to reason's cautioning call, Tina filled her hands with the silky strands of his hair, shivering to the feel of it sliding along the sensitized skin between her fingers.

"I love you. I have always loved you. I will always love you." The voice was feminine, and young . . . but certain.

"I know, love." Dirk's restless hands molded her hips. "I've been your brother, protector, best friend." Tina could feel the motion of his chest against her legs as he drew a calming breath deep into his lungs. When he spoke again it was as if the words were torn from his throat. "Now I must be your lover."

"Yes." Tina's response drew a shudder from Dirk. "Oh, yes, please!"

The entreaty in Tina's voice drew his long, sinewy body up the length of hers. Finding her mouth, he drank deeply of her passion, drawing it into himself

259

with the searing brand of his hardened, hungry tongue.

"Now I know why your hair is such a deep red," he murmured into her mouth. "You're a living flame, my Tina." Taking infinite care, Dirk joined their bodies, absorbing her moment of discomfort with his own strength, soothing her with stroking hands and beguiling whispers.

"There will be no more pain now, love." His body moved against hers gently. "Trust me, my Tina."

Tina's fingers flexed, nails biting into the smooth, vibrant skin of his shoulders. Her action was all the reply Dirk required. The motion of his body increasing, he lowered his face to hers.

"Burn for me, my flame." The lure of his enticing whisper drew Tina into harmony with his rhythm.

Her eyes closed to savor the rush of torturous pleasure sweeping through her in ever-powerful waves, Tina heard and responded to the urgency in Dirk's voice.

"Yes. Yes, love. Beautiful. Perfect. Now!"

"Now!" The five-year-old echo of Dirk's strained cry reverberated inside Tina's mind, causing quakes throughout her body. Caught up in the memory of that long-ago afternoon, she was beyond awareness of the here and now. Her body trembling with the need for one man's touch, she covered her face with her shaking hands and sobbed her despair into the silence of the room.

"I love you. I have always loved you. I will always love you." The sound of her own voice, like the scream of an animal in agonizing pain, brought reality into sharp focus. Exhausted, yet shimmering with the first real flow of life she'd felt in five years, Tina bared her soul . . . to herself.

"I will always love him."

The insistent trill of a ringing telephone later drew Tina from a shallow slumber. Prying her swollen eyes open, she frowned with the effort of remembering exactly when and how she'd gotten into bed. She lay frowning long after the phone stopped ringing.

A deep crease connecting his eyebrows over the bridge of his nose, Dirk listened impatiently to his caller for several minutes before rudely interrupting.

"Dammit, Derek! I told you to reschedule that appointment! Now do it!" Not bothering to wait for another protest from his usually dependable assistant, Dirk went on ruthlessly. "I'm leaving. Not for the rest of the day. Not for the rest of the week. But until I feel like returning. Do you read me?"

"But, Dirk! What can I possibly tell—" That was all the time Dirk allotted Derek Saunders, his very ambitious, very competent second-in-command.

One pithy expletive said it all before Dirk slammed the receiver onto its cradle.

Leaning back into the soft leather of his desk chair, Dirk smiled slowly as his thoughts replayed the phone conversation he'd had with Beth Harkness less than an hour ago.

"Well, of course she's still here," Beth exclaimed. "Where else would Tina be, for heaven's sake?"

"I'd thought, perhaps, that she'd returned to the city," Dirk dissembled, a grin of sheer relief softening the forbidding line of his lips. "To take care of business or something."

"No." Beth paused, then went on. "She did confiscate the extension phone from your room yesterday to call the shop, but she said nothing about the need to go back. Apparently that manager, or stylist, or whatever he is, is handling everything at the shop for her." Again she paused before offering, "Would you like me to call her to the phone?" Before Dirk could reply, she added, "I'm really surprised that she's not up and out by now. She was back from her jog by this time yesterday."

Dirk was intrigued. "Tina jogs?"

"Yes." Beth chuckled. "Like a fanatic! She was sweating like a workhorse when she came in yesterday morning . . . ate like one too."

A vision of Tina, her long, elegant limbs gleaming with exertion-drawn moisture, sent a zinging shaft of fire to Dirk's loins. Gripping the plastic receiver with suddenly slippery palms, he drew a silent breath into his aching chest.

God, he wanted her. At that moment, all the longing that he'd endured for the past five years culminated into one throbbing ache that spread to every cell in his body.

"Dirk?" Beth's confused tone cooled the rush of Dirk's hot blood. "Are you still there?"

Hanging on by my teeth, Beth. Dirk smiled derisively at the explanation he silently gave the innocent woman. Aloud, he gave her reassurance. "Yes, of course. I was . . . ah . . . thinking." The grin doubled in size, lending his austere face the glow of recaptured youth. "You said Tina talked to Rambeau?"

"Yes. For quite a while, at that."

Dirk's smiling lips flattened with displeasure. If that bogus excuse for a Frenchman has had her, I'll break his fingers! Dirk promised himself grimly. Then we'll see how great he is as a mincing stylist!

"I see." Dirk's smooth tone betrayed none of the emotions churning in his guts.

He was about to go on when Beth exclaimed, laughingly, "I hear her moving around now. Do you want to hold on until she comes down?"

"No!" Then, more calmly, "No. It won't be necessary. I'll see you both soon."

262

Now, anticipation growing in his mind and body, Dirk sighed with the realization that he would be seeing Tina within hours. Breathing steadily in a bid to slow the racing beat of his heart, Dirk mentally set a seal on Tina's future. She was his first. She'd be his again. There wasn't a power on earth strong enough to take her away from him this time. Tina could run her little mercenary heart out, but she couldn't run fast enough or far enough to outdistance him. She had played at life and love long enough. It was time to face the real world . . . and him.

As Dirk's thoughts coalesced into concrete determination, the breath that had seemed to be permanently constricted inside his chest eased out through nostrils flaring with passion.

Revitalized, Dirk shot to his feet. He was through screwing around! Enough is damned well too much, he decided harshly, silently issuing the order that set him into dynamic motion.

Go get her. No matter what it takes, make her yours.

Tina's running shoes slapped rhythmically on the wet sand. Her breathing ragged, she mentally dodged the ramifications of her enlightenment of the night before. This morning, Tina was dodging ineptly.

She would not, could not, love him. She had hated Dirk Tanger for years . . . nothing had changed the situation between them. She was still financially dependent upon his less than benign guardianship. He was still a ruthless bastard.

Status quo. Everything the same. Nothing changes, especially not Dirk.

Tina should have listened to her own thoughts.

On reaching the end of the beach, where tall sea grass swayed to the eerie tune of a fresh rising breeze, Tina flung her depleted body onto the sand. Drawing her legs up, she encircled them with her arms, rested her chin on her knees, and tried to sort out her tumultuous thoughts by staring at the undulating sea.

More tired from the racing of her thoughts than the punishment she'd meted out to her body, Tina was simply not up to keeping memory barred from her conscious mind. Taking control as completely as the encroaching waves took over the beach at high tide, remembrance swept her emotions, drowning her resistance in their swirling eddies.

Dirk had loved Tina through what was left of that long-ago afternoon and into the blackness of midnight. Seemingly insatiable in his hunger for her, he'd brought her to ultimate pleasure time and time again.

Perhaps the very fact that Dirk had given the appearance of never wanting to let her go made his abrupt rejection of her the devastating blow that it was.

"I can't go back to school now," Tina had cried, reeling from the adamant tone in his voice.

"You can, and you will." Dirk's bright sapphire eyes were shuttered, concealing whatever feelings—if any—he had. "And I have to go back to Germany," he continued flatly.

"Back to Germany?" Tina closed her eyes in fear of revealing the anguish he was causing her. "Dirk, please." She choked. "Please take me with you."

"I can't do that, and you know it." Unmoving and immovable, Dirk stood before her, coolly beating her girlish dreams of a forever-love to death with his hard tone. "You have to finish college. I have conferences to attend."

His gaze swept her stricken face and for a moment his tone softened. "Last night was a mistake, Tina. A mistake that, at my age, I should have avoided. I came to you to offer comfort." For an instant his tone faltered. "And stayed to steal the most precious gift you had to give to a man of your choice."

Very slowly, Dirk drew in his breath, as if girding himself for the hardest blow he'd ever have to bear. "I made you a woman." His lips twisted—with what? Tina had always wondered. Disgust with her or self-reproach? "Whether you were ready to become one or not. The damage can't be undone." Dirk's voice roughened. "But I can make damn sure it doesn't happen again before your maturity catches up with your body!"

Dirk stared at her through eyes gone dead, all expression drained from his features, leaving a stranger to observe her reactions. "Go back to school, Tina. Go do whatever it is young girls do at your age. I'll take care of all the school costs and send you an allowance."

"Dirk! No!" That was all the time he allowed her to protest.

"What happened last night was an accident," he went on, as if she hadn't breathed a word. "An unfortunate but understandable accident. Tina, we're both grieving and needed to share that grief. Now it's time to go on with our lives as planned."

Dirk's final words slashed into Tina's heart like a rapier: "I won't be returning to Cape May next spring."

At that moment, had Tina not blinked repeatedly against a rush of tears, she'd have seen the lines of intense pain etching Dirk's face. But Tina had blinked, fighting to restore at least a part of her pride by refusing to weep or beg him to change his mind.

By the time Tina returned to college, she had her tattered pride repaired and firmly in place. But gone was the laughing, outgoing teenager who had attended the school mere weeks before. In that young girl's stead was a woman with coolly assessing, sherry-brown eyes who had learned how to make exquisite love and how to hate with a vengeance.

During the two years that followed what Tina would secretly think of as her mental breakdown, she absolutely refused to respond in any way to overtures, written or phoned, from Dirk. She spent the money he sent her freely, carelessly, and made frequent, imperious demands for more. Dirk supplied the additional funds, and then one day she stood before him during his one and only visit to her at school; she coldly stared through him, blatantly refusing his attempt to reach her.

"Tina, please try to understand." Dirk had finally shaken her to center her attention. "I did what I had to do. You weren't ready for me two years ago. Hell! You weren't ready for a boy, let alone a full-grown man with an overactive libido!"

Dirk had not been attempting humor . . . which was just as well, for Tina wasn't amused. Narrowing her eyes, she allowed him a glimpse of the glittering hatred she held for him. The glittering hatred of a mature woman.

Stepping back, Tina shrugged out of his grasp. "You will never touch me again. Is that understood?" Her voice was as brittle as tiny shards of glass. "You rejected me once. Rejected the friendship of our past, and the might-have-beens of our future. You will never get the opportunity to do that again, either. Is *that* understood?"

"Oh, Tina." Dirk sighed deeply, smiling with infinite sadness; Tina refused to hear or see. "I did not reject you, our past, or our future. I *had* to let you go, give you time to grow to the point of making an *adult* decision, not an emotional one." There was a long pause, then he sighed again. "You're not listening to a word I'm saying, are you?"

Lifting her head regally, Tina smiled at him as if he were a stranger . . . as indeed she thought him.

"Go to hell, Tanger." Turning gracefully, Tina walked away from him, not to see or hear from him again until that first time she was forced to go to him to appeal for money. By the time that meeting materialized, Dirk no longer heard or saw *her*.

Adrift in the ebb and flow of memory, Tina was unaware of the changing tide until the first wave lapped at her running shoes. Startled out of introspection, she jumped to her feet with a muttered "Damn fool!"

Unwilling to decide whether her foolishness was connected with her reminiscence or with her nocturnal acceptance of her love for Dirk, Tina pivoted and ran back to the safety of the house and Beth. The scene that greeted her as she rushed into the kitchen was decidedly not one of safety for her.

Dirk was sprawled on a kitchen chair, a steaming cup of coffee clasped in his hand, a relaxed smile curving his lips into lines of shattering attractiveness. Tina felt every muscle in her body tense at the heart-wrenching sight of the only man she had ever really loved. Felt it and denied it at the same time.

"Well," she drawled with what she considered commendable sarcasm, "home is the hunter, home from the hills . . . and the banker back from the . . . whatever," she paraphrased dryly.

Sapphire-blue eyes pinned Tina where she leaned with deceptive ease against the frame of the doorway. Crossing one ankle over the other, she angled her chin at him defiantly while cautiously swallowing the wad of dust that appeared to have lodged in her throat.

"Feisty this morning, aren't we?" Dirk's glance

slowly raked her indolent form, then came back to drill directly into her eyes. "What have you been feeding this hellcat, Beth? Rusty nails and pieces of wrecked boats?"

"Now, Dirk, don't tease," Beth scolded laughingly. "Tina is probably starving." Beaming at Tina, Beth invited, "Come have some coffee before you go up to shower, dear. You must be exhausted. How in the world anybody can run for two hours is a mystery to me."

"Yes, Tina, come tell us all about the benefits of running one's, ah, tushy off." Dirk's tone was heavy with mockery.

"I think I'll pass." Smiling sweetly through gritted teeth, Tina strolled out of the room, calling over her shoulder, "Give me ten minutes, Beth."

The minutes required for Tina to both bathe and prepare herself for whatever Dirk had in store for her —and she didn't deceive herself for an instant that his reason for being there was strictly relaxation—tallied up to thirty-five. And during the entire time, she taxed herself to near distraction over what he was up to.

Dirk had sought her out, coolly and deliberately. That fact was obvious. But why? And why now? Those were the considerations that had Tina gnawing on her lower lip. Fortunately, for that lip and her peace of mind, she finally forced herself to return to the kitchen, minus answers, but with a myriad of related questions. It was enough to stir an urge to walk sideways and bury herself in the sand exactly like a crab did when frightened.

The urge intensified as Tina reentered the kitchen to discover Beth missing and Dirk at the stove.

Actually sidling into the room, Tina eyed Dirk warily. "Has Beth gone somewhere?" A silent groan rang in her head at the edgy sound of her voice.

"It's Thursday." Dirk made the pronouncement without turning away from the stove.

"Thank you, Mr. Answer Man," Tina snapped, beginning to feel surrounded even with six feet of tile flooring separating them. *"Has* Beth gone somewhere?" she repeated.

"Beth quilts with a group of friends every Thursday." Turning slowly, Dirk pierced her with a mocking glance. "I assured her I would be more than happy to prepare your meal."

"What are you cooking?" Tina mocked back. "Toadstools and holly berries?"

The smile that curved Dirk's lips sent a panicky shiver skittering down Tina's spine.

"Don't need 'em," he murmured. "Before too many days have passed, Tina, I just might decide to love you to death."

CHAPTER SIX

"Close your mouth and sit down, love. You're in no immediate danger."

Tina's jaws came together with a snap that shattered the bemused trance Dirk's earlier taunt had locked her into. The jolt also brought awareness of her surroundings with it, the pale sunlight slanting through the window over the sink; the wind-tossed dance of barren branches on the trees beyond the glittering glass; the sizzle and spit of bacon frying in the black pan on the stove; the happy gurgle of coffee perking; the soft thunder of her own life-force rushing wildly along her veins. And centered in that awareness, the instigator of her chaotic condition, his burnished hair reflecting sparks of sunlight, his tall body seeming to quiver with anticipation, his jewellike eyes riveted to her arrested, incredulous face.

"Lord!" Dirk's mocking drawl shuddered through Tina's bones all the way to her toes. "I'm glad no part of my hide was under those snapping teeth!"

Poised for flight, tension shimmering the length of her nervous system, Tina delved desperately into her reserves for composure. Surprisingly, she found some.

"You have a rather bizarre sense of humor, Dirk." Raising one delicately arched eyebrow, Tina slid into the chair she had been hanging on to for dear life. "Bizarre, and a trifle dark in color."

His bleached brows arching every bit as elegantly as Tina's, Dirk gave her a crooked grin before turning back to the stove. "An integral part of frustration," he rejoined, only half jokingly.

Tina frowned at his broad, neatly tapered back. He was a fine one to talk about frustration, she sneered inwardly. *She* could easily write a thousand-page tome on the subject—with Dirk Tanger as the main cause!

"In the mood for an omelet?"

Tina blinked her eyes to refocus her attention, sheer amazement flooding her face and mind. Was Dirk serious about cooking for her? Obviously, he was, for he was already beating eggs in a spotted blue-and-white mixing bowl.

"Ah . . . an omelet will be fine, thank you." Tina's reserves of composure went on strike. "But it really isn't necessary for you to make it." Pushing the chair back, she scrambled to her suddenly less-than-graceful feet. "I'll do it!"

His back to her, Dirk slowly poured the egg-and-milk mixture into an omelet pan. "Sit down, Tina"— he didn't even bother to turn his head—"before you trip over your own feet and break one of those gorgeous dancer's legs of yours."

Ridiculously flustered by his left-handed compliment, Tina subsided into the chair, watching his competent movements as he sprinkled chunks of onion, green pepper, ham, and mushroom into the pan as he slid it rhythmically over the gas jet.

"You really do know what you're doing there," Tina murmured, a hint of respect in her voice, "don't you?"

As her question had been uttered rhetorically, Tina was not expecting an answer, and certainly not the one Dirk sardonically tossed over his shoulder.

"A man foolish enough to marry a butterfly has absolutely no reason to be surprised if she refuses to risk singeing her wings by fluttering too close to the stove."

"Is that your abstract way of telling me your wife couldn't cook?"

"Not at all." Finally, he turned to her; his contemptuous expression made Tina wish he hadn't. "It is my direct way of telling you my wife adamantly refused to cook." A derisive smile slashed his face. "She did give me a choice though," Dirk went on dryly. "She said I could either hire a professional cook or learn to cook for myself."

Before Tina's amazed eyes, Dirk folded the mixture over, held the pan motionless an instant, then gently slid the golden brown omelet onto a plate. A satisfied smile softening his harshly drawn lips, he placed the perfect omelet in front of her.

"That's beautiful," Tina smiled, genuinely impressed.

"It's an egg." Turning from the table, Dirk walked to the counter to fill two heavy mugs with coffee. "Surely even you can cook an egg?" he taunted.

Tina sampled her first bite of the fluffy mixture, chewing appreciatively. "Hmm." She nodded, swallowing. "Delicious!" she pronounced before answering him directly. "Actually, I'm a very good cook. I took a course on gourmet cooking as an elective in my junior year of college."

"Your junior year." Dirk regarded her from darkened eyes. "The year I made my one and only visit to your school."

Tina wet her lips nervously. She could see Dirk's expression settling rigidly with the memory of that bitter visit, could feel the anger tensing his body. She watched warily, all the nerves in her body knotted, as

272

Dirk placed the mugs on the table, then dropped onto the chair beside her.

"If I recall correctly," he drawled in a quiet, dangerous tone, "you told me to go to hell that day."

I was young. I was upset. I was hurt. All these and more excuses flashed through Tina's mind; she discarded every one of them. Lifting her chin defiantly, she met his glinting blue eyes steadily.

"That's right."

A flicker of admiration feathered Dirk's eyes, then he veiled them again in frost. "I should have pulled you out of that damned school then and there." Dirk raked her body with a searing glance. "You really never used the degree you went for anyway."

"Never used it!" Tina exclaimed sharply. "Of course I used it . . . I'm still using it!"

"You need a certificate in physical education to curl some bimbo's hair?" Dirk sneered. "You need that certificate to employ some limp-wristed—"

"Dirk!" Tina's sharp tone sliced across his jeering words. "Paul Rambeau is not some limp-wristed *anything*! Paul is a very talented hairstylist." Pausing to control her rising voice, Tina literally threw her fork onto the tabletop. "And I do not cater to bimbos!"

Dirk snorted.

Tina saw red. Incensed, she leaned close to him, spitting her words into his face.

"I use my certificate every day, in a hell of a lot more ways than I would have done by becoming a high-school physical education teacher. And I make a hell of a lot more money at it too."

"Indeed?"

Had Tina not been so consumed with outrage, she would have recognized the trap Dirk had set for her. But as she was outraged, thoroughly outraged, she walked right into it.

273

"Yes," she enunciated clearly. "Indeed."

"Then, perhaps you'll explain to me just why you're always in such dire financial straits."

Tina could have screamed with frustration. Instead, she sputtered with indignation. "I—well, I need the money for—"

"All your creditors?" Dirk interrupted. "And to meet all the forever expenses like heat, electricity, water, and the phone bills?" He shook his head wonderingly. "Then, of course, let us not forget the exorbitant rent on your apartment, your penchant for rather expensive but terribly darling little sports cars, and the absolute necessity of being seen in the very latest designer fashions." Dirk smiled sarcastically. "Is that what you were going to say, love?"

It was not until later that Tina realized how very close she came to retaliating with a physical blow. It was also not until later that Tina realized how very fortunate it was for her that she only retaliated verbally; as it was, Dirk reacted in a way that stunned her.

"You really are a cynical bastard, aren't you?" Tina flung the accusation at him hotly.

Dirk pushed his chair back forcefully. "I've had enough of your curses, Tina." Grasping her roughly by the shoulders, he jerked her to her feet, knocking the air from her chest as he pulled her against him. "You've been cursing me in one way or another for five long years—and I'm sick of it."

"Tough!" Sheer bravado prompted Tina's sharp reply. Her bravado earned her a punishing kiss.

Muttering a rather colorful expletive, Dirk crushed her lips under his own, forcing them apart ruthlessly. When Tina began to struggle to free herself, he anchored her head by running his fingers into her hair. Still, Tina attempted to free herself by squirming frantically. Dirk merely tightened his hold and ground his mouth into hers.

Then, slowly, subtly the kiss changed, becoming coaxing, beguiling. With a groaning murmur, Dirk played at the corners of her mouth with his tongue, teasing a response from her lips that Tina was suddenly powerless to control.

Sweeping his hand down her spine, he spread his fingers at the base and drew her body up and in to meet the urgent thrust of his hips. Binding her to him with one hand entangled in her hair and the other caressing the small of her back, Dirk evoked near delirium in Tina by stroking his tongue over hers.

All the fight went out of her on a softly expelled sigh. Raising her hands to clasp his head, she let her body glide sinuously against his hard angles, shivering with the hungry groan her action elicited from deep in his throat.

By the time Dirk slid his lips from hers to trail moist kisses down the arching curve of her throat, Tina was making incoherent, urgent sounds of enticement.

"Oh, Tina." The words were torn from Dirk's soul. "Oh, God, Tina! Do you feel it? Do you feel what you do to me? Never, not with any other woman, is my response so immediate or so very painful." Running into the barrier of her shirt collar, Dirk released his grip on her hair to slip the buttons from their holes with trembling fingers.

Tina knew she ought to stop him, knew that if she didn't she would soon not be able to. The brush of his fingertips over her already heated skin decided the emotional issue. She arched back in silent invitation and cried out with remembered pleasure when his lips tasted her quivering flesh at the edge of her bra.

She had to touch him, she *had* to. The demand, more impulse than formed thought, impelled her fin-

275

gers to the gathered hem of the sweater Dirk was wearing. Sliding her fingers beneath the fine knit, Tina sighed with the sensation of warm skin on skin. Slowly, deliciously, she stroked her hands upward, delighting at the moan of pleasure that rumbled from Dirk's throat as he arched his spine against her caressing palms.

It felt so right, all of it so very right. The heat of his mouth on her breast, the warmth of his body under her hands, the lassitude as her senses swam with the clean, tangy male scent of him. It all felt so perfectly right that being swept from her feet into Dirk's arms, the journey up the curving staircase, was all part of an exciting flight to paradise. Even the jarring crash of the door Dirk closed by a backward kick of his booted foot failed to alarm Tina.

Drowning in the widening pool of need expanding at her core, Tina reveled in the urgency of his arching body, the restlessness of his searching hands, the hot moisture bathing her skin, his hungrily seeking mouth.

Moving, moving, Dirk's lips blazed a trail of stinging fire from her breasts to her neck, then to her face.

"I want to take hours and hours to love you," he murmured against her ear, his tongue darting in and out evocatively. "But I can't. I can't. I've dreamed about this so long . . . so very long." His parted lips slid over her cheek to the edge of her mouth, setting a flame dancing along her nerve endings. "I need to take you now, Tina. I must have you now."

Yes. Yes. The sound of surrender was a silent moan that quivered through Tina's soul. It's been so long, so long, and I've waited, wanted . . . always, just you . . . only you . . . ever you. Even with Chuck it was always . . .

The hazy thoughts fragmented, dropping like

276

weights into Tina's consciousness, rippling outward, gaining strength until she had to face the stark reality of their content: even with Chuck it was always Dirk she had wanted.

Oh, God.

Awareness brought a shudder of self-revulsion, and then an icy withdrawal. Feeling her stillness, Dirk lifted his head to gaze down at her, his eyes cloudy with passion and a building confusion.

"Tina?"

Opening the eyes she'd closed in pain, Tina stared into his blue depths, and down through the years to the afternoon he'd made her a woman . . . and his own.

All the dodging and twisting she'd indulged in, all the furious physical activity she'd applied herself to, all the mental gyrations she'd performed had been to one end: the desire not to face the demeaning truth.

But now the truth was staring at her out of eyes that were midnight-blue with passion.

"Tina?" A thread of concern laced Dirk's voice. "What is it?"

You. Me. Mostly me. The thoughts tumbled around Tina's brain, bringing not more confusion but clarity. Me, and what a fraud I really am. You're disgusting! Tina flung the accusation at herself silently before it erupted clearly and concisely in a whisper of self-condemnation. "You're disgusting."

His hands caressing her shoulders flexed, fingers digging into her flesh spasmodically. "What the hell are you trying to do?" Dirk stared at her as if she'd sprouted horns.

Twisting out of his grasp, Tina fumbled at the buttons on her shirt. "I—I'm sorry. I can't. I'm not—"

"What do you mean you can't?" A dangerous combination of sexual frustration and flaring rage chilled

Dirk's tone. "A few moments ago you wanted me as much as I wanted you!" His body taut with suppressed anger, Dirk stepped toward her. When Tina backed nervously away, he lashed out bitterly. "What the hell kind of tease are you? Do you get your kicks by turning men on only to watch them suffer? Is that why your husband was trying to set the record on the number of women he could lay?"

Tina recoiled as if Dirk had struck her. Her eyes horrified, she shook her head, unmindful of the mass of hair that veiled her vision; vision that might have noted the lines of self-reproach scoring Dirk's strained features. But Tina probably wouldn't have noticed anyway; she was no longer looking out, she was looking in, and she hated the woman she was looking at.

The buttons on her shirt fastened, if unevenly, Tina jerked away, running for the bedroom door. Scooping her bag and jacket from the straight-backed chair just inside the door, she made her escape while Dirk stood, momentarily too stunned to move. Tina was clattering down the stairs when she heard Dirk's voice from the doorway.

"Dammit, Tina! Where do you think you're going?"

Where was she going? Biting her lip in an attempt to stem the gathering pool of tears blurring her vision, Tina shook her head. Where could she go to hide from the truth, when the truth was inside herself? She had been cheating for the last five years, cheating everyone . . . but mostly herself.

Shrugging into her jacket as she dashed down the veranda steps, Tina glanced at the elegant silver Seville parked behind Paul's Nissan. The car made a bold statement for the rewards of wealth. Tina knew without doubt that the car belonged to Dirk.

Digging into her bag for her car keys, Tina heard the door of the house open, and an instant later the grating sound of Dirk's voice. "For God's sake, Tina! Will you wait?"

Sliding behind the wheel of the little car, Tina jabbed the key into the ignition. A moment later the car jerked into motion and roared down the quiet street with a grinding of gears.

Will you wait? Will you wait? Dirk's cry echoed inside Tina's head as she made the turn onto West Perry and drove toward the Point. A sad smile curved her trembling lips as she realized her destination. From the time she'd learned to drive at sixteen, Tina had escaped to Cape May Point whenever she wanted to work out a problem or cry out a hurt.

Her eyes dry but gritty, Tina ran a swift glance over the lighthouse to her left as she sped by, wincing at the memory of the first time Dirk had taken her there, giving her an outing while at the same time a history lesson on the importance of the light to seafarers.

Her direction now focused, Tina drove too fast as she made for Sunset Beach. She was out of the car and walking before the vehicle had ceased shuddering from the sudden stop. Head bent, she continued toward the water, her only reaction a mild shiver when she heard the screech of tires braking to an abrupt halt next to the Nissan.

Deserted of the summertime tourists happily examining stones in hopes of discovering one of pure quartz known as a Cape May diamond, the pebbly beach offered solitude and peace.

Tina felt that peace seep into her soul as she stared sightlessly out over the water to the *Atlantus*, the old ship lying half-sunken within a stone's throw of where she stood.

"I'd like you to tell me what happened back home."

Tina's lashes fluttered as they swept down to momentarily shadow her cheeks. Home. Dirk's use of the word, his achingly familiar, quiet tone, brought home very close.

But not the home of the bed-and-breakfast establishment that Tina had just fled. The home settling softly on her mind now was the home of her childhood, years of happiness and laughter with her parents, years of safety and security, years of hero worship and romanticism.

Years of Dirk.

"Has it sunk any deeper, do you think?" Tina's gaze rested on the hull of the old ship.

"Not noticeably." Dirk's response held the exact note of consideration Tina's query had. And in the same way it had a lifetime ago, his arm came to rest lightly across her shoulders.

Home.

Tina smiled around the thickness in her throat. She was so very tired of fighting and felt so very vulnerable. Gone was the ruthless Dirk who would see her lose everything she'd worked so hard for. Gone was the aggressive businesswoman guarding her bruised emotions behind a facade of fierce independence.

On Sunset Beach, staring out at the ship, were Dirk of the teasing eyes and protective arms and Tina of the gentle glances and grateful acceptance of any spare moments he had to offer her.

"I'm sorry for that crack about your husband." Even Dirk's voice had a different ring, echoing the tenor of the younger man.

"It was true," Tina said softly. "Even if I was, classically, the last one to know."

"I'm not apologizing for what he did," Dirk corrected her gently. "I'm apologizing for using my knowledge of it to beat you with."

Tina's lips quirked with genuine amusement. Her old Dirk had returned indeed, scolding gently when she displayed obtuseness. As always when Dirk chastised her, Tina moved closer to his protective warmth. And, as always, she told him the scrupulous truth.

"I failed him."

"How so?" There was no hint of condemnation in the question, merely a request for clarification.

"I accepted his marriage proposal."

The soft swish of the lapping waves grew loud in the silence that fell between them. After Tina's stark statement, there was really nothing else to say—at least on that particular subject. Dirk introduced a new-old topic.

"How many times have we watched the sun set from this exact spot?" he asked, a thread of laughter weaving through his tone as he spoke of remember whens.

"Four thousand, two hundred and seventy-seven."

"Are you sure?"

"Positive."

The hand grasping her shoulder tightened. "I could have sworn it was only seventy-six." After the near violence of their earlier exchange in Tina's bedroom, the relief in Dirk's voice was obvious.

Tina's tone mirrored his. "No," she said earnestly. "I always kept a running count. It's definitely seventy-seven."

"Hmm." Tilting his head, Dirk playfully frowned at her. "Is that including or excluding today?"

Tina frowned back. "Since we haven't seen the sun set today, it must be excluding."

"Good point."

Once again silence reigned, a relaxing, tension-dissolving silence. When it was next broken, Tina was indulging in remember when.

"How many times were you forced to tell me the stones I'd found weren't diamonds?"

"At least a million." This time the glance Dirk

slanted at her was openly affectionate. "Poor mite, you never did find one, did you?"

"No." Tina shook her head. "But that didn't matter. The fun was in the search."

"Like the mystery hunts you and your giggly friends were always trying to involve me in?" Dirk chuckled. "You girls certainly did come up with some winners."

"You mean like the time we buried the 'treasure' of old costume jewelery our mothers had given us and told you we'd found a genuine treasure map?"

Dirk laughed outright, the sound shimmering on the air around them, tugging the deepest part of Tina's heart.

"What a bunch of fluff tops you all were." His eyes danced. "There wasn't an ounce of seriousness to the pound in any of you."

Their voices blending, sometimes overlapping, they recounted memories as the sun trekked toward the horizon and descended spectacularly beyond the sea. Their voices faded, then stilled as the sun, reflecting an illusion of a pedestal, seemed to rest on it a moment before surrendering its glory to the encroaching dusk. Awed by the panoramic beauty, Tina shivered. Dirk was immediately solicitous.

"Come on, kid. Time to go home."

His arm still clasping her shoulder, Dirk turned them both in the direction of the two cars.

"Drive back at, or under, the limit." A chiding grin tugged at his lips as he handed her into the car. "If you wrap this pile of metal around a pole, they'll have to pry you out of the debris with a can opener."

"Charming thought." Tina wrinkled her nose.

"No, it isn't." Her gaze flew to his face at his rough tone. "It's a sickening thought. So drive carefully." Turning abruptly, Dirk moved to the Seville, leaving a bemused Tina staring after his rigidly straight back.

The warm bemusement lasted throughout the drive home. Tina, sedately following the taillights of Dirk's car, smiled dreamily at the visions their ruminating created inside her mind.

Drenched in the past, their past, she parked the car and hurried to join him where he waited for her on the sidewalk, slipping under his extended arm as though there had never been a harsh word uttered between them.

Oh, it felt so good being close to him again. How had they lost that precious camaraderie they had shared from the first day her father had brought him home?

Tina's thoughts muddied the calm waters of her contentment. She knew exactly how they had lost their empathy for each other. Dirk had ruthlessly taken all the love she'd had to offer, then discarded it and her.

Carefully disentangling herself from Dirk's encircling arm, Tina hid her renewed bitterness by fussily hanging their jackets inside the small foyer closet before turning abruptly to the stairs.

"Hey, kid!" Dirk exclaimed, startled. "Where are you going? I was about to offer to make a cup of tea for you."

And sympathy? Tina paused on the third step, glancing at him over her shoulder.

"I'll be down in a minute. I want to wash up." As hard as she tried to hide it, her tone reflected the chill permeating her thoughts.

"Tina?" Dirk's sharp gaze saw more than she wanted to show. "What is it? What's wrong?"

"Nothing!" There was an edge of panic there, an edge Tina knew she must control. "Nothing, really. I simply want to freshen up. You . . . you go put the kettle on. I'll be down in a moment." Tina was moving with her last word, taking the stairs two at a time.

Inside the comparative safety of her room she stood, shoulders slumped in dejection, wondering where she'd find the courage to go back downstairs again. Dirk was up to something, she knew, but what? Shaking her head, Tina walked to the dresser. Pulling a brush through her wind ruffled hair, she stared deeply into her reflected eyes.

Dirk is completely in control, and he knows it. After years of cold withdrawal, why was he suddenly donning the cloak of friendship again? The solemn brown eyes in the mirror held no answers, only worried confusion.

Dirk wants something from me. The realization turned Tina cold to the marrow. When had it happened? she protested mutely. When had she relinquished the reins into his hands? *She* had come home to rest and devise a plan by which she could wrangle something from *him*. At what point had she lost the impetus?

The tremulous mouth in the mirror smiled knowingly. Observing the movement of her own lips, Tina winced. She knew darned well exactly when she'd started to fall apart. Her eyes shifted slightly to the spot in the room where Dirk had so recently held her to the burning hardness of his body. The sight disappeared as Tina slowly closed her eyes.

All this time, she moaned inwardly, all the years I've hated him and kept myself motivated by hating him, I have really been hating myself. And with good reason.

Tina's conscience squirmed. At twenty-four, a finally *honest* twenty-four, Tina could appreciate Dirk's actions of five years ago. She had been so terribly young, so terribly green, so terribly naive. Her lips twisted wryly. Was it any wonder he'd run from her as though from the plague? Today, nine years difference in their ages was of no account. Five years ago it was a chasm. And because he had not fettered himself with that green girl, Tina had spent every one of those years punishing every person who dared come too close, especially her husband.

Suddenly feeling too weary to stand, Tina sank onto the edge of the bed. What an absolute waste, she thought sadly. A waste of time, and effort, and, yes, money . . . her money.

Had she married Chuck with cool, if unconscious, deliberation?

A shudder tore through Tina's slender frame at the thought. While it was true that Chuck was unfaithful as well as unprincipled, it was also true that Tina had never been stupid. Hadn't she known, from the very beginning, exactly what she was letting herself in for with Chuck? The probing thought straightened Tina's spine.

Then another, more disturbing conjecture chilled Tina's stiffened back. How had Dirk said it? *I'm apologizing for using my knowledge to beat you with.* The phrase revolved in Tina's mind.

In effect, hadn't she used Chuck to beat Dirk? Hadn't she known, while refusing to know, that Chuck would make demands for money from her? Money that she would have no choice but to ask Dirk for? Hadn't she also known that, by giving passive rather than active participation in her marriage bed, Chuck would seek satisfaction elsewhere, thereby saving her the shame of facing the unpalatable fact that while the man in her bed was her husband, the man in her heart and mind was Dirk?

"Rustle it, Tina!" Dirk shouted from the foyer. "Your tea is getting cold."

The tea wasn't the only thing. Tina shivered.

"Coming." Tina's response was threaded with anxiety and defeat. How could she face him? Not only face him but beg him to save her from the results of her own vindictive actions? But, Tina thought frantically, she had to get him to release her money. She couldn't lose the shop now, it was all she had left.

Reluctance making her movements stiff, Tina rose and walked slowly to the door. She hadn't washed her hands, she thought with bitter whimsy, but she'd done a fairly good job of scrubbing her grimy conscience.

"Tina!" Dirk's impatient call came from the kitchen as she reached the foot of the stairs. Not bothering to answer, she continued her slow pace to the doorway of the room.

"Where the . . ." Dirk's words trailed away at the sight of her strained features. His body tensed as if preparing for a blow. "I don't know, honey," he murmured, shaking his head as he examined her face closely. "But for some reason, I have this nasty suspicion you're withdrawing from me again." Dirk's head lowered with resignation. "Okay, let's have it. What have you decided I'm guilty of now?"

CHAPTER SEVEN

Tina smiled . . . at least made the attempt to smile. "Same old story, I'm afraid." She shrugged. "I need money. You refuse to release it to me. Instant antagonism."

Standing on the other side of the table from her, Dirk ran an assessing gaze from her gleaming red hair to the tips of her dusty boots.

Watching him scrutinize her, Tina felt a frisson of unease move through her at the contemplative spark that flared in his eyes before he concealed his thoughts by narrowing his lids. That brief flare convinced Tina that, whatever his thoughts, they meant trouble for her.

"There *is* one way," he began, then frowned when the phone rang shrilly. "Damn!" With a murderous scowl, he crossed to the phone and jerked the receiver from the hook. "Hello?" he barked into the mouthpiece. Turning his head sharply, Dirk pinned Tina with a blazing stare. "Yes, she's here." Even as he spoke, his jaw grew rigid with anger. "If you must," he finally snarled, holding the receiver out to Tina.

"Do I recognize the pleasant tone of your benign banker?" Paul drawled the moment she responded.

"Yes."

"How lucky can one woman get?" he wondered in

an awed voice. "First the man with the iron tongue, and now me, bearing tidings of financial woe."

"I'm almost afraid to ask." Tina sighed tiredly.

"Have you somehow overlooked the paltry sum of seven thousand dollars still owed on Chuck's car?" Paul asked brightly.

Tina had. Groaning softly, she rested her head against the cool wall. How could she have forgotten her agreement to pay for Chuck's import when she'd made the agreement in a last-ditch effort to get her divorce? It had been blatant blackmail on Chuck's part, of course. But at the time, Tina was so desperate, she was willing to do almost anything.

"Tina?" Though soft, Paul's voice was sharp with concern.

"I'm here."

"Look, beautiful, don't go into a tailspin. I paid it for you. You can pay me back when you get it." Paul spoke quickly in an obvious bid to relieve the tension he could feel humming through the wires.

"Oh, Paul!" Close to tears, Tina bit her lip. "I . . . I don't know what to say."

"Say good-bye."

The order came from behind Tina, not through the receiver. And it was decidedly an order, one Dirk fully expected her to obey. Paul had heard the command as well.

"Is that guy for real?" The steellike quality of Paul's tone was new and surprising to Tina; Paul *never* became perturbed. "And is he looking for a rap in the teeth?" he demanded, convincing Tina he did, at times, become perturbed.

"It's all right, Paul, I—" Tina cried out as the receiver was wrenched from her hand, then slammed onto the hook. "How dare you?" she shouted. "You have no right to inter—"

"I'll tell you how I dare!" Grasping her by the upper arms, Dirk dragged Tina close to him. "I dare, love," he sneered, "because *I* hold the purse strings. Remember?"

"Have you ever once let me forget?" Tina sneered back.

"No." Dirk shook her in an oddly gentle way. "And I'm not about to start now." Then, quietly, too quietly, "What did Rambeau want?"

"Money, what else?" Tina laughed shrilly, then wished she hadn't when his hands tightened painfully.

"You pay him?"

All the fight drained out of Tina, leaving her limp in his grasp. "Of course I pay him. He works for me."

"That isn't what I meant," Dirk said insinuatingly. "And you know it. Do you pay him in the same way you paid your husband, for services rendered?"

"No." Tina closed her eyes against the sickness welling in her throat. She heard his muttered curse an instant before he gathered her into his arms.

"Tina, don't. Oh, honey, don't look that way." Dirk crooned into her ear as he bent over her. "I'm sorry. Baby, please, stop trembling." Tina both felt and heard the deep breath he dragged into his lungs. "Why must we always claw at each other?" Lifting his head, he gazed at her tenderly. "We didn't always blindly strike first and ask questions later. Did we?"

"No." Tina sniffed. "Not before I grew up."

Raising his hands, Dirk cradled her face and tilted her head up. "Is that what happened?" Dirk's smile brought tears to Tina's eyes. "You grew out of your braids and into your bra." The spasm that moved over his face spoke of pain. "And shot a hole in my ego by discovering boys your own age."

Appalled by the very idea that she might have hurt him, no matter how innocently, Tina rushed to explain. "I never meant to hurt you, Dirk. You were always my knight in shining armor."

"Yeah, but when your father died, I rusted it."

And there it was, out in the open at last after festering in silence for five long years. As scalding moisture slipped over the edge of her eyelids, Tina closed them and lowered her head.

"Oh, Tina." Dirk's groan held the weight of every one of those years. "The worst part is that I can't make myself feel sorry it happened. I've never been touched so deeply as I was that afternoon, or felt so completely satisfied afterward." His hands less gentle, Dirk lifted her face again. "I wanted you very badly then." Slowly, irrevocably, he lowered his mouth to hers. "I want you even more now."

"Dirk, please, no—" The protest was lost inside the moist heat of his mouth, as Tina was lost inside the need that had been a constant companion for five years.

Time, place, self, spun away and drew Tina along in the whirlwind. There was nothing but a void beyond the safe haven of the only arms she ever wanted to surround her. Greedily drinking from his parted lips, Tina surrendered her soul into Dirk's keeping. She was his now, as she'd ever been his . . . whether he knew, or cared, or wanted her or not.

Dirk's actions made it clear that he definitely wanted her—at least the physical her. Murmuring of a need too long denied, he unfastened the buttons on Tina's shirt for the second time that day. When the material was at last brushed aside and the front clasp on her bra disengaged, Dirk burned her skin with his passion-fired gaze. Then, with excruciating slowness, he lowered his mouth to her breasts.

Her throat arching as her head fell back, Tina whimpered a sensual "Yes" as she speared her fingers through the silky strands of his hair and drew his lips to one aching nipple.

The raspy grate of Dirk's tongue on her sensitized skin sent shards of desire into the lower part of Tina's body. The gentle but urgent draw of his suckling lips wrenched a cry of sheer ecstasy from her throat. The sudden, jarring ring of the phone elicited a groan of protest from both of them.

"If that's Rambeau again, I will personally travel to New York and strangle him!" Dirk snarled savagely, drawing Tina with him as he stepped to the phone. Before attempting to answer, he breathed in deeply several times.

"Hello?" Even with the calming breaths, his voice betrayed impatience. Clasped to his side, Tina felt the tension seep out of him before he spoke again more evenly. "No, Beth, I'm sorry. I, ah, was occupied." As Dirk listened to Beth his glance covered Tina's face, then went caressingly to her still-heaving breasts. "No, of course not. Go, enjoy yourself." A sensuous smile curved the corners of his lips. "Tina and I will find *something* to eat."

When Dirk hung up he allowed his smile to grow enticingly. "Beth is going out to dinner with the girls and she was concerned about us." His glance danced over Tina's body, and along her nerves. "We could always devour each other," he suggested hopefully.

With that outrageous suggestion he was back, the Dirk Tina had adored forever, the Dirk of the laughing eyes and teasing quip. Her sense of humor struck, Tina skipped out of his loose embrace, drawing her shirt closed as she went. Tossing her now wildly disarrayed hair back, she smiled beguilingly.

"I'd rather have lobster." Tina fluttered her eyelashes exaggeratedly. "And a mound of French fries.

291

And a Greek salad with feta cheese. And hot crusty rolls. And—"

"Hey, kid!" Dirk contrived to look stern. "You eat much more than all that and you'll be sick."

Tina threw him a prim look. "I was going to say: and a tall glass of gin and tonic—heavy on the tonic."

Dirk was suddenly serious. "The mood's gone . . . isn't it?"

"Yes." Tina smiled tremulously. "The mood—or madness—is gone." Almost fearfully, she watched to see if the ruthless Dirk would return. Tentatively, she held her hand out to him. "Still friends?" she asked, unaware of her pleading tone.

Taking the two steps necessary to reach her, Dirk curled his fingers around hers. "Yes, love, still friends." His eyes clear, he stared down at her. "We're going to have a long talk, if not over dinner, then after it. Our differences have to be resolved, Tina."

Tina wet her suddenly parched lips, tingling all over when his gaze avidly watched the tip of her tongue. "I" —she cleared her throat—"I know. But let's not think about it now." Sliding her hand from under his, she took off at a run. "I'll bet I can be showered and dressed before you," she challenged in the same impudent manner she had as a girl.

"You're on." Dirk accepted, close at her heels. "Name the stakes."

Tina hesitated at her bedroom door. "The loser buys dinner?"

"Done." Dirk was disappearing into his room as he spoke.

Surprisingly, Tina won the bet, if only by some thirty seconds. Dirk was still grumbling about the possibility of her having cheated by not showering as they left the house.

"Do I look like the type of woman who would splash

292

on half a bottle of perfume and call myself bathed?" Tina laughed, walking to the side of the car.

"No," Dirk admitted sourly. "But how the hell *did* you get ready so fast? If I remember correctly—and I do—it always took you forever to get ready for anything." A grin denied his earlier sourness. "Even to go to the beach, where you *knew* you would immediately become messy with suntan oil and sand."

"Owning and running a business keeps me clicking along," Tina admitted seriously. "I have my grooming time almost down to a science. Now it's habit. It never takes me very long to get my act together, regardless of where I'm going or who I'm going there with."

Dirk's appreciative gaze roamed slowly from her shining hair to the three-inch heels on her Italian sling-back pumps. "And you get your act together very well," he murmured, smiling at the flush of pink that tinged her cheeks. "I like the dress." Dirk indicated the soft rose-tinted wool sheath that caressed her body, his smile growing in time with the color highlighting her skin. "Will you be warm enough with that?" Lifting his hand, he tested the material of the gray cape Tina had thrown around her shoulders.

"Yes." Possibly too warm, Tina added silently, breath quickening from the heat suffusing her body. Deciding two could play at this game, she examined his attire, fighting to hold an air of detachment.

Her examination only increased the flow of heat coursing through her veins. In truth, Dirk always looked good to her. Dressed to go out, he looked magnificent. His newly shampooed hair gleamed with burnished-gold streaks; his freshly shaven cheeks displayed the sheen of a year-round suntan. His pristine white shirt contrasted beautifully with the Harris tweed jacket that enhanced the breadth of his shoulders; the diagonally striped tie expertly knotted at his collar added a dash of color and panache. Even the knife-pleated chocolate-brown slacks that encased his long, muscular legs were an enticement . . . to what, Tina shakily refused to acknowledge, but her detachment slipped alarmingly. Swallowing in an effort to moisten her suddenly dry throat, she moved jerkily toward the car.

"Okay," Dirk drawled with amusement. "How would you rate me? On a scale of one to ten?"

Fifty-two. Tina could not deny the smile that curved her lips at the number that sprang to her mind. She had no way of knowing her smile hinted at her thoughts.

"That good, huh?" Opening the car door for her, Dirk leaned over quickly and brushed his lips over her cheek. "For that unspoken compliment, I'll happily pay for dinner." His eyes sparkling with laughter, he boldly assessed her exposed thighs as Tina slid onto the car seat. "And for that glimpse of the cradle of heaven," he whispered, "I'll even dance with you after we've eaten."

The car door closed with a solid thunk, effectively covering the gasp that escaped Tina's parted lips. The cradle of heaven? Tina smoothed the skirt of her dress down over her thighs with nervous fingers. The cradle of heaven. Was that what Dirk had found with her? A heaven of physical completion? The thought was both upsetting and exciting.

Tina's pulse hammered erratically. Was she supposed to respond to that blatantly sexual overture? A delicious tension holding her still, she slanted a guarded glance at Dirk as he slid behind the wheel.

The look Dirk returned was loaded, as was his observation. "There's no need for you to look so uneasy, love. You know I'm a smooth . . . ah . . . *gentle* dancer."

Tina stopped breathing altogether at his thinly veiled innuendo. Liquid fire suddenly racing out of control through her veins set a spark to her imagination and memory. For one brief, glorious instant she could actually feel the ecstasy she'd experienced while "dancing" with him on that long ago afternoon.

"You've always loved me."

Snapped into the present by Dirk's softly voiced but adamant statement, Tina stared at him out of anguished eyes.

"Yes." Feeling oddly defeated and triumphant at the same time, Tina straightened her spine and met his assessing regard fearlessly. "Yes," she repeated clearly. "I've always loved you."

"As a brother?" Dirk arched one golden-brown brow.

"Yes."

"As a lover?" His voice lowered seductively.

"Yes."

"As a man?" Tension filled his tone.

"Yes."

Inside the island of the plush Seville, Tina held her breath as Dirk's sapphire eyes scrutinized her features one by one. When those jewellike eyes captured hers, she released the breath in a sigh of surrender. She was his. She had always been his and, deep down, had always known it. Now he knew it too.

"I told you earlier that there was a way . . ." Dirk's voice trailed away, leaving tracks of question.

Bemused as she was, Tina knew what he was referring to at once. Dirk had said the words to her that afternoon just as the phone rang with the call from Paul. His response had been to her plea for money. Now, searching his face for a clue and finding none, Tina nodded her head in understanding.

"And that way is?" she asked softly, expecting, from his preceding hints, to be propositioned.

"Marry me."

Tina stared at Dirk in astonishment, but his austere expression left no doubt whatever about his seriousness. Why had she never considered the possibility? she wondered blankly. A tiny smile of bitterness tugged at her lips but was quickly gone. Why should a man buy something he can get for nothing? The old admonition silently mocked her. The light in her eyes diminished as Tina gazed at Dirk knowingly. Had he reached the conclusion that she would refuse to dance until he paid the band?

"Well, Tina?" An edge now serrated Dirk's tone.

"Is your need that great?" Tina blurted.

"Yes." The edge bit her savagely. "Is yours?"

Tina closed her eyes. It was obvious that Dirk believed he was referring to two entirely different types of need: in his own case physical, in hers financial. Lifting her shoulders in a tired shrug, Tina opened her eyes to stare into the blue depths of his. What did it matter? she asked herself, the pain she felt cutting into her heart. If she was his, she was his—whether she was with him or not. Now, given the choice, Tina knew she'd rather be with him than anywhere else on earth. What difference did it make as to why he wanted to be with her?

"Yes." Tina's softly uttered agreement was affirmation to both his questions; yes, her need was great, and yes, she would marry him to alleviate that need.

"When?" Dirk's gaze bored into her.

Attempting insouciance she was light years from feeling, Tina flicked her hair off her shoulders with a toss of her head.

"Whenever," she responded flippantly.

Dirk's eyes narrowed over a revealing leap of flaring

anger. "All right." His too-even tone sent a chill that feathered Tina's nape. "Next Thursday," he decided with a grim smile. "It will give us an added something to be thankful for on Thanksgiving."

Tina had completely forgotten that the holiday was only one week away. Gazing into his flinty eyes, she lowered her head in acquiescence. "Whatever you say."

"Look at me, Tina."

At the almost coaxing sound of his voice, Tina raised surprised eyes.

"We've both tried to make it with others and failed." Lifting his hand, Dirk drew an uneven line over her cheek. "I don't know." He shrugged. "Maybe our lives are too entwined." The soft laughter that broke from his lips held scant humor. "My wanting you feels almost incestuous. You were always like a sister to me, much more of a sister than my own ever was."

"Dirk." Tina's protest went unheard and unheeded.

"But I do want you." Dirk's tone hardened. "Thoughts, dreams, and the longing for you have tormented me long enough. The torment will end one week from today."

Or will it really just be beginning? The consideration dropped into Tina's consciousness like a stone into water, sinking into the very depths of her being. Suddenly cold, she drew her cape around her to contain the shiver that rippled the length of her spine. Dirk felt the shiver in the tips of his fingers.

"Dinner," he decided firmly, removing his hand and turning in his seat. "You're chilled from sitting here too long and you're probably half starved." His features relaxing, he sliced a teasing glance at her. "My care of you thus far hardly recommends me as husband material . . . does it?"

"You always took very special care of me," Tina reminded him quietly.

"Because you were always special to me," Dirk responded immediately, flicking the key in the ignition with a twist of his long, capable-looking fingers.

And Dirk's fingers were capable, Tina knew. In fact, Dirk had proved capable at everything he'd ever attempted, from sailing a boat to reeling in the fish he'd caught over the side. He could ride a horse with the best, ride a wave when it was up, ride a hunch that made an enormous profit for him. Bring a woman straight to heaven.

A sensuous thrill ricocheted along Tina's spine. Yes, she had glimpsed that heaven Dirk could offer a woman. And she had craved more of it every day for the last five years.

Into her own thoughts, Tina was only superficially aware of the motion of the car until it came to a stop mere minutes after they'd pulled away from the house. Drawn out of her reverie, Tina glanced around in confusion. The car was parked in the lot of the imposing Marquis de Lafayette Inn. Frowning, she turned to Dirk, who was watching her, an amused smile curving his lips.

"We're having dinner here?" Tina's brows arched.

"Obviously." Dirk's brows mirrored hers. "Would you prefer to go somewhere else?"

"No." Tina shook her head vigorously. "This is fine. I was just wondering why we bothered with the car."

"Because it will probably turn cold before we're ready to leave." Dirk ran a meaningful glance over her cape. "And I doubt you'll be warm enough in that." Not waiting for a response, he opened his door and stepped out. Tina was standing on the macadam before he'd circled the car.

"Liberated, are you?" he drawled, sliding an arm around her waist.

"Of course." Tilting her head to glance up at him, Tina wound her arms around him and gave him a quick hug, laughing softly at his contemplative look.

"Brazen too," Dirk decided dryly, setting her into motion by striding briskly. "I hope you don't make a habit of draping yourself around men in parking lots . . . or anywhere else, for that matter."

"Only the ones I've known for almost twenty years," Tina quipped, yelping when he retaliated by suddenly tightening his hold on her waist.

Laughing easily together, they entered the Inn and went directly to the Top of the Marq restaurant on the sixth floor. It was over five years since Tina had stepped foot into the restaurant, yet they were greeted with the warmth and friendliness accorded regular customers.

When Tina saw the table they were being ushered to, a small pang twisted in her chest. She could vividly remember seeing Dirk at that same table on the July evening her father had brought her to the restaurant for dinner. The spear of pain stabbing Tina was two-pronged. The memory was both bitter and sweet.

Preoccupied, Tina was blind to the searing scrutiny of shrewd blue eyes.

Innocently unaware of the fact that it would be the last time she'd dine out with her already ailing father, Tina had looked forward with glowing excitement to their dinner at the Marq. Within minutes of being seated at a window table that afforded a panoramic view of the ocean, however, all the excitement faded from the evening, and all the expectation Tina had secretly harbored concerning Dirk died an agonizing death.

Dirk had not occupied the table across the room

from Tina and her father in lonely isolation. The woman sitting very close to him was unfamiliar to Tina. The woman was a stunner: blond, suntanned, beautiful, and obviously enthralled with her escort.

To the silent death knell of all her girlish dreams of a happy-ever-after with Dirk, Tina had observed the couple from her window table. Intent on the menu, her father never noticed Dirk and his lovely companion. Intent on his companion, Dirk never noticed Tina and her father. Sadly, to this day, Tina could not remember what she and her father had talked about that evening, or what she'd ordered and subsequently eaten. Of course, the identity of the meal was unimportant; the conversation had been the last of any length she'd had with her father.

"Tina, where are you?"

Startled out of the past, Tina gazed solemnly at the Dirk of the present. How incredibly naive she'd been, she thought. So naive she hadn't even considered the idea that Dirk would enjoy, let alone need, female companionship. Seeing him with a woman hanging on his every word had shattered Tina's fantasy bubble. A tiny bittersweet smile shadowed her lips.

"Tina?" Though Dirk kept his voice pitched low, the edge of concern reached her. "I asked where you'd gone off to?"

"To an evening five years ago," Tina told him. "The night Dad brought me here for dinner." She sighed. "It was the last time he took me out. And the first time I ever saw you with a date."

"A date?" Dirk gazed at her in confusion. "Who was she?"

Tina shrugged. "I haven't the foggiest. I'd never seen her before." Since it was obvious Dirk didn't remember the woman, Tina smiled. "But she was a knockout; blond, tan, and gorgeous."

"Blond, tan, and gorgeous." Frowning in concentration, Dirk repeated the description. "Hmm, I wonder . . ." He smiled reminiscently as his voice trailed away. "Ah, the disco queen!" he exclaimed, laughing softly.

"Disco queen?" Intrigued, Tina raised a questioning eyebrow.

Dirk shook his head. "All that chick wanted to do was dance," he explained. Then, his laughter taking on a hint of sensuality that annoyed Tina, he qualified. "Well, that isn't quite *all* she wanted to do."

"She liked to swim?" Tina inquired sweetly around a patently false smile.

"Only if it was on top of a water bed," Dirk retorted dryly. "I swear, that woman was—"

"I don't want to hear it," Tina cut him off sharply, feeling her cheeks grow warm when he roared with laughter. "And I don't see anything funny, either!"

"Oh, Tina." Dirk sighed. "You haven't changed at all. You're still a very prim and proper young lady."

"And you have changed completely," Tina shot back. "You never were an arrogant bas . . ."

"I warned you about the name-calling once, Tina." Dirk's quiet tone was coated with ice. "I have no intention of spending my married life being cursed."

"Are you threatening me?" Tina asked in amazement, beginning to feel all the old anger churn in her stomach.

"Merely warning you, love," Dirk corrected gently. "I'm usually a patient man, but my patience doesn't extend to listening to my wife swear at me."

"You haven't got a wife yet." Tina glared at him. "And at this rate, you just may not get one—at least not this one." She stabbed one long-nailed finger against her chest.

"Really?" Dirk was obviously unimpressed by her

tirade. A sardonic smile curving his lips, he leaned back lazily in his chair. "Then," he actually purred, "whatever will you do to get the money you need to bail yourself out of debt?"

Square one. Tina could really have sworn at him then. Fortunately, the waiter chose that moment to bring the drinks she'd never even heard Dirk order. Reflecting his careless attitude with forced composure, she watched him warily while sipping the cool white wine.

"No quick comeback?" Dirk drawled with chiding humor. "No protestations of numerous financial sources? No assurances to the effect that you don't need me—for anything?" The sensuous curve played over his lips again.

He knows full well how very much I need him. The realization of her own vulnerability drained all the fighting starch from Tina's stiffened spine. How she longed to put Dirk down with a verbal slap. But some inner knowledge warned her that, should she attack, Dirk would retaliate harder, and she was simply too tired to deflect his verbal blows.

A self-effacing smile on her lips, Tina raised her glass in salute. "To the victor . . . and all the rest of it," she toasted him bitterly. "We spoils will endeavor to control our tongue."

The sensuous curve to his lips grew a wicked twist. "Not in *every* situation, I hope. There are times when the application of one's tongue can be quite exciting."

"You are absolutely unbelievable!" Tina exclaimed softly.

"Horny too," Dirk admitted blandly. "But then, I think I demonstrated that quite effectively on two separate occasions today, didn't I?" Not bothering to wait for a response from her, he raised his glass in a return toast. "To the blessed end of five long years of horniness."

Humiliation, shame, and pure rage combined momentarily to choke Tina. She loved him to the point of adoration, and he only wanted the use of her body. Collecting her outraged sensibilities, Tina retaliated in the only way that presented itself at that moment. "On our wedding night," she added to his toast, experiencing a small sense of revenge at the spasm of shock that flashed across his face before he could impose control.

"You're really going to make me wait?" he asked, almost teasingly.

"I'm really going to make you wait," Tina repeated.

"I might be agreeable to releasing your money sooner," Dirk suggested. "Or have you forgotten your creditors?"

"I'm really going to make my creditors wait as well." Tina emptied her glass with a few deep swallows. "Look at it this way," she advised mockingly. "Next Thursday, you and my creditors will have something to be thankful for."

Expecting a range of reactions from rage to sarcasm, Tina was amazed when Dirk laughed. She was just beginning to wonder if she should feel insulted when he squashed that idea as it formed.

"Okay, Tina, let's drink to Thanksgiving Day." Once again he raised his glass. "The feast will be all the more enjoyable for the anticipation of it."

Unable to join him in the drink, Tina merely touched her empty glass to his, thinking drolly, And in this case, I'm the turkey.

CHAPTER EIGHT

Methodically chewing a piece of his rare prime rib, Dirk contemplated the infuriating, tantalizing woman seated across the table from him.

Doing justice to a rather large lobster tail, Tina appeared sublimely unaffected by either his perusal or his presence.

Swallowing a curse along with the mangled piece of beef, Dirk stabbed his fork into the steaming baked potato on his plate. The very idea of blackmailing any woman into marriage was galling. The fact that he was applying force against this particular woman was actually creating a growing sickness inside.

All these years, all these years. The refrain revolved continuously in Dirk's mind. Years of caring, and protecting, and loving Tina. Tina, his sister, his friend, his confidant.

But Dirk no longer regarded Tina as his little sister, and therein lay the root of the conflict that ate at his conscience, setting him against himself.

Dirk loved Tina; there was no question about that. The question tormenting him was, In what way did Dirk love Tina?

Ostensibly viewing the unique mural of "Old Cape May" the Inn was proud to display, while actually observing Tina closely, Dirk consumed his dinner without tasting it, and his wine without feeling its effects.

Smiling inwardly, he watched as Tina daintily devoured her meal, a tremor quaking through him as the tip of her tongue flicked at a glistening drop of melted butter on her lip.

Damn. There certainly was no question of how he wanted to love Tina. Dirk had long ago admitted to himself that he wanted to feast on her like a starving man at a banquet table.

Though Dirk had mentally dodged the knowledge for months, he had finally faced the truth the winter between her sixteenth and seventeenth birthdays. And that truth was that he, Dirk Tanger, the pride of his parents and the private school he'd attended, the shrewd live wire, up-and-coming banker, the no-nonsense businessman, lusted after Tina Holden, the teenaged daughter of the man who'd been more of a real father to him than his own.

Suddenly dry, Dirk drained the full-bodied red wine from his glass. How many women had he used in a vain attempt to quench his thirst for Tina that winter? More than a few, he acknowledged ruefully. And not only that winter, either.

Lord! Dirk now thought in amazement. From the summer Tina was sixteen until that September afternoon when she was nineteen, he'd spent almost as much time hopping in and out of bed as he had amassing the fortune he now possessed. But where the business deals had been satisfying, the sexual indulgences had not. He realized now he had been trying to escape the hold Tina had on him; there was no escape.

Ignoring the remains of his dinner, Dirk refilled his glass, then bleakly watched Tina over the rim, sipping slowly as she finished her lobster.

God, she is so beautiful! So elegant in appearance. So gut-wrenchingly desirable. If anything, Dirk wanted Tina more now than he had before he had experienced the total fulfillment she could give him. And the bottom line of truth was, he'd used his wife as ruthlessly as every other woman in his determination to avoid facing his own reality.

Of course, as his wife had also been using him, Dirk forgave himself that transgression. What he couldn't forgive was his own weakness, which drove him not only to possess Tina physically but to own her soul. And that was exactly what he intended . . . he would own her, completely.

"Is there something wrong with your dinner?"

Dirk's gaze rested on Tina's lips as she posed the question. "No." Raising his glance to hers, he narrowed his eyelids to conceal the flow of desire reflected there. "I guess I'm not as hungry as I thought I was." At least not for beef and potatoes, he amended silently.

"You look . . ." Tina shrugged lightly. "Pensive. Are you feeling a little down?"

Quite the contrary, Dirk thought wryly. "I'm fine, Tina," Dirk assured her. "I'm just not very hungry." A teasing smile charmed his lips. "But you obviously were." A nod of his head indicated her plate.

"I love lobster tail." Tina smiled. "You, of all people, should know that."

"Yes, I know that, darling." Dirk returned her smile." I introduced you to it when you were six. Remember?"

"Yes."

Tina's whispered response and the dreamy expression on her lovely face combined to send a shaft of pain through Dirk's heart.

Whenever Tina thought of the past, their past, her features softened into that dreamy expression, and she became once again his own beautiful little sister. But there were other times, times like the day he'd confronted her on the beach, when her eyes glittered with the hate she bore him in the present.

Dirk was nothing if not honest with himself about this. He knew that their former relationship bound them together in an intensely emotional way. He also knew that by stepping over the line from brother to lover, he had irreparably damaged that precious relationship. And yet the emotional ties endured, twining around them both, the loose ends of love and hate binding them securely one to the other.

With new insight, Dirk followed the trend of his thoughts. He was not alone in the hell of inner conflict; Tina also suffered the effects of emotions straining in opposite directions.

He loved her, needed her . . . and hated her for having created, however innocently, the insatiable hunger he had for her.

Tina had admitted to loving him, needing him . . . and hating him, not only for shattering her young dreams, but for the subsequent control he'd held over her through her inheritance.

He thought her a grasping mercenary, prepared to use any means or any man in her determination to succeed as a businesswoman.

She thought him a coldhearted ruthless womanizing bastard.

And so they hated each other.

And so they loved each other.

Dirk's thoughts settled fatalistically. Marriage to each other would very likely be both heaven and hell. But it was the only arrangement he'd accept, because he knew from experience that living without her was just pure hell.

He'd live with it, Dirk decided. They would both have to learn to live with it . . . and each other. Raising his glass, he tilted it in a silent salute to his bride to be. It was better that they destroy each other than still more innocent bystanders along their way.

"What are you drinking to?" Though Tina's voice was light, her eyes betrayed wary confusion.

"Us." Though Dirk's tone was smooth, his painful thoughts were centered on the real reason for his toast. To the revenge we'll wreak upon each other, love, he mused darkly. Revenge achieved by legally binding our futures. And if the pill we mutually swallow is bitter, we'll have the bleak consolation of knowing that the coating is very sweet.

"Dirk." Tina's concerned voice drew Dirk from the depths of black despair. "What is it? You look so . . . so pained!"

Sighing deeply, Dirk shook off the residue of bitter speculation. "It's nothing, honey." He grinned to back up his denial. "For a moment there, a specter was dancing on my future grave."

Future grave? Tina shuddered. What an odd thing for Dirk to say. Sitting forward, she examined his eyes and skin color for signs of a brewing cold or flu. Dirk's color was not only good, it advertised glowing health, and his eyes were blue and clear. Still . . .

"Why are you peering at me like that?"

"I'm not peering." Sitting back, Tina frowned. "I was trying to determine if you were coming down with some sort of illness," she explained worriedly.

Dirk laughed reassuringly. "I'm perfectly all right." Then, knocking back the last of his wine, he set the glass on the table and rose to his feet. "And to prove it," he continued teasingly, "I'll chase you around the floor." Extending his hand, he smiled. "Come on, honey. Come dance with me."

Stepping into Dirk's arms was like stepping into yesterday. Sighing contentedly, Tina obligingly moved closer to Dirk's strength when his arms tightened about her waist. Her senses drowning in the intoxicating masculine scent of him, she allowed her suddenly heavy eyelids to flutter down. Immediately Tina was transported back in time to the only other occasion when Dirk had held her while dancing.

It was late spring, the evening of Tina's senior prom. Excited, she'd finished dressing long before her date, the good-looking boy who sat behind her in English, was due to arrive. Too keyed up to remain in her room, and eager to see her father's reaction to her appearance, Tina had swept down the curving staircase with all the elegance of an antebellum debutante, her wide, belled skirt swishing against the spokes in the stair railing.

Weeks before, to George Holden's mock pleas for mercy, Tina had scoured one shop after another for the perfect gown. The dazed expression on her father's face as she waltzed into the living room made the exhausting search worthwhile. But in truth it was the unexpected blazing gaze of sapphire blue that put the final stamp of approval on the billowing yards of virginal white tulle.

Off the shoulder and with a snug bodice, the dress drew the eye to the budding maturity of Tina's breasts and her tiny waist. The snowy white against her skin enhanced the creamy glow of her neck, shoulders, and arms.

Poised in the doorway to the living room, Tina held her breath while waiting for the two most important men in her life to offer an opinion. She hadn't had to wait very long.

"Is this beautiful creature my skinny Tina?" George asked in an awed tone.

From where he'd been sitting by the narrow window, Dirk walked to her slowly. "You look like every man's fantasy come to life." His oddly hoarse tone drew her startled eyes to his face.

For one brief moment, Tina thought she saw a flash of intense pain flicker in Dirk's eyes. Then it was gone, banished by a smile that warmed her all the way to her toes.

"Since your date hasn't arrived yet," Dirk murmured, opening his arms wide in invitation, "I'm claiming the first dance."

The music wafting around the room from the stereo was slow and romantic, perfect for that moment. Dirk held her lightly and maintained several inches of space between them during the brief ballad. Yet at that distance and in those fleeting moments, Tina realized two very important things. One was that she followed Dirk's lead as easily and naturally as if they'd danced together hundreds of times. The second was that, even with the distance separating them, she would rather dance with Dirk than any other man on earth.

The appearance of Tina's date was the anticlimax to her evening. Tina had gone on to the prom, her corsage of white and pale green orchids gracing her slender wrist, and she had thoroughly enjoyed her evening. Still, while she laughed and conversed with friends and danced with different partners, she carried an inner vision of being twirled around the small confines of her living room within the thrilling embrace of her one and only hero.

"At least this time there's not a mile of material between us." Dirk's murmured observation sent a tingle feathering Tina's spine. The brushing sensation of his lips moving over her temple drew goose bumps of excitement to the surface of her shoulders and arms. "This time I can feel your body moving with mine." His breath whispered into her ear, cutting hers off entirely.

310

Attuned in memory and motion, oblivious to the other couples on the dance floor, they swayed to a more evocative, more basic rhythm.

Flushed, her blood rushing through her veins in time to the music, Tina placed her slightly parted lips against the curve of Dirk's neck and caressed him gently with the tip of her tongue when he drew in a quick, sharp breath.

"Are you trying to get tumbled on the dance floor, woman?" Dirk's whispered growl was nearly Tina's undoing. "Maybe it's time to get out of here before we scandalize the decent folk of this fair city." His tone was laced with amusement and a broad vein of sensuality.

Responding to his mood, Tina glanced up at him through her partially lowered lashes. "Did you have a destination in mind?" she asked guilelessly, teasing him by combing her fingers through the fine hairs at his nape.

A visible shiver ran the length of Dirk's spine and his arms flexed in reaction. "We could continue the dance at home," he suggested softly. "In my bedroom . . ." A sexy smile curled the corners of his lips at the gasp that escaped Tina's guard. "I can guarantee you'll love the beat of the music."

For a moment Tina forgot to breathe. Her insides and her resolve melting, she closed her eyes in defense against the luring gleam in his. The temptation to fling caution to the winds was great, but not quite great enough. Piercing the web of sensuality Dirk was weaving around her, a smidgeon of common sense urged Tina to think.

She loved him, and although she would trust him with her life in a threatening situation, she could not trust him with her future. Dirk wanted her now, wanted her enough to make her his wife, and by doing so make not only her inheritance but his own fortune available to her. But if she were to allow him the physical satisfaction he craved before they were legally bound, what assurance did she have that he'd carry through with his promise?

Absolutely none. The answer came from deep within Tina's consciousness. The temptation to end her five-year hunger for him was great . . . but not quite great enough.

Shaking her head, Tina swirled out of Dirk's embrace. "I think we'll take a moonlight stroll on the promenade instead." She laughed, eyes bright with mockery. "Something tells me you could do with some cooling off before crawling into your bed . . . alone." Slanting a come-hither look at him over her shoulder, Tina made for their table, her body swaying invitingly.

A bemused smile softening his lips, Dirk trailed in Tina's scented wake. After paying the check, he escorted her from the Inn, draping the cape securely around her shoulders as they crossed Beach Drive to the deserted promenade.

The night air was cold and heavy with salty moisture that tantalized the nostrils and clung to the eyelashes. Drawing the distinctive odor of the seashore deep into her body, Tina was again transported back in time.

How many times had she walked this path with Dirk by her side? she wondered dreamily. The soft murmur of the curling waves seemed to whisper an answer: more times than can be counted.

The feel of Dirk's arm circling her waist, drawing her close to the warmth of his body, was a familiar sensation. Tina settled naturally into his easy, loping stride, more at home within the curve of his arm than in the house she'd grown up in.

"Shall we take a stroll along the silvery moonlight

path?" Dirk's teasing question was as familiar as his protective embrace. Tina's gaze sought the undulating strip of silver on the inky darkness of the sea. With very little imagination, one could believe it possible to follow that path to the horizon.

"Where will the path lead us?" Tina responded as she always had, bringing her moonlight-brightened gaze back to his face.

Dirk's eyes were dark with the memory of how very often he'd answered Tina's question. "A carefree place, filled with light, laughter, and love." He repeated the words he'd first spoken to Tina the summer her father had drawn him into the circle of love surrounding the Holden family. "A place glowing with all the colors of the rainbow."

Tina blinked against the rush of hot moisture that filled her eyes, pitying the five-year-old dreamer who had believed that such a place could exist. Smiling sadly, she shifted her gaze back to the lure of the restless sea.

"Growing up is a bitch, isn't it?"

Tina came to an abrupt stop at the harsh bitterness in Dirk's tone. What did *he* know of bitterness? The thought incurred renewed anger. Denying the need to burrow closer to his strength, she slipped out of his encircling arm, spinning away from him.

"Tina!"

Ignoring the entreaty in Dirk's commanding tone, Tina ran down the steps to the beach, unmindful of the abrasive grains of sand that insinuated themselves under the narrow straps of her sandals. She hadn't a hope of outrunning Dirk and she knew it, yet Tina fled on wobbly high heels, heading for the shoreline. Her breath a raspy sound in her ears, Tina didn't hear Dirk as he gained on her. His grasp of her shoulder came as a shock, though it shouldn't have.

Wildly angry, and not even sure why, Tina tried to shake off Dirk's detaining hand. His hold tightened, his arm jerked, and then she was falling, pitching to the ground, pulling him down with the impetus of her body. He landed with a thud beside her.

"What the hell is the matter with you?" Dirk's ragged voice growled into her ear.

"Nothing! Everything! I don't know!" Tina deplored the uncertainty threading her own gasping voice. Her arms flailing, she attempted, unsuccessfully, to scramble to her feet. Utterly spent, she lay still, staring up at the star-tossed sky. "Why did you ask me to marry you, Dirk?" she whispered.

"I think you know the answer to that." Dirk's emotionless tone was chilling.

"Yes." Closing her eyes against the brilliance overhead, Tina shuddered at the memory of his hot mouth searing her skin. "We'll destroy each other, Dirk." Her toneless statement still managed to convey despair.

He was lying so close, Tina felt the sigh he expelled. "Very likely." Dirk was quiet a moment, then he pushed the upper part of his body up to stare directly into her eyes. "But there's no turning back, no getting out of it." His trembling fingers contradicting the fierce determination blazing out of his eyes, he tenderly brushed the hair back at her temples. "Like it or not, Tina, there is a bond between us. An emotional and physical bond. I've never believed in predestination, but . . ." His voice trailed away, and he shrugged. The smile that played with Dirk's mouth had the power to wound. "Who knows"—he shrugged again—"maybe we're both working off our individual karma on each other."

Predestination? Karma? Tina shuddered. Inching away from him, she struggled to her feet. Closing her mind to the possibility of what he'd sardonically suggested, she brushed vigorously at the sand clinging to her dress.

"That's ridiculous." Tina wished her voice held more assurance. "We control our own destiny, and you know it."

"Do we?" Chuckling softly, Dirk sprang to his feet before her startled eyes. "Then how do you explain the lure that keeps drawing us back together?"

"Sexual attraction." Speaking each word distinctly, Tina lifted her head proudly. "A violent reaction of our respective body chemicals."

Dirk's soft chuckle expanded into a full-throated laugh. "I'll say!" he exclaimed, choking back a fresh burst of laughter. "And if you think I'm going to deny all those chemicals going berserk inside my body, you're crazy." Grinning wickedly, he slid his hand around her neck and tugged her rigid body into contact with his own. "Sexual attraction, chemistry, or whatever, you are going to marry me." His lips teased the corner of her mouth. "Aren't you?"

Tina felt the tingle begin at the inside of her mouth, then slowly radiate throughout her body. Sighing softly in defeat, she moved her head the fraction of an inch necessary to fuse her lips with his. Disappointment racked her nerve endings when Dirk lifted his head slightly, refusing to kiss her.

"Aren't you?" he insisted, tormenting her by flicking the tip of his tongue over her lips.

"Dirk." Tina's cry was part protest, part plea.

"Aren't you?" His tongue slid fleetingly into her mouth.

"Yes." Clasping his head with her hands, Tina drew his mouth to hers. "Yes," she moaned, parting her lips for the invasion of his. Melting into him, she gave herself to the thrill of his thrusting tongue. "Yes." Her whisper was lost inside Dirk's mouth.

To what conclusion the embrace might have led, Tina had no idea—nor did she care. Swept into abandonment by the fiery onslaught of Dirk's mouth, she was soon past the point of rational thought or even instinctive self-preservation.

Not merely pliant but eager, she threw all her longing and frustration into the kiss, as if trying to absorb the essence of him into her entire being. It was Dirk, an obviously shaken Dirk, who saved Tina from herself.

Tearing his mouth from hers, he held her away from him, his breathing rough and uneven as he stared down into her passion-glazed eyes.

"Good Lord, Tina!" Dirk's whispered exclamation held a note of pain. "Now dare to tell me the only thing between us is *physical* attraction!"

Tina felt the intensity in Dirk through the tremor in the fingers gripping her upper arms. Her breath coming in shallow gasps, she closed her eyes. "Dirk . . . I won't . . ." That was as far as she got, fortunately, for she hadn't thought of one word with which to plead her case.

"You will." Dirk enforced his words with a light shake of her shoulders. "You will admit it because, like me, you have no choice."

"You're wrong!" Tina's eyes flew wide in reaction to his statement. Staring up at him, she longed to lower her lashes again, to shut out the heart-wrenching image of him with moonlight striking burnished glints off his hair and sparks of blue fire from his piercing eyes. The glinting streaks in his hair rippled as he shook his head.

"No, Tina, I'm not wrong. I could control simple physical attraction, and I'm sure you could as well. But what we're dealing with here is much stronger, much more involved, and you know it." The smile that feathered his lips sent an ache radiating through Tina's chest. "No, darling, what we're dealing with here has the scent of obsession."

"Dirk!" Tina's cry of protest rang on the cold night air.

"Hush, love." Drawing her to him, Dirk cradled Tina's trembling body close to his hard strength. "Accept it. We've had a taste of the forbidden fruit. The obsession is to devour the entire apple."

Obsession.

The one word stood between Tina and sleep. Alternately hot then cold as she lay on her bed, she restlessly drew the covers up to her chin only to throw them off again moments later.

Was she obsessed with the need to possess and be possessed by her friend, her hero, her one-time lover? Flopping onto her side, Tina raised her hand to wipe impatiently at the tears gathering in her eyes. Now was not the time for tears; now was the time for some heavy thinking.

When had her mental waters become so muddy? Sighing tiredly, Tina rolled to her other side. On leaving New York, her goal had been clear-cut, her thinking decisive. Confident in her determination, she'd never really doubted her ability to get what she needed.

Of course, with perfect hindsight, Tina now saw the two glaring errors in her calculations. In the first place, she had conveniently forgotten how adamant and stubborn Dirk could be. And then, compounding her foolishness, she had actually convinced herself that the emotion that ran rampant inside whenever she thought of him was hate.

Grimacing with astonishment at her own self-delusion, Tina slowly shook her head. If she lived for a thousand years, she could not hate Dirk. She could resent him, and she did, sometimes violently. But hate?

A sound, half sob, half laugh, shattered the early-morning stillness of the room. Surely even a moderately intelligent person could define the difference between resentment and hate. Unless, of course, Tina admitted with ruthless honesty, that person wanted to avoid the unvarnished truth that lay beneath the resentment.

And yes, that truth was a love so enduring that even Dirk's coldness failed to freeze it. Did that make what she felt obsessive?

Yes.

Scrambling off the bed, Tina prowled around the dark room like a caged animal; the bars caging her were all mental.

A perfectly normal urge to run gripping her, Tina dropped to her knees beside the bed, groping for the suitcase she'd stowed there on her arrival. Had it really only been a few days? she marveled, sweeping her arm along the carpet. Lord, it seemed like weeks since she'd left her apartment.

Common sense gained control as Tina's fingers brushed the supple leather case. What would running accomplish? Her turmoil was inside, it was emotional, and there was no way to run from it. No, she decided, shaking her head as she got to her feet; running was out. In a sense, hadn't she been running for the last five years? Could she face the idea of running in place for the rest of her life?

No! The cry came from deep within. She knew she had to stay and follow the path connecting her life to Dirk's to its natural conclusion.

Sliding onto the bed, Tina steeled her resolve. With luck, and a lot of hard work, maybe, just maybe, she and Dirk could make a life together . . . *if* they could reconcile their past with the present.

Tina hugged that vaguely hopeful thought to her heart as she drifted into an uneasy sleep.

Behind another closed door across the hall, Dirk lay awake and thoughtful. Had he convinced her? he wondered. Had he managed to convince himself?

Giving up on the hope of sleep, Dirk rose, raking a hand through his hair as he walked to the window to gaze sightlessly at the deserted street below.

Damn, he groaned silently. How had something that had begun so simply become so complicated?

Looking back with his mind's eye, Dirk could see himself, young, lonely, eagerly following George Holden into the house to meet his family for the first time.

Smiling softly into the night, Dirk relived the welcoming warmth Tina's mother had given him, and the glow of love that had appeared to surround the three members of the Holden family. Unstintingly, they had drawn the impressionable youth he had been into that circle of love. And he, as a man, had betrayed George Holden's trust.

Dirk's smile gave way to the bitterness that twisted his lips. And now, with cool deliberation, he was about to betray his friend a second time.

His movement violent, Dirk spun around to stalk the length of his room.

George, forgive me, Dirk pleaded mutely, but I must take your most precious possession and make her mine.

Dirk was still pacing his room, still waging war with himself, when the first streaks of dawn lit the horizon. Stepping out of his brief shorts, he shrugged into a terry robe and strode to the bathroom. His course was set and there was no going back: Tina would be his.

The plan sprang into Dirk's mind, full blown, as he stood under the stingingly cold shower spray. A satisfied smile tugged at his lips as he mulled the idea over while drying his body with a large white towel.

Tina was vacillating, and Dirk knew it. His own mind set on the necessity of a legal union between them, he'd worried over the possibility of Tina's balking, perhaps even running before he could marry her.

Now Dirk's smile expanded into a confident grin. He knew exactly how to proceed with her. And the answer was so damn simple too.

Pulling on his robe, Dirk left the bathroom, whistling softly as he strolled to his bedroom. Inside his mind a vision lingered, a vision of Tina, her features softened by memories, her eyes faraway and dreamy.

His voice low, Dirk sang the words to the ballad he'd been whistling. As he dressed in casual slacks and a finely knit sweater, the song's lyrics gave way to a rumbling chuckle.

Pulling on his scuffed desert boots, Dirk swung out of his room and ran lightly down the stairs. His battle tactics clear in his mind, he took the final two steps as one and pivoted toward the back of the house. All that is now required, he thought smugly, is to put the plan into action.

Dirk was again whistling as he sauntered into the bright kitchen. The sight that met his eyes stole the whistle from his lips and the smugness from his mind.

In much the same manner as Mrs. Holden had so many years before, Beth was standing at the stove, preparing a meal. But the figure that arrested Dirk's glance and attention was tall and slim, all graceful motion as she bustled around the table with dishes

320

and flatware, one fiery braid bouncing merrily on her back.

The breath catching painfully in his throat, Dirk experienced an eerie sensation of déjà vu.

Completely unaware that his eyes had clouded with memory and were caressing the slender woman poised expectantly by the table, Dirk moved like a sleepwalker into the room. Having planned to steep Tina in memories throughout the week to keep her amenable to his wishes, Dirk now found himself caught in the very same web.

"Good morning, scrawny." The husky murmur was all Dirk could get past the tightness in his throat.

CHAPTER NINE

At her first glimpse of Dirk as he paused in the kitchen doorway, Tina felt a rush of warmth tingle through her body. At his murmured greeting, all her bones seemed to melt. Ensnared by the smoky blue of his eyes, she clutched the edge of the table to keep from sliding into a heap on the tile floor.

Within the instant required for him to cross the room to where she stood, Tina was held breathless in a time warp. She was five years old again, quivering with the expectancy of hearing her father's robust voice introduce the golden-haired young man to her smiling mother.

"Breakfast is almost ready." Beth's amused voice broke through Tina's memory warp. "And if you could coax her to eat more, Tina wouldn't be so scrawny."

Simultaneously, Tina and Dirk blinked themselves back to the present, then exchanged smiles of secret communication. Once again attuned to each other's thoughts, they moved in unison to finish setting the table, their gazes tangling when their hands, briefly touching, set off sparks of awareness between them.

"Did you sleep well?" Dirk's low tone flowed over Tina like a healing balm.

"No," Tina admitted frankly, with a rueful smile. "Did you?"

"No." A self-derisive smile shadowed Dirk's lips.

"Not at all, actually." A frown drew a line across the bridge of his nose. "Did you run this morning?" Scraping a chair back from the table, he seated her before moving to the stove to help Beth.

"Yes, for a little while." Tina smiled into the arched glance Dirk threw at her over his shoulder. "I wasn't up to the long haul."

"Considering the meager amount of fuel you put into your body, I'm surprised you can run at all!" Beth exclaimed scoldingly, carrying a plate of crisp bacon to the table.

Trailing in Beth's wake with an oval serving dish heaped high with fluffy scrambled eggs in one hand and a plate of stacked toast in the other, Dirk grinned at Tina wickedly.

"Shall we confine her to her room unless she cleans her plate?" he asked Beth dryly.

"It's an idea, but it probably wouldn't work," Beth responded in kind. "What Tina needs is someone to take care of her, twenty-four hours a day!"

"A keeper?" Tina exclaimed, laughing.

"Or a husband," Dirk inserted smoothly.

Beth's shrewd glance shifted from Dirk to Tina. "Is there a husband in the offing?" she asked bluntly.

Tina felt the heat of a flush in her cheeks, but before she could reply, Dirk stole the initiative from her.

"Yes." Dirk equalled Beth's bluntness. "Me."

For long moments the room seemed to hum with tension, then Beth beamed her approval, lighting her face and lightening the atmosphere. "That's wonderful!" she cried, reaching out to grasp their hands. "When was all this decided? And when will the wedding take place?"

"It was all decided yesterday." Dirk supplied the answer, again beating Tina into speech. "And the ceremony will take place next Thursday, Thanksgiving Day." His tone was as dry as Tina's throat.

"Thanksgiving," Beth exclaimed, "how absolutely perfect!" In that moment, Tina was positive she could see Beth mentally shift gears. She was proved correct when Beth added enthusiastically, "We can have a small reception right here!"

Stunned, Tina and Dirk stared as Beth jumped out of her chair and bustled to a drawer in the cabinet next to the sink. Exchanging confused glances, they tried to make sense of the housekeeper's excited chatter.

"A reception?" Tina whispered, appalled. "Must we have a reception?"

Dirk was already shaking his head, frowning as he glanced back at Beth. "We didn't want any fuss, Beth," he said carefully, not wanting to hurt the older woman's feelings. "I thought the three of us could have a meal out, after the ceremony."

Tina felt her body relax with relief, only to tense again at the shocked expression on Beth's face when she returned to the table, a pencil and pad in her hand.

"Eat out?" Beth's lips pursed sourly. "The three of us?" she repeated in an outraged tone. "Dirk Tanger, you have some very good friends in this town!" The look she leveled at Dirk reminded Tina of a stern teacher . . . her sixth-grade teacher in fact. Hiding a smile brought on entirely by nervousness, Tina forced her attention back to the chastising Beth. "Not to mention your family and friends in Wilmington."

Displaying patience Tina didn't know he was capable of, Dirk smiled at Beth. "But you see, Beth, Tina and I prefer—" he began gently, only to be interrupted by a now incensed Beth.

"And you, Tina. What about your friends? Don't you think they'd feel slighted if you just sneak off and get married?"

324

"Sneak off?" Tina and Dirk responded in unison, their voices loud in the quiet kitchen. With a brief nod of his head, Dirk allotted the floor to Tina.

"Beth, we are *not* planning to sneak off anywhere," Tina explained as calmly as she could. "But we both prefer a quiet, simple ceremony. I mean, really," she went on, contriving a laugh she was a long way from feeling, "neither one of us is exactly dewy-eyed. We've both been married before."

"So what?" Beth snorted. "Is it chiseled on stone somewhere that a second marriage can't be celebrated?" As the query was obviously rhetorical, Beth didn't wait for a response. "Good grief!" she scolded. "Every living soul is entitled to one mistake, and most have countless numbers, come to that! You're getting married, for heaven's sake! I'd think you'd want to share your happiness with all your relatives and friends."

"Oh, Beth, you don't understand," Tina protested weakly, turning to Dirk for support. At the contemplative expression on his face, she felt a knot grow in her stomach. The knot expanded with the glittering light that flared in his eyes.

"You know, love, I'm beginning to think Beth's right."

Astounded, Tina just stared at him. Surely he couldn't be serious, she thought wildly. After a brief hesitation, Dirk set her straight on that score. Oozing charm, he leaned toward the now smiling housekeeper.

"What did you have in mind, Beth?"

Beth took off like a Chinese rocket. "Well, I thought I'd prepare a buffet. You know, all the traditional Thanksgiving foods, but with slight variations because it's also a wedding. Using the dining room as well as the living room, I'd estimate we can squeeze about forty or so people into the house."

"Forty?" Tina's squawk went unnoticed as Beth continued talking to a very interested Dirk.

"Of course, there'll be no time to send out formal invitations, but I'm sure your secretary can do the inviting by phone." She raised a narrow eyebrow at Dirk. "Can't she?"

"Certainly," Dirk drawled, obviously amused by Beth's ardor.

"Dirk!" Tina might as well have saved her breath for all the notice her companions paid her.

"I'll need a list of names from the two of you," Beth murmured, scribbling what appeared to be a grocery list on the pad of paper she'd brought to the table. "And I'll need it today." She glanced up to frown at first Dirk, then Tina. "And you also have some arrangements to make, don't you? I mean, blood tests, marriage license, and so forth?"

"Right." Getting swiftly to his feet, Dirk walked around Tina's chair, giving a gentle tug on her braid. "You heard the lady. Let's get crackin', kid."

Feeling slightly punchy, Tina rose and followed him out of the room. Partial rationality returned as she stood meekly in the front hall, watching Dirk remove their jackets from the closet.

"Where are we going?" she asked, shaking her head as if to clear it of cobwebs.

"Beth was right, Tina, we do have things to do." Stepping behind her, he held the garment as she docilely slid her arms into the sleeves. "We have to get a blood test and apply for the license. There's a three-day waiting period. Remember?"

"Yes, but . . ." Tina came to life as he moved around her to zip up the jacket. "Hey, wait a minute!"

she objected. "I have no makeup on, and I should brush out my hair."

Already at the door and holding it open, Dirk ran an encompassing glance the length of her body, from the shiny red braid to her scrubbed face, over the sweater that outlined her breasts and down to the jeans that encased her hips and legs. When he brought his gaze back to hers, Tina imagined she could feel the heat blazing out of his eyes.

"Tina." Dirk's low tone was husky with sensuality. "If we don't leave this house right now, I'm going to pick you up and carry you to my bedroom." Arching one brow, he taunted, "I'd as soon stay here. The choice is yours."

A soundless moan shivered in Tina's throat. Suddenly feeling vulnerable and very tempted, she stared at him wistfully, her eyes drinking in the sheer masculine appeal of him as he leaned lazily against the door.

A quick awareness of his sharpened gaze alerted Tina to what he was about to say.

"Honey, you better make your choice," he warned softly, "while the choice is still yours to make."

Coming to her senses, Tina dashed past him and through the open door, tingling to the rumble of the laughter that followed her. As he joined her on the porch, Dirk's laughter subsided to a teasing grin.

"Coward," he murmured into her ear as he slid his arm around her waist.

Sniffing disdainfully, Tina walked sedately down the steps, automatically heading for the little Nissan. Long fingers flexing into her flesh brought her to an abrupt halt.

"I think we'll take my car." The gritty edge on his voice caused an altogether different kind of tingle along Tina's spine. "At least I know mine is paid for."

"So is this one." Tina indicated the sports car with a wave of her hand. "And it's not mine anyway."

Dirk's entire body went still; Tina's heart began to race erratically.

"Not yours?" A deceptive silkiness increased the thumping in her chest. "May I inquire to whom it belongs?" he asked with frightening formality.

For a moment Tina could barely articulate past the thickness in her throat. Then a rush of impatient anger swept by the obstruction. Who does he think he is? she fumed, glaring at him.

"It's Paul's," she said tightly. "*My* car was repossessed weeks ago . . . thanks to you!"

"Thanks to me?" Dirk's jaw tensed, lending an arrogance to his features that chilled Tina. "In what way, precisely?" he demanded.

Shrugging out of his grip, Tina hastened to the side of the gleaming Cadillac. "You knew perfectly well in what way," she snapped, mourning the loss of their shared camaraderie.

"Tina, stop this!" Walking to her, Dirk grasped her by her upper arms and shook her lightly. "You know why I've guarded your money so carefully."

"Oh, sure." Incensed now, Tina struggled to free herself; Dirk merely tightened his hold on her. "You were determined to keep Chuck from squandering it. Well, I've got a news flash for you, Mr. Banker. I'm this"—she held her thumb and forefinger apart a quarter of an inch—"far from losing everything I've worked so very hard for!"

"Poor management," Dirk pronounced pedantically, sending Tina's temper soaring.

"It was not poor management!" Tina had to pause to keep herself from screaming at him. "I could have handled it, if—" Realizing what she was about to admit, Tina caught herself up short.

"If Chuck hadn't demanded more and more money from you," Dirk finished for her. "Is that what you were about to say?"

All the fight suddenly drained out of Tina, leaving her feeling excessively tired. How many times had they had this same argument? she wondered bleakly. How many more times would they plow over the same barren ground?

Deflated, she watched as he unlocked the door on the passenger side of the car, and obediently she slid onto the seat at his impatient gesture. Sighing softly, Tina caressed his lithe form with dulled eyes as he circled the hood of the car to the driver's side, sadly aware that he possessed the power to arouse her even when she was furious at him. Futility left a bitter taste in her mouth and she grimaced as he slid behind the steering wheel.

"It's over, Tina." Though quiet, Dirk's tone was hard with finality. "One week from today you can write any number of checks to pay off your debts." His chest heaved with a roughly expelled breath. "And for any other whim that might take your fancy." Reaching out, he caught her chin with his fingers, lifting her head to stare into her eyes. "But the first one had damned well better be a car of your own." His fingers tightening spasmodically, Dirk bent to brush her lips with his own, muttering fiercely, "I want that vehicle returned to Rambeau as soon as possible."

Running the tip of her tongue over her lips to savor the elusive taste of him, Tina fought back a growing excitement. Was that the ring of jealousy she heard in his commanding tone? she asked herself in amazement. Her ebullience went flat with the verbal pin Dirk stuck into her ballooning hopes.

"You belong to me now, Tina. Exclusively." Eyes narrowing dangerously, Dirk visually pinned her to the plush seat. "I don't share my private property with other men. Do I make myself clear?"

Warring emotions of frustration, anger, and crushing disappointment kept Tina silent. She could feel Dirk's mounting anger in the fingers now bruising her tender flesh.

"Do you understand?" he grated in a terrifyingly soft tone. "As long as you wear my ring, there will be no other men in your life."

Sheer rage provided the strength that enabled Tina to jerk chin out of his grasp. Dirk's insinuation concerning her lack of morals ran through her system like poison. Her chest tight with pain, her breathing shallow, she lashed out at him in a choking snarl. "You pompous bastard, I will be no man's private property!" Twisting around, she groped for the door release. "Do you understand *me?*" she flung over her shoulder.

Dirk stopped her flight by the simple method of catching hold of the braid that seemed to fly right into his hand with her swift movement. Tugging it sharply, he drew a cry of pain from her compressed lips. "Be still and you won't be hurt," he advised remotely. "I did warn you about cursing me. Didn't I?"

"Let me go, Dirk." Tina kept her face averted to conceal the tears blurring her vision. "I've changed my mind. I won't marry you." Being deliberately cruel, she added scathingly, "I'll find another man to tide me over until my birthday."

"Stop it!" Dirk's voice rang with the same authoritative tone he'd always used when she'd had temper tantrums as a girl. Responding to that tone, Tina quieted and closed her eyes as his hand released her braid and curled around her neck. Sighing, she allowed him to draw her back against him.

"You know you're going to marry me—so spare me

the histrionics, please." Tilting her head up to meet his descending mouth, he added, softly, "Be a good girl, darling, and part your lips for me."

"Dirk . . ." Tina's attempt at protest was swallowed by Dirk's mouth.

The very gentleness of his kiss disarmed her. Carefully, tentatively, his lips explored hers until, feeling the resistance ease out of her rigid body, his lips hardened possessively while he staked his claim with his raking tongue.

When Dirk raised his head to gaze down at her, all the anger was gone from his eyes and expression. "We're already bound to each other, Tina." His fingers trailed lightly over the satiny skin on her arched throat, leaving a path of fire in their wake that evoked a tremor Tina was beyond concealing. "The legalities are just a formality," he murmured, stroking the fluttering pulse in her throat with his thumb. "And you know it."

"Yes."

Hours later, the legalities Dirk spoke of set in motion, Tina sat at the kitchen table mulling over their hectic morning while she played with her lunch, Dirk and Beth's conversation swirling unheard around her.

"Well, I think that if you're going to do it at all, you may as well do it right. What do you say, Tina?"

"What?" Glancing up, Tina blinked. "I'm sorry, I was thinking about something."

Beth frowned. "I asked if you wouldn't rather be married by a minister than a judge?"

"Oh." Tina's frown mirrored the older woman's. "I . . . I don't see that it makes any difference. As Dirk pointed out earlier, this isn't the first time for either of us."

Now Dirk frowned, making the expression around

the table unanimous. "But it will be the last," he said flatly. "So perhaps you're right, Beth." He smiled at the older woman. "Okay, you win. Call your pastor and ask him if he'll officiate."

Rising with deceptive laziness, he arched a brow at Tina. "Does that meet with your approval, darling?" he asked smoothly.

Tina shrugged her shoulders; what difference did it make who actually said the words over them? "Yes, of course," she murmured, then she qualified, "but I really don't want a lot of bother." Sliding her gaze to Beth, she cautioned, "Tell your pastor we'd prefer to be married in his study—or for that matter, right here in the house."

"Why, Tina," Beth cried, "that's a wonderful idea!" Jumping up, she whipped around the table to bestow a fierce hug on Tina. "And since the lists you two gave me are so skimpy, we can invite everyone to the wedding as well as the reception!"

At the mention of the lists, Dirk smiled dryly at Tina. Beth had scolded both of them about the meager number of people they wanted present. Nevertheless, they had remained adamant and the guest list Dirk had relayed to his secretary by phone had numbered less than twenty.

"Okay, is that it for today?" Dirk fixed a look on Beth that said it had better be.

"Yes, I think so. Why?"

"Because Tina and I are going to take a brisk stroll on a long boardwalk, that's why." Dirk's tone brooked no arguments. "Let's go, kid," he ordered a blank-faced, openmouthed Tina.

"But . . . but . . ." Tina stuttered as Dirk grasped her arm to pull her from the chair. "Dirk!" Digging her heels in, she planted her hands on her hips defiantly. "What are you talking about?" she demanded, thoroughly exasperated. It *had* been a strange morning. "What boardwalk?"

"Atlantic City. I'm taking you to dinner and then a show." Dirk grinned. "And if you're good, I might even give you a little money to play with."

"Atlantic City?" Tina's voice betrayed the excitement beginning to curl inside; she'd been longing to see the hotel casinos for ages. "Really?"

"Yes, really," Dirk drawled. "So suppose we adjourn this conclave and get ourselves ready."

"Now?" Tina frowned. "It's only one-thirty. I thought you said we were going for dinner?"

"We are, my sweet." With a strong hand at the back of her waist, Dirk steered Tina out of the kitchen, Beth's chuckle trailing them. "But I also said we were going to stroll the boardwalk." Reaching the stairs, he urged her up the curving treads. "A good brisk walk will whet our appetites."

The trip to Atlantic City was a huge success and the start of the most enjoyable five days Tina had ever lived through. Leaving all the wedding arrangements in Beth's capable hands, Dirk and Tina drifted through the days in a world all their own, most times steeped in memories of the past they'd shared.

On one exceptionally mild day they went sailing, Dirk laughing as Tina scrambled around relearning skills she'd nearly forgotten.

And on one blustery afternoon they wandered around the ruins of the old lighthouse and gun battery, Dirk indulging Tina by playing hide-and-seek with her as he'd done when she was ten.

They walked the beach and the promenade day and night, in all kinds of weather, holding hands and reminiscing about family and friends and other such walks, countless in number.

In the mornings, Dirk ran beside Tina on the damp sand, his teeth flashing in the bright fall sunlight in an endearingly familiar grin.

Ensnared by silken threads of memory, Tina was happier than she'd been in years. Not at any time did she notice the occasional glance of assessment Dirk slid over her or the shadowy smile of satisfaction that fleetingly touched his lips.

By the time Thanksgiving—and her wedding day—dawned, bright with holiday sunshine, Tina was not only amenable to any and all suggestions Dirk made, she was anxiously looking forward to becoming his wife.

The morning was spent in a happy if hectic continuation of the communion she and Dirk had shared throughout the previous five days. Smiling secretly at each other, they performed the last-minute tasks Beth assigned them without demur, slipping out of the housekeeper's sight at regular intervals to touch with their eyes or hands or lips.

Late in the afternoon, as Tina dressed in a winter-white soft wool suit and a lacy blouse that matched the sherry color of her eyes, she tilted her head whimsically, examining the dreamy-eyed young woman reflected in the mirror, vaguely surprised at the change five short days had wrought in her appearance.

The woman staring back from the looking glass had no need of the artifice of cosmetics Tina had used mere weeks ago to conceal the taut lines of strain around her eyes and mouth. Her skin glowed with the dewy freshness of a late-blooming rose; her soft lips smiled easily with the relief from tightening stress; her eyes sparkled with anticipation.

Turning from the mirror, Tina's gaze slid over the narrow bed, then returned, a delicious tingle igniting her nerves and senses. No longer would she lie alone and lonely on that single bed, she mused, her smile growing sensuous.

Glancing at the watch that encircled her delicate wrist, Tina's lips trembled. Within a few hours she would be climbing the curved staircase again, only this time to share the wide bed of her friend, hero, lover, husband.

Even as Tina stared at the face on her watch, the hands moved and it was time for her to leave the room of her childhood, close the door firmly behind her, and go to meet her future.

Though short, the wedding was beautiful. Tina knew simply because everyone told her it was. For herself, she was too distracted by her groom to take more than surface notice of the solemnly intoned service. She repeated her vows sincerely, if automatically, only coming fully aware as Dirk bestowed the traditional sealing kiss.

Tina had invited only Paul and two of her other employees from the shop as guests. Besides his parents and sister and brother-in-law, Dirk's list had consisted of his personal assistant, who acted as best man, and two married couples from Cape May, all of whom Tina knew casually from her younger days. Beth proudly stood beside Tina as matron of honor.

After congratulations, the shaking of hands, and the kissing of the bride, the guests eagerly attacked the sumptuous array of foods Beth had so lovingly prepared, washing it all down with the champagne Dirk had supplied by the case.

Except for a hurried, serious conversation she had with Paul in the relative privacy of the kitchen, Tina hadn't the vaguest idea of what she talked and laughed about with her guests during the three-hour reception. All she remembered was wishing it would all be over, and that everyone would simply go home.

Tina's new in-laws were the last to leave. When, finally, after pitching in to help clear away the party debris and bestowing still more kisses and well-wishes, they did depart, they took a tired but happy Beth with them to drop her off three blocks away at the home of her best friend.

After waving them on their way, Tina stepped back into the hall, smiling a trifle shyly at her new husband as he closed the door with telling firmness. Her smile faltered as Dirk turned to her, his eyes colder than the night air outside.

"What was that little tête-a-tête between you and Paul in the kitchen all about?" he demanded tersely.

Dirk's tone dispelled most of the euphoric haze that had clouded Tina's thinking throughout the previous days. A frown marring her smooth brow, she shook her head as if to clear it.

"There was no tête-a-tête, Dirk." Lifting her chin, Tina faced him confidently. "For some reason, Paul thought I was considering selling my business. He made me an offer for it."

"For some reason?" A sardonic smile curled Dirk's lip as he softly repeated the words. "How naive of him," he muttered.

"What?" Tina's frown deepened.

Dirk shrugged as he moved into the living room. "Never mind. Did you accept his offer?" Turning slowly, he pierced her with eyes now glittering with blue fire; Tina was too surprised to notice.

"Of course not," she exclaimed. "Why would I even consider it?"

"Why indeed?" Dirk's expression settled into sharp lines of austerity. "Unless, of course," he went on chillingly, "you thought to consider the fact that the business is in New York, while our *home* will be in Wilmington."

Oh, Lord! Tina's teeth caught at her lower lip. Not once had she given even the tiniest thought to where they'd live. And in all fairness, she could not possibly expect Dirk to make his home in New York while conducting his banking business in Delaware. But give up her business? Everything inside Tina rebelled at the idea.

Distractedly raking her fingers through the mass of red waves, Tina stared at Dirk, mutely beseeching him to solve the problem.

"Well?" Dirk merely stared back stonily.

"I . . . I don't know." Tina shrugged her shoulders helplessly. "I suppose we'll have to work out some sort of arrangement." It was hardly a satisfactory solution, and Tina knew it.

"I see." His sardonic smile was back, causing a twisting pain in Tina's chest.

"Dirk . . ." she began, not even sure of what she was going to say. Her voice faded as he turned abruptly, heading for the dinning room.

"I'm going to lock up," he said, not bothering to look at her. "You go up, I'll be there in a few minutes."

Feeling dismissed, and angry for it, Tina hesitated briefly, then ran up the curving stairs, unconsciously dashing into her own bedroom.

Dirk was angry with her, very obviously angry, and he had every right to be. Where *had* her mind wandered off to this last week? Tina berated herself, absently beginning to undress as she paced the floor.

Images of the laughing, companionable days she and Dirk had spent together flitted in and out of her mind. Instead of playing, she sighed, they should have discussed their future—all aspects of their future. And because they hadn't as much as mentioned the future, they were facing their very first crisis on their wedding night.

Her eyes bright with threatening tears, Tina was hanging her suit in the closet when the door to her room was flung open forcefully.

"What the hell are you doing in"—the sharp edge of Dirk's voice softened as he caught sight of Tina—"here?" he finished hoarsely, his eyes devouring the look of her body, clad skimpily in a white-satin teddy, sheer hose, and sling-back high heels.

"Oh, God, Tina, you're so beautiful!" A blue flame leaping in his eyes, Dirk slowly crossed the room to her. Raising his hand, he slid his fingers into the thick waves that tumbled to her shoulders, lifting one tendril to his lips as he bent his head. "And now you're mine!" Brushing her hair back, he sought the curve of her neck with his mouth.

Tina knew she should stop him; they had to talk, come to some kind of understanding. She knew it and yet, at the touch of his moist lips against her skin, she chose to forget what she knew. Closing her eyes, she let her head drop back, giving him access, and invitation.

"My Tina." Dirk's warm breath sensitized the nerves close to the surface of her skin. "Finally," he muttered, sweeping her into his arms and carrying her to his room across the hall.

There was no hesitation, no awkwardness, no fumbling. Within moments Dirk had removed Tina's scanty clothing and his own, tossing everything carelessly to the floor. Then, his eyes worshiping her flawless form, he lowered her gently to the bed.

Covering her quivering body with his own, Dirk proceeded to drive Tina wild with his lips, his hands, and the exciting murmurs he growled deep in his throat.

"I've waited so long, so very long." Tina shuddered as Dirk's tongue tasted every inch of her. "Oh, love, the nights I lay awake, aching for your softness, for the

338

way you fill my senses, for the sweet taste of your mouth."

Time and time again he brought her to the very edge of ecstasy, only to soothe her, calm her before arousing her unbearably once again, whispering raggedly, "I want to make it last for ever; I want it perfect for both of us."

Gasping, her mind lost to reason, needing his possession more than she would have believed it possible to need anyone or anything, Tina clung to Dirk, returning his caresses.

And when finally Dirk's hair-roughened thighs eased between the silkiness of hers, Tina cried out with joy.

Becoming one, their loving was hot, and sweet, and at times savage, so very starved were they for each other. And then, their oneness complete, they slept in each other's arms.

CHAPTER TEN

"Are you on the pill?"

Still lying curled against his warm strength, barely awake, Tina blinked as she gazed up into her husband's calm face.

"What?" she asked softly, shaking her head to dispel the lingering wisps of sleep.

"I asked if you've been taking a birth control pill." Dirk's voice was as calm as his composed features.

"No." Tina frowned; what was he getting at? "Why?"

Dirk's chest heaved in a deep sigh. "Well, it's too late to do anything about last night," he said wearily. "But from now on, until you can see a doctor to get a prescription, I'll see to it."

Thoroughly confused, and oddly fearful, Tina gazed at him in amazement. "Dirk, I don't understand. What difference—"

"I worried myself sick that other time, after your father died," he interrupted in a faraway tone. "I called myself all kinds of a fool for being so careless."

As Tina listened to him, her eyes widened in stupefaction. How strange, she mused; usually it was the female who worried herself sick. At the time, crushed by his rejection and consumed with resentment, Tina hadn't even thought about the possibility of becoming pregnant.

"But, Dirk," she chided gently, "that was a long time ago. Why would we need to be careful now?"

"I could say it's because I want you all to myself," he said, expelling his breath on a very weary sigh. "And although that would be the truth, it would not be the complete truth." Disentangling his legs and arms from hers with obvious reluctance, Dirk slid off the bed.

Her still slumberous eyes cloudy with confusion, Tina stared up at him blankly. "Dirk, I . . . I don't understand."

"I think it would be better for all concerned if we agreed not to bring children into this marriage," he explained in an oddly thick voice.

"No children?" Tina repeated dully, then shocked: "No children! But why?" This time Tina's blink was against the hot sting of tears. Through the blur, she missed the spasm of pain that flickered over Dirk's face.

"Tina . . ." Dirk raked his fingers through his hair agitatedly. "Honey, you must admit that you're not the same type of woman your mother was," he said distractedly.

"My mother?" Tina echoed flatly. "Dirk, what does . . ." Her voice trailed away as he turned away from the bed.

"I know what it's like to grow up in a house where the mother is so terribly busy with her own pursuits, remember?" Sublimely unconcerned with his nakedness, Dirk strode restlessly around the room. "For all the delight and enthusiasm my parents displayed last night, you know as well as I do that they could never really be bothered with the day-to-day problems of raising children."

Spinning to face her, Dirk smiled humorlessly. "Oh, I will grant that they love me in their own fashion, but in any competition with *his* work and *her* civic duties,

341

both my sister and I ran a poor second. The closest thing to a real home I ever knew was in *this* house."

Every bitterly anguished word Dirk spoke was true, and Tina knew it. Hadn't she heard her father voice the same opinion to her mother numerous times while she was growing up? But still, what did that have to do with *their* marriage? Tina felt even more confused than before. She would have expected Dirk to be almost fanatic in his determination to be a good father—but not to want children at all? That didn't make any sense. And what had he meant about her mother?

"Dirk?" Her eyes wide, Tina sat up as he rummaged in a drawer for underwear, a pair of jeans, and a shirt. When he paused to glance over his shoulder, she blurted, "Where are you going?"

"For a shower," he muttered. "Then for some coffee." Turning away, he reached for the doorknob.

"Wait!" Now Tina was on her knees in the center of the bed, disregarding her own nudity. Though he paused again, Dirk held firm to the doorknob.

"Well?" he asked with tired patience.

Hurting for him, and herself as well, Tina drew a steadying breath. She had to have an answer. "I'd like to know what you meant by saying I'm not the type of woman my mother was."

"Oh, Tina." The eyes that met hers were bleak. "I would think, after last night, the answer would be obvious. You hadn't even given any thought to where we'll live." His eyes closed briefly. When he opened them again, they were remote. "Or for that matter, if we'll even live together."

"But—" Tina began, flushing.

"I know," he interrupted. "Your career and business mean everything." He smiled sadly. "And that was what I meant by the comparison with your mother. The only thing your mother ever asked for from this life was this house—with her husband and daughter safely inside it. She was the homemaker-mother type." His smile vanished, leaving his mouth unrelentingly tight. "On the other hand, you need the challenge of a career—at whatever cost." Shrugging, he twisted the knob and swung the door open, unaware or unheeding of Tina's low gasp of pain.

"Dirk!" Once again her cry halted him. "I've—I've worked so very hard for it!"

"I know. I've accepted it. I won't ask you to give it up. Not the challenge or the excitement or any of it." His chest heaved with the depth of his sigh. "You're not the homemaker-mother type, Tina. I prefer not to bring a child into the unstable marriage situation we've bound ourselves to." Stepping into the hall, Dirk shut the door quietly behind him.

Tina stared at the door until the flow of tears obliterated the carved wood panels. What had they done? What had *she* done? Distractedly, she combed her fingers through the long mane Dirk had tangled during his impassioned lovemaking. More to the point: What were they going to do now? Everything Dirk had said was true—as far as it went. She did love her career, and the challenge, and the excitement. But she loved him too. She *wanted* to bear his children. Didn't Dirk realize that?

How could he? She silently answered her own question. Did they really know each other anymore? Tina sighed; how could they have gotten to know each other again? All they'd done was spar and jab at each other.

What was she going to do? she wondered, gazing around the room where she'd discovered the meaning of the word *bliss*.

They had to talk, she decided, slipping off the bed and drawing a robe over her chilled body. She should

343

have insisted they talk things out *before* she so mindlessly agreed to marry him.

Wiping ineffectually at the tears still running freely down her cheeks, Tina sank onto the edge of the bed. Why hadn't they discussed the everyday details of marriage? Frowning, she carefully retraced every minute she and Dirk had spent together since he'd first mentioned the word marriage.

Tina's tears lessened, then stopped completely as enlightenment slowly dawned. Incredible, unbelievable as it was to accept, the realization hit her that Dirk had seduced her a second time . . . only this time he'd seduced her with memories. And she, fool that she was, had succumbed every bit as easily the second time as she had at the untried age of nineteen.

Her lovely features settling into rigid lines of anger and self-disgust, Tina shook her head slowly. Denying the pain that seemed determined to tear her apart inside, she faced the truth squarely. Not only had Dirk seduced her twice, he'd rejected her twice, the first time when he'd sent her back to school after making her a woman, and just a few moments ago, by rejecting her worthiness in mothering his children.

What kind of life could they possibly have together? Tina wondered dully. Unable to bear thinking about the barren emptiness of that life, she scrambled to her feet and fled to the now vacant bathroom.

Some thirty minutes later, carefully attired in her finest wool slacks and a complementing sweater, with her hair brushed into obedience and her tear-ravaged face camouflaged with expertly applied makeup, Tina strolled into the sunny kitchen determined to appear her best before her husband.

Dirk was sitting at the table, his hair gleaming almost copper in the ray of sunlight streaming in through the window, his hands curled around a steaming mug of coffee.

As she entered the room, he glanced up and Tina felt her breath catch painfully in her throat at the weariness on his beloved face.

And it always had been, and always would be beloved to her, Tina acknowledged sadly as she crossed the room to pour herself a cup of coffee. Whatever her future, Dirk would have to be part of it. Tina had tried denying that truth once, she simply wasn't up to the subterfuge any longer.

Carrying the cup to the table, Tina sat down opposite Dirk, who had watched her every move through shuttered eyes.

"What are we going to do?" she asked with what she considered commendable calm.

"Do?" Dirk raised one burnished brow. "Why, we're going to enjoy our honeymoon." He shrugged. "At least for the next ten days," he qualified dryly. "I have to be back in Wilmington a week from Monday." Then, the sardonic smile Tina was quickly growing to hate curving his lips, he said, overpolitely, "And don't you have some financial matters to see to?"

"Yes," Tina admitted tiredly. "That is, if you release my money."

"I have." The coldness edging his tone chilled Tina to the marrow. "Any other questions . . . my love?" Dirk drawled with quiet insolence.

Refusing him the pleasure of seeing her flinch, Tina employed every ounce of willpower she possessed to retain her composure. "Just one," she responded steadily. "Are we going to see each other at all? I mean, after we leave here next Monday?"

"Of course," Dirk replied unhesitatingly, if dryly. "I suggest we meet here on Christmas Eve and stay through the first week of the new year." Again one brow arched quizzically. "Isn't that what you had in mind as a 'sort of arrangement'?"

Tina opened her mouth to protest, then closed it again. She *had* made the suggestion, and even if she hadn't meant it the way Dirk had interpreted it, what difference did it make? For even though Dirk had said *their* home would be in Wilmington, Tina now realized he couldn't care less whether they shared a home permanently or a bed every few weeks or so.

"Does that *arrangement* meet with your approval, Tina?" Dirk insisted grittily.

As she raised her cup to her lips, Tina lowered her lashes to conceal the shimmer of tears blurring her vision.

"Yes," she whispered, gulping the hot brew in a vain hope that it would warm her frozen insides.

Tina held little expectation for the remainder of their time together. Confounding her yet again, Dirk proved her assumption incorrect as soon as they left the breakfast table.

For the rest of that day and the nine days that followed, Dirk wrapped Tina in a glorious mantle of happiness. And if at times his laughter seemed a trifle strained and his lovemaking a bit desperate, Tina was far too bemused to notice.

By the time she found herself behind the wheel of the Nissan, approaching New York City, it was much too late to ask questions. Dirk had left the house in Cape May hours before she'd awakened that morning.

Her hands gripping the wheel as she had a near miss with a cab, Tina felt her cheeks glow with the memory of the reason she'd overslept.

They'd returned to the house very late after a last fling in Atlantic City, and Tina had literally danced into Dirk's arms with buoyancy, flushed with the thrill of winning fifty-five dollars at roulette. Laughing with her, Dirk had swept her into his arms and up the curving steps. But the laughter subsided, replaced by the repeated murmur of her name as he slid onto the big double bed beside her.

Throughout what was left of the night and into the pearly gray dawn, Dirk was a flame in her arms, a flame burning out of control, igniting an answering blaze deep inside Tina.

Now as Tina made her way back to her empty apartment, and her emptier life, she sighed for what might have been for her and Dirk—if the love she knew he carried for her only outweighed the bitterness she also knew he harbored.

Away from Dirk, time dragged endlessly for Tina. But the slowly moving hours produced one positive resolution in her mind. Tina wasn't even sure exactly when that resolution occurred, but midway through the three long weeks of separation following their honeymoon, she realized she had lost her resentment for Dirk. Now she merely loved him.

When she'd awakened that last morning of their honeymoon, alone and already lonely, Tina had bridled at the terse note Dirk had left on his pillow. The note had consisted of four demanding words. In a slashing scrawl, Dirk had ordered: *Christmas Eve. Be here.*

Disappointed, disheartened, Tina crumbled the note up angrily, only to smooth it out again after she was packed and ready to leave. It wasn't much, just a small scrap of paper, but he'd scribbled his name across the bottom, and it was all she had of him to take with her. Folding the wrinkled note carefully, Tina slid it into a zippered compartment of her handbag; she'd carried it with her everywhere since then.

As the tension and anticipation of the approaching holiday accelerated, Tina's spirits swung from low to rock bottom. The glittering decorations, the joyous music, and the trills of excited laughter all combined to instill depression and longing in her.

Telling herself she absolutely would not do it, Tina nonetheless found herself pushing her credit card across a counter for a beautiful handmade cableknit sweater for Dirk for Christmas. As she had already written out Christmas bonus checks for her employees, her only other purchase was a lacy shawl imported from Spain for Beth.

Sleeping little and eating less, Tina was beginning to resemble the Ghost of Christmas Yet to Come as Christmas Eve drew closer. As the holiday business was always frantic, Tina was working herself to a frazzle when, surprisingly, Paul Rambeau decided he'd had enough of it. Lingering in the shop after one particularly frantic day, he peremptorily closed the account book Tina was laboring over.

"I want you to get out of here," he said quietly when Tina shot him an angry look.

"What?" Tina muttered, shocked by his action and his advice.

"And I mean all the way out," Paul went on assertively. "Look at yourself, Tina!" Frowning, he ran an encompassing glance over her drawn features and thin frame. "For God's sake, you're so fragile—physically *and* emotionally—you look like you'd shatter at the lightest touch."

"I'm all right," Tina insisted.

"No, honey." Paul shook his head pityingly. "You are definitely not all right. You're on the verge of crumbling, and I don't want to witness it. I think it's time to go home."

"To an empty apartment?" Tina choked through her tear-clogged throat.

Paul smiled tenderly. "No, Tina. To your banker."

"Paul, you don't understand."

"That's right, I don't. But I understand this: If you don't do something about the problem between you two, you're going to wind up in a hospital." Paul bent over Tina to grasp her chin and raise her face to his. "There are only two days left before the holiday. I can handle everything here. Go home, Tina. Home to Cape May. Make peace with your husband . . . and yourself."

Peace. Yes, Tina decided sometime around three A.M. that night, perhaps it was time to make some sort of peace with Dirk. She had endured five years of undeclared war, both hot and cold, and she was simply too weary to maintain the battle. Paul was right; it was time she went home.

The next morning, tired, nervous, filled with trepidation, Tina called the shop and asked to speak to Paul. The moment he came on the line, she blurted her question.

"Do you still want to buy the shop?"

"Yes," Paul responded promptly, reassuringly. "Are you ready to sell?"

Tina's response was equally prompt. "Yes."

Paul's long sigh of relief sang along the wire to Tina. "I'm positive you're doing the right thing, honey. Every man likes to believe he comes first with his woman." He laughed softly. "And as tough as Dirk obviously is, I doubt that he's any different from the rest of us closet chauvinists. And I know he loves you."

"Can I come cry on your shoulder if he proves you wrong?" Tina asked tremulously.

"I'll go you one better," Paul said quite seriously. "If you like, I'll come there and flatten him for you."

Paul's promise was the one bright ray in an otherwise gloomy and overcast day. With the lowering clouds threatening snow, Tina loaded her suitcases

and the two exquisitely wrapped presents into the un-
sporty compact she'd bought the week before and,
without a backward glance, drove out of the city.

A fine, light snow began falling as Tina left the Garden State Parkway and turned onto Lafayette. The
pavements wore a dusting of white when she parked
the car in front of her house.

"You're early!" Beth exclaimed happily, hugging
Tina as she urged her into the warmth of the house.
"Dirk told me to expect you both on the twenty-
fourth."

"I needed a holiday," Tina explained, laughing to
keep from crying.

Stepping back, Beth ran an assessing gaze over
Tina's slim body. "I'd say you needed one very badly,"
she murmured despairingly. "Tina, are you ill?"

"No! Of course not." Shrugging out of her cape,
Tina walked to the fireplace to warm her hands near
the crackling fire. "I'm just tired. I've been busy at the
shop the last few weeks. All I need is some rest." And
to be close to Dirk, she added silently.

"The house looks beautiful, so Christmasy," she
complimented Beth, gazing around at the natural decorations of pine boughs, fruit and nut arrangements,
and flickering candles. "And the tree is magnificent!"
she exclaimed, staring at the shimmering six-foot blue
spruce. "And"—Tina drew in a deep breath—"I'd
hazard a guess that you've been baking up a storm!"

"Only the usual." Beth dismissed her efforts, while
still beaming with pleasure. "Cookies, mincemeat pie,
and fruit cake."

"It smells like home." Impulsively hugging the
older woman, Tina sniffed. "It feels like home too."

Much too close to tears, Tina hurriedly collected her
things and headed for the stairs, positive that unless

350

she moved away from Beth at once, she'd be sobbing out her unhappiness on the older woman's shoulder.

By the time Tina finished unpacking in the room she and Dirk had so passionately shared for ten days, she was wound as tight as a spring. Pulling on her jogging outfit, she determined to run off her tension. As she left the house, Tina assured Beth she'd be back shortly.

The beach was deserted. Tina's sole company was the muted roar of the waves and the occasional caw of a gull. Tina was never certain, afterwards, when she lost sight of her intention to run for only a half hour or so. Depressed, fearful of yet another rejection from Dirk, her mind revolving with images and impressions of all the times, happy and bitter, they had shared, she began running, and forgot to stop.

Her feet rhythmically slapping the wet sand, Tina ran on and on, past pain and into near euphoria. On and on, unaware that she was practically staggering, she was unsure if the call came from within or without the first time she heard her name, sounding like a cry of pain swirling in the wind-tossed snow.

"Tina."

Frowning with the effort to concentrate, she kept on, unable now to stop, unaware and uncaring.

"Tina!"

Dirk. Oh, Dirk. Sobbing, yet no longer knowing why, Tina stumbled to her knees. Her tortured breaths a sound of agony, she closed her eyes as her head dropped to the sand.

"Oh, my God. Tina!"

She vaguely heard the beloved, familiar voice as she slid into the comforting arms of oblivion.

When Tina opened her eyes she was in the big double bed and the room was flooded with morning sunshine. The details of how she'd gotten back to the house, let alone into the bed, were a mystery to her fuzzy brain. One thing was certain; it *was* morning. The morning of Christmas Eve? Tina asked herself.

Christmas Eve. Dirk was coming today!

Flinging back the covers, Tina sat up, groaning at the stiffness in her muscles. Then, her mental fuzziness dissipating, she remembered bits and pieces of the day before; her foolish overexertion on the beach, the sound of someone calling to her, her collapse on the sand. Had it really been Dirk calling to her?

Ignoring the aches in her body, Tina rose, scooping up her robe and sliding her arms into the sleeves as she hurried from the room.

She found Dirk in the kitchen, sitting at the table, a cup cradled in his hands, in much the same manner as the day after their wedding. However, today there was one glaring difference in his appearance. This morning Dirk looked overdrawn and exhausted, his face pale, his eyes shadowed, and perhaps the most startling thing of all to Tina, his clothes rumpled as if he'd slept in them.

As she entered the room, Dirk glanced up quickly and Tina's breath caught in her throat at the haggard, harried look of his face. The eyes that observed her passage into the room were dark and rimmed with red. Had he been crying? she wondered.

Shaken, yet unable to accept the idea of Dirk crying for *any* reason, Tina continued in a straight line to the coffeepot.

"How are you feeling?"

The hoarse, hesitant note in Dirk's voice arrested Tina's hands midway to the coffeepot. Was he coming down with a cold? she speculated, completing the action of pouring the dark brew into a cup. A cold would explain the rough edge to his voice *and* the redness in his eyes. Staring out the window above the sink, Tina answered without looking at him.

"I feel stiff and achey, and more than a little foolish." Turning slowly, she met his burning stare directly. "Was it you I heard calling to me? Did you bring me home and put me to bed?"

"Yes. Beth helped me get you into bed. She was pretty upset." Dirk sighed tiredly. "And I was scared out of my mind."

Though Tina had to bite her lip, she managed to face his brooding expression. "I . . . I'm sorry, Dirk."

"What the hell were you trying to do?" Dirk demanded raggedly, scraping the floor as he pushed back the chair and jerked to his feet.

Beginning to tremble in reaction, Tina bit down harder on her lip. "Nothing. I . . . I don't know."

"Are you so very unhappy, Tina?" There was an odd sound to Dirk's voice, as if there were something caught in his throat.

"Yes." Unconscious of the pain, at least in her lip, Tina's teeth sank deeper into the tender flesh.

"Is it me?" Dirk asked very softly.

"Yes." Tina was shocked at the sudden taste of her own blood as her teeth pierced her lip. With a distracted flick of her tongue, she removed the ruby drop that welled there, her gaze intent on the spasm of pain that passed over Dirk's features.

"Because I forced you into marriage?" he said huskily.

"No," Tina replied sadly, "because you don't love me."

"Not love you?" Dirk's amazed expression might have been funny if his features hadn't revealed pure agony. "I adore you. I've always adored you." His body rigid with tension, his face pale, Dirk went on

353

harshly, "Ever since the first day I walked into this house, into this very room, I've adored you!" Moving jerkily, he started toward her. "Tina, I—"

"But that's not the same thing!" Tina cried over his bitter voice. "It's not the same kind of love a man feels for a woman!" All restraint gone, Tina made no attempt to contain the tears that trickled down her face. "I'm not a little girl anymore, or even a teenager. I'm a woman and I need—Dirk!" she cried out as he grasped her by the shoulders and pulled her into his arms.

"I have needs too," Dirk muttered, rubbing his cheek over her hair. "I need you. Oh, Tina," he moaned, seeking the sensitive skin on the curve of her throat. "Tina, hold me. Love me. These last weeks have been sheer hell without you." Lifting his head, Dirk brushed his lips over hers, then paused to draw her lower lip into his mouth, the tip of his tongue testing the texture of the delicate inner flesh.

A heady combination of hope and sensual excitement bubbling through Tina sent her hands up to cradle his face. Capturing his teasing lips with her own, she let her deep kiss and her softening body convey the barrenness of her own last few weeks.

Even though Tina knew it would solve nothing, she didn't protest when Dirk swung her into his arms, murmuring deep in his throat of a hunger raging out of control. Clinging to him, she buried her face in the curve of his neck as he strode through the house to the stairs.

"Beth." Tina remembered the housekeeper as Dirk attained the landing at the top of the staircase.

Dirk's arms tightened around her tensing body. "Beth left a little while ago to spend today and tomorrow with her sister and brother-in-law in Wildwood Crest," he murmured tersely. "Even though she spends the holiday with them every year, she was undecided this morning whether to go or not. She was very concerned about you, Tina," he chastised softly as he continued on into the bedroom and sat with her on the bed.

"I . . . I'm sorry." Tina lowered her lashes in shame.

"You should be," he chided gently. "You frightened both of us very badly . . . and we both love you, you know."

Tina's lashes swept up. "Do you, Dirk?" she asked tremulously, gazing into his eyes steadily. The tender expression on his face caused a thickening tightness in her throat.

"Yes," Dirk answered simply. "In one form or another, I always have." Raising his hands, he cradled her face in his palms, drawing her to him as he lowered his mouth to hers. "Yes, Tina, I love you," he whispered against her lips. "I suppose I always will. Oh, Tina, please say you love me too."

"I do," Tina sighed, seeking fuller contact with his mouth. "Dirk, you know I do."

Their avowals were repeated, at times in impassioned gasps, at others in replete murmurs through what was left of the morning and into most of the afternoon.

The late afternoon sunlight spilling through the bathroom window struck burnished highlights off Dirk's wet hair, and made Tina's slick body gleam as they lathered each other between bouts of laughter and consuming kisses.

"For a man who had practically no sleep at all last night, I'm feeling pretty damned good," Dirk declared, grinning as he stepped out of the shower and onto the bath mat beside Tina. "You feel pretty good too," he teased, skimming his hands over her water-beaded breasts.

"If hollow from hunger," Tina laughed, slipping away from his enticing fingers.

"Good Lord, that's right!" Dirk's stricken gaze skimmed her too slender form. "You missed dinner yesterday and you haven't eaten a thing at all today." His expression a study in self-reproach, he shook his head. "You know, you were right. I am a selfish bas—"

"Dirk," Tina exclaimed, her feeling of well-being expanding at his obvious concern, "I refuse to listen to you talk that way about the man I love. The problem is easily solved—that is, if there's anything to eat in the house?"

"Anything to eat?" Dirk laughed. "Beth ran amok preparing things for us. The refrigerator is on the point of bursting."

"Well, then, what are we standing around for?" Tossing her sodden towel into the hamper, Tina dashed out of the bathroom, Dirk at her heels. "Let's throw some clothes on and go relieve the poor thing of some of its burden." Inside the bedroom she paused to give him a contemplative look. "On second thought, let's relieve it of a lot of its burden. I feel like I could eat my way through a supermarket!"

An hour and forty odd minutes later, the remains of their feast littering the table, Tina, her robe sweeping the floor, walked to the coffeepot to refill their cups as Dirk sliced thick wedges of fruitcake.

Glancing casually out the window a soft "oh" whispered through Tina's lips at the scene that met her gaze. Approximately two inches of glittering white snow covered the ground and clung to tree branches and fence posts.

Though her exclamation of appreciation was barely audible, Dirk heard it.

"What is it?" he murmured, sliding his arms around her waist as he came to a stop behind her.

"The snow." Sighing, Tina rested her head against the warmth of his hard chest. "Isn't it beautiful?"

"Yes," Dirk agreed readily, then qualified, "Almost as beautiful as my wife."

His wife. For the first time since he'd slipped the narrow platinum band on her finger, Tina truly felt she was Dirk's wife. Loving him until she thought she'd die from the joy of it, Tina leaned against him, reveling in the strength he exuded, growing light-headed with the musky masculine scent of him.

"Darling?" Dirk's soft voice, close to her ear, enhanced the glow warming Tina from the inside out.

"Hmm?" Snuggling closer, Tina rubbed her cheek against the soft cotton T-shirt he'd pulled on along with washed-out jeans, luxuriating in the play of muscles in his chest and the natural body heat emanating from him.

Absently, reciprocally, Dirk caressed her hip with one palm. "Honey . . . ah . . . have you seen a doctor for a prescription for birth control pills?" he asked in an uncharacteristic hesitant tone.

Sudden tension drew Tina's nerves taut again. "No," she finally responded honestly if breathlessly.

"Good." Dirk expelled the word softly on a long sigh.

Eyes wide with surprise, Tina twisted around in his arms to stare up at him. "You're not angry or upset?" she asked in astonishment.

"No, darling, I'm not angry or upset." Closing his eyes for an instant, he swallowed—noticeably. "I can't describe the relief I'm feeling at this moment," he said hoarsely.

"But, Dirk"—Tina gaped in sheer amazement—"you were so adamant about not wanting a child!"

Dirk's hands gripped her waist reflexively. "No. No, honey." He shook his head in denial. "I never said I didn't *want* a child. I do—rather badly, as a matter-of-fact. And not just one, but several."

Tina frowned. "Yet you didn't have any with your first wife," she murmured. "Why?"

Tina's amazement grew as a faint flush spread from Dirk's neck to his cheeks, and he wet his lips as if suddenly suffering from a dry throat.

"I . . . well, you see . . ." He smiled in self-derision. "Oh, dammit, Tina! I didn't want children from her! I wanted them from *you.*" At her shocked gasp, he smiled softly. "I couldn't give her a child, honey." He shrugged. "Not that she wanted one, she didn't. But even if she had, I . . . I couldn't."

Alarm shot through Tina's mind; was there something wrong with him—something he hadn't told her about? She didn't get the opportunity to ask. Reading her expression, Dirk laughed a little ruefully.

"No, Tina," he assured gently. "I'm perfectly capable of making a child. The problem has been that I have this vision of what my child will look like." Releasing her, he raised a hand to curl his fingers into her hair. "In my vision, the child is a beautiful, scrawny little girl with one braid bouncing on her back."

Though Tina blushed with pleasure, she frowned from confusion. "Dirk . . ."

"Honey, I've spent the majority of the last few weeks cursing myself for telling you I'd prefer not to have children." Raising his hand, he drew his fingertips over her flushed cheek. "I want us to have children, love. I long to watch our child grow inside you." Tilting his head back, he ran a frowning glance over her slim form. "That is," he qualified in a deeply concerned tone, "after you've put some sustaining weight on your body. Have you been overworking and undereating these last weeks?"

"Yes," Tina answered simply. "But most of all, I've been pining for you."

With a strangled groan, Dirk closed his arms around her tightly, as if actually afraid to let her go. "Oh, God, love!" he murmured grittily. "What we've been doing to each other these last five years is criminal." He pressed his lips to her forehead, breathing deeply. Then, raising his head, he smiled gently. "Come, love, it's time to straighten out this mess we've made of our lives."

Clasping her hand, he drew her to the table. "We already know that the physical side of our marriage works." He grinned as the color tinged her cheeks again. "Now we've got to work out the practical side."

Her eyes misty with unshed tears, Tina watched him hungrily as he returned to the counter for their coffee cups, filling them again after pouring the now cold brew down the sink, then joining her at the table.

"When I said I loved you, I meant it. I wasn't mouthing the words in the heat of the moment." Dirk's chest heaved with a deep sigh. "I've been in love with you since the summer you turned sixteen, Tina."

"Dirk!" Tina carefully placed her cup on the tabletop. "You never—"

"Let me finish, love," Dirk again interrupted gently. "Then you can have your say. Okay?"

Staring at him from glistening eyes, Tina nodded. "Okay."

Dirk swallowed a sip of coffee before continuing, tersely. "I was already a man by the summer you were sixteen. I was more than a little shaken to realize I wanted you as a man wants a woman." His lips twisted derisively. "I fought my share of guilt battles for my thoughts. Then after your father died, and I held you in my arms, I lost the mental battle . . . and my control. Believe me, the guilt trips I'd suffered before that day were nothing to the one I went through the morning after we made love."

"So you compensated for your guilt by rejecting me," Tina concluded when he paused for breath.

"No!" Dirk's denial held solid conviction. "I never rejected you. I sent you back to school to give you time, Tina." Reaching across the table, he grasped her hand with trembling fingers. "Honey, I wanted you to have all the things young girls are supposed to have. Dates and fun and . . . well, all the things that you deserved."

"But all I wanted was you!" Tina wailed in objection.

"Honey, I thought you were too young to know what you wanted." Dirk squeezed her hand. "You were vulnerable, and you trusted me. I betrayed not only your trust but your father's as well. I . . ." A spasm of pain swept his face and he closed his eyes briefly. "I sent you away because, by looking at you, I had to look at myself—and I hated what I saw.

"When I came to visit you in your junior year, I came to ask you—beg you—to marry me." Again his lips smiled derisively. "I had to come, I couldn't fight myself any longer. You told me to go to hell," he finished thickly.

"I was hurt, Dirk," Tina explained. "I was lashing out. I wanted to hurt you too."

"Oh, you succeeded, love, believe me." Dirk shrugged. "And you continued to hurt me, with your extravagance and, worst hurt of all, with your marriage to that . . . that parasite." His lips tightened almost painfully.

Lowering her eyes, she admitted, "I know . . . now . . . that I chose Chuck deliberately. I used him, Dirk." Raising her eyes, she met his gaze squarely. "I used him to hurt you."

360

"And all the other men since him?" Dirk muttered raggedly.

Tina stiffened with sudden indignation. "There were no others," she said convincingly. "There was only Chuck. And"—even though she felt her face flush, Tina knew she had to tell him the whole truth—"and even when I was with him, there was only you. Do you understand what I'm saying?"

A smile of commiseration softened his lips. "Only too well," he replied softly. "I used my wife the same way."

"What an utter waste," Tina observed sadly.

"Yes," Dirk concurred. "But I'm through wasting time, or lying to myself, or playing games." Releasing his grip, Dirk began stroking her fingers. "I came back here yesterday prepared to beg you for a real marriage between us."

"But that's—" Tina was about to tell him that that was the same reason she'd come home early, but once more he wouldn't let her finish.

"Honey, I know how much your business means to you, but God, I need you with me!" Leaning forward, he asked, earnestly, "Couldn't you open another salon in Wilmington and make periodic trips to New York?"

"No." A shadow passed over his face at her flat refusal. Aching for him, feeling his pain, Tina rushed to explain. "I have no shop to make periodic trips to New York for, darling. I agreed to sell the business to Paul yesterday. I also gave notice that I'd be vacating my apartment." A smile tugged at her lips when she saw the look of amazement on her husband's face. "As of the end of January, this house is the only home I have."

Kicking over his chair as he jumped to his feet, Dirk circled the table to pull Tina into his arms.

"You could always come live with me, scrawny," he teased in a suspiciously tight voice.

"On one condition," Tina said adamantly.

"Name your terms of surrender." He laughed in relief.

"By next year at this time," Tina said softly, "I want to be decorating a nursery as well as a Christmas tree."

A slow, excitingly sexy smile curved Dirk's lips as he gazed down at her, his blue eyes glowing with love.

"Both here and in Wilmington," Tina added as an afterthought.

"You're a demanding woman, love." Dirk's arms tightened, making Tina thrillingly aware of his need of her. "But as I was planning to keep this house as our getaway anyway, I'll meet your terms . . . on one condition of my own."

"And that is?" Tina asked, molding her soft curves to his angular frame.

"That is"—he paused to kiss her deeply, meaningfully—"we get started on your terms immediately."

Futuristic Romance

Love in another time, another place.

DESTINY'S LOVERS

By FLORA SPEER

Janina the Priestess was a maiden whose golden purity must remain untouched. Reid was the stranger whose life was spared to improve the blood lines of the village. He was expected to mate with any woman, but he desired only the one who had heralded his mysterious appearance. Irresistibly drawn to one another, Reid and Janina broke every taboo as they lay tangled together by the sacred pool. But in the heat of their heady desire they forged a bond that no man could put asunder.

_2985-5 $3.95 US/$4.95 CAN

Futuristic Romance

Love in Another Time, Another Place...

FROM THE MIST

By Saranne Dawson

For generations the men and women of Volas had been separated. Their only dealings were for purposes of procreation, and they were strictly scientific rather than sensual. But fiercely possessive Jorlan swore he would restore the women of Volas to their men, particularly the fiery beauty Amala, who had chosen him as her long-distance mate. But Amala wanted no man to dominate her, not even the charismatic Jorlan, who filled her with a strange longing to taste the forbidden pleasure of love.

___3083-7 $3.95 US/$4.95 CAN